DEVIL'S KISS

A DARK MAFIA ROMANCE

SAVAGE LEGACY BOOK 1

KHARDINE GRAY

FAITH SUMMERS

Copyright © 2022 by Khardine Gray Please note : Faith Summers is the Dark Romance pen name of USA Today Bestselling Author Khardine Gray

All rights reserved.

Devil's Kiss Book 1 in the Savage Legacy Series Copyright © 2022 by Khardine Gray

Cover design © 2021 by Book Cover Couture

Photographer- Michelle Lancaster

Cover Model- Lawrence

Graphic image- Babelast

No part of this book may be reproduced in any form or by any electronic or mechanical means, including information storage and retrieval systems, without written permission from the author, except for the use of brief quotations in a book review.

This work is copyrighted. Apart from any use as permitted under the Copyright Act 1968, no part may be reproduced, copied, scanned, stored in a retrieval system, recorded or transmitted, in any form or by any means, without the prior written permission of the author, except for the use of brief quotations in a book review.

This is a work of fiction. Names, characters, businesses, places, events and incidents are either the products of the author's imagination or used in a fictitious manner. Any resemblance to actual persons, living or dead, or actual events is purely coincidental.

The author asserts that all characters and situations depicted in this work of fiction are entirely imaginary and bear no relation to any real person.

No part of this book may be reproduced in any form or by any electronic or mechanical means, including information storage and retrieval systems, without written permission from the author, except for the use of brief quotations in a book review.

The following story contains mature themes, strong language and sexual situations.

It is intended for mature readers. All characters are 18+ years of age and all sexual acts are consensual.

For my husband Daniel Gray, always and ever the Viking.
Thank you for inspiring me, always.
You are most definitely worthy of Valhalla.

DEVIL'S KISS

Savage Legacy Book 1

USA Today Bestselling Author
Khardine Gray
writing as
Faith Summers

ALSO BY FAITH SUMMERS

Series

Dark Syndicate

Ruthless Prince

Dark Captor

Wicked Liar

Merciless Hunter

Heartless Lover

Ruthless King

Dark Odyssey

Tease Me

Taunt Me

Thrill Me

Tempt Me

Take Me

Original Sins

Dark Odyssey Fantasies

Entice

Tease

Play

Tempt

Savage Legacy

Devil's Kiss

Duets

Blood and Thorns Duet

Merciless Vows

Merciless Union

Cruel Secrets Duet

Cruel Lies

Cruel Promises

Novellas

The Boss' Girl

The Player

Standalones

Deceptive Vows

Deadly Games

Iuramentum est vita
nostra et mors nostra
R
RAVENTHORN
Blade
Cypress
Erebus
Iapetus
Gael
Adriel
Amergin
Myrrdin
Erik
Raventhorn

RAVENTHORN

AUTHOR NOTE

Please note Faith Summers is the Dark romance pen name of USA Today Bestselling Author Khardine Gray

DARK ROMANCE NOTE

Dear reader friend ,

Thank you so much for picking my book to read. I hope you enjoy it.

I just have to warn you that this book is a dark romance.

It contains scenes that may be triggering to some readers .

Best of wishes xx

BLURB

In a world where the secret society and the Bratva reigns, villains and monsters own you from birth.

I was torn between two hearts:

The devil who stole me.

And the man I was promised to.

I was supposed to marry Viktor Volkova, heir to one of the most powerful families in the society.

But his older brother stole me on our wedding day, just as we were about to take our vows.

Like a hellish wild card, Desmier Volkova stormed into my life, seeking revenge for my father's sins.

He forced me to marry him, dragging me into his game of lies, revenge, and deceit.

Then our twisted arrangement turned into something else neither of us saw coming—

Obsession, passion, and a war between three hearts.

A war that will either destroy me.

Or the man I choose to love.

Everything spirals out of control when skeletons from the past unleash dark secrets and whispers of death.

Then the real war starts, and I won't just be risking my heart.

Devil's Kiss is a dark mafia enemies-to-lovers arranged marriage romance, which is part of the Savage Legacy series.

This book is a 125K word standalone romance that contains dark themes, dubious situations, mature content, and graphic violence some readers might find offensive and/or triggering.

PROLOGUE

DESMIER

Russia, 16 years ago

The thud of heavy boots echoes on the concrete floor outside the room, making my heart thump with vicious panic.

He's coming.

The monster is coming.

He killed Mom, and now he's going to kill me. Just like he promised yesterday.

Fear slows my thoughts, and my mind struggles. I never knew my life would end at twelve years old, or that I'd helplessly watch my mother die, unable to do anything to save her.

I grip the metal bars of my cage and look around the dark dank room the monster has kept me in for weeks.

Last night, he beat me to a pulp and broke my leg the same way he snapped Mom's neck.

Mom and I were never going to escape him.

And this was always going to happen to me just for being Desmier Volkova.

The door creaks open, letting in a sliver of light, and the beast-like man walks in.

The light is just bright enough to highlight his pale, ghost-like eyes and the mean-looking scar running from his left eye to his jaw.

He smiles when he reaches my cage.

"Time to die, you fucking little shit."

"No!"

He opens the cage door, then yanks me out, sending unbearable pain shooting up and down my body.

"Let me go, now!"

"Shut up." A punch to my face delivers more pain, and I see stars.

The monster tosses me over his shoulder and carries me outside to the old barn. This was where he burned Mom's body. And made me watch.

He opens the door and throws me inside. I fall to the ground in so much pain I can't move, I can't see, I can't do anything.

The sinister sound of the door slamming shut lets me know I'm trapped.

Tears stream down my cheeks as I try to move, then I smell smoke.

Thick smoke pours in from under the door.

Seconds later, orange flames swallow the smoke, rising all around me and I scream.

Mom, I'm sorry I couldn't save you.

Or myself...

CHAPTER ONE

ANASTASIA

Boston, present day

Today is my wedding day.

I can't believe this day has come around so quickly. Yet it feels like I've been

waiting forever.

I'm standing in the bridal dressing room at Grantham Hall, one of the most

prestigious wedding venues in Boston.

Staring back at my reflection in the floor-to-ceiling mirror wall, I take in how grown-up I look.

My face is made up like I'm ready to walk the red carpet

at the Oscars, and my wild platinum locks have been teased into loose waves beneath my veil.

In this dress my father bought for me, I look and feel like a fairy-tale princess.

Unlike the medieval-looking wedding gowns worn by descendants of the Brotherhood of Knights, my dress is from Vera Wang's iconic bridal collection.

The strapless draped bodice has a sweetheart neck and a swirling frothy full-length skirt which reminds me of the sea of white roses in the courtyard at home.

In a matter of minutes, I'll walk down the aisle to marry Viktor Volkova, a man known throughout the country and Europe for his family's wealth, power, and status.

Even though the contract for our marriage was signed and sealed in blood before I was born, the idea of our union never felt arranged to me. Not with him.

Although I'm nineteen and Viktor is nine years older than me, we've always been close, and I can't wait to marry him.

Everything is perfect. But I'm nervous.

And it's not the wedding or Viktor making me feel this way.

It's my nightmares.

They've gotten worse.

Seven months ago, when I started my Psychology degree at Raventhorn University, the hellish nightmares I experienced as a child after a car accident returned.

Sleepless nights followed, and I haven't managed to push aside the wretched feeling telling me my nightmares might not really be *nightmares*, but fractured memories of something horrific that happened to me.

Something different to the car accident, and something more I can't remember from the past.

Just the thought sends a chilling shiver through my body.

The creak of the door draws my attention away from the mirror and my sordid thoughts. When Mira, Viktor's mother, glides in, my spirits lift.

As usual, she looks like a goddess with flawless makeup on her alabaster skin and her salt-and-pepper hair in a perfect chignon. The elegant emerald gown flowing around her body matches her eyes and makes her look at least ten years younger than her fifty years.

She looks me over, bringing her dainty hands up to her cheeks.

"Anastasia, oh my gosh, look at you." The deep emotion in her voice almost overpowers her slight Russian accent. "My dear girl, you look absolutely beautiful."

"Thank you."

She pulls me in for a loving hug, and I sink into her embrace.

"No need to thank me, dear. It's true. I couldn't ask for a more beautiful daughter-in-law, or a better one."

"I feel the same about you."

Mira—the lead psychiatrist at Massachusetts General—was not only the inspiration for my career, but she helped me after my accident. Because we knew each other, it wasn't therapy; I just checked in with her. She's also been my rock, like a mother to me since my mom died.

"We're lucky to have each other."

"We are."

She touches the veil, and as I watch her expression, the only word that comes to mind is *nostalgic.*

"I remember when you first laid your eyes on my veil. You were eight years old, playing dress-up. You asked me if you could have it."

"And you said when the time was right, you'd give it to me." I fill my voice with false pride, pretending I remember what happened like I always do.

"It means so much to me that you remember."

"I know." As lies spew from my lips, guilt writhes in my soul.

The truth is, I don't remember anything. It's normal for people to forget childhood memories, but the accident stole mine. My parents were told I'd have permanent memory loss, so I have no memories from before I was nine. Nothing whatsoever—not events, or even people.

Nearly ten years have passed since, and I still feel like I'm walking around in a universe someone made up for me. Raising me didn't exactly help my mother's depression, and I worried I drove her to kill herself. It must have been awful having a child who can't remember you're their mother.

I push the heartbreaking thought out of my mind along with my nerves and give Mira a smile. I promised myself I wouldn't spoil the day by thinking about the past.

I just need to get through today, then find a way to get back on track. The last thing I want is to start my marriage off on the wrong foot when Viktor had so many women falling at his feet.

Mira takes my hands in hers and gives them a gentle squeeze. "Enjoy today, my love."

"I will."

"I'm sorry Evgeni can't be here." The light in her eyes dims as sadness invades her expression, making her look fragile.

"Me too."

Evgeni, her husband and Viktor's father, had chronic heart failure. Three months ago, he had a heart attack and has been in a coma ever since.

We wanted to postpone the wedding with the hope he'd get better, but Mira insisted we go ahead because the chances of him coming back to us are slim. She knew Evgeni wouldn't have wanted us to delay the wedding for him.

"He would have loved to witness your wedding. So, on behalf of the both of us, I'd like to welcome you to the Volkova family."

My heart swells with warmth, and I feel like I'm going to be okay. "Thank you so much. That means a lot to me."

She kisses my cheeks and says, "Munu sterkr smár einn."

I love this blessing of strength in the Old Norse language, the language the Knights still use. I love that women like Mira speak it because of their thoroughbred linage which goes right back to the founding fathers from the Viking era.

I dip my head, appreciating her words. Since I was raised in the Bratva, the only other language I speak apart from English is Russian. But thanks to Mira, I can understand a few Old Norse words.

The door opens again, and my best friend and maid of honor, Lorelai, walks in.

Like me she's in her first year at Raventhorn University.

She's doing a performing arts degree and wants to be an actress. From as far back as I can remember, my friend has always entered a room as if she's the leading actress in a Hollywood film. Today is no different, and in her long golden bridesmaid's dress that looks like it was painted on her slender frame, and her waist-length ebony hair swishing around her shoulders, she looks every bit the part.

Although she saw me get ready, awe still brightens her face as she looks at me. It's the same adoration I feel for seeing her look so good too.

"It's time." Lorelai's voice is infused with excitement. "Are you ready?"

Releasing my breath, I nod. "Absolutely."

"Then let's go." Lorelai claps her hands together and Mira smiles.

She leads the way out, and Mira and I follow.

We join the wedding party waiting for us by the entrance to the hall where the wedding will be conducted.

I go to my father and take his hand. His curly hair, unruly as usual, is smoothed back today. Despite the crude scar on his cheek, the look gives him a refined edge. But he still reminds me of an older Sirius Black from Harry Potter.

Dad looks like the proud man he always shows the world, but nervousness lurks in his eyes.

I understand the nerves. I'm not just his only daughter, I'm his only child.

My dad kept me wrapped in a silk cocoon before Mom died, but after her death, he tucked me away in a glass house, keeping me safe from cartels and drug lords and any guy other than Viktor.

I give him a big smile of reassurance, letting him know

I'll be okay. He leans in and kisses my forehead just like he used to do when he tucked me into bed at night.

"You look beautiful, my daughter." His voice holds heartfelt emotion he never shares with the public. As head of the enforcers in the Bratva, he would never risk showing any weakness.

"Thank you, Dad."

The grand doors open, and harp music playing *The Wedding March* filters out into the hallway.

Dad and I link arms then proceed into the hall.

There are over a hundred guests here who are mostly officials from the Knights, but the moment we step inside, my eyes land on Viktor standing at the altar waiting for me. He looks so handsome and not nervous at all.

Aleksander Ivanov, leader of the Knights, is in the center ready to officiate. Because Viktor's family is part of the elite group in the Knights, Aleksander will marry us.

Next to Viktor are his two younger brothers, Zakh and Malik. Like the rest of the men here from the Knights, they're all wearing the black knight's tunic, which has the silver Raventhorn crest embossed on the chest.

I try to focus on how handsome and happy Viktor looks, but seeing him in that uniform reminds me that the Knights are a secret society.

A powerful one dating back to the Viking age who formed the Komarovski Bratva. As well as leading the Knights, Aleksander Ivanov is also the Pakhan of the Komarovski and the man we all answer to.

I never tend to think about those parts because everyone is so normal—and of course no one talks about the Knights unless behind locked doors.

I think of it now because my family have always been part of the Bratva, and me marrying Viktor is a great honor for us. I'll be the bridge that will link my family to the Knights. The same rules and oaths that bind Viktor will bind me, too.

On top of that, Viktor is about to inherit his father's empire and take over his position in the Bratva, so he'll be the Pakhan's second-in-command. As his wife, a lot will be expected of me. I must be proper, obedient, and, most of all, compliant.

When we reach Viktor, Dad gives him my hand, and we face each other.

I look into his deep brown eyes, feeling like we were always meant to be.

Aleksander starts with an Old Norse blessing, and I smile as Viktor runs his thumb over my palm.

"Now repeat after me." Aleksander raises his hand and his voice. "I—"

The door at the back of the hall smashes into the wall.

We all turn and stare at a tall muscular man standing in the doorway. He's at least six foot four with shiny black hair cut into a sharp faux hawk and a neatly trimmed beard covering his chiseled jaw.

He's wearing a black biker jacket and leather pants, which make him look like a drifter. But the lines of muscle along his huge arms suggest he might have served in the military. Or did time in the state penitentiary.

He walks in carrying a large brown envelope, and his expression is don't-mess-with-me angry. Everything about him is rough and rugged with the potent air of danger I'm used to from the ruthless men in the mafia.

Thick raven brows lower when he gets closer and Viktor steps in front of me.

The gesture makes the man narrow his eyes and clench his jaw like he's gearing up for a fight.

Despite his menacing vibe, there's a storybook prince thing about him that's alluring and compelling. When his striking hazel eyes meet mine, our gazes lock. And I feel a connection.

As if he read my mind, his stare intensifies, turning into something sinfully scandalous. He does a full sweep of my body, giving me an I-could-fuck-you-if-I-wanted-to look.

A spike of heat darts to my groin, and for a moment, I'm so lost, I forget where I am.

The stranger, however, doesn't even bother to hide the obvious fact that he's checking me out. Or how inappropriate he is. Surely, he can see I'm about to take my vows.

"Can I help you?" Aleksander stares the man down with raw scrutiny.

His question snaps my thoughts back to reality.

"Yes, you can, Pakhan." The man dips his head respectfully. I notice he speaks with a slight accent I can't quite place. At first, it sounds like the mixed Russian/American most of the men I know speak, but there's a difference. "I am Desmier Volkova."

"Volkova?" Viktor drops my hand. His whole body goes rigid. And I see surprise, then disbelief, before he shuts down.

"I object to this wedding." The man's voice sounds like thunder, sending a shockwave through my heart.

"Why?" Viktor's voice is just as demanding, just as powerful.

"This wedding cannot continue because *you* are not Evgeni Volkova's eldest son. *I* am." He holds up the envelope. "As per this contract, it is *me* who is supposed to marry this woman. And *me* who is next in line to inherit all that our father owns."

CHAPTER TWO

DESMIER

Blood drains from Anastasia Sidorov's already pale skin when she hears my venomous words of objection.

As her full lips part in shock, I instantly think of her mouth around my cock, and I find myself smiling like the psycho I am.

I know how strange I must look to all the stunned people observing me, but I don't care. Stealing Anastasia is just the beginning of what I plan to do.

My brother's betrothed is just a pretty emblem of his imminent defeat and the first of many trophies I will be taking.

There, there, Princess. This monster won't be eating you just yet. But I do plan to very soon.

Anastasia is truly beautiful and tempting, even to a man like me who's had his fair share of women.

Her eyes are a bright crystal blue, like the Icelandic glaciers I love sailing around, and that hair of hers is cotton white like the old Norse paintings of Valkyries. There's a fire burning within those eyes that's fitting to the description, and I'd bet underneath that dainty princess exterior, she wishes she could claw my eyes out.

Or maybe she has other things in mind for me. I didn't miss the arousal that sparked in her gaze when she first looked at me. If she's the kind of girl who acts innocent on the outside but is secretly thinking of fucking, I'm game. The dress hugging her decadent body highlights all the parts of her that make a man think with his dick. I can't wait to force her to her knees and train her to please me.

The thought widens my wicked smile.

"Clearly, this is some fucked-up misunderstanding." Viktor walks up to me with his hands balled into solid fists.

I was already prepared for him to challenge me. And I'm sure he didn't like the way I looked at his woman either. But even I have to accept that his reaction is completely understandable. Hearing you're about to lose everything to the half-brother you never knew about can't be easy. That's, however, as far as my consideration goes.

I'm four months older than him. That was my ticket to today. This motherfucker had everything I never did growing up.

He's about to find out how it feels to have those privileges taken away from him.

"I assure you, *little brother*, this is no misunderstanding." My voice is infused with mockery that makes his nostrils flare.

"Little brother?" With his fists raised, Viktor steps into my personal space. A big mistake. If I didn't have a grand plan, he'd be dead. "Who the fuck do you think you're talking to?"

"Want to fight me?" I'm not here to fight, but God knows I'll gladly do it. "I assure you, you won't win."

Viktor charges me, but Zakh and Malik grab his arms, holding him back.

At that moment, I see how similar we all look. We all have the same height, build, high cheekbones, and distinct facial features that make us look like brothers. We're also similar in age with Zakh being twenty-seven and Malik, twenty-six.

The only differences are our eye and hair color. Viktor, Zakh, and I have the same dark hair, but Malik's is blond like his mother's. And I have my mother's eyes.

Despite the differences, one look at us tells you we're related.

"Fucking let me go," Viktor snarls.

"Calm your damn self," Zakh chides, tightening his grip on Viktor's arm.

"This asshole is no brother of mine." Viktor glares at me.

"I don't like it either, but it is what it is." I smirk.

"We're going to need more of an explanation to stop this wedding," Aleksander interrupts us.

On his word, Uncle Leif—the real underdog of this siege—steps forward, fulfilling his final part in *our* plan. More shock registers on my brothers' faces when he walks up to Aleksander and whispers into his ear, telling him truths the others will eventually hear. For the moment, they know that Leif knew something they didn't.

If not for him, I'd be dead. He's my father's younger brother and the only ally Mom and I had. It was him who rescued me from the burning barn that should have killed me.

When we were being hunted, Mom called him for help.

Leif was too late to save her, but he didn't stop looking until he found me. It was nothing short of some miracle that he got to me before the monster burned me alive. I didn't, however, escape unharmed.

Everyone watches his exchange with Aleksander with curiosity, taking note of Aleksander's reactions. The widening of his eyes, the displeasure intensifying on his haggard face, and finally a nod.

He looks at everyone else, including the guests in the congregation. "This wedding will be postponed until further notice," he announces, causing audible gasps to ripple across the room like a Mexican wave making its way through a crowded stadium. Aleksander then flicks his gaze back to me. "I expect a report once this matter is resolved."

The order is another stab in Viktor's heart because he knows it will be me who gets the Sovientrik—second-in-command—position in the Komarovski. Not him.

Just. Like. Everything. Else.

"Yes, Pakhan." I bow my head with reverence, and Aleksander's eyes drift down to the tattoo on my wrist, where his gaze lingers.

All the men in the Knights who pass The Reaping at the age of sixteen receive the Viking Futhark rune for defense tattooed on the underside of their wrist. They then receive the Greek Sigma symbol once they're initiated into the Brotherhood. I have neither because not only should no one know of my existence and lineage, but I was supposed to die that night seventeen years ago.

The tattoo I have on my wrist is of Odin's rune, which means the training I received and rites I have undertaken surpass all others, even Aleksander's. My mark tells him he just barely has power over me because if I wanted to, I could challenge his position and take everything from him, too. Since I haven't, I'm sure he knows it's better to be on my right hand than my left.

Aleksander gives me a curt nod then disappears through the exit behind him.

With his departure, the tension increases. Good. It's showtime, and all the key players are here. There's the princess, who is still glaring at me, Viktor, who looks like he's about to summon the Four Horsemen of the Apocalypse, Zakh and Malik, who wear the same questioning expressions, Mira—the *wife*—who has gone ghostly white, and last but never least, Uther.

Uther Sidorov, Anastasia's father. The monster.

The fucking monster who killed my mother. He thought he killed me too when he set the barn on fire that night so long ago in Russia.

He's staring at me. Afraid of *me* now, because he knows what I could do to him with just one word.

Since death is too good for people like him, I planned a special punishment.

A special *game*, like the ones he used to play with me that made me fear for my life. The game begun today as he walked his daughter down the aisle, knowing from our little encounter days ago what was going to happen to her next.

"You, Leif. You knew about this. Didn't you?" Viktor spits, glaring at Leif. "You planned this."

"I did." Leif sets his shoulders back. Unfazed by Viktor's

rage, he stares at him as if he's ready to charge like a wild bull. He might be sixty, with a head and beard full of gray hair, but he can still snap any motherfucker in half no matter their age.

"How the fuck could you do this to me?"

Leif gives him a hard stare. "I suggest you stand down and remember I still hold the authority here, until it passes."

That tones Viktor right down because he knows what's at stake for his defiance. Under the Rites of Inheritance, Leif will never inherit the empire or the position of Sovientrik to the Pakhan, but he acts as an executor would, holding all the authority and decision-making power while the inheritance is being transferred.

"I'm aware of that, *Uncle*."

"Good, then we should relocate to the meeting room and talk, away from the guests." Leif gestures to the door on our left.

"Yes, I think that's best," Mira agrees with a weary voice.

"Perfect." I cut her a glance and give her a crude smile.

Of course, my father's wife wants to talk in private. I've already embarrassed her in front of her nearest and dearest. Everyone here today would have been important members from the Knights and the Komarovski. They'll have questions, but most of all, I've tainted the prim and proper image Mira Volkova seems to be upholding.

I know she's probably as nice as she appears to be, but sometimes the good must unavoidably suffer with the bad.

As if on cue, my two personal guards, Jayce and Zane, come in from my right.

"Zane, please see the guests out." I point to the door I used to enter. "And, Jayce, take the girl to my house."

"What?" Anastasia suddenly finds her voice. "I'm not going anywhere."

"Sorry, Princess, but you are." I give her a daring smile, willing her to defy me.

She looks away, turning to Viktor. When he gives her a defeated shake of his head, she rushes over to her father. "Dad, don't let him take me."

Uther slips an arm around her. "It will be okay." His voice is soothing and so unlike the monster I know him to be.

"How can it be okay?"

"Anastasia, please. Just go with them. I will sort this out as fast as I can."

Sort out? Oh no, no, no. The prick shouldn't make promises he can't keep or give her hope when there is none. He already knows there's nothing to sort out. All cards have been laid on the table, and decisions have been made.

Anastasia is mine, no matter what anyone says or tries to do to set her free.

"Okay?" Uther cups her cheeks and leans in closer, making a lock of his shaggy gray hair fall over his eye.

Anastasia glances at me then looks back at her father, nodding reluctantly. "Okay."

"I will walk you to the car."

Jayce makes his way to them, and this time when Anastasia looks over her shoulder, she stares at Viktor. The man who almost became her husband.

Is that love in her eyes?

Most likely. If it is, love just makes this vendetta that much sweeter. Perfectly in keeping with the saying that revenge is a dish best served cold.

Zane ushers the guests out as I watch Anastasia go, wishing I could take her home myself. Seeing my new toy later will, however, have to do. My job here isn't finished yet.

When I turn back to face my father's family, I don't miss the hatred in Viktor's eyes.

"This way, everyone." Leif gestures to the door again and leads the way out.

Mira, Viktor, Zakh, and Malik follow him.

Triumph surges through me as I trail behind and acknowledge that I have everyone right where I want them. Even my father on his deathbed.

I've waited a long time to share my story and avenge my mother's death.

I'm no longer the helpless boy who was kept a secret.

I'm Desmier Volkova. The man. And their reckoning.

CHAPTER THREE

ANASTASIA

The wedding is off.

God, what a nightmare.

And now I'm being taken to Desmier Volkova's house.

The thought weakens me, and I feel so fragile I fear I may shatter into a million pieces.

Thank God Dad's arm is still around me. If he weren't holding me up and moving us down the corridor toward the car, I don't think I could do it myself.

The echo of my heels against the marble floor is a welcome distraction from the turbulence in my mind, but I can't stop myself from freaking out about what will happen to me. And Viktor. I've never seen him look so defeated, and so powerless.

I'm desperately trying to hold it together, but I can't.

How the fuck must I? What the hell are the chances of

my life being ruined by Viktor's long-lost brother? And surely, he can't be serious about marrying me.

Every time I try to process it, I feel like I'm losing my mind.

When we walk past the stunning hall decorated for the reception, my heart gives a hard squeeze. From the rose-gold tablecloths and the covered chairs with giant bows on the back to the white Calla lilies surrounding the pewter candlesticks on each table... Everything is magnificent.

This glimpse is all I'll be seeing.

I lean even more on Dad. "I can't. I just can't."

"It will be okay."

My dad always fixes things when they go wrong, but this...? Viktor? Desmier? Me?

I want to believe Dad or Viktor will be able to sort this out, but the tension in my gut is telling me otherwise.

Our footsteps become louder as we continue to the adjoining hall. Once there, Jayce—I think that's his name—is joined by three more guards. All are armed.

I'm quite aware of the dark underworld of danger I live in. Where all of society's rules bend and break for men with power.

When you live in a world like mine, where the Knights and the Russian mafia are God, anything can happen because they are the law. Things can change drastically from one moment to the next and leave you trying to crawl your way out of hell.

I saw the way Desmier looked at me. I saw how he undressed me with his eyes, and I noted the seductive promise lurking within them.

I don't want to go to his house.

When I get there, what will happen next?

What will Desmier do to me?

Even though there was seduction in his eyes, his entire presence and show of power were filled with vengeance.

We walk outside into the drizzling rain.

"Syuda," Jayce speaks in Russian and points to a black Ferrari parked by the entrance to the parking lot.

Once we reach the car, he opens the door and gestures for me to get in. When I think of leaving my dad and disappearing into the unknown with these men, I feel an invisible hand around my throat. It squeezes tighter and tighter, stopping the air from reaching my lungs.

Jayce clenches his jaw, instantly looking pissed off. "Get in."

"Wait, please." I'm not ready for this.

"We need to go now, Miss Sidorov."

"Please, I just need to talk to my father."

"Anastasia, please go with th—" Dad starts, but I interrupt him by grabbing his arm.

"No. I need to know what you plan to do." I need to know *something. Anything.* "Surely, this Desmier doesn't seriously mean to just take me and keep me. Right?"

I can't imagine that happening. Not with so many powerful people around me who should be able to fix this. People like my father. But Dad just stares back at me.

"My love, Desmier has the marriage contract."

"But that contract was for me marrying Viktor."

He releases a heavy sigh, and his expression turns as soft and caring as when Mom died. "The contract was for you to marry the eldest Volkova son. That's Desmier."

My heart triple beats. "But surely, you can revoke it. You

made the contract. There must be some law or something that can help us."

"No, there's nothing." He rests his large hands on my shoulders. "Look, Anastasia... there are some things you don't understand."

Dad glances at Jayce, and a moment of understanding appears to pass between them. Then something hits my mind. It's a sort of realization I didn't sense before because I was too deep in my shock to notice anything else.

It's how Dad looks. Or rather, how he doesn't look.

Dad wasn't surprised or shocked like everyone else when he saw Desmier.

He didn't even argue when the order was issued to take me to Desmier's house. He was completely compliant.

The overprotective father I knew would never hand-deliver me to people he doesn't know. Men he doesn't know. *Dangerous* men with guns.

Dad wouldn't even let me go to the mall or Lorelai's house, or, fuck, the heavily guarded college campus, without a bodyguard.

Yet here he is, sending me off without any of our guards, telling me he can't help me.

It's like he knew. Knew these people, knew I'd be taken.

Jesus Christ. Did he?

My heart jumps, then gallops, and I wish I could run away with it.

I search Dad's eyes. But I find nothing to tell me I'm wrong.

"What do you mean, there are things I don't understand?" I hate that my voice shakes.

His head drops for a moment. When he returns his eyes

to mine, he looks weak and drained, opposite of the man I know him to be.

"Desmier Volkova has certain powers not even I can work my way around."

"Oh my God. You knew this would happen today. Didn't you?"

His eyes hold mine in place, and I feel in my soul that everything he says next is going to hurt me.

"I'm sorry, my girl. My hands are tied."

Now my heart pounds like it's trying to break through my ribs. "But you're the Senior Enforcer." My voice is high and pleading and desperate. I grab his jacket, pulling on the lapels.

"Anastasia, please calm down." He loosens my hands.

"Are you kidding me? Calm down?" I take a few steps backwards, every instinct telling me to run. Run now before I can't. Run now before it's too late.

But Jayce walks toward us, raises his gun, and cocks the hammer. He taps the silver barrel to the side of Dad's head, and everything inside me goes numb.

"You need to get in." Jayce jerks his head toward the car.

"This is wrong," I choke out, sounding like a little mouse.

He answers with a devilish smile. "Just so you know, I'm not required to keep your father alive. He's not needed for anything, but you are. Do you understand?"

I understand completely. The translated version of what he's saying is he'll kill my father right here and now if I don't do as I'm told.

The message my heart receives is that I'll lose another parent.

The memory of Mom's cold, dead eyes filters into my mind, and dark dread fills me. I nod my acquiescence, making my legs move so I can get in the car as quickly as possible.

When I slide in, Dad grabs my hand and squeezes it. That's all he gets to do, though, because Jayce pushes him away and closes the door.

He gets in next to me while the other men pile into the car. One on my other side and two in front.

The car starts up and pulls out of the driveway, taking me deeper into this nightmare, but I don't look away from my father's rigid form standing on the pavement with his shoulders sagging.

He said his hands were tied.

There's only one way to tie a man like my father down to beat him, and that's to hold something so powerful over his head that his only option is to bow.

So... Desmier must have something like that. Something big.

What is it?

Or maybe the better question is *why*.

Why is Desmier doing this?

And what exactly are his plans for me?

CHAPTER FOUR

DESMIER

Leif takes us to the closest meeting room, which is just as ornate as the rest of the building.

I'm the last to enter and close the door. My guests don't sit. They stand together facing me, waiting for answers.

"Well, start talking," Viktor demands.

"Yes, I'm eager to find out how I have another brother I never knew about," Malik says, and Zakh nods.

"My mother was Fryeda Polinsky," I begin. "She and our father grew up together in Moscow. He was with her before your mother." I pause, glancing at Mira, who looks more ghostly than before. Leif told me everything about the past and never shied away from the possibility that Mira was at least aware Mom existed and was involved with my father. She didn't know about me, though. No one did. "They broke up when he was promised to Mira, but he didn't know she was pregnant with me. She didn't tell him until I was twelve. However, things didn't go as expected. She didn't know that my existence as his firstborn son threatened his business relationship with Mira's family. Or that he would order our deaths."

"What?" Mira sucks in a sharp breath, and her entire being trembles. "Evgeni did that?"

"Yes, he did." That's the truth I've had to live with. My father sent Uther to kill my mother and me. "My mother was killed, but I survived."

Mira's eyes grow larger. "I can't believe what I'm hearing."

"It is the truth." Mira's family business mines diamonds in three different countries, and the Volkovas have a shipping company that practically owns the seas. It was a match made in heaven and the reason for their combined success today. Success my father wanted to protect, but I'll take all of it now. "Once your father died and signed over the remaining parts of his company to my father, losing the business was no longer a threat to my life."

Her father died two years ago. After that, Leif and I waited for the right moment to strike. We already knew of the plan for Viktor to marry Anastasia so the Sidorov family property development business could join the Volkovas' already flourishing fortune. But Leif wanted me to get everything else. The door was opened with the news that my father's heart condition was terminal.

"How did you escape when you were a boy?" Mira asks, compassion filling her eyes.

"Leif saved me."

She looks at Leif in disbelief and shakes her head. "How could you keep this secret from us?"

"It was for his safety." Leif clenches his jaw. "And I vowed to avenge Fryeda's death. I grew up with her, too. All Evgeni cared about was his business. So much so that he was willing to kill a woman who loved him, and his own child. People who knew Fryeda and Desmier believed they died at their home in a fire. That's the story Evgeni went with all these long years. I took Desmier to Denmark to keep him safe. Then I waited for the right time to reveal the truth and see that he obtains his rightful place as heir to the Volkova legacy."

"And what about me?" Viktor challenges.

"I'm sorry, my boy, but it is Desmier's birthright."

Viktor's brows shoot up. "And today was the right time? My wedding day?"

"Marriage to Anastasia Sidorov is part of the empire transfer." Leif's face softens. "And as you are aware, the ninety-day transition period under the Rites of Inheritance ended at midday today. That means your father is out of the picture now. So, yes, today was the right time. The bottom line is, it's time to choose a new leader. And I have."

"So, he gets everything?" Mira asks weakly. "My business included?"

"Yes, he does."

"This is an outrage," Viktor spits. "You know it is."

"And you know there's not a goddam thing you can do about it." I take back the reins. People can talk and mouth off about shit, but they know the law of the land and, worst of all, the law of the Knights.

"You're taking absolutely *everything*?" Zakh's dark eyes search mine.

By everything, he means anything with the Volkova name. But it's not like my seizure will mean they'll be homeless-on-the-street poor. They were each given a sizable inheritance from Mira's father, and they'll receive another once our father passes. However, none of that comes close to what I'm taking.

"Yes, I am taking everything. But there are some things that will remain the same. I'll let you know what those are in due course." That will be things like their homes in some cases, and other assets.

God knows I would prefer to kick them all out and burn everything to the ground. I want them to suffer the way I did when Mom had to clean toilets and go through all kinds of shit to take care of me.

"What about the subordinate selection?" From the apprehensive look in Viktor's eyes, I can tell that's what he's most worried about. They all are. My arrival means there's only one more position of power left.

As the soon-to-be Sovientrik, and under the unique circumstances of the Knights' law, I have the authority to choose the Obshchak, which is the third member of the Bratva elite. The man who holds that position is the chief financial officer of not only the Bratva but the Knights too.

Leif wants me to pick one of my brothers, and he also wants me to allow them to keep their jobs at Volkova Inc.

I'm not overly fond of that part of the plan, but I'm following Leif's advice.

A king has to wear his crown with honor and know how to protect his conquests. I'm not a fool, or vengeful enough to fuck up a billion-dollar business by thinking I can run things on my own and allow the empire to fall apart.

"You'll find out at the inauguration ceremony." That's in a months' time, so they will have to wait. I need time to think and figure out who's who in real life, not just from the records Leif has given me.

"This is complete madness." Viktor steps forward and glances at my tattoo. He knows, just like Aleksander did, what it means, but he's showing he doesn't care.

"Well, it's happening, *brother,* whether you like it or not." I square my shoulders. "Now, if you don't mind, I have things to do."

On that note, I bow my head, give them a victorious smile, then Leif and I walk out, leaving them to stew in the pile of shit I just launched them into.

I can imagine what they'll be talking about now, and how they'll probably want to keep the truth about my father under wraps. Mira in particular won't want to destroy my father's highly-esteemed reputation in the Knights. Or hers. Even though no punishment will be issued because of who my father is, what he did to Mom and me is despicable and disgraceful even by the Knights' standards.

When we reach the end of the corridor, I stop when my name is called. It's Uther.

He rushes up to me, out of breath. His face is red, and his eyes are filled with panic.

"This can't work. You can't take my daughter. She's an innocent in this." He shakes his graying head, contorting his face so his scar becomes more pronounced. "There must be something else I can do."

I give him a radiant smile, enjoying his trepidation the

way he enjoyed mine when he tried to kill me. "Uther Sidorov, you know there's *nothing* else you can do. You also know what will happen if you try."

This motherfucker knows my threats aren't empty, nor are they something to be trifled with. I've already taken Anastasia and his business through the marriage contract. I will also be relieving him of his senior position in the Bratva. Meaning the fucker will lose everything. I would have loved to kick him out completely, but I didn't want to raise any red flags.

He knows if I unleash all the serious dirt I have on him, he'll have more than just me to fear. And more than himself to worry about. His weakness is his daughter, but he wasn't thinking of her when he got up to all sorts of shady shit that would get him in trouble with the Pakhan and drag her in, too.

"I think we're done here." I tap the lapel of his jacket and turn away to leave.

Desperation must have made him crazy because he catches my arm and pulls me back, looking like a helpless animal who's been caught in a snare.

Glaring down at his fingers, I seethe, and he releases me.

"Please don't tell her what I did." His voice comes out in a hurried rush. "She won't understand. She's good... Not like me. Please don't tell her."

I laugh. I can't help it. The asshole doesn't want his sweet daughter knowing he's a monster. "What shouldn't I tell her, Uther? There's so much."

"None of it."

"We're part of a secret society and the Russian Mafia.

I'm sure she knows you're not a good man." The princess didn't look like she'd been kept in the dark.

"This is different."

I agree, but why should I do him any favors? I don't owe him shit.

There's bad, there's evil, and there's soulless—those whose souls are so tarnished and dark there is nothing human left in them. That's Uther, and by the end of this, it might be me, too.

"Worry about yourself, Uther. Not your daughter's opinion of you."

The only reason I won't tell Anastasia everything is to protect my plans to punish him. No one must find out about that, because knowing what I know would make me liable too. The Knights' law contains ways of punishing people like him, but he would only be accountable for the dirt I found on him. Not the crimes against Mom and me. Because our deaths were ordered by my father, they'd consider Uther as acting within his duties. That's why I'm taking matters into my own hands

The best part is no one will ever know, unless I choose to tell them.

To everyone, even if they have some suspicion that I have a vendetta against Uther, I'll just look like I'm honoring the marriage contract and securing a partnership with Sidorov Developments.

"She'll want to see me. You have to let me see her."

"How about you don't tell me what I have to do."

"But I—"

Uther's words die in his throat when Leif steps forward and grabs his shirt. "Enough, Uther Sidorov. I believe my nephew has given you a sufficient answer. Be grateful we've allowed you to keep your life. You will see your daughter at the wedding, and not before." Leif stares him down. "You will not contact her or make any further demands. Do you understand me?"

"Yes."

"Good. Now fuck the hell off."

My uncle may seem like the placid type, but he's far from it. He's silent and deadly and has wanted Uther's head for years.

When Leif rescued me in Russia, Uther was already gone, but I was able to identify him when I recovered. I begged Leif to leave him for me to deal with when the time was right.

This is my time now, and I plan to destroy him.

"Please don't hurt her, Desmier." One last plea from the loving father, but it falls on deaf ears.

Leif and I leave him standing there, drowning in the sea of worries he created for himself.

We make our way outside into the burst of crisp fresh air and rain, but I can still feel Uther's eyes burning holes into me.

I have the upper hand now, but I know I need to watch him. No matter what dirt I have or how powerful it is, Uther will be trying to find some way of getting his daughter back and restoring his plans. He undoubtedly loves her, but she was his biggest investment. Now he's broke and trapped under my thumb.

When Leif and I reach the parking lot, we stop and look at each other, silently acknowledging the ball of destruction we just set in motion.

We did it.

This secret plan we plotted for years is finally done, and now I'm fully a part of the world of the Knights.

I've shot straight to the top, and it feels like I'm right where I should be. Even though this isn't my world, it is my legacy and the thing my mother died for because my father didn't want me to have it.

"It's done," I breathe.

"It is done," Leif agrees, giving me a weary smile.

I can't help but notice that he looks like he's aged. I know the whole encounter was heavy for him because now his family knows he's been playing sides all these years. Nothing was ever as it seemed, and he knew their fates were never going to be what they worked for.

"You okay, Uncle?" I interchange between calling him Leif and Uncle, opting for the latter during these moments when we can just be ourselves and let down the shields of defense.

"As good as I can be. Let's hope by the end of this, we'll still be worthy of Valhalla."

Always the Viking. I swear Leif lives during the wrong time. Or maybe the universe got it right and he exists now so that people like me don't forget the old ways. Leif favors the way of life our ancestors led before they became Knights and were just Vikings.

Sometimes, I wish I could be like that, but there is too much darkness in me, and I'm not honorable enough to care where my soul goes—Heaven or Hell, Valhalla or Niflheim.

All I want is retribution for my mother. Until I get it, I don't really give a fuck what happens to me or any part of me.

Dragging in a breath, I clear my head of the haunting memory and return my focus to the present.

"I would still prefer if we did everything ourselves." I wish I could change Leif's mind. "I don't want any of my brothers to be my subordinates."

Brothers. I don't even want to call them that. The word feels wrong in my mind and my mouth.

"That was how it was meant to be." Leif presses his lips together. "Our family has never had an opportunity like this before, so it needs to be this way."

He's talking about the new structure of the Komarovsky. Months ago, after three members of the elite on the Knights' Council went rogue, the Pakhan took the opportunity to streamline the leadership. The Volkovas were chosen because of Aleksander's long-standing relationship with my father and the established lineage of power and wealth. In our family, positions of power are inherited, thereby keeping everything contained within one body. So, if the Pakhan and his heirs were eliminated, we would be able to take over the entire operation.

Prior to my father's unfortunate state, he was the Sovientrik and Viktor the Obshchak. Although the Sovientrik can choose whomever he wants as a subordinate, the intention was to keep it in the family between father and son or between the brothers.

"You will need allies, Desmier. Allies you'll find in your brothers."

I smirk, not bothering to hide my sarcasm. "You were in there. You saw how they looked at me. There isn't anyone in there I can trust."

"We'll see, boy. I knew this day would pit brother

against brother and create enemies, but they're men like you. They won't want to walk away empty-handed. Better to have some power than none, even if that means falling in line and being a subordinate instead of the leader you thought you were going to be."

As always, my uncle sounds wise, so I nod respectfully. "Alright. I guess we'll see."

"I'll catch up with you later. I have a few more legal matters to attend to for the assets being transferred to your name."

"Okay. Speak to you later."

"Well done for today." He smiles proudly.

"You too."

He taps my head like he used to when I was a boy, then he walks to his car while I head in the opposite direction to jump on my motorcycle.

I have a few things to do, too, before I head home to get acquainted with the princess. Then I have one other thing I promised myself I'd do before midnight.

I just returned to the States a few days ago after being at sea for over six months. Before that, I floated between Denmark and Russia, where I'm predominantly based. That's where Leif and I would meet over the years. I've hardly ever come to Boston because I wasn't ready. Now I am.

I wonder what the princess is doing now. Is she scared?

She should be, although she looks like the type to try and fight fear.

I sense that fire I saw earlier is a taste of what I'm up against.

Uther looked unhinged, so I can only imagine he must have said a thing or two to his darling daughter.

The darling daughter I can't wait to get my filthy, dirty outcast hands on.

This is the dawn of a new era, where those like me who walk in the dark reign.

God help anyone who stands in my way.

Or tries to take what's mine.

CHAPTER FIVE

ANASTASIA

Resting my head against the satin wall, I stare at the sea in the distance through the long casement windows. I'd think the intricate carvings in the wood were beautifully designed if I weren't trapped behind them like a bird in a cage.

My mother believed patience was the most powerful of virtues.

I always agreed. But there are some situations where not even the highest level of patience can help you.

Mine is without a doubt one of them.

Two hours ago, I arrived at the massive compound of Desmier Volkova's mansion on Cape Cod. The house is one of the old-style Tudor homes you'd normally find in Salem, but his is ostentatious and has a haunted vibe.

The idea of being in a haunted mansion is creepy enough, but I feel like I'm trapped in one of my nightmares.

When I got here, a rude-looking woman with silver hair and an upturned nose met us on the driveway. Then, without a word, she escorted me to this huge master bedroom I knew straightaway belonged to a man. It's the décor. Dark colors surround me, from the navy wallpaper to the long curtains at the window, and the black silk sheets covering the king-size bed.

The only touch of difference is in the white Persian rug in the center of the room.

The woman left me in here to my thoughts—the first being that the room belongs to Desmier.

There was really no question about it. His scent, a mixture of the forest and the sea, clung to the air with the same power he exuded when he walked into my wedding and turned my world upside down.

To confirm my suspicions, I looked inside the wardrobes and chest of drawers. When I found men's clothing that suited his style, I knew I was right.

As the time drifted by, my thoughts have become a chaotic mess.

I even tried to come up with an escape plan but realized all too quickly there was no way out for me—except the way I came in. The house and grounds are heavily guarded with armed men who look like they could form their own Bratva. And even though I was captain of the girls' swim team in high school, I don't think I could jump in the sea and swim out of here. Doesn't mean I wouldn't try; I just know the chances of escaping that way are slimmer than slim.

Dad, of course, hasn't left my mind, but my biggest worry is what will happen when Desmier eventually graces me with his presence.

When I see him again, it will be in here. In this bedroom. And I will be all by myself.

I'm trying to balance my thoughts, but I feel just as unhinged and manic as when I found my mother lying dead in her bathtub—her body lifeless and gone forever, the water bloody from her slit wrists, and a bottle of pills scattered on the floor beside her.

It's an image I'll never get out of my mind. I don't think anyone would, much less a fourteen-year-old who adored her mother to the ends of the earth.

I feel like I'm in that same limbo and my worries are chewing up my insides. Whatever Dad did is going to dictate what happens to me next.

With Dad, this mess could be about *anything,* and I know he has his secrets.

My father is an important man with a job that has taken him everywhere. Sidorov Developments is just the ordinary day-to-day job he inherited from my grandfather, but his power lies in what he does for the Bratva. The range of what that includes is vast and way beyond my scope.

Like most men of status who keep women out of business, my father did the same.

Trying to figure this out is going to be like a fruitless attempt to pick a needle out of the sea. It doesn't help either that while I was carted off to this prison, everyone else went to talk, leaving me in the dark.

I wonder if Viktor's hands are tied too.

If not, would he fight to marry me?

I've always thought of us as a couple, even though Dad only allowed us to start dating when I turned eighteen. I knew I wasn't the only woman on Viktor's arm, and I didn't expect him to be a virgin like me either.

I'd seen him with women multiple times at events like fundraisers, and I'd heard things from Lorelai. Things I didn't want to hear.

Now I wonder if he loves me enough to challenge Desmier and rescue me.

I know how the Knights operate when it comes to oaths and blood contracts, so Viktor might not be able to do anything, regardless of how he feels.

But would he try?

Even if he did, it might not help me right now.

As it stands, the only thing I can do for myself is find out more information.

When I see Desmier, I'll ask what's going on then try to negotiate my freedom.

Surely, I can make him see this can't work and people don't do shit like this anymore. This isn't the Viking age or the time of sea pirates when a man would just grab a woman and keep her under lock and key.

It's—

My thoughts are invaded by the ominous sound of the door opening. Even before I look around, I know it's not the rude woman coming in. There's a shift in the air, like an omen of danger.

So when I meet the bright hazel eyes of my captor, I'm ready for him. And I can see straightaway from the stern expression on his face that talking to him is going to be difficult.

He walks in, and the door swings shut, the sound of the

click lingering like a reminder that I don't know who I'm dealing with.

The biker jacket is gone, but he still has the same drifter look, enhanced by the expanse of muscle on his arms, which I can clearly see now, bulging against his fitted T-shirt.

My eyes flick to the clothes folded in his hands. I spot a gray T-shirt and something stretchy like yoga pants. I assume those are for me, and my stomach drops.

The beginning of a smile tips his full, sensual lips, revealing dimples that make his already handsome face more striking. I stare back at him, trying to figure him out, but I can't. His personality seems to have several things going on, and I'm not sure what part of him I'm going to get.

From the predatory vibe emanating from him, I know to stay focused because despite everything, he's dangerous. All the Volkovas are, but this one is the one to watch.

Especially with that rune on his wrist.

The only time I've ever seen it was in books about the Viking gods and paintings of Raventhorn, the Viking founder of the Knights.

Desmier stops paces away, his smile coming to fruition and his scent wrapping around me.

"Alone at last, Princess." A twinkle lights up his eyes as he holds out the clothes for me to take. "These are for you to change into. Your clothes will be brought over tomorrow."

Over my dead body. I want to tell him just that, but I hold my tongue. It's best not to start my negotiation with a hostile attitude. At the same time, I don't want him to think I'm weak.

Ignoring his outstretched hand, I set my shoulders back and glare at him.

"What is going on?" At least I sound more confident than I feel. I've always been good at that, and I'm glad to see some things haven't left me.

"I was right. You are as fiery as a Valkyrie." His voice takes on a sing-song edge, irritating me. "I wonder what else I'll find out about you."

"*Nothing.* I want to know what is going on."

"You were at the wedding, weren't you, Princess?"

"Yes, I was, but there's more, isn't there?"

"Yes." Casually, he sets the clothes on the wooden chair next to me, never breaking his gaze from mine.

"Okay, so tell me. Tell me why you've suddenly come on the scene like a damn wild card and how come you've existed all this time with no one knowing about you. What are you planning? What are you planning for me?"

Something darkens in his face as he studies mine. He leans closer, as if trying to intimidate me, and although my nerves spike and scatter like darkness being chased away by light, I stand my ground.

"None of those are things you have to concern yourself with."

My blood heats at his lame-as-fuck answer. "If your plans involve my life, I need to know why you're doing this to me."

"Because I can." The cool nonchalance in his voice is as cold and uncaring as his Arctic stare.

"You can't just take me and think you're going to get away with it."

His sinful lips spread into a full smile that borders on psychotic. It makes me think he is.

"My dear Anastasia, I've already gotten away with

everything I wanted." His eyes bore into me. "What? Were you expecting someone like your precious Viktor to come and save you?"

"Viktor isn't going to allow you to do this to me. I was going to be his wife."

Desmier steps closer. This time, I try to put some space between us by backing away, but I come up against the wall, feeling like a little mouse when I gaze up at him. Next to this hulking man, my little heels barely add a few inches to my five feet and three inches. I feel even smaller when he barricades me in by resting his hands on either side of me, trapping me further. Then, like a predator, he inches much closer, hovering a breath away.

I try to appear calm, but my heart pounds frantically, hammering out of cadence.

Can he see it?

Hear it?

"Baby girl..." His voice lowers a notch and deepens, making the adrenaline hammer through my veins. Lifting a lock of my hair, he allows it to coil around his finger, all the while keeping his eyes on me. "You've been at my home now for over two hours, and no one has come to save you. When I walked into your wedding and took you, not even the Pakhan could stop me. Believe me when I say there's not a damn thing Viktor can do to get you back. He's as useless to you as your father."

"My father?" At the mention of Dad—where I was only echoing his words—his face takes on a savage edge.

"Yes, baby girl."

"This is crazy. You need to let me go. Whatever my father has done is nothing to do with me."

"Maybe so, but you're key to my plans."

"How am I key?" My voice shakes.

"Because like it or not, you are your father's heir and one of his assets. Since I'm taking everything he owns, that includes you." His mocking grin returns with a vengeance. "Your father has nothing, Anastasia."

My God in heaven. "Nothing?"

"Not a goddam thing. Not his home, his company, and not you. Everything he owns is mine."

That's entirely different to what the marriage contract stipulates. He's not supposed to own anything.

"You are mine now. Mine to Fuck, whenever, however, and wherever I want."

Terror writhes through my being as I realize how much danger I'm truly in, and panic seizes my soul. I want to run out of my skin, or tear it off—anything to get away from him.

"I'm not yours." I try to imbue my voice with the strength I summoned before, but it's evident I'm scared.

"Say whatever you want. Truth is truth. Now change out of that dress and come downstairs for something to eat."

I shake my head. "No. I don't want anything from you. I want to go home."

"This is your home now."

"Fuck you!" I shove at his granite chest, hurting my wrists.

He laughs, mocking me again. "Fuck me? Is that a request, Valkyrie?"

The pet names—*princess, baby girl, Valkyrie*—just enrage me.

"You fucking bastard. You know it's not a damn request. Let me go."

"I said no, and this is the last time I'm going to tell you to take off that dress."

"Fuck. You."

I don't even get to entertain my next thought. Desmier shoves me hard against the wall, grabs the top of my dress, and tears it right off me like a bodice-ripping pirate. The delicate material shreds under his savagery, and I scream, barely registering that I'm topless. The dress had a built-in bra, and now my breasts have fallen out, bouncing into his chest as he presses against me.

The pirate-man then tears off my panties and throws them to the side, assaulting my dignity.

With my bare pussy on show and nothing left to cover me, I panic further. More disbelief hits me because he's the first man to see me naked, and I don't even know him.

I don't know what he's capable of or if I've only accelerated his seedy plans for me.

Grabbing my wrists with one large hand, he pins them over my head and holds me down so I can't move. He then does a full sweep of my naked body, his eyes roaming over my breasts.

"My fiery little sexy-as-fuck Valkyrie." His warm breath tickles my skin as he inches in toward me again, moving to my ear. He licks over the lobe and tugs on the edge, making something weird stir deep in my core. It feels far more intimate than it should, and my nipples harden. He notices, and I sense a smile on his face even though I can't see him properly. "Do not think I didn't notice the way you looked at me earlier."

"I don't know what you're talking about," I pant, embarrassment filling my cheeks because I know exactly what he means.

"I never figured you for a liar, so let's not kid ourselves. You wouldn't have looked at me like you wanted to fuck me if my brother were getting the job done."

His crass words send a bolt of electricity through me, and my eyes snap wide. He shuffles, meeting my gaze, and leans in so I can feel his arousal pressing into my belly.

"Feel my dick, Valkyrie." He smiles, pushing his cock harder into my skin. On feeling his size and rock-hardness, moisture gathers in my pussy.

Shit. I'm wet and growing wetter than when I touch myself in the private confines of my room.

My mind goes deeper down the rabbit hole when he traces a finger down the length of my stomach and lingers at the start of my mound.

"What are you going to do to me?" I whisper.

"I don't think you're ready for that yet." A deep chuckle rumbles in his chest. "But here's what I have in mind: me, fucking you hard against this wall. You, screaming my name. Begging for more."

Wildfire flicks over my entire body, and I know not even I can deny the thrill of this. Whatever *this* is that's happening between us.

Tilting his chin, he gives me a shit-eating grin. The kind I imagine a shark would display before it devoured its prey.

"At least I'm not a liar," Desmier says. "You don't have to wonder if I want to fuck you. You can feel it, and I'll tell you like I just did."

"You're a vile, crude asshole."

"Yes, but you like that, even though you shouldn't."

"You're completely deluded if you think that." As heat and embarrassment continues to consume me, I'm not sure who I'm trying to convince. Him. Or me.

He looks at me as if he can see straight through my words to what is probably nothing but lies. "Let's get a few things straight, shall we?" He brushes his nose briefly along mine, his warm breath doing things to my body I can no longer ignore. "This is your new life now, and there's nothing you can do about it."

I stare back at him, feeling the weight of my world crumbling all around me. I know there's nothing I can do to fix it, but I need to know why this is happening.

I need to know what Dad did.

"What power do you have over my father to do this to us?"

"Enough to bury him." He uses the same icy tone as before. A steel weight drops in my soul, pulling me under. "I have enough for the Knights' Council to force him to his knees and execute him. And everyone in his family. Starting with you. One word from me, and that's it—death."

My heart stops like someone switched off all the power. When it starts beating again, it's pounding faster and faster and faster, and my brain is paralyzed with terror.

Dad, what the hell did you do?

Execution?

For all of us?

Him first? No. I can't lose my father.

I can't.

Not that way. Or *any* way.

"No. Please. Don't let them kill him." I'm begging with

my heart and soul because this is so much worse than I thought. "Please. I'm sure he's sorry for whatever he did. He's not a bad person. I swear it. He's not bad. He's my father."

I'm pleading with everything in me, but his icy glare tells me I'd have more luck talking to a wall.

"That means nothing to me." Hatred radiates from Desmier's eyes, telling me exactly how he feels about my father. I've never seen hate like that on anyone. It's crippling and frightening, and making me realize that Dad must have done something terrible to him. That's the only thing that makes sense, and explains why Dad said his hands were tied.

"What did he do to you?" My voice is barely there, but the question seems to stall him.

There's a moment of silence when he looks like he's contemplating an answer, then the hardness returns to his face.

"You don't have to worry about that now."

"But I should know."

The mocking smirk comes back and he leans in again, his chest brushing over my nipples—a reminder that I'm naked.

"Believe me, princess, it's best you don't know. So do not ask me again." He moves back and his eyes drop to my lips then float down to my heaving breasts. Lust—more intense than at the wedding—ignites when he looks back up at me. It's too much. Too intense. Too overpowering. "All you have to worry about is pleasing me. You will do as you are told and *when* you are told. Fuck with me, and I won't hesitate to punish your father, or you. You understand?"

I nod slowly, looking away from him.

Quickly, he catches my face and guides it back to his. "Look at me and tell me you understand."

"I understand."

"Good girl. Now you can get yourself ready for our wedding."

My God. No. "Our wedding?" I can barely get the words out.

"Yes, Valkyrie. In five weeks, you'll be my wife."

CHAPTER SIX

DESMIER

By the gods, Anastasia Sidorov is fucking beautiful.

I don't know how the fuck I'm standing over her perfect naked body with her tits looking as ripe as they do and managing to restrain myself.

Me.

Me, whose primary hobby includes fucking, is bridling the beast inside that wants to ravage her body.

It would be so easy to bend her over the desk and fuck her senseless now that I have her all to myself. We're not in a room full of people, and she's not holding Viktor's hand.

It's only us within the four walls of my bedroom and the savage force of wild attraction rippling between us.

But business first, then fucking when I see fit. Right now, I'll settle for my fascination with our attraction, and her fire, which extinguishes as she processes the fact that I have her father under my thumb and she will be my wife in five weeks.

"You're serious about marrying me?" Her voice is weaker now.

I've watched her go from strong to weak in a matter of minutes. The transition has been fascinating.

"I don't joke."

When her mouth opens and no words come out, I release her and step away. It's best that I do. I will fuck her, but not today. She doesn't have to know that,

though.

She can be afraid of me. That's perhaps the wisest thing for us both. Fear will keep her in line and me in check so I remember the role she plays.

When I allow my gaze to skim over her body, I realize keeping myself in check might be more difficult than I anticipated.

The Valkyrie folds her arms over her ample breasts and tries to close her legs tighter to hide her pussy, but it doesn't work. She could cover herself with the entire house, and it wouldn't wipe the memory of what she looks like from my mind.

Like the asshole I am, I feel another surge of triumph for getting one more thing over Viktor. I've not only robbed him of his wedding and the legacy he thought he was going to have, but I've stripped his bride naked on the day he should have feasted on her, whether for the first time or not.

One look at her decadent body, and I'm sure there's no way she's a virgin, or that today would have been the first that Viktor got to be with her. I'm sure my dear brother would have taken his fair share. And now I will.

Anastasia will certainly be my entertainment in more ways than one. Until I'm done with her.

"Put on the clothes I got you and come downstairs. Ehlga will give you food."

She doesn't answer. She just stares at me, unmoving and unblinking, so I take one last look at the soft flesh of her fully rounded tits before I walk away.

I leave to regain control of my mind, and tamp down the temptation to tell her the truth about her father.

The clever girl figured out that this was personal. I kind of thought she would.

It would have been sweet to tell her that her father isn't the good person she thinks he is, but I'm walking away.

Sure, I need to protect my plans above everything. But I can see for myself that she's good and not like Uther.

I saw it in her fear as she begged for his life, and there was something about her pleas that evoked the last shreds of humanity in me.

Her innocence and love for her father is like that of a child. Learning a vile truth like what I have to share would be like death. Death of trust.

Maybe I like her just enough not to do that to her *yet.*

Or maybe it's more than that and it's me. Maybe these are all excuses and I'm not as ready as I thought I was to talk about what Uther did to me.

Right now I've told Anastasia all she needs to know. Nothing else is important.

What's important is already happening. Today was a victory, and I have to take a moment to acknowledge that.

When I walk into the corridor, I release a haggard breath and adjust my cock so I'm not so obvious.

Ehlga is preparing dinner, but I asked her to make Anastasia a snack if she goes down for food. I already know she most likely won't, so I've instructed Ehlga to bring food up later.

Later, when I'm not here.

Ehlga has been my custodian since I bought this house, but I've practically known her all my life. She's originally from Russia but lived in Denmark.

When Mom was killed, Leif hired her to look after me, so she became my guardian. She's the only other person apart from him whom I treat like family. As one of the people Leif trusted, she knows my story. Years ago, when I decided it was time to establish a base in Boston, I hired her to work here.

Ehlga is not overly fond of Anastasia being here because she knows whose daughter she is. But since she's always and ever loyal to me, she'll do what I need her to do.

I make my way downstairs to the study, where I find my crew waiting for me.

There's Jayce, Zane, and Gytha sitting around the table in the center. Well, Gytha is actually on the table with her legs crossed, the leather mini skirt she's wearing barely covering her panties. She has her slick black hair in a ponytail and is wearing bright red lipstick. She's my femme fatal assistant and has been other things, too, over the years.

We've all known each other for a long time. Jayce and Zane are sons of two of Leif's men. I met them in my late teens. We all met Gytha years after when she was looking for the man who killed her father. I helped her get her retribution, and she's stayed with me since.

The four of us linked up as a team five years ago when I

decided to set up my own company and traffic items on the black market. But my main job has actually been on the Volkova Inc. cargo ships. As Leif manages that side of the business, I've worked there covertly since I was eighteen years old under an alias. Over the years I worked my way up and secured connections—a lot through my black market friends in different countries across the world—so I manage all the contract negotiations for our clients.

I still plan to go back, without the alias. People will now know who I am and wonder why I still choose to get my hands dirty and live at sea for most of the year, but that's me.

The sailor. The perpetual God of the Sea. Like Poseidon.

While I'm away, the crew takes care of the other business. Jayce and Zane are the muscle and do everything I do. Gytha takes care of my clients, but more importantly, she's a hacker unlike any other I've known. She gets the dirt I need on people.

It was *her* who got the dirt I have on Uther and all the intel I needed on everyone else.

A smile spreads across her doll-like face as I pull up a chair and plant myself in it, looking at each of them. They all look happy. They should be. They all worked hard to make today possible.

"We did it," Jayce states.

"We did." I smile, bumping my fist with his.

"Shouldn't we be having champagne?" Gytha asks, raising one perfectly arched brow. "Or something along those lines?"

"We will." I meet her serpentine eyes, which are fixed on me with wild seduction. This is one of those times when we'd usually end up in bed, or anywhere we could get lost in each other, to destress. "For now, how about you each get those bonuses I promised?"

"Fuck, yeah," Zane replies, pumping his fist once in the air then snapping his fingers. "And that's why I fucking love working for you."

I'd like working for me, too, if I added a bonus of ten G onto an already high five-figure monthly salary.

Given my poor upbringing, sometimes it feels unbelievable that I'm able to do this. Me at twenty-eight years old being in charge of what I've already been doing without the Volkova fortune.

"Don't go wild just yet. The job is still ongoing." That's why I've summoned them here for a brief check-in. "We also need to plan the next steps."

"Oh, we know," Jayce agrees, lighting up a cigarette and puffing on it. "We fucked with the big boys today. Can't screw with people like that and not expect them to bite back."

"We knew this would happen, though," Zane concedes.

"We did. That's why I need each of you to keep your eyes open even more than before."

My brothers and Uther are nothing in comparison to our previous encounters with mafia groups and other low-key organizations.

Fucking with them is like screwing with the Knights themselves. Everything is older, more deep-rooted, and involves the deadly combination of wealth and power. There will also be people who won't like that I'm in charge because their business relationships will be affected.

"What next, boss?" Gytha asks, noticing my deep concentration.

"I think I'm going to need Zane backing Jayce up on surveillance. I need solid eyes on my brothers and Uther. I need to know what they're up to twenty-four seven." I want to know everything no matter what it is. Whether they spit, shit, or sleep. "I will also need you guys watching my father's men." I'll inherit my father's personal guards as well, and his task force. I undoubtedly have to make sure they can be trusted.

"We can do all that," Jayce says, and Zane dips his head in agreement.

"And me?" Gytha asks.

Zane tries to sneak a peek between her legs when she sits forward. He looks away quickly before she catches him, schooling himself. He's always liked her, but he wouldn't go there because of me. No one is ever certain when we're friends and when we're lovers.

"You're with me," I answer, ignoring the warning in my heart to beware of her. Working closely with Gytha may not be the smartest choice when I need clarity. But despite what we are and what we aren't, I don't trust anyone else to do what she does for me.

"You?" Her eyes sparkle with hope.

"I'll need help with the company once I start." I'll be at the headquarters of Volkova Inc. bright and early Monday morning, doing the parts of the job I don't give two fucks about. "I need you to check out all the workers and keep an eye out for anything I might need to be aware of."

I especially need her because at the end of all of this, Leif is retiring. That was another reason he wanted me to work with my brothers.

He projected that our work should take about two months to complete. By then, he'll have finished teaching me what I need to know. He plans to return to Russia. I'll leave months later when I have everything up and running, then head back out to sea.

"That sounds like I got the easy job." Gytha chuckles.

"Don't be quick to judge. The company is huge, and I need to make sure there's no dissension in the ranks, or shit."

"Okay, boss." She makes her tone sound purposely sweet. The complete opposite of what she is.

"That's all from me for now. I'll need a report from you guys every six hours for the next few days."

"Got it. See you later." Jayce stands, and Zane follows his lead.

When the two leave, I look at Gytha because she hasn't moved. She continues to stare at me, the fire of mischief dancing in her eyes.

"I thought I'd double-check to make sure you didn't need me for anything else. Right now." She straightens and makes a point of parting her legs so I can see her panties.

"I don't need anything else." We go through these cycles, she and I. One moment we're up, the next we're down. Sometimes it's fun, other times not.

"You did so much to get to this point, though. Seems a shame you aren't at least celebrating with me like we used to. Remember the last time?"

"Yes." I'm not likely to forget because I considered making her mine officially.

That was a year ago. At the time, we'd been exclusive for months and I took her on a getaway to Morocco. I saw it as the start of something more. But she didn't. I don't know if I got too close, but she pulled back, and the same week we got back home, she cheated on me.

I caught her in the act, and she behaved like she didn't do anything wrong. No apologies were offered, and we've been in that gray area since, not even being the fuck buddies we used to be. She has, however, been working hard to get back in my bed.

"If you remember, then what are we still doing here?" Her smile grows wider.

"No." I shake my head, and the smile fades.

"No?" She hops off the desk and glides over to me, resting her hands on my shoulders when she steps between my legs. "Are you sure, boss?"

"I'm very sure."

"I guess the girl must have made quite an impression, then."

"We both know this is not about *the girl.*" Although I make the clarification, my dick has other ideas, stirring at the thought of being buried deep in Anastasia's sweet little cunt.

"You forget I know you, Desmier Volkova," she teases.

At that moment, something catches my eye. It's the slightest movement through the railings on the stairs outside the room. A glimpse of a lock of white-blonde hair floating back up the stairs proves my earlier assumption wrong. The Valkyrie came down after all.

Well, well, well.

And she was watching me. Maybe trying to listen in, too. If I were her, I'd definitely be doing that.

She wouldn't have heard anything because of the distance between the stairs and the room. I wouldn't have met my crew in here if I'd wanted to talk about something more private. I might not have even done that here at the house.

Gytha follows my gaze to the stairs, then we both look back at each other.

The sly smile tilting her glossy red lips is one of her forced smiles. A sign I've pissed her off.

"The guys said she literally looks like a princess. Maybe that's what you're into these days, regardless of whose daughter she is, or whose bride she almost was."

I don't give her the satisfaction of an answer. She doesn't deserve it.

"Let's not mix business with pleasure."

"Okay, Desmier," she adds with light laughter. "When you're ready for the queen, you know where to find me."

Lowering her head, she plants a kiss on my forehead and leaves.

I look at the stairs again, tempted to find Anastasia, but I stave off the urge.

Today was the longest day ever, and there is still one last thing I have to do. One more thing I've been putting off.

Meeting my father.

THE BEEPING SOUNDS of machines fill my ears as I walk into my father's hospital room.

Not that I wanted to come before, but I might not have gotten past his guards at the door. Now that they're mine, I have free reign of where I go and when I do it.

Dim lights create a heavenly glow in the room. I make my way to the bed in the center, where my father lies motionless.

I stop at the edge of the bed and stare at him, finding myself fixated on his face. This is our first meeting. Him being kept alive by machines, unable to see me, and me full of vengeance.

Earlier, I noted how similar my brothers and I look, but seeing my father now throws me off balance.

I look just like him. Like a clone. Like his younger self. I've seen pictures of him, so I should have been prepared. But I'm not.

Mom told me who my real father was only days before she died. Prior to that, I didn't know. I even had her surname. I suspected Leif was my father because he was always in my life. I'd never seen him show affection to my mother, though.

Leif was married and never had kids because his wife couldn't.

I still assumed he was my father, especially because he always came to see Mom no matter what country she lived in. When we lived in Boston, Mom worked as a live-in maid for a family called the Butyrskayas. My mother came from a servant family who'd always worked for the founding families of the Knights. That's how she met my father and Leif.

The house I live in now belonged to the Butyrskayas. I was practically born there and lived there until I was ten. At that point, Mom decided to move to Russia. It was in that house that I was hidden away like everything else the Butyrskayas kept secret as part of their job. They kept Mom's secret, however, because they loved her like she was part of the family. They disappeared many years ago and have been presumed dead.

I came here tonight to meet my father before he dies.

It's a fucked-up thing for a man like me to know his father ordered his mother's killing and allow him to live. But this slow death will suffice.

Right now, I want him to hear my voice before he departs from this world. I want him to know he didn't win.

Reaching out, I cover the cold skin of my father's hand with my own. The gesture is almost loving, like I'm the worried son.

"Father, my name is Desmier. Desmier Volkova. I only took your name because Leif wanted me to have it." I drag in a breath and lift my chin higher. "I needed you to know you didn't kill me all those years ago, but it was a nice try. Now I live to avenge my mother. You took her from me. Now I will take everything from you and your family. Thank you for turning me into a monster. I won't disappoint you."

CHAPTER SEVEN

ANASTASIA

I rest my head against the wall and gaze at the clock on the desk across from me. The next few seconds tick by, heralding the start of another hour—eleven o'clock.

It's been night for a while now, and I've been sitting on the floor with my back against the wall in the spot Desmier found me when we had our little encounter.

I returned to it when I saw him with that woman. I didn't see her face properly, but I could tell she was involved with him in some way.

As I haven't seen him since, I'm guessing he's with her.

I hurried upstairs when he noticed me, so I don't know what happened after. I regret that I was foolish enough to go downstairs in the first place.

It wasn't to eat. I needed some ice-cold water after the bomb he dropped on me. Passing the bathroom with a perfectly working tap of running water, I simply wasn't thinking when I went down the stairs.

I'd dragged on the stupid clothes he left for me, which I'm still wearing, and I really hope they don't belong to that woman.

I didn't think I'd see him again so soon, let alone find myself watching him. I'd heard male voices seconds before, so I thought he was talking to Jayce.

In the grand scheme of things, none of that matters. Nor the obvious fact that the asshole I'm supposed to marry in a mere five weeks is already cheating on me.

What matters is all the confirmations I've received of how screwed I truly am. Everything is fucked.

Every damn thing. And I don't know what I'm going to do.

As the time has gone by and I realized no one was coming to save me, raw terror settled in my soul.

I wasn't stupid enough to think Desmier was lying or trying to scare me, but that didn't stop me from hoping things would be resolved. Or praying some miracle would happen to free me from this situation before the end of the day.

I'd give anything to be curled up in my bed at Dad's house.

It's Dad's house now, no longer the place I call home. My home was going to be with Viktor. Now I feel like a nomad because this isn't home either.

And as for earlier—as in Desmier stripping me naked and his talk of fucking—I don't know what to think of my reactions to that either.

I'm sitting all the way over here because I don't want to

be anywhere near that bed. Plus, I'm near the door. I figured I could run if I needed to. In this big house, there must be somewhere to hide.

Could I hide from him, though?

Somehow, I don't think so.

I swallow hard and hold back tears. I hate crying because it reminds me of how I fell apart after Mom died. I've been holding back and holding on to the last shreds of sanity, but my mind keeps drifting back to Dad.

I worry that something will happen no matter what I do, or how I try to *please* Desmier and he'll hand my father over to the Knights.

They always kill those who cross them. The Bratva is ruthless enough, but add in the eerie secret society, and you know there's not an ounce of hope if you find yourself in trouble.

Then it will be death for me too depending on if I'm married to Desmier or not. In the Knights, if I marry him I become his property.

I'm already his property and apart from knowing his name, his hatred for my father, and that we'll be married in a few weeks, I don't know anything else about him. I don't know if he plans to keep and punish me forever, or if this captivity is just for a certain amount of time. If so, will he let me go after that? Or will his vendetta against my father mean he'll send us both off to the gallows?

Footsteps sound outside the door and just like earlier, I know it's not the rude woman—Ehlga. She brought me up some dinner, which I ate, and she came back to clear the plates. That was at least three hours ago.

As Desmier walks through the door, my entire body

tightens. But instead of the deep-rooted trepidation I was feeling only seconds ago, the memory of how he looked at my naked body earlier enters my mind.

Upon seeing me on the floor, he gives me a narrowed stare and continues to watch me as he walks further into the room.

What's he going to do to me now?

The hour I feared has come, and I'm no more prepared for it than I was when I first realized I'd be sleeping with him tonight.

"Comfortable?" He smirks.

"I'm quite fine, thanks." My voice sounds hoarse, as if I haven't spoken for centuries.

He chuckles, allowing his jacket to slide down his shoulders. Then, without taking his eyes off me, he pulls off his T-shirt and I see that those muscles I imagined weren't imaginary. They're absolutely real.

Deep lines of rigid muscle run down the length of his torso beneath smooth tanned skin perfectly kissed by the sun. His pecs, sharp shoulder blades, and overbearing biceps look like a drawing of the perfect specimen of a man.

I no longer think he got the body he has from lifting weights in the state pen—not that I know any ex-cons. Desmier's body looks more like an athlete's. His muscles are too defined to belong to someone who only loves working out.

His tattoos are just as captivating. On his left arm is a swirl of roses, perfect for a wedding bouquet. His pec on the same side has the tattoo of the Volkova family crest. It's a Viking-style sea dragon with the sword of Myrridin going down the center. Myrridin was their Viking ancestor and one of the twelve founding Knights who formed the Brotherhood.

The crest is well known. I've seen the tattoo on the other brothers before, and I've seen it on the company design logo. It's just strange seeing it on Desmier and thinking that he makes it look good.

And shit, I'm just staring at him. Gawking at the wrong Volkova brother. The man who's not my fiancé, or anything to me but the devil.

My cheeks burn with embarrassment, and he grins, seeing my debacle.

I look away from him and focus instead on the swirling patterns of the plaster cornices.

"Baby girl, if it pleases you to look, then look." His voice is deeper.

Showing him I don't care, I return my gaze to him, giving my best poker face. "I take no pleasure in looking at you."

He responds by undoing his belt buckle then shoving his pants and boxers down his legs, freeing his enormous cock.

At the sight of his length and thickness, my mouth falls open and my mind checks out. I don't have the ability to look away and there's a thickness in my throat I can't work past, making my mouth pool with saliva.

He steps out of his clothes and pushes them, along with his shoes to the side, his cock bobbing and growing with every move he makes.

I feel like I should say something, but I wouldn't know what. And I wouldn't want whatever I say to push me deeper into this hellhole I've fallen into.

So, I yield to my body and continue staring, taking in the

line of Viking-style tattoos going down his strong, strong legs.

Desmier doesn't say anything else. He turns, and when I see his back, more shock flies through me.

For the most part, the skin is as smooth as the rest of him with a huge tattoo of a compass spreading across the center.

But at the base of his spine and a good four inches of the surrounding area is a burn scar. One that could have only come from having a third-degree burn.

The scar doesn't diminish anything from his beauty, but its presence alludes to another story. Another bad story that couldn't have ended well.

What the hell happened to him?

Desmier doesn't look back at me as he makes his way into the bathroom while all I do is stare at his body, looking from the scar to the solid definition of his ass. I watch until I can't see him anymore.

The sound of water breaks my stupor, and I guess he must be in the shower.

Earlier, when I tried to ask where he'd been all this time, he shut me down, but I'm curious.

I listen to the water flowing for at least ten minutes. When it stops and he walks back out, my previous worries return.

With his cock swinging between his legs, he moves closer to me, and my nerves spike.

"Give me your hand," he orders.

"My hand?" I'm not following on why he wants my hand.

"Give it. Now!"

I give him my right hand, but he shakes his head. So, I give him my left, and my heart breaks just a little more when he pulls off the engagement ring Viktor gave me.

The oval-cut diamond ring belonged to his grandmother on his mother's side. Mira was only too happy for me to have it. She felt I deserved it.

I've been doing a good job of keeping the tears at bay, but this gets me. So does watching Desmier place the ring on the nightstand as if it means nothing.

"What are you going to do with it?"

"I will see that Viktor gets it back. Now get up and get on the bed."

Oh my God, this is it. And there I was, feeling sad over my ring. He's going to seal the savagery of the day by ripping away my innocence the same way he ruined my life. I never imagined my first time would be like this.

"No." I shake my head and steel my spine. I can't lose my shit now when I've been strong all day.

"Anastasia." It's the first time he's said my name and I truly loathe that I like the way it sounds on his lips.

"No. I'm not getting in that bed with you."

"If you don't get on the fucking bed, I'll throw you over my knee and spank your ass and pussy so hard you won't be able to sit on anything for a month."

His crude crass words blaze over my skin like fire. What the hell is wrong with this guy? Nobody has ever spoken to me like that before, and I've never met anyone so rude and abrasive. I've never met anyone like him. Period.

I wish I could argue, but as with everything else, I know he's serious. He'll do exactly what he's threatening. So, my options are: defy him and have him brutalize my body, or get on the bed and let him fuck me. *And* brutalize my body.

"Get. Up. Now." His voice is harsher. It pierces through me, and I realize there are no options here besides following his orders.

So, I stand.

I stand with my body trembling and all my fears colliding in my mind. Shaky legs carry me to the bed, and I crawl onto it.

He moves the covers away so I can get under them, then he gets in next to me and switches off the light.

Engulfed by darkness, I can feel my heart pound inside my chest as I try to visualize how this will play out.

I don't consent to this, so will he hold me down? Will he fight me? Will he beat me?

His heavy hand rests on the flat of my stomach, and I shudder.

"Go to sleep." His mouth is at my ear, his hulking presence surrounding me. "I'm not going to hurt you any more today."

A momentary blast of relief floods me, but I take note of what he said.

Hurt me any more...

What a bastard. And who could sleep in this situation?

Tonight is my wedding night, but the man I'm lying next to is not the one I was supposed to marry.

Desmier Volkova is the monster who stole me away.

CHAPTER EIGHT

ANASTASIA

Bright light shines down on me.

It's too bright, too powerful, too harsh.

I force my eyes open and find myself staring at Ehlga pulling open the curtains on the other side of the room.

It's morning. *Sunday morning*.

I survived the night. I'm not sure when I actually fell asleep, but thank God I did and there were no nightmares. Maybe because I'm living in one.

Desmier isn't in here, and I can't hear him in the shower. It's just Ehlga.

Looking at the older woman, I straighten at the same time she faces me with that disgruntled expression on her face.

I don't think Ehlga likes me. She hasn't said anything to make me think it; I just assumed from the haughty glare she keeps giving me. I can't stand people who judge you when they know nothing about you.

"You need to get up. Breakfast is almost over." She speaks in a thick Russian accent. I get the feeling that she and Jayce only speak English when they need to.

"What time is it?"

"Nearly midday."

I straighten even more. "I didn't realize I slept for so long."

"Master Volkova allowed you to sleep. However, he wants to speak to you now before he leaves for the day. After breakfast, I'll show you around and help you sort your things out when they arrive." She sounds so official. As if she's about to train me to start a new job.

"Okay."

"Five minutes. There's another T-shirt and yoga pants in the bathroom for you."

"Who do the clothes belong to?" It might be petty on the scale of things to worry about, but I want to know.

"They are a few things his aunt left behind before she died."

"Do you mean Polina?" Polina was Leif's wife.

"Yes, I do."

As Polina was a lovely woman, I don't feel awkward wearing her clothes. I do wonder, though, about all the secrets in this family. That part is none of my business, but since I'm here, I'm wondering who was ever truthful. Clearly Polina knew about Desmier and never said anything to anyone.

"Five minutes," Ehlga reminds me, and I nod. "I will

wait for you in the hallway and take you down to the dining room."

"Thank you."

When she leaves, I steal a minute to gather myself.

Instead of being here, I should be with Viktor in the Caribbean on our honeymoon for a two-week cruise.

But I'm in *his brother's* bed.

If not for Dad, I wouldn't be here. I love my father with all my heart, but this is his fault. When I think of what the hell he must have done to get me wrapped up in this disaster, I feel like screaming and running through the walls.

I thought I had problems before with my nightmares, but damn, that was nothing.

I look at the nightstand and notice my engagement ring is gone. That's the first sign that today will undoubtedly have its own set of challenges. I hope Desmier wasn't spiteful enough to throw it away, the same way he disposed of my dress. Ehlga cleared away the pieces of fabric when she took my empty plates last night.

With Desmier wanting to speak to me, I can't help but fear what new bomb he'll drop on me to shake my already fragile state. There's a lot to talk about and the same amount of things to think about.

At the top of the list is my freedom, which is getting further away from me.

There has to be a way out of this—a path I have to find. So, I need to see what I'm up against and keep my eyes open for opportunities.

With that reasoning, I head to the bathroom, shower quickly, and change into the clothes that were left for me. I leave my damp hair down so it can air-dry.

When I'm done, I look at myself in the mirror, noticing the dark circles under my eyes. My usually vibrant blue irises don't even look blue anymore. My eyes look like someone placed a toner in them to fade the color, and my skin is blotchy. The glow I had from the facials I did at the spa with Lorelai only days ago is gone.

In a nutshell, I look like shit dragged in from the highway. But at least I'm alive and still have my virginity intact.

I walk away from the mirror and make my way out to the hallway, where I find Ehlga.

She leads me down the stairs on the opposite side of the landing. They lead down to a section of the house I didn't see before. This part feels older, and the decoration is more fitting to the period style of the house.

Ehlga shows me into a grand dining room fit for royalty or some A-list celebrity. There I meet Desmier's scrutinizing stare.

Today, he's wearing a white button-down shirt with the sleeves rolled up his forearms. He's dressed like he's going to work in an office.

Tearing my gaze away from his, I look around the room and take in the oil paintings of pirate ships and beautiful landscapes. There is a row of antique plates on one wall with images of ducks.

The large, long mahogany table holds a delicious spread of pastries that remind me I'm starving, but when I return my gaze to the dangerously handsome man sitting at the head, my appetite disappears.

"Sit here." He points to the chair next to him.

Pulling in a deep breath, I make my way over and lower myself into the cushioned seat.

Ehlga leaves us, but the door is still open and I can hear people milling about in the other rooms.

I keep my breathing measured so I can think about all the things I need to ask. This is an opportunity for me to talk, too. And surely, there's no way he can think it's acceptable for me to blindly follow along with this charade without more information than he's given me.

"Sleep well?" He sets his elbows on the table.

My eyes flick down to the tattoo of the rune on his wrist. "As good as can be."

He sits back and stares at me. "Eat. You'll need your strength."

That makes me want to eat even less than I did before. "What will I need my strength for? You do realize you haven't actually told me what you plan to do to me, except for this ridiculous notion of marrying me."

"Why is it so ridiculous? Your marriage to my brother was arranged."

"Yes, but I've known him all my life. There's a massive difference." And I know Viktor's not psychotic. This guy is. "He also didn't treat me like an animal."

Desmier chuckles, bringing a hand to his temple. "Good for him. Sounds like a real gentleman. I can assure you, I'm nothing of the sort."

I want to tell him I could have guessed that without being given any clues, but I think better of it. He has the type of arrogance that's deadly, and I'm no match for it.

He reaches down next to him and lifts a little bag I recognize instantly. It's one of the bags I took to Grantham Hall. It has my personal things inside, like my phone.

My God, I completely forgot about my phone. What kind of girl does that?

My phone is something I check a hundred times a day, so I can't believe I haven't even thought of it once during the time I've been here.

Instead of giving me the bag, Desmier opens it and takes out the little box of my contraceptive pills. Since he knew to find it in the secret pocket, I assume he's searched through my bag and has looked through my things.

My blood boils when he flips the lid of the box open and takes out the blister packet containing my pills.

"What are you doing?"

He tilts his head to the side. "The days are all mixed up."

"What's your point?" I don't know why he's concerned with such a thing. Not keeping track of dates is a bad habit of mine and the same reason diaries and calendars don't work with me. It's not a problem for my pills because I take one a day religiously.

"Did you take yesterday's pill?"

"Why is that any of your business?"

"Everything you do is now my business, and I don't want other miniature problems on our hands."

God, I'm so naïve. Of course, he's concerned about my pills because he doesn't want me to get pregnant.

The light of lust burning in his eyes sparks thoughts of him taking me in the hardcore way he said he would. Quickly, before it can take root in my mind, I shove the explicit image away.

The last thing I should do is entertain any thought of him like that. Especially when he's a complete jerk.

"So, back to the question." His expression takes on a stern edge. "Did you take a pill yesterday?"

"Yes. I did."

"Good girl. Make sure you don't miss any."

Asshole. He doesn't have to worry about me missing anything. I won't make such a mistake.

Finally, he hands the bag to me. I quickly check inside to make sure my phone is still there. It is, and so are my other things, like my purse, wallet, and keys for my car.

"I've allowed you to keep your things for the moment."

"For the moment?"

"Yes, keeping them is dependent on whether you can obey me and follow orders without that smart mouth of yours pissing me off. Right now, it's fascinating. I love a woman with a little fire. But you, my dear Valkyrie, are of a different kind. I can imagine you getting on my wrong side quite quickly. That's less fascinating but might be entertaining in other ways."

The darkness in his eyes sends a shiver crawling down my spine and the longer I look at him, the more I can tell the sadistic bastard is getting off on the idea of me being on his wrong side.

The words *obey* and *follow orders* make me clench my teeth, but once again, I try to calm myself.

"What do you actually want to talk about?" I decide to keep my tone level and my words basic.

"My expectations and my rules."

Can he actually hear himself? Does he realize how he sounds? As if he's talking to a petulant child who's just arrived for their first day at a strict boarding school.

But damn it, it's me who's silly. Of course, he knows how

he sounds. Men like him are born dictators. The only language they know is their own.

"You can return to your daily activities and college," he informs me. "I've canceled the original vacation leave you had planned for the wedding but allowed you this week to get used to the house and settled in. There will be nothing special about our wedding, so we don't need any time off."

Our wedding. Those words still sound so strange to my ears, and wrong.

And of course, there's no sentiment in him. I didn't expect anything special. It just stings to hear how little he cares about something that should be important.

"Well, I didn't expect you to take me on my Caribbean cruise." I don't even bother to hide my sarcasm.

Desmier smirks and raises his thick brows in amusement. "Fuck, is that where Viktor was going to take you?"

"Yes, he was. Viktor wanted to take me all over the world. He booked the cruise so we could explore a variety of islands, and in the same breath, he had another getaway planned to Paris at the end of next month."

"Well, at least the asshole isn't cheap."

"He's not an asshole. You are."

"Trust me, your beloved is just as much an asshole as me." The conviction in his deep accented voice infuriates me.

"You don't know him."

"I don't need to. I knew he was a motherfucker before he even opened his mouth to speak to me."

This conversation is getting me nowhere and it's pointless. It's also probably best to stop pushing him because there's still more I need to know, and I haven't negotiated the important things yet. “Can I see Viktor or my dad? Or at least call them?”

“No.” His tone is cold, his stare icier.

“Why not? They’re my family.”

His nostrils flare. “Viktor is not your fucking family.”

“Even you can’t think this is okay.” I glare at him, wide-eyed, pleading. “Desmier, you just took me as I was about to make my vows. That was it. I at least got to say some sort of goodbye to my father, but I didn’t get to say anything to Viktor.”

He sits back, his expression emotionless as he steeples his fingers, staring back at me in silence. Not the kind of silence you expect from a person contemplating something important, but definitely the kind when they aren’t.

It’s clear whatever mission he’s on has stolen his humanity.

“Please,” I add.

He blows out a ragged breath and presses his lips together in displeasure.

“One visit. One text to arrange it. He can come *here* for a few minutes. I don’t want you meeting him anywhere I can’t watch you.”

“Okay. When?”

His face turns to stone. “Not in the next three weeks.”

God, that’s a crazy, crazy long time. Anything could happen to me. “*Three weeks*?”

“Take it or leave it.”

“Alright.” What choice do I have? “I also see his mom sometimes. She teaches on campus, and we meet up for work experience sessions. She’s kind of like my mentor. Please can I continue to see her?”

"That is fine. You can keep your relations with people like that and other friends."

"Thank you." It feels so weird to be thanking him, but here's hoping I can see Mira when I return to campus.

"As for your father, it's an absolute no. The next time you see him will be at the wedding and possibly other functions. No other time before or after."

"That's it?" I can't imagine that. As bad as my father is, I know he loves me. He's never treated me badly, and I can just imagine how this is killing him. "But he's my father. I have to see him."

"Baby girl, you're pushing your luck with me. Be grateful I allow you to see him at all. Enough talk about him now."

"But—"

"I said *enough*. I need to leave, and you need to know the rest of my rules."

I would rather continue pleading, but I guess I'm not completely defeated as I have something to work with. "Fine, what are they?"

"The wedding planner will be here in the next few days. You aren't to give her any trouble. Ehlga is my custodian; she will take care of whatever you need. You will have guards with you at all times when you leave the property. Some will include Jayce and Zane, whom you've already met."

Zane must have been the other guard who came in with Jayce at the wedding.

"Anything else?" I clench my jaw.

"I think it goes without saying that you aren't to speak with anyone I wouldn't want you to speak to, or try to defy me. Your phone is chipped, so I'll know. Your car will be delivered here sometime during the week. I'm having a tracker fitted in, but I prefer if you use my drivers."

Jesus. I really am a prisoner. "So, I have no freedom?"

"I think I've given you enough *freedom*."

I allow myself the withering stare I issue him. "What about after? After the wedding? Do we have our happily ever after in this house with our kids?" I'm being completely sarcastic again. He knows it, but his expression becomes more intense.

"You and I are not having kids." His voice is even colder than before, dripping with disgust. "I won't be having a child with a Sidorov, or anyone else. Get that straight. Once I wrap this up, I'm going back to sea."

"To sea?"

His face softens. "I'm a sailor."

My eyes automatically scan his body. That explains the muscles and the hard-ass look.

"Once the wedding is done, you will stay here and live your life, and I will return for a few months a year." He sighs and clenches his jaw. "We need to stay married for two years."

Fuck. Two whole years.

My God. I guess now I have the information I wanted to know most.

I just don't know how I'm supposed to get married to him in the first place, then stay that way for two years.

"Is that seriously how long you plan to keep me?"

He chuckles—cruel, wicked, and low. The sound raises my nerve endings, and I realize I've missed something.

"Baby girl, I never gave you an end date." His dark brows rise into a rigid line. "That timeframe is simply to meet the business terms of inheritance for Sidorov Developments. Even though I'll own the company, you still have shares and inheritance rights. All we're doing is ticking a box."

My mouth falls open. "So, you don't plan to let me go, ever?"

"That part is debatable. I have a lot in store for you people. Giving Uther Sidorov's daughter her freedom wasn't really part of my plans."

I hate the way he talks about me as if I'm some species he's classifying.

"So, my life is just collateral," I rasp in a hushed tone. I can't believe I really am little more than a pawn in this and he truly doesn't care.

"I think I've told you all you need to know."

"How?"

"Don't push me, Anastasia. Yesterday, I informed you of the looming threat hanging over your head. If I were you, I'd be grateful no one worse than me discovered your father's extra-curricular activities. Believe me, if they had, you'd both be dead."

I've definitely thought of that, but as for being grateful —no. I'm not grateful to this asshole because everything is all bad and he hasn't exactly said he won't throw us to the lions when he chooses to.

"So, dear wife-to-be, you need to watch yourself." He smiles, switching back to the cynical version of himself. "Lastly, Ehlga will be taking you to the doctor tomorrow morning. Make sure you comply with that, too."

"Why do I need to go to the doctor?"

"For your sexual health tests."

My tolerance evaporates into the air, replace by fury unlike I've ever known. "Excuse me? I will do no such thing."

"Yes, you will." He leans in closer as Ehlga walks in with a pot of coffee. When she sets it down and leaves, the hard line of his jaw softens, and he continues. "I assure you, my dear Valkyrie, I don't fuck like a gentleman. Condoms won't work with me. When I fuck you, I want to feel you come undone around me."

Blood surges from my fingertips to my toes like a raging river in a tempestuous storm. Then wild sexual images flood my mind, each one hitting me harder than the one before.

Desmier's seductive stare intensifies, and his raw masculine presence lulls me like a drug, enticing my body to betray me. His closeness doesn't help either.

One corner of his sensual lips turns up, and he angles himself so he's a breath away.

"Maybe you'd like that. Or you will." His breath caresses my skin, turning up the heat burning through me. "Don't people say good girls prefer bad boys? I'm as bad as they come, Valkyrie." He shows me the tattoo on his wrist. The sight makes me wonder what he must have gone through to get it and how many he had to kill.

"Oh, I definitely believe you're as bad as they come." I nod.

"Glad we're on the same page, because I also heard good girls love to be fucked hard and dirty. Is that how you want it, baby girl? That's how I like it."

I'm already on fire, but I shock myself further when I realize moisture is beading between my thighs. My God, I'm actually aroused by this man and his dirty words, and I shouldn't be.

What the hell is wrong with me?

Guys like him would usually be an instant turn-off, but maybe being held against my will by this psychotic man is throwing my mind out of sync.

"You are vile," I grate out, swallowing past the lump clogging my throat.

Moving so that we're eye to eye, he rivets his gaze to mine as if he can see through to my most secret thoughts.

"Am I? I'm simply making an observation based on the scent of your fear and needs."

He searches my eyes. I try to pretend he's not affecting me, but I know I fail. I know he knows, too, because there's something strange between us— him and me. Something wicked and alien to me.

It feels like attraction, but it can't simply be that. There's no way.

Attraction feels like too meager a word to describe this... entity.

This entity my soul warns me to be careful of.

Schooling my thoughts, I think of a way to tone the conversation down.

"Your observation is wrong."

"I am never wrong." He chuckles. "You have that test done, and we'll see how right I am."

"Are you going to do a test?" I can imagine him being the kind of man to live in a brothel where he can eat, sleep, drink, and breathe women.

Desmier straightens, and I'm able to breathe properly again.

"I'm clean. I don't need a test. It's you who needs to follow my rules, not me."

"But I'm clean, too." I'm as clean as could be.

"I need to be sure. I don't want to catch anything my brother might have given you. Unless he hasn't gone there yet."

I should tell him I'm a virgin, but I don't. I noticed earlier that any talk of Viktor irritates him, so I decide to piss him off a little more.

"Oh, we've gone there many times." I imbue my voice with strength I don't feel.

When that darkness drifts into his eyes, I realize I'm right.

But what in the ever-loving fuck did I just do? I got carried away and lied. If I can't get myself out of this mess—*and it's not looking like I will*—he'll know the truth soon enough.

"I guess that's all the more reason for you to go to the doctor."

The sound of someone clearing their throat has us turning toward the door.

The sultry silver-blue eyes of a tall model-like woman with long straight hair stare at me. She's wearing an elegant black strapless jumpsuit, and her makeup is perfect enough to allow her to stand in line with the Kardashians in a photoshoot. I peg her to be in her mid- to late twenties, but her makeup makes her look ageless.

She's the woman from yesterday. I didn't see a whole lot of her then but recognize the little daisy tattooed on her wrist.

In the few seconds it takes for her gaze to flick from my face to Desmier's, I learn a few things. One is that she doesn't like this situation any more than I do, presumably because of her recognizable interest in Desmier. The next thing is her standoffish, scrutinizing attitude—and she hasn't even said anything yet.

"I'm ready when you are," she tells Desmier.

When he nods, she walks away, but not without glancing back at me first.

"Who is that?" I ask. I shouldn't bother, but I want to know.

I look back at Desmier and wait for his answer.

He pushes to his feet. "That's Gytha. My assistant."

Assistant?

I wonder what she assists him in doing exactly. I doubt it's paperwork.

"See you later, Valkyrie. Don't do anything stupid." He gives me a thin smile, then leaves to join Gytha.

I shouldn't feel the stab of annoyance burrowing its way into me, but I do.

Ehlga returns with a tray of pastries. I notice straight-away that her face seems less harsh than earlier, and I guess she must have heard a thing or two.

"I thought you might like these." She waves her hand over the rows of croissants and pains au chocolat.

"Thank you. I appreciate that."

"I'm glad. Eat up, and I'll show you around in about an hour."

I nod. When she leaves, I get my phone out.

My heart shrinks when I see how many messages I've received. There are over twenty.

The bulk are from Lorelai and a few from my other friends who were at the wedding, all of them wanting to know what's happening. The most heartfelt message, however, came from Viktor. He said he was sorry he couldn't stop me from being taken.

I send Lorelai a message and decide to wait to respond to Viktor. Since I'm only allowed one message to him, I need to make it count and say all the things I need to say to arrange when we can meet, and essentially say goodbye.

There's nothing from my father, but I know that's because he's most likely been told not to contact me.

I eat the pastries then fall into a slump of going through the motions when Ehlga starts giving me the tour of my new prison.

Although the grounds of Desmier's home are truly beautiful, I'm not paying attention to anything, and I'm sure Ehlga knows. There's no way she thinks I'm sufficiently okay to act like I'm on a school trip when the truth is looming over my head.

We walk along the beach, which—I was right—is private and enclosed between the walls of the cliff so you can't see what's on the other side.

From here there's nothing for miles and miles but the sea.

I might be a good prisoner, but that doesn't mean I'm not looking for a way out.

I'm looking through the woods for a passage, at the sky for the heavens to open up and take me, and the ground to swallow me whole.

I'm looking at anything and everything because I've never felt so unsettled and ensnared in my life. But of course, my heart sinks as I find nothing but the truth telling me I'm trapped here. Even if I did find a way out, my defiance would get Dad killed.

Ehlga takes me to the top of the cliff and starts talking about the Savannah sparrows and larks that come by during the summer. When she points to the ivy-covered stone walls between the garden and the cliff, every muscle in my body goes rigid as my gaze lands on a crest of a wolf's head and a crescent-shaped moon next to it, carved into the stone.

My eyes bulge, and I wonder if I've slipped into another nightmare because this is the only other place I've seen this particular crest.

I stop short and gaze at it, goose bumps crawling down my skin. My mind flip-flops assessing the design and contemplating the possibility that I could be mistaken.

But I know I'm not. And I'm awake. What I'm looking at is real.

It's just that, this thing is not something I remember seeing anywhere in real life.

Closing my eyes, I tap into the horrific scenes that have been plaguing my mind for years, and there I find the crest carved into a dark surface, like a door or a wall. I've just never been able to determine so before because the monsters rush out of the shadows and kill me.

Warm fingers tap my shoulder, and my eyes snap open.

Ehlga stares back at me with concern filling her pale gray eyes.

"Are you okay, dear?" she asks. "You've gone pale."

"Um..." I stutter, unsure what to say because, no, I'm not okay. Not by a long shot.

Up until now, I'd believed everything in my nightmares was figments of my imagination. Now that one of them is staring right back at me, I can't help but question if this is something from my missing memories.

But this is the first time I've been to this house. And the crest I see in my nightmares is the same, the same design, just smaller and darker.

"Anastasia?"

I steady my thoughts and look back at Ehlga. Maybe I could ask her about the crest. "Ehlga, that crest over there." I point to it. "Can you tell me about it?"

"Of course. It's one of the Butyrskaya family crests."

"Butyrskaya?" I don't know anybody by that name, and I've never heard of them either. "Were they part of the Knights?"

"Yes."

"Do you know them?"

"No. Desmier's mother worked for them as a live-in maid. This was where they all lived before moving to Russia."

"So, this is their house?"

"Yes, because he and his mother were so close to them, he bought the house and even decided to keep most of their things."

Wow, she's told me more about Desmier in those few words than he has.

"Isn't he in contact with them anymore?" Maybe I could speak to them.

Ehlga shakes her head. "I'm afraid not, dear. They all died many years ago."

"Oh." Disappointment squeezes my stomach.

I look back at the crest, taking in the intricate design. It's as real as I am standing here.

So...what else is real inside my nightmares?

CHAPTER NINE

DESMIER

I'm at Raventhorn Hall, the headquarters of the Knights. It is situated on the grounds of Raventhorn University.

This is the place where the Ritual of Initiation is conducted. Here you take the Oath, pledging your life to the Knights to live and die by the vows you make.

I walk into the ritual hall and make my way down the path where Aleksander Ivanov stands at the head.

When I gave him my report last night, his one request was for me to do this—take the Oath again in front of him and the Knights' Council.

That report included the entire truth about my father. As I am going to be Aleksander's second-in-command, Leif thought it wise to tell him, and I agreed. I need this man to trust me, so I will tell him all the things I feel he needs to know about me.

Aleksander is standing between the stone statue of

Raventhorn and the Fountain of Promises, symbolic of the river the Viking Knights used centuries ago for rituals like this.

Around Aleksander, the twenty-four members of the Knights' Council are assembled. Leif is one of them. He is judge number eight. With the changes in the structure, he assumed the role at the same time my father got the Sovietnik position in the Bratva.

Next to Leif are my brothers, who stare at me the same way they did yesterday, with curiosity and an air of trepidation.

Everyone, me included, is wearing the Knights' tunic.

The last time I was dressed like this was years ago when I went through the same ceremony. Except mine was conducted under the old pagan ways at the Knights' temple in Uppsala, Sweden.

Although this hall is underground, the reverence is the same as at the temple, and the same emblems bind them together. The main one being the Raventhorn Crest, which sits high above me on the center of the ceiling. It has two blue ravens on either side of a shield and the letter R engraved in the middle, along with a golden fleur-de-lis banding the ravens together. Around the crest are black carvings of the Elder Futhark runes, paired with their Greek counterparts: Alpha, Zeta, Sigma, and Omega. Those represent the four factions of the Knights.

I, like my brothers, am a Sigma. They are tasked with the first order of knighthood, which is protection and defense against enemies.

As I continue my procession toward Aleksander, all eyes

are on me—the man no one knew about who could overthrow everything if he wanted to. Because of my rune.

The law of Odin's Rune exists to show that things can change. Something can come along to challenge the life you know, the riches you hold, and the world you think you've built. It's like having a reset button.

The tension coming from those wondering what my intentions are is so thick it could choke me.

I cut Viktor a glance as I walk by. The scent of his thirst for vengeance is like acid in the air, and I wonder what stolen opportunity he hates me for the most—the legacy I seized from him or the woman I took.

Both losses must be eating him alive in equal parts. I know I'll be enjoying both ventures. Especially the woman.

Anastasia Sidorov has plagued my mind from the moment she walked into the dining room this morning. With her perfumed hair damp, face free of makeup, and her helplessness hanging on her sleeve, I found her even more beautiful than she already is.

It's nearly nine at night, and I'm still thinking of what those pillowy lips would feel like around my cock.

All day, my fucking cock has stirred at the memory of how she looked when I taunted her.

I knew from the moment I left the house that this attraction between us—which I know she's acknowledged, too—is going to be a problem for us.

A problem I shouldn't be concerned about, along with her declaration that she's been with Viktor *many* times. Surprisingly, that irritated the fuck out of me, but it's something I need to shove out of my mind. I'm too old to be thinking with my dick. Everything I've done so far is the art of war at its finest. Many years have been put into my plan, and no part of it must fail.

When I reach the Fountain of Promises, Aleksander and I bow to each other respectfully. He picks up the ceremonial blade and holds it out to me.

"Desmier Bjorn Volkova, do you swear your life and allegiance to our cause?" Aleksander keeps his gaze fixed on me as if he's trying to see into my mind.

"I do." I raise my right hand and pledge.

"Then please take the Oath."

"Luramentum est vita nostra et mors nostra," I say in Latin, which translates to: *The Oath is our life and our death.*

Aleksander dips his head, but he still eyes me with scrutiny. Although taking the Oath before him tells him I pledge to him as my leader, I'm aware he doesn't like the idea of me. He doesn't know me, and he's just as threatened by my presence as everyone else. When he chose my father for this role, he knew he was choosing the Volkova line. In our family, roles like this are inherited from father to son or brother to brother. It was an act signed in blood that can't be relinquished now, no matter how he feels.

"Give me your hand."

I do, and he slices a thin line across my palm. Blood trickles from the wound and drops into the fountain, renewing my vow to the Knights.

When I took this oath before, I decided it was one I would live by because it was the anchor to my past, present, and future. As I take the Oath now, I consciously make the decision to do the same thing.

It's what my mother would have wanted, so my oath is for her. She came from a family who would always be servants. Me becoming a Knight is something that would have made her proud.

When I was growing up she always told me stories about the old Viking Knights who were led by Raventhorn, the leader who started all this when he and his men worked for Vladimir the Great as secret assassins.

"We as a brotherhood accept your pledge and the service of your life for our cause." Aleksander bows his head again, and I do the same. When he rises, he looks at everyone else. "You may all go."

All except me. He wants me to stay behind and speak with him. Talking to me in this sacred hall is like binding me again. Everything I say will be held as part of the Oath.

The men bow and leave, but the tension remains.

Aleksander continues to keep his face stern and gaze unwavering until

we're alone.

At fifty-one years old, he's considered to be one of the younger leaders in the alliance, but there's a natural ruthlessness in his eyes that makes him look much older.

He glances at my rune, then flicks his gaze back to mine. "What are your real intentions here?" The question in words and tone cuts to the chase.

"They are what you see." That's the actual truth, no matter what my other plans entail.

"You took the Oath in front of me, and you're going to be my second-in-command. That means you don't bullshit me."

"I'm not."

"Then answer me this: how will you fulfill your role if you are at sea for most of the year?"

I knew I'd get asked about that at some point, but I'm not worried about my duties to the Knights. The benefits of me being away outweigh my presence here.

"You won't have to worry about that. I will be here whenever you need me. While I'm away, whoever I choose as Obshchak will act on my behalf. My work on the ships is integral and ensures business runs smoothly for clients like you who use our company."

That should shut his question down. He knows what I do on the ships and the benefit it will be if I continue my responsibilities.

"Alright, that is acceptable for the moment, but I request a review of this arrangement in a few months when you return to sea."

"Of course."

"And what of the Sidorov girl? Do you still intend to adhere to the marriage contract and take her as your wife? Although the wording of the contract pertains to you as the eldest Volkova son, that contract was made with Viktor in mind. Given that I have the power to dissolve it."

I was aware of his powers; I just never thought he would offer it. Nevertheless, it doesn't change anything. "No, I intend to adhere to the contract and continue everything as originally planned."

A touch of suspicion invades his expression. "Are you sure? It would be far more suitable for a Knight of your status to marry someone with a lineage from the Knights. There are plenty of women to choose from with better family businesses to align yourself with."

"I am sure. I'm satisfied with the one I have." I sound convincing to my own ears.

"Then I accept your decision. Welcome, Desmier, son of Evgeni, descendant of Myrridin." He puts out his hand to shake mine.

I shake it, but I sense he's still in two minds about me. "Thank you."

"I'll see you in a few weeks for the Bratva inauguration."

"Indeed."

With another dip of my head, I leave and find Leif waiting for me in the hallway. We're in the corner so we have privacy to talk.

"How did it go?"

"As good as it can be. He suspects me."

"Of course, he does, but he's not someone you have to worry about."

"No." We took measures to keep what we know about Uther's crimes under wraps. There's no way of Aleksander finding out what he's done and trying to incriminate me for blackmail. Everything I have is hidden so deep, I'd need the type of clearance to get into Fort Knox to access it—that's the benefit of having someone like Gytha working for you.

"Alright, my boy." Leif smiles and rests a hand on my shoulder. "Tomorrow is another big day. I will see you then."

Tomorrow, I get Volkova Inc. and everything my father owns with the Volkova name attached to it. "See you then, Uncle."

With another smile, he pats my shoulder and walks in the opposite direction.

I turn to leave but stop when I feel eyes on me.

I look up and find myself staring at Zakh on the third-floor balcony, watching me. I can't quite see his face properly, but from what I can tell, he's assessing me.

A good couple of seconds pass with us just staring at each other, and I don't know what to make of it—whether it's good or bad.

He breaks eye contact first and walks away.

As weird as that was, he's the first of my brothers to have any interaction with me.

I guess I'll find out what his assessment is soon enough.

THE SILVER MOON shines over the automatic garage doors as they open for me.

I drive my Mustang inside, and the door lowers once I'm parked.

When I bought this house, the garage was like the ordinary type you'd find on a house this old. I modernized it to what it is now and extended the space to accommodate my cars and my bike.

Although I haven't been here much over the years, I always feel privileged to own this home. It's been mine for the last five years. The house was being maintained by Pavel Butyrskaya's great aunt. Just before she died, I approached her and bought it. She was the last living Butyrskaya relative on this side of the globe.

Apart from my work on the garage and improving the surveillance, I kept everything pretty much the same and either sold or stored away what I didn't need. The house was big enough that I didn't need to hire a separate storage unit.

It may seem odd that I kept their things, but I did it because they meant a lot to my mother. She grew up with them here after her mother died. When I came along, they took care of me, too.

They were a family of three: Pavel, Vittoria, and their son, Elmier who was five years younger than me.

Both Mom and Leif lost contact with them after we left for Russia because they moved the following year and their jobs took them all over the world.

It always saddens me when I think of what might have happened to them. They disappeared around the time I turned nineteen. In our world, when you vanish the way they did, it means you either took yourself off the grid, or someone with above-board skills killed you and disposed of your body in such a way that no one would be able to find you ever again.

According to how the Butyrskayas left things behind, people assumed the latter, and quite rightly so.

Because of the covert jobs Pavel did for the previous Pakhan, and the consistent traveling, he and his family could have met their end anywhere.

I shouldn't know this, but Pavel was part of the Knights Secret Force. The division consists of an elite group of enforcer assassins who only go by a number. No names.

In some cases, they don't even know who their peers are. The concept was borrowed from our Italian mafia allies.

I get out of the car and head into the house.

When I reach the hallway, the sensor lights snap on and my footsteps echo on the marble floor, disrupting the blanket of silence covering the house. Most of the staff have either left for the day or are sleeping. Ehlga won't be sleeping, though.

Knowing exactly where to find her, I make my way into the kitchen. She's inside kneading dough for her special bread. She's wearing a dressing gown, and her hair is piled neatly into a bun on top of her head.

"Baking at this hour?" I raise my brows.

"I thought it would be nice to wake up to freshly made bread."

Since I hardly eat bread, the gesture means she's taken a motherly shine to Anastasia.

"I'm sure *she* will like that." I let her know I'm aware of what she's up to.

Ehlga gives me a warm smile, and the light in her eyes sparkles. "I thought so."

Something must have happened today to tone her down because she was completely against the entire idea of Anastasia.

"Was everything okay today?"

"Yes. All Anastasia's things are here now. I'll help her go through them tomorrow when we come back from *the doctor*." She enunciates those words because she hates the grittier parts of my plan.

"I can send her with someone else, if you wish."

"Like Gytha?" Her brows rise. "Not even I can be that cruel."

Ehlga doesn't like Gytha and puts every woman who takes an interest in me under the same scrutiny you'd expect from a caring mother.

"What's wrong with Gytha now?" I incline my head, getting ready for her to bitch at me.

"What was she doing here, Desmier?" She gives me a hard stare. She's the only person I allow to speak to me this way. "I know you two have this on-and-off relationship, but it's completely inappropriate to have her here when you're planning on getting married in a few weeks. I'll always be here for you whenever and wherever you need me, but some things are wrong."

"We're off. We've been off for nearly a year, and I'm not planning on being on again. It's just work."

"Does *she* know that?" She blinks several times.

"Yes."

"Does she accept it?"

That's a different story. "She will have to."

"Good. I get this whole plan, and of course I'm on board, but please don't forget you have to know when to show compassion. Anastasia may appear strong, but I sense something is broken inside her. Something that doesn't feel like it's about this."

I narrow my eyes, curious for her to elaborate. Something must have definitely occurred today for her to say that. "Did something happen?"

"I'm not sure, but I think you should be mindful of her. She's Uther's daughter, but she's a person as well. What's happened to her is a big deal, but it feels like there's something more underneath all that."

I've read Anastasia's medical and psych reports, so I'm aware she had a difficult childhood. When she was nine, she was hit by a car and left in a coma for six months, then rehab for two years. Just as she was able to return to some sort of normal, her mother lost her mind, eventually killing herself. Anastasia was only fourteen. It was she who found her mother dead.

I haven't told Ehlga about Anastasia's background, and I think it's best I keep it that way. I don't want her to open her heart any more than she's already seemed to.

"I don't want you to lose yourself in this." Ehlga's eyes fill with concern.

I won't disappoint her by telling her I was lost a long time ago. Ehlga thinks she saved me, and I will honor that. When Leif first put me in her care, she'd just lost both her husband and her son in an accident, so we seemed to become each other's family.

"I will consider all things."

"That's good to hear." She stops kneading the bread, and judging from the pensive look she gives me, I know she has more to say that I most likely won't like. "You're going to have to tell her about her father one day, you know?"

I was right. I don't like this conversation. "I know."

"I understand the reasons for keeping the truth from her, but she's going to be your wife soon."

"I know, but it has to be this way for the moment." I'd be hellbent on getting answers if the situation were reversed. I've only told Anastasia just enough to terrify her into complying, but I haven't hit the core. And I told her not to ask me again. "Right now, I don't want her to know anything about me."

Nothing at all, not even about my father. When it comes to her, one story can't be told without the other. Those who know what my father did aren't going to be concerned with knowing which of his men he sent to carry out the hit on

Mom and me. Anastasia, on the other hand, will figure out that it was her father.

"Really?"

"Yes. But I promise I will talk to her when the time is right." Whenever that will be.

"Okay. I respect that." Ehlga nods, and the light returns to her eyes. "Go, get to bed. That's enough talking for us."

"Don't stay up too much longer."

"I'll be in bed within the hour." She chuckles, seeming more relaxed.

I leave her and head upstairs to my room. When I get there and notice the light shining from underneath the door, I wonder if Anastasia is still awake. I open the door, and my gaze settles on the beauty asleep in my bed.

All that hair of hers that I want to run my fingers through is sprawled out around her, and the moonlight mingles with the room light shining over her body.

She really is beautiful, even in her sleep.

Unlike last night, she's wearing a loose nightshirt that shows off just the right amount of her breasts and her slender body.

When she shuffles, I move closer to her, and her scent wraps around me within seconds. It's a combination of nectar and roses and underlying feminine mystique that makes me want to pick her apart layer by layer.

Her brows wrinkle, and I expect her to wake up, but she doesn't.

She shuffles again, parting her lips to mumble something, but I can't tell what she's saying. I realize then that she's dreaming. Or possibly having a nightmare, judging from the worried expression on her face. Maybe she's dreaming about me and I'm terrifying her even in her sleep.

Poor little princess. There's no one to rescue her from me.

I want to strip her bare again, but this time, I want to see deeper than the surface. I want to see the wounds that created her invisible scars.

It wasn't Gytha who gave me Anastasia's records. It was Leif, because Anastasia had lost her mother, too.

Is that it?

Was the loss of a mother what broke her?

That's what broke me.

Along with the betrayal from a father I never knew.

When my mother told me about him and who I really was, I was nervous to meet him, and disappointed Leif wasn't my father. But my heart was open because Mom was happy. At the time I went by Desmier Polinsky—using Mom's maiden name. I thought that might change.

We were supposed to meet my father that night at the park, but before we even left the house we were under attack. Uther and his men smashed down the door and told her my father had sent them to kill us.

Our neighbor heard the commotion and intervened. That was how we escaped. Unfortunately he was killed. We jumped in Mom's car and then we were on the run for days. We ended up in a little cottage in the countryside, where Uther caught up to us. There we had no chance.

Uther killed Mom, and only took her body with him because he didn't want to leave any evidence behind.

He burned her and made me watch just because he

could. He wanted to show his cruelty. Then he wanted to show me he was god when my time came to die and he set the entire barn on fire.

That made up story about Mom and me dying in a fire at our home was the cock and bull shit my father hid behind. Nobody knew the truth, and still no one really knows what I went through, because until this day I can't talk about it.

The torture Uther put me through was unbearable, but nothing will be able to rid my mind of the horror I experienced of watching my mother die. Nothing.

Sometimes, I can still hear her screaming in Uther's arms, and I can still see that emptiness of life in her body and the light of the living leaving her eyes when he snapped her neck.

That image will always stay with me.

I wonder if Anastasia has memories of her mother like that, too—the terror of witnessing the death of a loved one and knowing there's nothing you can do to either save them or bring them back.

If she does, we have something in common, and misery loves company.

I sense there's more to her, though. More secrets.

Secrets she might have shared with her beloved Viktor.

Does he know what lies beneath the layers of her porcelain skin that I want to peel away?

Maybe.

Does it make me a petty bastard that I want to take everything from him— *including the woman he loves*—just because I can?

Anastasia shakes her head and rolls onto her side, trapped in her mind.

Trapped in what I've decided must be a nightmare.

Another touch of humanity sparks inside me. I step away, deciding to give her some reprieve. I won't add to her darkness tonight.

Perhaps my action is a kindness a Sidorov doesn't deserve, but I do it anyway, retreating to the room I used when I was a boy.

Everything will happen in its own time, but it's so much better when you're the master of your own destiny.

CHAPTER TEN

ANASTASIA

I stare at the rustic red brick wall before me, tapping the bricks with my fingertips to that song in my head.

Run and catch, the meadow's calling you home...

I tap one, two, three, four, five, six, seven, eight.

On the eighth count, I blink, then I'm running through the meadow. A bird flies high in the sky, and the sun feels bright and warm on my skin, tempting me to chase it. I run toward the sun, but it disappears, and blackness swallows me whole.

It's so dark, I dare not breathe. I'm too scared that I'll disappear. But I walk on the unseen path before me, terror ravaging my soul.

Darkness fills my mind like a thick fog of smoke, suffocating me with the

ominous feeling of imminent doom.

Patches of light flicker in the darkness, and I see it—the crest with the wolf and the moon engraved into it.

I try to get closer, but shadow monsters rush out of the darkness, howling and gnashing their teeth like evil souls trapped in the pits of hell.

Faceless faces push out of the darkness, and a million screams wrap around me.

Blood pours from the sky. And a knife plunges into my throat, stabbing me again and again and again.

I SCREAM, jumping out of the hellish nightmare, right into Ehlga's grasp.

She grabs my shoulders, steadying me as if anchoring my mind to this world.

"You're okay, dear. You were just dreaming." Her voice is gentle and soothing, but it doesn't stop the terror from pumping through my blood.

I fasten my eyes to hers until the hellish images of shadow monsters fade from my mind.

When my breathing calms, Ehlga releases me and grabs a glass of water from the nightstand.

"Here, drink this."

She hands me the glass, and I take a few sips, savoring the water's cool temperature soothing the dryness in my throat.

"Thank you."

"You're welcome. Are you okay?"

Am I? No. Apart from everything that's happening, seeing that crest has jarred me, and I don't know what to do.

"I just feel silly for screaming." I decide to lie because it's easier.

"Don't. We've all had bad nightmares." She gives me a

sympathetic smile and takes the glass, then her eyes brighten. "Your friend Lorelai is here."

My spirits soar on hearing that, but I suck in a sharp breath as I glance at the clock and see it's past ten thirty.

Shit. I overslept. I was supposed to be up hours ago.

I called Lorelai last night to arrange this visit and planned to get myself together before she arrived. Our time is limited as it is because I have to go to the stupid doctor in less than two hours.

Ehlga stands and continues to give me her sympathetic smile. "I'll leave you to get ready. I've prepared breakfast in the garden for the two of you."

I feel more at ease hearing we can go into the garden. It means we'll have some privacy to talk. "Thank you."

"No worries. See you downstairs."

She leaves, and I jump out of the bed to get ready. I can't wait to see Lorelai.

Seeing my best friend will be like a safe haven for my soul and a refuge from this horror my father has pushed me in.

"My God, Anastasia, it feels like I haven't seen you in years." Lorelai hugs me hard. I savor the safety I feel in her warm embrace.

"I'm so happy to see you." Because my phone is chipped, I couldn't say much to her last night. Seeing her face to face now means I can really talk to her.

"You too." She holds me tighter, like she knows how

badly I'm trying to keep myself together and stop the pieces of my mind from falling apart.

If anyone knows how I feel, it's her. She knows me inside out, and we've been friends for so long we think of ourselves as sisters. Since the only sibling she has is her older brother, Leo, and I'm an only child, that works perfectly. We met at Raventhorn Academy when we were twelve years old. Although that was years after my accident, my mind was still fragile and unstable. Like it is now.

When we pull apart, we sit opposite each other on the wicker chairs Ehlga set out. Between us is a table with a delicious spread of pastries and homemade bread.

It looks like a feast to die for, but all I want to do is talk to Lorelai.

"He hasn't hurt you, has he?" Worry fills Lorelai's eyes, and she speaks in a hushed tone, glancing over her shoulder to check no one is listening.

"No, I'm not hurt." Unless I factor in the blow my pride and dignity took when Desmier tore off my wedding dress and stripped me naked.

"Tell me what's happening." She rests her hands on the table between us. "I'm sure Desmier knew you'd tell me *something*."

She's right. Even though he never gave me the full rundown, I'm sure he knew that by allowing me to see my friends, I'd have to tell them something. He also knew I wouldn't tell anyone anything I wasn't comfortable sharing. Like the things about Dad.

"I can tell you, but please don't say anything to anyone."

"Anastasia, come on." She frowns and places a hand over

her heart. "You know your secrets are completely safe with me."

"I know. It's just that the stuff I have to tell you is quite bad, and I need you to promise me you won't even tell your family." Her father is one of the Pakhan's brigadiers, and her brother is on the enforcement team. I'm putting myself at risk by even breathing the mere words I've said, but I'll go crazy if I don't talk to someone I trust.

"I swear on my life I won't tell a soul. Okay?"

"Okay." I take a moment to think before I tell her everything. All that I know.

"Jesus, Anastasia. That is crazy." Her face pales like the time she nearly got expelled from school for smoking pot in the locker room. "Do you have any idea what your father could have done to Desmier?"

"No. And I don't think he's going to tell me. Or he would have by now."

Her shoulders sag. "And he seriously won't allow you to speak to your father?"

"No. I don't even want to find out what will happen if I try to make contact with Dad. Things are bad enough as it is, so I'm going to play it safe."

"How are you feeling about your father?" She issues me with the same I'm-here-for-you stare she gives me every time I've had problems with Dad.

I inhale the fresh air wrapping around us like a blanket, allowing it to soak into my lungs and loosen the tension. Normally, I can open up and talk freely about how I feel. Today, I don't know how to answer her question without breaking down.

Lorelai is aware of the intense awkwardness I've experienced with my father since my mom's death. I've told her how he became more overprotective and secretive. But this disaster has driven a wedge in my heart.

"I feel betrayed and disappointed." My voice is so fragile a gentle breeze could shatter it.

"I'm so sorry. This is truly awful."

"I know." I take another gulp of air, hoping it will ease my mind. "I hate feeling so trapped and knowing there's nothing anyone can do."

"Viktor tried to get you back," she offers with an encouraging smile.

My heart flutters on hearing that. "Did he?"

"Yes. He even came to my father for help, but everything they thought of turned out to be a bust." Her father has connections that can be useful sometimes. It's unfortunate he couldn't help me.

"Thank you for telling me. It means a lot."

"I thought it might. I don't have the best opinion of Viktor most of the time, but I thought it was sweet he tried to get you back."

"It was. Please thank your father for trying, too."

"I will. It's just unreal that no one knew about Desmier." She bites the inside of her lip. "The news of another Volkova son has shocked everyone, but it hit Mira the hardest. Desmier is only about four months older than Viktor."

My eyes widen. "I didn't know they were so close in age. And poor Mira."

"Yes, poor Mira."

I've tried to figure out if Evgeni cheated on her or if he just didn't know about Desmier. We can't even ask him. The man is on the verge of death.

"Has anyone said anything about Desmier's mother?" I bite the inside of my lip.

"No. Nothing at all."

Then where is she?

I assumed she was in the background somewhere, pulling strings. Or if no one is talking about her, maybe she's not around anymore. Like mine.

"I heard Desmier has practically taken everything. The company and all the Volkova assets are going to be signed over to him today."

Well, at least I know where he is. I didn't see him last night.

When I started wondering if he was with that woman —*Gytha*—I was completely pissed off at myself. I suppose if he's at work, she's with him. But there's no way she's a real assistant. Maybe she's there to suck him off whenever he snaps his fingers.

"Must be a great day for him. I've never met anyone so obnoxious and cold."

Or... shocking.

When I think of his overly masculine naked body and his lewd words about fucking me, an unwanted tingle ripples through me, but I tamp it down, knowing I have to be careful. Desmier Volkova is not the sort of man to get weak-kneed over, no matter how gorgeous he is. The only good thing he's done for me is arrange to get my clothes. They were at Viktor's house. And it was so much worse because I had my things hanging in the walk-in wardrobe Viktor had made for me.

"He sounds awful. I hate that you're being forced to marry him."

There's far too much emotion in her tone for me to ignore that she could be talking about the *secret* she hasn't shared with me but is one I know.

Lorelai is promised to marry Dmitri Konstantin, but she's been seeing Zakh Volkova. I saw them kissing in his car after the same meeting where her father made the marriage contract to Dmitri.

Their marriage is supposed to bridge the gap between their families after a hundred-year-long feud. The situation is made worse because Zakh is her brother's best friend.

I keep waiting for her to talk to me, but each time she seems like she might, she doesn't.

"Maybe more will be explained eventually." Lorelai taps my hands and gives me a supportive smile. "Right now, everything is vague and weird."

The words vague and weird makes me think of the crest.

Lorelai couldn't be a better person to share my thoughts with because she knows I thought my nightmares were based on real memories.

"There's something else." I grit my teeth.

"What is it?"

"I saw something here from my nightmare."

"What?" Her mouth drops open. "What did you see?"

"The crest." She's as well-versed in my nightmare as I am, so she knows what I mean. "It was engraved on the side of the cliff."

"Are you sure it's the same thing from your dreams?"

I nod. "I am extremely sure. The only difference was the size and the location. The crest I saw was a lot smaller but the very same design. And I think it could have been on a door. Ehlga explained that the previous owners of this house were the Butyrskayas and the crest is one of theirs."

"Oh my God. I didn't know *this* house belonged to them." Her skin flushes like it does when she knows more to a story than everyone else.

"Do you know of them?"

"Not really. But I know the husband—I think his name was Pavel—worked for the previous Pakhan. Dad worked with him once, long before I was born. I heard the family disappeared."

"Disappeared? Ehlga told me they died." Disappearing is way different than just dying.

She bites the inside of her lip. "Well, that's kind of the same thing in our world when it looks like you've been killed and no one can find you. It was also many years ago."

A knot twists my stomach. "Do you know how long?"

"No. I don't think anyone can be specific." She leans in closer and lowers her voice. "I think the man worked on the secret squad."

I widen my eyes. "Really?" I don't know much about the secret squad other than that they're *secret* and only the Pakhan knows who belongs to it.

"It's just my thought because things don't add up. The guy also worked all over the world and wasn't in touch with anyone apart from the Pakhan. I only know that because of Dad. I heard him talking. It seems to be one of those situations where they could have been gone for years before anyone realized they were missing."

"That's awful."

"And strange that you'd be dreaming about their crest."

. . .

"I CAN ONLY THINK my father must have taken me somewhere the Butyrskayas owned. Maybe something happened to me there."

Given my situation with Desmier, there's every chance Dad's position in the Bratva could have exposed me to all sorts of things. Or one particular thing my parents kept from me.

Every time I brought up my nightmares, they brushed it off like it was nothing but my imagination. Thank goodness Mira helped me work through it until they went away. But now they're back.

"Since the crest is real, I've been thinking I could be right about the rest of the dream." I sigh. "The parts where the shadow monsters kill me. Of course, I'm not dead, and I know the monsters weren't monsters, but if I had a bad experience, I want to know what happened."

Worry washes over her face. "Do you think you should? I mean, maybe that's why your parents didn't want to talk about it when you brought it up."

I nod slowly, feeling a little defeated. "I guess, but I just want to know."

"Anastasia, I think you need to take each day as it comes and one problem at a time." She reaches out and covers my hands with hers. "Things are already intense enough with Desmier. You've been thrust into this new life where you're not with Viktor and you can't speak to your father. Don't take on anything that's going to add to that stress."

"You're right." Playing Nancy Drew is not what I should be doing now with everything else going on.

"At the same time, I'm not saying you shouldn't do

anything, because maybe you can ask Desmier. But be careful."

"I will."

"And remember I'm here for you."

"Thank you."

We hug again, then fall into talking about college. Time flies by way too fast, and soon she has to leave.

Ehlga comes out to get me moments after, but the person I see walking alongside her has my skin crawling.

It's Gytha.

She's not with Desmier like I imagined.

Today, she's wearing a fitted skater dress with thigh-high leather boots. While I look like I'm appropriately dressed to rummage through the snack aisle at Walmart, she looks like she's ready to sign a modeling contract with Dior.

Jesus, what's wrong with me?

Why am I comparing myself to this woman? I've never worried about my looks before. All my life, people have told me how beautiful I am. At one point, I got tired of it, especially the comments I'd get about how blessed I was to inherit my mother's hair color and her ice-blue eyes.

Gytha zeroes in on me like a cat about to pounce on an unsuspecting canary. Ehlga, on the other hand, has a put-out expression on her face. Although I don't know this for sure, I get the impression she's not overly fond of Gytha.

I sensed it yesterday after my first encounter with the *La Femme Nikita* wannabe.

"I'm ready to go," Ehlga announces, forcing a smile.

"And I just wanted to introduce myself properly before

you leave," Gytha cuts in, looking me up and down, sizing me up.

"Anastasia, this is Gytha." Ehlga points to her. "I told her Desmier would have introduced her like he has with all the staff, but she felt it more appropriate to do it herself, as you are going to be his wife."

I almost laugh when Gytha cuts Ehlga a crude stare, clearly disliking what she said.

"That's not entirely true, but it doesn't matter. I wanted you to know I'll be trading places with Zane this week, so I'll be around more."

"Okay, I'll bear that in mind."

"You need to because Desmier and I have a past you might not be aware of yet. When I'm around and we're together, we don't like to be disturbed. Let's just say I'm queen of the castle. Always. No matter who you are or what you are, wife or not, that will never change."

What a fucking bitch.

"I see." A pang of hurt goes straight to my heart. It's not for Desmier. It's for what I lost with Viktor.

I want to tell her she can be queen if she wants but don't. I already feel like someone could break me into a million pieces, so I don't have the strength to argue with a woman who's telling me she's my husband-to-be's mistress.

"Good, glad you understand, *princess*." Gytha smiles, revealing perfect white teeth beneath her crimson-painted lips, then she turns on her heels and walks away, swaying her womanly hips.

"Don't mind her," Ehlga says, looking at me apologetically.

"It's hard not to."

"Try not to worry about her. She's not very nice." Ehlga confirms my prior thoughts. "I have an idea. If we leave right away, I can take you to my favorite Continental coffee shop. It's on Main Street. They have a great selection of European tea there. Do you like tea?"

The offer surprises me, but I'm grateful for it. She's done a massive turnaround since the other day. As she's in charge, I would have hated to have any contention with her.

"I love tea."

"Ahh, that's good. Then it looks like we'll get along just fine." There's a warmth beneath her gaze. "My grandmother was a gypsy. She could tell the future by reading tea leaves. I'll teach you how to do it."

"That would be really cool." I can see she's trying to make me feel better, so I won't spoil things by telling her I already know my future looks like shit.

"Come, let us go." She places an arm around me, and we head out.

When we drive off the grounds, it feels good to be away from the house, but my worries follow me, haunting me like my mother's ghost.

CHAPTER ELEVEN

DESMIER

"This is the last thing to do." Leif beams with a radiant smile, tapping the company ownership documents on my desk. The lawyer just dropped them off. "Everything officially belongs to you now. All you have to do is sign the documents."

"Thank you, Uncle." I shake his outstretched hand, savoring the surge of victory. My new reality became real for me the moment I stepped inside Volkova Inc. earlier this morning.

We're in my new office, on the fifteenth floor at the very top of the building.

It used to belong to Leif. He felt I'd be more comfortable here than in my father's office. He was right.

At the moment, my father's office is closed. No one is using it out of respect. Everyone knows he's not expected to make a return to the world of the living, but they won't do anything with it until after he's gone.

I'm only honoring that because I want to make a good impression and I've already caused enough upheaval.

All eyes were on me when I arrived earlier, and as Leif gave me the tour of the building, people looked on curiously, wanting to catch a glimpse of Evgeni's long-lost son, and their new boss.

I was also right about the family wanting to protect my father's name. The story going around is that my father never knew about me, and I've suddenly come about as the rightful heir to claim the empire.

"I'm so proud of you," Leif says, his eyes glistening with the pride he speaks of, once again assuming the role of the father I never had.

"I hope I can make you even prouder."

"You know you don't have to do anything more than you already have. It's been a long journey, and I'm glad I got to see this day."

"Thank you for sticking with me." *And for saving me.*

Leif chuckles and taps my knuckles before releasing my hand. "As if I wouldn't. I just wish your mother could have been here to see this and know you made it, know you're okay and you got this far."

"Me too." No matter how tough I am or how iron-clad my skin is, any talk of my mother hits me hard. "This is for her. For you, too."

"For you both, my boy. I've had my glory days. I wanted you to have that, too." He smiles briefly before a frown wrinkles his brows. "It doesn't feel like it's enough. We planned all this, but it still feels like more should be done to avenge Fryeda's death."

It's moments like these when I think I'm right, that my mother meant more to him than what he's ever told me or allowed me to see. I've never asked him, but I've wanted to, long before my mother was killed. It felt like the question was always inappropriate for one reason or another. It stopped feeling that way after his wife died a few years ago. But I still haven't managed to muster the courage to ask him.

"It's not enough. However, destroying my father's greatest desire is something," I assure him. "He wanted to ensure his legacy through the sons he had with Mira, and that never happened. We have to take that as the real victory."

He nods, agreeing. "Spoken like a true warrior."

I touch my heart and bow my head. "I'll sign the documents and get them back to you before lunchtime."

"Good. Have you thought more about who you'll be choosing as your subordinates?"

"No." I need more time. I'm using today for that reason. We have a board meeting before lunch. My brothers will all be there. I'll take the opportunity to assess them a little more.

"That's fine. I just wanted to know."

"Have my brothers asked you anything?" I can just imagine the stress he's had to deal with from everyone else.

"Of course, they have. But they will have to wait."

"Yeah." Right now, I wouldn't know who to start with, and I'm not interested enough either.

"Alright, I've got to run. I have a few calls to make before the meeting. Let me know if you need anything else."

"Of course."

When he leaves, I relax my shoulders and stare at the documents. There are fifteen of them, one for each asset that belonged to my father. I need to read through them thoroughly before signing.

I hate paperwork, but this is something I'll gladly review. I want to make sure no one can try to screw with me because of some obscure term or shit.

But before I do anything, I need some more coffee. Something strong like a triple espresso to keep me going for the next few hours.

Straightening, I head out to the break room. Each floor has its own break room equipped with soft black leather sofas, a good view of the Boston skyline, and good coffee.

Not even a minute passes after I grab my cup that I hear footsteps behind me.

When I turn around, I find myself staring at Viktor. In his crisp black Armani suit it's he who looks the part of the esteemed CEO.

I'm dressed the part, too, but the bulk of muscle on my shoulders makes me look more like someone's bodyguard —*his* bodyguard.

Viktor still looks like he wants to fight me. If that's the case, I'm still game, and he *still* won't win. I was trained to kill when I fight, regardless of who my opponent is. So, I'd have no problem ending this guy.

"Enjoying your new position?" Viktor's tone is infused with sarcasm.

"Yes, thank you for asking."

He shakes his head at me. "You're loving this, aren't you?"

"What do you want?" I don't have time for this shit. I have things to do, and he's the last person I want to speak to.

"I want to talk to you about Anastasia."

"Why?" A spark of annoyance pulls at my insides, but I tamp it down.

"Really?" His eyes blaze. "Are you serious? It's obvious I'd ask about her."

"*What* do you want to know?" I don't give a fuck how riled up he is, or about his attempt to point out the obvious. He can't do shit, so if he wants an answer from me, he needs to answer the fucking question I'm asking him.

"I want my girl back."

His girl.

Hearing him call her that shouldn't create any response in me other than the pleasure I already feel for cutting him down. But something akin to rage stirs in me.

"Keeping her is ridiculous, and so is marrying her," he sneers. "You have Volkova Inc., and I'm sure you can find some way to take Sidorov Developments as well. Surely, we can come to some agreement for you to give Anastasia back to me."

Could we?

Should I?

This is definitely the ultimate pissing match, where I'm being the greedy motherfucker by keeping his woman. On the other hand, I myself admitted Anastasia was a distraction. That's a good enough reason to let him have her. Right?

As soon as the reasoning takes residence in my mind, I

conjure those pouty lips, her face flushed with arousal, her nipples ripe, begging to be sucked. All for me. Not him. In those moments, she wasn't thinking of him. She was thinking of me.

Whether I like it or not, that wild attraction exists between us. But that's not why I'm going to keep her. Nor the mere fact that I want to keep her because Viktor wants her. I need to keep her to punish Uther and avenge the dead.

"Well? What's it going to be?" he demands, his question grating on my nerves.

"No," I reply flatly, much to his dismay. I reach into my back pocket and pull out the engagement ring he gave Anastasia. His face colors fiercely when I hold the ring up so he can see it, then place it in his pocket. "She won't be needing this anymore."

"You motherfucking bastard," he grunts. "You won't get away with this. I don't care who you are. I'm not going to let you get away with any of it. Taking my girl and my company."

"Dear Viktor." My voice takes on a sing-song edge of mockery. "Bring it the fuck on. I'll be waiting for you."

He scoffs at me and walks out. *Good.* There is no reasoning here, nor the chance to come to any agreement. At least now I'm certain of his hostility toward me.

Leif can tell me to keep my mind open all he wants, but I already know the Obshchak position won't go to Viktor.

Everyone has had the weekend to think about which side they're on. Clearly, he's chosen to set himself against me, and that's fine by me.

I glance at the no-longer-steaming cup of coffee in my hand and top it up with some hot water. I then head back into the hallway and stop mid-stride when I find Zakh leaning against the wall, looking like he was waiting for me.

The stern stare he issues me confirms he was. With one ankle crossed over the other, he appears jovial, like he would be the light-hearted one of the bunch, but there's a dangerous vibe about him. I sensed it straightaway when we first met, and it was there last night at Raventhorn Hall.

As such, I wonder if this is round two with brother number two.

"Come to say your piece?" I ask when he continues to stare.

"Maybe. But I'm not a man who wastes words." His voice is rusty, a little like that of a smoker.

"What kind of man are you?"

He looks me up and down with scrutiny. Not the kind that displays arrogance, but the kind that suggests he's assessing me because he wants to determine if he can trust me.

"The kind who isn't stupid."

"What exactly does that mean?"

He chuckles and gives me a wide grin. "Viktor means it, you know," he states, letting me know he was listening in and ignoring my actual question. "He'll destroy your ass for taking his woman."

"I didn't doubt him."

"Good."

"Is that seriously what you wanted to tell me?" I quirk a hard brow as I try to figure him out.

"No. It's not." He straightens to match my height and looks me up and down again. "Viktor loves Anastasia. He fucks around all the time with all sorts of women, but he does love her."

Hearing the confirmation of love rouses what is undoubtedly jealousy. I could almost laugh at myself. "I gathered that."

"He loves her, but that's not the only reason he wants to marry her. Nor is it because of gaining partnership with Sidorov Developments. She's a little more valuable than that, and she doesn't even know it."

My interest piques, rocketing to the sky. "What kind of value?"

"How about you find out? I think it will be better that way. Take a good look at her inheritance. At the vineyard her grandfather left her."

"The vineyard?" I give him a deadpan look. I'd seen details about the vineyard in her records, but it didn't really look like it was that valuable. Just a little family business in the Russian countryside.

"Yes, the vineyard. When you find out what I'm talking about, remember it was me who gave you the information. Then maybe you can trust me, *brother*. I'm away until next week. We can talk then."

Pressing his lips together, he turns and walks away, leaving me with that interesting bit of news I'll be looking into straightaway.

CHAPTER
TWELVE

ANASTASIA

"Do you need anything else, dear?" Ehlga asks, closing the wardrobe doors.

She has that heartfelt expression again, a sign she still feels bad about today.

Not just for the horrid encounter with Gytha, but also for the barbaric experience at the clinic.

"No, I'm just going to turn in for the night." It's a lie. There's no way I'm going to sleep. My head is a damn mess.

"I'm going to do the same. It's been a long day."

She forgot to say it was fucked up, too, but I don't think Ehlga uses words like *fuck*.

"Any news on when Desmier will be back?" It's just after ten. If he's coming back tonight, I want to be prepared.

"No. But I'm sure he'll be here in the morning, if you need to speak to him."

"Alright." I do need to speak to him, but maybe it's best I

don't tonight. I'm too worked up, and I'll only get myself in trouble.

"See you in the morning."

"Good night."

As soon as she leaves, I sulk down onto the bed, resting my head in my hands. I allow all the tension to drain from me and take deep breaths to calm my mind.

I've never been more humiliated in my life. The doctor Desmier sent me to works for the Knights, which means his methods for sexual health checks are as archaic as in the Middle Ages. Whatever the hell tests that asshole conducted on me were barely a step away from a purity test. In fact, he actually asked Ehlga if he should do one because he had a few minutes to spare. Thank God she said no, but that asshole doctor just made me feel worse than I already do.

Now that I'm alone, the weight of everything sits on my shoulders like a fifty-ton trailer. And I haven't stopped thinking about the crest.

I know I'm adding to my stress, and Lorelai would tell me off if she were here. But I don't think I can help feeling like I should be trying to find out more information.

Regardless of what that is, it's pieces of a life I was told I'd never remember.

Desmier's arrival has unearthed that reality.

Lifting my head, I stare at the wardrobe, and something occurs to me.

Ehlga said Desmier had stored some of the Butyrskayas' things.

What if I found the room and looked through their stuff?

Okay, that would definitely be asking for trouble, but in for a penny, in for a pound. Finding something like a photo album with a picture of the crest from my dreams might at least help me with a location.

And I have an idea where I could start looking. When Ehlga showed me around, there was a section of the house she said was out of use, so she didn't take me there.

My guess is the room is on that side. And since Desmier isn't here, tonight might be the best time to look around. Who knows what could happen tomorrow, or the next day, or the day after? This might be my only chance, providing, of course, the guards don't stop me.

If I get caught, I could say I got lost, but that might not go down so well.

Fear, however, isn't enough to stop me from trying.

With that reasoning, I wait for fifteen minutes to make sure Ehlga has gone to her quarters and I won't run into her. Then I make my move, slipping out of the room and walking down the corridor as if I'm just taking a leisurely walk—I need to look legit for whoever is on surveillance. Not like I'm up to no good.

I head over to the stairs that lead to the older section of the house, which is in a separate wing. As it makes sense to store things in a room on the ground floor, I head downstairs, carefully creeping along the passage once I get there. I'm wearing ballet flats, but they can make a squishy sound against the marble floors when I put my full weight on my feet.

The lights down here are dim, and there doesn't seem to be anyone around.

I also noticed there aren't as many security cameras as on the other side, so maybe no one can see me.

That would be good.

I relax a little when I don't notice any more cameras, but I still maintain my awareness just in case I miss one.

When I arrive at the end of the corridor and turn toward the next, a weird feeling comes over me that I can't quite describe.

There's a presence. As if someone's here, or waiting for me.

The more I advance down the passage, the more intense the feeling becomes. It's so strong I glance over my shoulder, searching for the source of the energy. Or the person.

But there's no one there. It's just me and the chill crawling over my skin.

I didn't believe in ghosts until Mom died. After she passed, it was like I could feel her spirit either with me or in the room where she killed herself. I know Dad felt it, too, because we moved a few months after.

All thoughts of ghosts dissipate when I turn the corner and am greeted with a full-size version of the crest on the wall ahead of me, which splits the path like a fork in a road. A light shines down on it like a halo, meaning I can see it more clearly than the engraving on the side of the cliff.

Eager to get closer, I quicken my pace, no longer worrying about the sound of my footsteps.

When I reach the crest, I search over the grooves in the carving, confirming that it really is what I see in my nightmares.

It's it. It's definitely it.

Being this close makes my nerves scatter and my heart-beat quicken. My curiosity ignites, and I'm even more keen to find out what my link to this thing is.

I stare for a few more moments, then I take the passage to my left, continuing my mission.

Down here, the lights are a little brighter and I can see doors along the wall.

Maybe the room I'm looking for is one of these.

I open the first door and find an empty room. The next few rooms are bedrooms, but the last door is locked.

From the size, it could lead into a hall or a bigger room, so it could be what I'm looking for.

Lorelai showed me how to pick a lock once. Her brother taught her. We broke into her aunt's office one summer night when I was staying over.

Little did we know her aunt had locked the door because she was having sex with her gardener. Needless to say, when we walked in and caught them, we got in so much trouble, but that was overshadowed by our discovery, which led to her aunt and uncle's divorce.

I hope a similar fate doesn't await me. I wouldn't want to catch Desmier and Gytha together.

I pull a hairpin from my bun and stick it in the lock. Then I push it up into the mechanism until I feel the clip and wiggle it around.

Just as I hear the clicking sound of the pin forcing the clip down, a heavy hand rests on the space above my head and warm fingers flutter over my waist.

Despite the warmth turning into fire, ice trickles down my body, and I shudder.

A low guttural laugh fills my ears, and I dare not move because I know the sound belongs to the pirate-man who stole my life.

Desmier presses his lips to the nape of my neck, but I keep my feet rooted to the ground.

"Well, well, my little Valkyrie." His breath caresses my skin like a lover's touch. One I don't want from him. "You must really have some balls if you think you can break into my office."

Jesus Christ. His office?

Oh, hell no.

What did I get myself into?

I whirl around out of his grasp, but he locks me back in, pushing me up against the wall. He gives me a salacious grin, his teeth looking whiter in this light.

The overly confident look on his face is the same one he wore when he waltzed into my life and stopped my wedding.

As his eyes roam over me, I think of what to say to get myself out of this, but nothing comes. I doubt he'd buy a lame-ass excuse like I was looking for the bathroom when I was obviously breaking in. The hairpin is still in the lock.

"I didn't know it was your office," I babble, as if that will help me.

"It doesn't matter. I'm going to enjoy punishing you." He reaches forward and yanks my hairpin out of the lock, then opens the door—*with his key*. "Now, then, why don't you step into my office, Anastasia?"

CHAPTER
THIRTEEN

ANASTASIA

The overhead lights come on as we walk into Desmier's office.

I take in the antique-looking furniture made of black walnut wood and the glass-paned bookcase to the left that takes up the entire wall.

The desk in the center commands most of the space, and rows of shelves filled with books line the wall behind the padded leather chair.

This office doesn't seem to suit Desmier. It would be more fitting to someone older. Like Leif. Or Jules Verne, judging from the volumes of classic literature on the shelf about adventures to the center of the earth, the moon, and the sea. There's also an ancient-looking pair of golden binoculars sitting on a tripod by the window.

It's all interesting, but I can see that I would have been quite disappointed if I'd succeeded in breaking in.

Desmier places his hand to the small of my back. The contact twists my stomach into more knots, and I wonder what the hell I'm going to do.

This is bad. Very bad. I don't know what to expect or what more to say to get myself out of trouble.

Before, all I did to piss him off was to exist as Uther Sidorov's daughter. Now I've really given him a reason to do something to me. Something he said he's going to enjoy.

Didn't he threaten to spank me only yesterday?

And the look on his face as he said it was like he was talking about eating some delicious meal. He seems to be one of those men who get off on things like that.

Shit. Why didn't I just stay in the room? I could have just taken a bath or tried to sleep; either option would have been better than this.

Desmier shepherds me to the desk and lowers to sit on the edge, setting me in front of him.

When he looks at me, I feel like a child who's just been dragged into the principal's office.

"How about you start by telling me what you were hoping to find?" His eyes brighten with malice, and his handsome face contorts into a devilish smile.

What do I tell him now?

The truth about the crest?

Given the fact that I think the bad memories are linked to my father, I'm not sure that's a good idea.

"I was just looking around."

"And the locked door tempted you to find a way to get in?" He quirks a hard brow.

"It wasn't like that."

"Then what was it like? Did you think you might find a gun in here?"

"No," I answer quickly, but he looks like he doesn't believe me. I guess, though, when you factor in my circumstances, me looking for a gun is the logical thought process.

"No?" His gaze drops to my breasts, lingers there long enough to make me blush from deep within, then flicks back up to meet mine. "So, maybe you thought you'd find answers in here. Answers to my secrets. If so, how furious do you think I am right now?"

I glare back at him, suddenly remembering it's me who's supposed to be furious. Today, I went from feeling like I was less than microscopic when his bitch girlfriend informed me of my place in the grand scheme of things, to feeling like a two-dollar hooker you needed to check for every disease under the sun.

"Why would I need to sneak around for answers to your secrets when I'm sure Gytha would tell me?" I steel my spine. Even if I have no power, it doesn't mean I shouldn't stand up for myself.

"Gytha?" His brows knit, and the sexual haze fades from his eyes.

"Your girlfriend, Gytha."

"Men like me don't have girlfriends."

I know what he means, so I have a good comeback for the asshole. "They certainly don't have wives either."

That makes him smile. "Sometimes they do."

"Not in the normal sense. Please don't tell me you think anyone would want to marry you."

He laughs, and it sounds different than the scarier ones he's given me so far. This is a real laugh. And even though he's laughing at me—because what I said is completely ridiculous because *hello,* he's gorgeous—the sound seeps into me, and I wonder what he's like when he's not evil.

Who is he when he's not the villain who thinks it's okay to steal a woman who was about to take her wedding vows?

"What did she say to you?" he asks, still smiling but with a hint of seriousness in his tone.

"I'm sure you can imagine given the circumstances. I'm here as some pawn you're marrying, and clearly, you're involved with her."

"Tell me what she said."

It hasn't escaped me that he didn't deny being involved with her. I don't care. None of it means anything to me because I shouldn't even be here.

"She said she was the queen of the castle, and I shouldn't disturb the two of you when you're together." There's more I could say, but that's enough.

The narrowed look he gives me suggests he's not entirely happy to hear what Gytha said.

"It makes sense that she's the queen, since I don't think you would have sent her to some whacked-up creep to have her probed like an animal." I had to find a way to say something about the doctor.

"Doctor Marchant comes highly recommended."

"I couldn't care less if God himself recommended him. The man is a dirty creep who touched me inappropriately. That was your fault. I'm not some slut who sleeps around."

His jaw clenches like he's furious, but all he says is, "What did you say to Gytha?"

I hate when he skillfully evades a conversation. "Aren't we talking about the doctor?"

"No, *you're* talking about the doctor, and I'm done. Now I want to know what you said to Gytha."

I smirk at his abrasiveness. "Nothing. What was I supposed to say?" Because I'm stalling and don't want to get myself in more trouble, I hold back on telling him he's not Viktor. If he were, I would have told Gytha to go to hell because she's obviously deluded. If we were talking about Viktor here, there would be no Gytha.

I know Viktor was with other women, but he was mine the moment he put his ring on my finger.

"Doesn't quite seem like you to keep quiet, baby girl."

Baby girl and Valkyrie. I just realized something. He seems to call me baby girl when he thinks I'm weak and Valkyrie when I show some defiance.

Both endearments feel like he's mocking me because I don't want to be anything to him.

"You don't know me."

"I know you were trying to get in here to find something." The lightheartedness fades from his expression, and it's like he slips on the evil mask again. "Now, enough talk about Gytha and your lame attempts to change the subject. Tell me what you were looking for."

Damn it. We're back to that again, and I never got to really bitch at him about the doctor. The whole Gytha thing didn't bother me nearly as much as the doctor did.

Now what should I say?

What excuse can I find for breaking in?

I think for a moment while he stares at me for what feels like eons.

Maybe the truth is the only option. All I'm asking about is a crest.

"When Ehlga was showing me around, I saw a crest on the cliff. It's also in the house. She told me it belonged to the family who used to live here." I try to keep my voice steady, but it doesn't help that his face hardens.

"That's correct. What about it?"

"I've seen it before. When I was little."

His gaze intensifies. "Where?"

"I don't know. I'm... missing memories." I don't know if he knows that part of my background, so I decide to give him some context. "I had an accident when I was nine that left me with permanent memory loss. I can't remember anything before that."

"Nothing at all?"

"No."

"Then how do you know you saw the crest when you were little?"

"I see it in my nightmares now." I'm surprised by how easily I said that to someone I don't know.

"Nightmares?" He looks at me with disbelief.

"Yes. It's a recurring nightmare I've had since my accident. Until I came here, I didn't think anything from it was real, but then I saw the crest."

"Is the cliff or the house in your dreams?"

"No. I was somewhere else. The crest was carved into something dark. I've always thought it could be a door, but I don't know."

"What else is in this nightmare?"

Although he's asking questions, he doesn't look like he believes me. I'm sure he won't and will just think I'm crazy the moment I tell him about the rest of the dream.

"Well?" His brows lift impatiently.

"It starts with me standing by a wall singing some kind of a nursery rhyme. Then I'm running through a meadow and everything gets dark, like when night comes down. And... " My voice trails off. This is the hard part.

"And what?"

I stifle a groan. "Monsters that look like shadows come out of the dark."

He chuckles, just like I thought he would. "*Monsters*?"

"I know it sounds crazy."

"It's fine to dream about monsters. Believing they're real is another story."

I roll my eyes at him and frown. "I didn't say they were real, but it feels like something happened to me."

"What do the monsters do?"

My heart quickens again. "Kill me."

"Have you ever told your father about this nightmare of yours?"

"Yes, millions of times, but he just thinks it's a regular nightmare."

He inclines his head. "Look, maybe it is just a regular nightmare. I also don't think you would have seen that crest anywhere in the circles you travel in. Maybe you're connecting it to something similar but not the same."

"What do you mean, the circles *I* travel in? They're the same circles you travel in. Maybe my parents knew the Butyrskayas."

"Maybe so, but I can't imagine Pavel Butyrskaya being associated with the likes of your father."

Of course not. How dare I forget my father is the scum of the earth in Desmier Volkova's eyes?

"What if he was associated with him?" Maybe now's a

good time to ask again if I can talk to Dad. "Would you allow me to call my father and ask him about it?"

"No."

"But—"

"No." His voice is harsher and just as hard as the cold expression tainting the beauty of his face.

From the shift in his demeanor, I realize I probably shouldn't have talked about Dad so much, or at all. Not if I hoped to save myself from whatever punishment Desmier has in store for me.

At the same time, I'm not going to allow him to make me think I'm mistaken about the crest.

"Regardless of the circles I'm in, I know I've seen that crest somewhere."

"Fine, believe what you want."

I will because I'm right. "Does this particular crest have a meaning?"

"Maybe." His expression deepens, but I know his lame answer is his way of shutting me down.

"Maybe?" I arch my brows. "That sounds like you know something and you're refusing to tell me."

"Valkyrie, I think you need to remember who you're talking to. Also, none of that explains why you wanted to break into my office."

"I told you I didn't know this was your office."

"What did you think it was?"

"A storage room. Ehlga said you kept some of the Butyrskayas' things." I don't think Ehlga would mind me telling him that. I doubt she'd say anything I couldn't repeat to him. "I was hoping to find a photo album or something like that with a picture of somewhere that might have the crest on it. Or maybe jog my memory by looking at their things."

He considers me for a moment as if weighing his words, then pulls in a slow breath. "There were no photo albums or anything like that when I bought the place. Knowing them, they would have kept everything of sentimental value close to them. I wouldn't know where those ended up. I also doubt seeing their things would help you."

"Why?"

"Because you're looking at some of their stuff now, and it doesn't seem to be doing much for you. This office belonged to Pavel Butyrskaya. It's pretty much in the state he left it."

On hearing that, I glance around the room, suddenly understanding why the office is more suited to an older gentleman who most likely loved exploring.

I can't hide my disappointment when I realize there's nothing in here that does anything for me.

"Am I right?" he prods.

I look around once more, just to be sure, but nothing comes. "What else do you have stored?"

"Furniture."

"Do you know if they had any other homes or business places?"

"People like them would have had lots of places all over the world. I've only been to a handful, and they all had giant crests like what you saw on the cliff and inside the house."

That definitely doesn't help me. "Can you tell me anything more about them? They must have meant a lot to you for you to keep their things."

"They did mean a lot to me, but all I can tell you is that

Pavel and his wife were good people who took care of my mother and me. My mother knew them all her life, so we were hardly different from family. We had a good life here. When we went to live in Russia, we lost contact with them."

Wow, he actually told me something about himself. And I'm surprised at my eagerness to know more. Although I guess most people would want to know a hell of a lot more than the little I do about the man I'm going to marry.

While he's sharing, I decide to ask more questions.

"You don't really sound Russian."

He smiles and allows it to linger. "I lived in Russia with my mother for a few years before I went to Denmark for fifteen, then back to Russia again."

That definitely explains the mixed accent. "How come you never came here? And no one knew about you?" The last time I asked anything close to that, I was issued with the threat on Dad's life and my own. Here's hoping I have better luck this time.

"It had to happen that way. Why? Wish you could have dated me?"

I raise my brows. "Remember, you don't date."

"You're right. We wouldn't have dated." He gives me a seductive grin. "I prefer fucking."

My pulse jumps, and I have to school my thoughts. It's typical of him to say something so lewd.

"I'm sure you would have gotten quite well acquainted with the female population."

"No. Just you, Valkyrie. Isn't that the point of the Promise?"

I'm thrown that such words could come out of a devil

like him. And hurt that Viktor never saw it that way until we were engaged.

The Promise in the Knights is sentimental. Parents signing the contract trust each other with their children's lives and hope that they'll find true love.

I hated hearing about Viktor's conquests from Lorelai, then feeling like shit after. And worse because I never asked him about it.

"No one really follows that. It's old."

"I would. Did you?"

"Yes, but some people think it's okay to sleep around until you're engaged."

His smile widens. "Is that what Viktor told you?"

"We're not talking about Viktor. He was good to me." It's time to change the subject. "How old were you when you went to Russia?"

He smiles again at the subject change. "I was nine."

"Didn't your mom like living here? The house is beautiful."

"Back then she had her reasons for leaving."

"Do I get to meet her?" That's my cleverly covert way of asking where she is.

The light in his eyes dims, and I know the answer just from the way he looks. I have the same look when anyone who doesn't know me asks me about my mother. I instantly regret the question, but it's too late to take it back.

"No. She was killed."

"Killed?" My insides squeeze, and I feel even worse.

"Yes." He stands and walks over to the windows to close the blinds, the only modern thing in the room.

"I'm truly sorry," I mutter, my voice frail and soft. "That's awful."

He turns to face me and leans against the wall, folding his arms. "I appreciate that."

A moment of awkward silence passes between us, and I can't think of anything else to talk about that's safe. More awkward seconds tick by, and I realize my time has run out.

So, when he smiles and mischief dances in his eyes, I know to prepare myself.

"All talked out?" He looks me over with interest and makes his way back to me.

Nervously, I shift from one foot to the other and try to keep my composure. "I'm tired now. Can I just go to bed?"

"Really?" He stops way too close. As close as he was before we came into the office. Except now I can smell his masculine scent beneath the cologne. It's jarring me and infringing on my ability to think past his overbearing dangerous presence.

"I told you what I was doing."

"But you were still breaking into my office." One corner of his lips turns up into a sexy smile. "If I make a mistake and kill a man because I thought he was someone else, that doesn't make him any less dead, does it?"

"No, but that's not the same thing."

"It's the same damn thing in my eyes."

"Well, not everyone is as psychotic as you."

Another real smile spreads across his face. "How about we find out just how psychotic I am, and I allow you to choose your punishment?"

"Me? Choose?" I almost feel relieved, but when I think

properly, I realize he's not going to just *allow* me to choose something that won't entertain him in some way.

Desmier inches even closer. "You get to choose from two things."

"What two things?"

"Either you let me fuck you against the wall, or you suck my cock."

CHAPTER
FOURTEEN

ANASTASIA

A wave of fire slides over my skin, and my body tightens with the numbness crawling through my nerves.

I want to slap him for talking to me like that, but my head is spinning and I'm shockingly conflicted.

My mind attempts to right itself, but the undeniable throb of arousal in my core is unashamedly curious to explore either of those options—*let him fuck me against the wall or suck his cock.*

Scandalous images come to my mind, doubling my heartbeat, and the tendril of desire dancing in my veins pushes me toward the dark side.

What would it feel like if I gave my body to this devil?

I think he'd take me ruthlessly and ruin me.

But would I like that?

Anastasia, no. What the actual hell are you thinking?

Stop right there. You cannot be turned on by this vile pirate of a man.

Just no.

The jolt of reality snaps me out of the sinful reverie and I straighten, standing a little taller.

"You fucking asshole. I'm not doing either," I tell him, but all he does is turn his smile up a notch.

He chuckles deep and low, mocking me again. "My dear Valkyrie, once again, you seem to be mistaken about our roles. Or specifically, yours. I still own you, and you are still indebted to me."

"*Indebted*? Are you kidding me? I haven't done anything to you. How can you hold my father's sins against me?" It's a fruitless question I've asked before, but I'm freaking out. "It's not fair."

Before I can continue my tirade, he catches my face, sending a bolt of fear rushing through me. That smile is still on his face, showing off dimples that should be illegal. I hope he's not psychotic enough to make me think he won't hurt me and then does.

"Baby girl, let's get this straight once and for all. I don't care how fair this is or isn't. You're mine. Now, you'd better find a way to get my dick wet before I choose for you. And just so you know, I may choose something a little more painful and not so pleasurable. Like whipping your ass. For all I know, you could be lying about your reasons for coming in here."

Oh my God. What the hell is wrong with him?

"I'm not lying."

"That's exactly what a liar would say. You're my captive. If I were a captive, I'd definitely either be looking for a way to escape, or a weapon. You should be grateful I've given you a choice. Now choose."

Damn it to hell. Why the fuck did I come down here? It wasn't worth it. Not one bit. Now I have to either let him fuck me or suck his cock.

As I'm not going to lose my virginity to him in here, I only actually have one choice. And I've never given anyone a blowjob before.

It serves me right. I was the one who said Viktor and I had done *many* things.

"What's it going to be, Valkyrie?" His voice takes on a deeper baritone, which makes me shiver from the outside in.

I try to look away from him, but he tightens his grip on me, gradually sliding his fingers down my neck until his nails dig into my skin.

"I'm waiting far more patiently than I should, so I think I'll choose—"

"I'll suck your cock," I cut in, feeling my strength drain just from saying those words.

Another chuckle rumbles in his chest. "Are you sure? At your wedding, you looked like you wanted to fuck me."

"I'm sure." The fewer words I say, the better. Or worse. I can't win. I'm playing a game where I'm just a participant. There is no scenario where I have an inkling of a chance at winning.

Desmier's pupils dilate, darkening with undeniable desire and pure sex. Watching him stirs a lusty feeling of forbidden need deep inside me, and I feel ashamed for it.

No matter what, I shouldn't feel like this. Everything is all too fresh for me to entertain these wild thoughts. And especially not when I should have been his brother's wife.

What does it say about me if I can flip-flop between emotions that should all have been reserved for Viktor?

Whatever it says doesn't matter now because I'm going to have to do this.

Desmier releases my face and pushes me to my knees, running his fingers through my hair until it comes free from the bun. My hair tumbles down my shoulders, and I gaze up at him, taking note of the animalistic hunger in his eyes.

The hunger magnifies when he unbuckles his belt then undoes the zipper and buttons on his pants. He pushes his boxers down, and his cock springs free. It's bigger than when I first saw it. I guess he wasn't as aroused then, and what I saw nights ago was already huge.

Now he's completely and utterly aroused, and his thick, veiny cock is so hard it looks like it could burst. As if his body can hear my thoughts, pre-cum beads at the tip.

With one finger, he swipes it away and holds it near my mouth.

"Lick."

Pushing aside my pride, I lick his finger, tasting his salty, masculine cum.

Heat uncurls in my belly, awakening the ache between my thighs, and I hate the way my body betrays me.

Before this, I was simply at his mercy. Now I have nothing left, not even control over the crazy emotions racing through me.

I hate it and I hate him and I hate everything.

Desmier reaches out to touch my cheek, but I swat his hand away.

"I hate you."

"So you should, Valkyrie, and I'd expect no different." Malevolence sparks in his eyes, and I realize he really doesn't care. "Now, open your mouth and suck my dick like a good little slut."

Lacing his fingers through my hair, he grabs a fistful and draws me closer to his cock.

My lips part, and when he pushes his thick length into my mouth, I forget I'm just feeling my way around as a first-timer. Having him inside my mouth feels different than I expected—although I'm not sure I know what that is.

He tastes like temptation. His male dominance steals away my thoughts the same way he stole everything else.

"Suck. Hard." He groans, the sound showing he likes what I'm doing to him.

It induces my mind back into that haze, and I start sucking.

Another primal groan pours out of him, making my nipples tighten. Then, using my hair, he grips tighter and deepthroats me.

I feel like I'm going to choke on his cock, but I adjust my mouth to take him, getting control of my gag reflex.

Everything in my mind vanishes when he starts fucking my face. The force at which he hammers into my mouth sets my body on fire, and every nerve sizzles. Lust overrides the blood in my veins, pushing straight to my pussy, and suddenly I'm soaked.

Soaked in a way that I've never been before, and I can no longer deny the need making my clit throb.

I know I'm treading in dangerous waters when this no longer feels like a punishment and I want him to touch me.

Touch me and take me.

Desmier lifts my face and stares down at me, our gazes locked. Him watching me sucking him, and me watching the pleasure on his face.

We maintain eye contact while we continue this carnal act of passion. It makes me feel wild and free, not like the Anastasia I was even days ago. That girl was restricted and felt trapped.

It's ironic that I'm actually trapped now, but I feel free.

Free and addicted to the thrill like an adrenaline junkie riding a sledge down Mount Everest.

He rocks his hips and angles himself so he can increase the pace. Tears spring from my eyes, but I don't want to stop.

I couldn't even if I tried to because he won't let me. His lock on my jaw means I will stay right where I am until he's finished with me.

"Fuck, you're beautiful," he grates through gritted teeth. "And perfect."

His cock stiffens in my mouth and his groans deepen, sounding more guttural and animalistic.

A savage roar then rips from his hard chest and cum hits the back of my throat. It coats it like hot cream, warming me up from the inside out.

The same savage energy wreaks havoc in my body, and I want to make myself come.

Desmier pulls out of my mouth, but he doesn't let go of my face.

Lifting my chin higher, he glares at me, his eyes still brimming with wild lust.

"Swallow." The command bends my will further, and my body instantly obeys.

His hot cream flows down my throat as I swallow, and his wicked smile of satisfaction scares me. It tells me he might have more in store for me.

My thoughts are confirmed when he tucks his dick back into his pants and lifts me up from the ground.

A touch of awareness returns, and I panic. "What are you doing?"

"We're not done yet." Knocking the stack of folders from the desk, he sets me down. "Open your legs."

Jagged pieces of fear slice through me.

"What are you going to do to me?" I can't keep the quiver out of my voice any more than I can the arousal.

I don't want to open my legs because I don't know what his plans are. And I don't want him to see how wet I am. I'm so wet my panties are slick and clinging to my mound.

"Valkyrie." The wicked devil chuckles. "If I was going to fuck you, I'd be buried deep inside you already and you wouldn't be able to walk. Now, shut the fuck up and open your legs."

One finger trails over the waistband of my skirt and tugs. It brushes over my skin, and that's enough to bewitch me back into the sexual haze.

I open my legs, and it feels like I've fallen deeper down this rabbit hole. The seductive look he gives me hooks me further, and I can't look away because I've never before had a man look at me the way he is.

As if he wants to devour every inch of my body and own me, leaving nothing behind.

Desmier smiles wider, a lock of that wild hair falling over his eye when he grabs my hips. He shoves my skirt up to my waist and loops a finger through the edge of my lace panties.

"Black lace," he husks, inching closer.

He crouches slightly to pull my panties down my legs and stops to gaze at them when he sees my arousal soaking through the fabric.

"Fuck me, you're soaked. Clearly, you picked the wrong form of punishment."

The pirate man holds up my panties, then he shocks me by sniffing them, making a point of showing me he's getting off on my scent. I gasp when his hot, slick tongue flicks out, and he sucks the juice soaking my panties.

My mouth drops open, and I want to say something, but all I can do is stare, mortified then wildly captivated when he pushes them in his back pocket.

I don't know what to make of him wanting to keep my panties, but I stop thinking all over again when he parts my legs wider and just stares at my pussy.

"Pretty here, too." He licks his bottom lip. When his eyes climb back to meet mine, he lifts the hem of my camisole top and tugs it. "Take this off, and the bra."

"Wh—"

"Do it. It's not like I haven't seen what you look like."

"Then why do you need to see me again?" That must be my brain's last attempt at preserving my sanity because I don't know where those words come from.

Of course, the bodice-ripping pirate responds by ripping

my beautiful top from my body as if it's a sheet of paper. Another wicked smile spreads across his lips, revealing the savage Viking he is. Much more than a mere pirate. And more like the devil.

Snapping the straps on my bra with a mere flick of his quick fingers, he rips that off, too, leaving me topless on his desk with my legs spread wide and my pussy exposed.

Before I have a chance to process the trepidation surging through me, he covers my breasts with his large hands and takes the left nipple into his hot, wet mouth.

My jaw drops, and a shudder wracks my body, rippling over me in a wave of consuming pleasure. Flames flick over my already-heated skin, and my head spins.

A moan I have no hope of restraining pours out of my mouth, and in that moment of helplessness, I crumble, giving him a piece of myself.

He fondles my right breast as he continues to suckle on my left, turning the barely-there pink color of my nipples a dusty rose.

His expression brightens, peppered with sin, as I arch my back, pushing my breast deeper into his mouth. He indulges me by sucking harder then moves to my other breast, wrapping his tongue around the nipple to tease it to life.

I pant, trying to catch my breath and hold on to what's left of my dignity, but neither feel like mine anymore.

Desmier moves away, stopping his wild suckle, and stares at me for a moment.

That's the only moment of reprieve he gives me before he dives in between my thighs and sucks on my clit. I cry out from the impact, a sound infused with pleasure and pain. Both are unbearable, but soon, they become the same. In an instant, I crave both like an addict who needs her next fix of a potent drug.

I don't want him to stop. I want this. I want more, and I want *him* to give it to me.

Shame fills me at the thought, but not enough to make me feel bad when I feel so good. And not when he starts eating me out, mixing up his actions between sucking, licking, and nibbling on my clit.

Unable to hold myself up, I grab his ripped shoulders, feeling the hard muscle beneath my fingertips for the first time.

Desperate moans hum from my lips as he continues feasting on my pussy, and I can't believe those sounds are coming from me.

One hard tug on my clit sends me into overdrive, and a bone-chilling orgasm reverberates through me, shattering my senses. My entire being quivers in total surrender, and I know the world as I knew it will never be the same again.

Desmier licks me clean, drinking every last drop. When he's finished, he pushes to his feet and my hands slip from his shoulders.

He straightens, and I notice the bulge in his pants straightaway.

We both stare down at it, but he smiles.

For a brief moment, my awareness returns, and I realize I'm practically naked. I try to cover my breasts, but he catches my hands and pins them to either side of me.

"Want more?" He pushes his bulge into my thigh, and as his pants are still undone, I can see the fat mushroom head of his cock poking out.

"I… I…" My words come out in a stutter as my mind continues to spin on a spiral of ecstasy.

"See what you do to me?"

Desmier moves closer, hovering an inch away from my lips like he's going to kiss me. His warm breath tickles my skin, making me entertain the thought of his lips on mine.

Instinctively, I lean in to receive the kiss, almost tasting him, but he moves away, severing the connection. Then his eyes become guarded, and he slips back into the devil I know.

"We're done for tonight," he says, even sounding like the devil. "Consider this round one."

Round one?

My brain snaps to attention when I process what he's saying. "What do you mean, round one?"

"I mean your punishment will be done when I say so." The grin sliding across his face is evil and mocking. *Mocking me.* "You will end your days with my cock in your pretty little mouth. Until I decide to change things up."

A stab of humiliation pierces through me, and I feel like a slut. This really is a game to him, and I'm just a toy.

"You can leave now, Anastasia *Sidorov*." The way he says my name in that hate-filled tone dripping with venom is to remind me that he hates me.

Hates *me*. Not just my father—me too.

In his eyes, Uther Sidorov's daughter is little more than a thing you treat like nothing.

I move away from him, grabbing the remnants of my top to cover myself. Then I rush through the door, fleeing his cruelty.

When I take the corner, I run past the crest, cursing it and my damn curiosity for the mess tonight became.

I run faster, wishing I could run out of here and far away to a place where no one can find me.

It's just a wish, a dream my heart wants, because right now, the only way I can escape is the same way Mom did.

Through death.

But I don't want to die.

CHAPTER FIFTEEN

DESMIER

I gaze out the floor-to-ceiling window of my office at Volkova Inc. watching the morning sun kiss the Boston skyline. The view almost has the same ambiance as when I'm at sea watching night turn to day, but this is different.

I still feel like an angry god trapped in the wrong dimension.

I'm certainly not acting like myself, and I know it's because of her.

Anastasia Sidorov.

My dear little Valkyrie.

I pull her panties from my pocket and sniff them. The scent still holds whispers of last night.

I can still taste her sweet nectar on my lips. Her pussy was as exquisite as fine wine, with the perfect provocative blend of arousal to give you that mind-fucked feeling you get when you're stoned on the good stuff.

Still, she managed to maintain the sweetness that comes with innocence. Even after I tried to pick her apart and tap into her inner crazy.

Now her essence lingers on my black soul.

I don't know if that's what made me overreact when I paid Dr. Marchant a visit at the crack of dawn. Or if it was because I never got to fuck her last night.

If she'd stayed around me a second longer, or if I'd gone to my room, I would have buried my cock deep in her sweet cunt over and over again.

I thought I stopped myself because I'd gone beyond my limits of control.

But it wasn't that.

Having had the time to think, I know it's because I actually want her.

The Valkyrie has poisoned me with that possessive streak that makes a man want to claim a woman and take everything from her.

Just from tasting her pussy, I knew one fuck to get the craving out of my system wouldn't be enough.

Anastasia wants me, too, but she has Viktor on her mind.

I won't fuck a woman I want when she's thinking about another man, even if it's to fuck him out of her system.

So she needs to be fixed. *Slowly, so that it's surely.*

Some things are more enjoyable when you take your time. Especially when the object of your desire has given you a way in.

So, the sexy punishment I've conjured for her will have to do. I can't lose my own game by allowing my dick to control me.

Pent-up lust had already turned me insane by the time I saw Dr. Marchant. Then again, the man gave the wrong answer when he told me he'd given

Anastasia a thorough internal examination. He then proceeded to tell me all that he'd done to make sure she was clean.

As I landed my fist in his face and rammed him into the wall, I knew I'd made one more enemy. But it needed to be done. He's clearly one of those old creepy fucktards who use their profession to get away with *other* things. Everything he said sounded like sexual assault. He's lucky I allowed him to keep his life.

Admittedly, I was also pissed because the motherfucker shouldn't have gotten to see the Valkyrie's pussy before me.

I can't remember the last time a woman fascinated me the way she has.

And that's just one thing.

Her revelation about the Butyrskaya crest divulged more about her than I expected to find.

I've purposely not been thinking about what she said about the crest because I don't know what to make of it. But I believe her. Despite my dig about not traveling in the same circles, I'd formed the same conclusion she had that her father, like many, must have known the Butyrskayas.

What's weird is her actually recognizing the crest, because it's no ordinary crest.

It's a crest the Butyrskayas placed on their safe houses and secret passages. Those are all places Uther and his family would not have known about. Especially since Pavel was on the secret squad.

The secret squad are almost like a separate brotherhood

who don't mix with the other enforcement divisions, or sometimes not even others in the Knights and the Bratva. I only know the things I do because Leif was part of them at one point. You are sworn to secrecy for life, but he told me certain things I needed to know.

The house I live in used to be one of the Butyrskayas' safe houses. The crest on the cliff and the one in the house both indicate secret passages that lead to a safe house in Salem, which I also currently own.

The only people who know what the crest really means and where the secret passages are located are Ehlga, Jayce, Zane, and Gytha. No one else.

My house stopped being a safe house when the Butyrskayas lived there, but they had many others I don't know the location of.

Because they left so long ago, most people around now don't even know that they used to live at my house.

The problem I'm having is, Anastasia has obviously seen a crest at one of the Butyrskayas' houses that she shouldn't know about.

It's weird as fuck and shady. Things that are not uncommon to Uther Sidorov.

Uther has more dark secrets than anyone I know. Since the Butyrskayas disappeared off the face of the earth and that was weird as fuck and shady, I can't help but wonder if there's some connection.

At the same time, I'm mindful that my hatred for the man could be driving my thoughts. I don't have enough information to form any real conclusions, but it's definitely something I'm going to look into.

I'll ask Leif about it when I next see him, but I'll also get

Gytha to do some digging around. If we don't find anything, I'll pay Uther a visit.

I don't want to alert him yet, just in case, which was why I told Anastasia she couldn't call him.

The sound of somebody clearing their throat in an exaggerated manner pulls me from my thoughts. When I turn around, I find myself facing Gytha, who is staring at the panties in my hand.

The fury and hurt on her face tone down the professional look she has going with the business dress she's wearing.

I hope I didn't look like that when I found her that night with some motherfucker balls deep inside her ass. I would hate to give anyone such control over my emotions.

I also hope that getup she's wearing isn't for me. After what Anastasia told me, it looks like I have to talk to Gytha again and make sure I set her straight. I don't need women problems, or any other right now.

One more sniff before I place the panties back in my pocket.

Gytha locks the door and comes closer, stopping paces away from my desk.

"I was wondering when you'd take her," she says, looking like she's doing her best to keep her composure.

"You shouldn't wonder about such things. It's not good for you. And while we're on the subject, I heard about yesterday. I want you to limit your contact with Anastasia."

Her nostrils flare. "This is ridiculous. The fucking girl is a pawn. She shouldn't matter to you. I didn't say anything to her that wasn't true."

"What, that you're the queen?"

"Wow, the little princess really did go running back—"

"Enough." I don't want to hear any more.

"You haven't given me a chance to fix things with you." She balls her hands at her sides. "I made my mistakes, and I can't take them back."

"I've already told you where we stand, and I won't be repeating myself." I raise my voice and stare her down so she sees how serious I am. "I don't have time for shit or games. Either you're in or out. Tell me now."

She stares at me for a moment, and I'm actually not sure what she's going to choose. It's not until a spark of hope enters her eyes that I know she'll stay, but I also know she's not happy about the situation. And it's clear no matter how many times I tell her our relationship is over, she won't stop trying to get me back until she decides it's time to stop. That can't be my problem.

"I'm in," she mumbles, pulling some documents from her bag and placing them on the desk.

"What's this?"

"More shit to deal with." She pulls up a chair and lowers herself into it. "The vineyard in Russia Anastasia is supposed to inherit isn't entirely a vineyard, and making wine isn't entirely the main business activity."

I straighten, raising my brows. "What do you mean?"

"It's an oil company worth billions."

My pulse jumps. "What the fuck?"

"It's actually Belzok and Co." She tilts her head to the side and presses her lips together.

"You're shitting me."

"I wish I were."

I bring a hand to my jaw and stare back at her in disbelief. Anyone who's anyone in the oil industry knows Belzok and Co. They're right up there with the best.

"I had to jump through all sorts of hoops to find this information and dig deeper than deep," she adds, and I can just imagine what she had to do.

"Tell me more."

"Nearly twenty years ago, when Anastasia's grandfather died, he thought he was leaving a small gift of property to his granddaughter. She wasn't even born yet. He'd worked on the vineyard with his family, and so had many generations of Sidorovs before him. It was considered something to keep in the family because of the special wine they made. Nobody knew the land had oil until three years after his death. Someone accidentally found it."

"Holy fuck." As far as weird things go, this is a good one. "Uther, that motherfucking bastard. He hid that well." This is the real reason he was shitting himself when I descended on him like a nightmare from hell and unearthed his dark, dirty secrets. Yes, there was the loss of his job with the Bratva and partnership with Volkova Inc., but this is most assuredly his greatest loss. A billion-dollar company at the tip of his fingers.

"Uther kept the company under wraps so it would look like he wasn't a part of it, but he's the executor of the business and of Anastasia's trust fund."

"No surprise there."

"No. Uther currently gets paid a monthly allowance, and the bulk of the money goes to Anastasia's trust fund because all profits, regardless of the business activity, are to go to her. It helps that the vineyard is still operating, but the real business gets transferred to Anastasia when she's nineteen, which she is, and after marriage. She and her husband will then co-own the company because it's meant to be a family business."

And that's where my dear brother thought he was going to fit in. This is what Zakh meant.

I wonder if Uther told Viktor what I have on him.

No... I don't think so. I don't know either of them well enough to guess their movements, but it doesn't make any practical sense for Uther to divulge that type of information. Viktor is loyal to the Knights. He wouldn't risk being linked to an accomplice whose crimes would cost him everything. Uther would have guessed that and definitely kept his secrets to himself.

This new revelation is something else. Another loss to them and another thing I would have stolen from Viktor.

"I guess I truly took a fuck of a lot from my brother."

"Uther too. This document here"—she holds up what looks like a contract— "shows Anastasia starting the transfer process back to her father so he would co-own the business with Viktor."

"And she seriously doesn't know what she's signing over?"

"No. They told her they were going to renovate the winery. There's nothing here to suggest she knew anything else, or that any of the other Volkovas knew. Apart from Zakh, of course. This was something of a side business to more than increase wealth for both Uther and Viktor."

Wow, I can just imagine their plans. The combined wealth of the companies between the two men would have been immeasurable because of the opportunities and assets that would flow from them.

"That's not a binding contract, is it?" I glance at the document.

"No, just the initial paperwork of what would have been."

"What are the termination and transfer of business clauses?"

"She's allowed to give her portion of the business to whomever she chooses, but the co-owner needs to agree."

Unfortunately for all those greedy motherfuckers, the new co-owner—aka me—won't be agreeing to anything.

"However, if she dies, the whole thing dissolves and everything goes to charity." Worry fills her eyes. "Desmier, you need to be careful here."

I sit back. "I know."

"Uther went to a lot of trouble to keep his daughter wrapped in a glasshouse. He even handpicked the man she would marry so he could get all of this. Your intervention is definitely a bigger loss to him than we knew. I'm sure you can see the only way he'd get back control is if you die."

Again. The asshole is most likely plotting my death as we sit here talking about his secrets. But I won't be that helpless twelve-year-old boy again.

The scar on my back is a constant reminder of what Uther did to me, but the scars on my heart drive me to keep fighting until I win.

"I've already factored in that he'll try to kill me."

"I know, but now you have the bigger picture. If Uther and Viktor are going to do something, they'll have a month from the day of the wedding to do it. It's a sort of cooling-off period. And rest assured something is on the horizon. Zane's team picked up footage of Uther meeting with someone in secret by the old warehouses."

"Did they see who it was?"

"No, but it wasn't Viktor. He was somewhere else with Zakh and Malik." She pulls in a haggard breath. "What are you going to do, Desmier? Are you going to confront Uther?"

"No. I don't think it's wise for him to know that I'm aware of this truth just yet. But keep watching him. I need all the info before I strike. Confronting either of them now might thwart their plans and leave me open for attack."

Also, under the Knights' law, if Viktor is trying to kill me, it's obviously sufficient grounds for death. The murder of another Knight is always punishable by execution. A plot to kill one who is part of the elite is also punishable by the same, except you get to kill the man who tried to kill you.

Which is why this needs to be kept secret. That includes keeping it from Anastasia, too. It's one more thing I have to hide from her, one more thing she should know the truth about and her precious Viktor, but I don't want her telling anyone and risk losing my leverage.

"Okay. I'll feed that back to the crew." Gytha nods. "That's all I have for you today."

"Thank you. You did good." Praise is due, and I'm a fair man, so I'll give it. The discomfort between us doesn't matter. Gytha always comes through with the impossible. That's why I still work with her, and I won't be an asshole thinking I could have gotten this information so fast without her.

"Thank you. Anything else you need from me?"

"Yes. Can you see if Uther might have worked with the Butyrskayas in the past, and if so, in what capacity?"

She narrows her eyes. "You think he worked with them?"

"Possibly. Or had some relations with them."

"Okay, I can look into that, but I think I've gotten all I can on Uther."

"Just have another look."

"Sure. Anything else?

"Just keep doing what you're doing."

"I will," she answers, but it sounds like a promise regarding our former relationship.

She rises and heads to the door, glancing once over her shoulder at me before leaving.

I push my concerns about her out of my mind because I need to. I was over her a long time ago. I think it was easy for me to move on because my feelings never ran as deeply as I thought they did.

I know the situation between us can only get more awkward, but right now, I need to process the intel she gave me.

And the man who gave me the heads-up.

There's no doubt Zakh wants the Obshchak position.

Regardless, it seems I found an ally.

I'll be speaking with him the moment he gets back.

Our meeting is one we'll need to have face to face.

CHAPTER SIXTEEN

ANASTASIA

I bolt upright, fleeing from the terror of another nightmare.

My heart is pounding hard, and I'm breathing like I've just finished swimming in the all state championship.

Feeling disorientated, I frantically look around, checking to see where I am.

When I see satin-covered cream walls, long embroidered curtains hanging at the window, and inhale that masculine scent of power clinging to the air, I get the answer I seek.

I'm in Desmier's room, sitting on his bed.

I'm not in the nightmare anymore, and shadow monsters haven't slashed my throat. No one is trying to kill me.

It's morning, and it's just me in here. Once again caught in the aftermath of another intense nightmare.

Damn it.

I don't know how much longer I can go through this.

Seeing the crest and not having any further information to work with has rattled my brain and put me in a stupor of confusion.

That thing has plagued my mind for years, smoldering like a volcano waiting to erupt. And worst of all, my little expedition the other night got me in more trouble with Desmier that I didn't need.

Just thinking about him heats my blood.

Like an idiot, I waited up late last night because I wanted to be prepared for him. The idea of falling asleep in the dragon's bed in my helpless state felt like I was just asking for more trouble. But I didn't see him, and sleep claimed me anyway.

I don't even know if he came back eventually and slept in here.

And I don't care.

I'm just glad I didn't end up with his cock shoved down my throat.

If I can avoid that asshole for as long as possible, I will.

I slide off the bed and make my way into the en-suite. A shower always helps calm me when I get worked up like this.

I'm not doing anything much today besides speaking with a wedding dress designer to pick a dress I don't want. That's supposed to be after lunch, so I have the morning free.

I shrug out of my nightshirt, loosen my hair, and step into the walk-in shower. I then adjust the settings so one of the jet sprays will blast cold water while the rest will keep me warm.

Pressing my hands against the smooth granite walls, I double over and allow the rapid stream of water to flow down over my head, soothing the section of my brain I hold responsible for my horrors.

I stay like that, keeping my eyes squeezed shut as I pretend I'm anywhere but here.

If everything had gone to plan, I'd be on that cruise ship with Viktor.

I was looking forward to all the fun we were going to have, but more than anything, I was looking forward to being with him.

I miss him with all my heart, and our sweet talks about the future. I miss talking about the two boys and two girls we were going to have—*Fredrich, Siegfried, Arabella, and Freyiss.*

I can't believe it's all over.

The moment I think that, fingers flutter over my back and my insides still.

The water flow over my head slows to a light spray, and a hand slides across the flat planes of my stomach.

Whipping around, I turn to see Desmier, and my heart lunges into my throat.

Fuck. He's in *here* with me.

And *naked.*

Naked naked.

Before I can even think of getting away, he barricades me in, setting his giant palms on the wall either side of me.

His big, strong biceps seem to ripple under the water's flow, and the vigorous definition in his muscles stops me from trying to break free. My hands would probably snap off if I braved the attempt.

Since I can't escape, I do the next best thing. I cover my breasts, lock my legs, and keep still like I'm playing possum, pretending to be dead.

"What the hell are you doing?" My voice chokes with the fright seizing my lungs.

"I was about to ask you the same thing, Valkyrie." A saucy smile flirts with his lips. "Your head was practically between your legs. Looked kind of kinky. Couldn't be sure, though. Never can tell with you daddy's-little-girl types. But your ass looked great."

Oh my God.

My nerves sizzle with annoyance and embarrassment. Every time this man speaks, he manages to shock me worse than the last time.

"I'm not a daddy's-little-girl type." Especially not now. I don't know when I'll ever forgive my father for what he's done to me.

"Yes, you are." He gives me a light chuckle, making me think this is the jovial version of him.

"Whatever. I'm bathing. Can't I at least have some privacy?"

"No, you can't. Everything is mine, including you. So, things like privacy no longer exist."

"You're such an asshole."

"Yes, I am." Flashing me a deadly smile, he straightens and runs a hand through his hair.

Then, against my better judgment, I allow my wanton eyes to drift over his body.

This is the first we've seen of each other since the other night, and for some ungodly reason, he looks hotter than he did before. It's his beard. It's fuller.

And with his wet hair sticking to his skin, it gives a better view of the precise sculpt of his angular face. I'm sure *FHM* wouldn't hesitate to christen him 'the world's sexiest' in their next issue.

I watch the water spraying over his body. His perfect, naked body with his cock already erect and massive, bobbing between his legs.

And oh God, I looked at it. Again.

I look away, but now Desmier is grinning at me because he caught me looking at his dick. My skin has turned several shades of crimson, so I can't even hide my embarrassment.

"I already told you if it pleases you to look, then look." He lowers his voice purposely, making it sound velvety smooth and sensual.

"It doesn't please me." He wouldn't know I'm looking because, of course he's hot, but he's the first naked man I've ever seen.

"Well, I much prefer you this way." He leans back in and pulls my hands away from my breasts, then parts my legs so he can look at my pussy properly. "Don't hide yourself from me."

The same wild look from the other night enters his eyes, and I'm glad the water is pouring over us because I can feel my arousal gathering between my thighs.

Something must be really wrong with me if I can be aroused by my captor.

The man is dangerous and will probably kill me when all is said and done.

I try to remember that, but when his gaze roves over me with slow seduction, a spark of desire sets off the nest of bats in my stomach.

My throat tightens with anticipation because I know his presence here *like this* can only mean one thing.

"What are you going to do to me?" I hate how small my voice sounds.

"Not sure yet. I'm thinking of how we can make up for last night."

Christ. I'm right. And I'm not prepared. I'm still shaky from my nightmare.

And I'm just not prepared.

He turns away to reach for the bottle of shower gel sitting on the double glass shelf near him.

As his back is turned to me, my eyes go straight to the burn scar, and for the millionth time I wonder how he got it.

When he turns back to me, he catches me looking and gives me a strange smile I can't figure out.

"Ugly, isn't it?" He pins me with an inquisitive stare.

"I don't think it's ugly."

"Well, that's good. I haven't had any complaints so far. Most women think a man with some scars is sexy."

They do, and his is, but a closer look speaks of more. More pain. More horror. "Did it hurt?"

"I nearly died. I'm lucky it's the only visible damage that remains."

It hits me that he's sharing information about himself again.

"How did you get it?" I'm eager for an answer, but he shakes his head.

"Story for another time, baby girl." The guard shielding his deeper thoughts slips for a heartbeat, and I pay attention to the soullessness and desolation in his eyes.

The last person I knew who looked remotely close to that was Mom.

Mom, the night before she decided she no longer wanted to be a part of this world.

When he blinks, the look is gone.

Gone and replaced with malice.

"Time to make up for last night." He winks, reminding me that he's an asshole.

I almost felt sorry for him. Anybody who looks like he just did must be broken inside.

I understand what broken feels like because I feel it every time I think of Mom. And every time I think something isn't quite right with me.

"Why do I have to make up for anything?"

"Because men have needs."

"Isn't Queen Gytha around to tend to your needs?" Mustering courage I don't feel, I lift my chin. But my courage becomes short-lived when he pushes me back into the wall.

"You're here. I had fun with you the other night. You had fun with me, too."

"You were punishing me." I harden my stare to avoid arguing because I have no other explanation for coming all over his face.

"You deserved to be punished." He traces a finger down my belly, and my

breath hitches. "And you still do. God knows what you could have stolen from my office."

"I told you what I was doing and why. Do you seriously believe I made up that shit?"

His eyes pierce into me. "No. I don't think that. I believe

that part. I think you have bigger things to worry about than making up a story about a family crest."

As sinister as his words are, hearing him say he believes me infuses me with an unexpected spark of hope.

"If you believe me, then stop punishing me."

He shakes his head. "No."

"Why?"

"I don't want to."

He stops my next words by continuing the fiery path down my stomach.

His finger goes down, down, down, stopping at my mound. There he strokes the skin, making my body fill with erotic expectancy.

It's almost unbearable, and I don't want to like it. But I do.

"I've just received the confirmation that you're clean." He looks from my pussy to my face.

My temper flares. "I told you I was clean."

"Now I know for sure. So, we can have more fun and play in other ways."

"Like...what?"

"How about we see where this shower takes us?" He squeezes some of the gel out of the bottle, cups my sex, and rubs it on my mound. My head spins, and I suck in a sharp breath, trying to stop myself from falling over.

Rubbing the gel in small circles until it foams, he works his way back up my stomach, then over my breasts, filling his hands with each globe.

My pussy clenches at his touch, and I feel like I'll go crazy if he stops.

As pleasure coils through me, my thoughts slip from my mind, rendering me useless to resisting him.

And he knows it.

I can tell from the flicker of triumph pressed into his smile that he knows what he's doing to me.

Desmier drops the shower gel and washes the foam off my body, touching me everywhere. Breathing is all I can do to keep myself from withering away.

A deep rumble rattles in his chest like a beast, and he lowers his head to nuzzle his face between my cleavage.

Like a savage, he sucks my nipple, sending pleasure sizzling through my body. Every nerve quivers with forbidden heat, warning me that I can't fight this. I've already entered his lair, and the only thing I can do now is play his game.

Desmier continues sucking my breast. *Shit,* it feels so good.

I press my hand against the wall, but it slips, so I grab his shoulders.

The gesture makes him suck harder, and a desperate moan slithers out of my mouth. He pulls away slowly, oh so slowly, fixing me with a merciless glare.

"You like that?" He sounds more like he's making an observation, not asking a question.

He looks at me as if he can see through me again, and I realize I can't do this.

I can't be like this with a man who isn't Viktor.

It's outrageous, and I can't allow Desmier to turn me into a fool because I'm afraid of him.

"I have to go now," I mutter, hoping he'll let me leave.

"Fuck that. You're not going anywhere." Without warning, he shoves two fingers into my pussy and strokes my clit, making my body go crazy. "Now tell me, Anastasia, do you like what I do to you? Do you like how I touch you? How I make your body feel? Tell me, baby girl."

His words have me arching into the wall, my senses shattered.

"Yesssss." My entire being comes alive with the answer.

He moves to my ear and nibbles on the lobe. "I don't think he touched you the way I do, did he?"

We both know the *he* Desmier is referring to is Viktor, so I don't need him to clarify.

"Answer me." His voice is more forceful, and so is his touch.

"No." As I hear myself, I know I just betrayed Viktor even more.

"Didn't he suck your tits and feast on your pussy the way I do?"

"No." Another betrayal, but this time, I think of all the women Lorelai told me Viktor was with. The part of me that hated that he couldn't have been true to me before we got engaged pushes through, wanting Desmier to continue.

"Don't worry, Valkyrie. I'll do it for you. We've only just started to get nasty."

He moves back down to resume his suckle, and the dangerous thrill of him liquifies my last resolve.

Taking my hand, he guides it to his cock, closing my fingers around his thick shaft.

"Stroke me," he grates out, and I obey, running my hand up and down his hard cock.

His body jolts at my touch, and I take one fleeting

moment to acknowledge the temporary power I hold over him. It feels good.

"Harder." His voice strains with the same pleasure spiraling through me.

I stroke his cock harder, but then he secures his hands to my ass and picks me up. Instinctively, I wrap my legs around his taut, muscular waist, and he carries me out of the shower and into the bedroom.

The next thing I'm aware of is my back hitting the silky sheets and Desmier on top of me.

Grabbing my waist, he rolls us over so I'm on top, but then he flips me around so my ass is in his face and his cock in mine.

My mouth drops when I realize what he's going to do to me.

One heavy hand lands on my ass as he spanks me hard and chuckles deep and low.

"Suck me, Valkyrie. Let's take care of each other's needs."

Before I can answer, he licks my pussy then grabs my ass so he can thrust his tongue deep into my needy passage.

I have to brace myself to take the impact of undiluted pleasure and the sight of his cock thrusting up in my face.

He starts eating me out, and I take his cock into my mouth, sucking him like the slut I made him believe I am.

Every stroke of his tongue sends a savage rush of electricity blasting over my body, and I feel him, too, growing harder and thicker in my mouth.

His gifted mouth pushes me closer to orgasm, and as he sucks hard on my clit, I come on his face, bucking against him like a madwoman.

I can't stop the moans from falling from my lips, nor gain control over the cacophony of emotions assailing me.

I have to release his cock as my body arches with the luxuriating sensation of my release. He waits then pulls me closer, setting me on my back again.

I'm so carried away and love feeling his hands on my bare thighs too much to notice what we're gearing up to do next.

It's not until I feel his cock pushing into my entrance that my senses return.

He's going to fuck me. I'm going to have sex with the same man I met five days ago, who kidnapped me from my wedding and is forcing me to marry him.

I'll no longer be a virgin, and he'll know I lied.

I should stop him, but I'm not.

I'm ... not.

I'm not doing anything but feeling him pushing into where I crave him the most.

"You're tight as fuck, Valkyrie," he groans, pushing his cock harder into my virgin passage.

It hurts like hell, but the infusion of pleasure keeps me there, wanting more even though in a matter of seconds, he's going to know why I'm so tight.

He pushes deeper, and I cry out, making him narrow his eyes.

Has he figured it out yet?

That I'm a virgin and he'll be the first man to have me?

I don't get to find out because a loud knock on the door severs the sexual haze and Desmier pulls out of me.

"Sorry to disturb you." It's Ehlga. "Mrs. Volkova is here to see you."

Mrs. Volkova?

As in Mira?

Desmier straightens, looming over me like a dark cloud of doom, his face filling with the vengeance I remember from our first meeting.

Hearing that Mira is here broke our lust-crazed spell and turned him back into the devil.

A closer look at his stony expression makes me realize it's not caused by her exactly.

It's who she represents—Viktor.

My stomach folds, twisting into knots of disgrace as I think of Viktor, too.

CHAPTER SEVENTEEN

DESMIER

H*oly. Fucking. Shit.*

I gaze down at the naked blonde beauty on my bed, lying exactly the way she would in any man's fantasy.

Her soft milky skin is flushed with the sheen of desire, her rose-blushed nipples diamond hard, her legs spread wide and her pussy glistening, begging to be fucked.

It's like I'm looking at an angel. An eroticized version of the angel I stole and brought to my unhallowed hell.

Hades—God of the Underworld—would have been proud, but dare I say that not even Persephone—the Goddess of Spring—was as enchanting as this being in my bed.

I got a mere taste of what it would feel like to be inside her, and I pulled out.

I actually pulled out.

Now I'm torn between slamming back inside her tight wet cunt or going to see what my father's wife wants.

Why the hell is Mira Volkova here?

Okay, I know why. That's a very stupid question.

It's more like it would be weird if she didn't come and seek me out to talk in private.

She could have spoken to Leif. I don't know anything he doesn't. But maybe I care less than he does about compassion, so I won't spare her feelings with the truth.

I maintain eye contact with Anastasia, feeling as aroused as I am pissed at the intrusion, along with the reminder of Viktor.

I noted the moment she thought about him, and I didn't like it.

She looked embarrassed.

"Desmier, what should I tell her?" Ehlga calls out again in a tentative voice, cutting into my thoughts.

Fuck it. I'm going to have to go down there.

I grit my teeth and straighten, hating all of this. "I'll be out in a minute."

When I slide off the bed, Anastasia covers herself as if just realizing she's naked.

Something must be wrong with my head to make me choose this over sex.

The Desmier I know would have chosen fucking and made Mira wait.

But perhaps this is more about my respect for Ehlga. She endured the worst of me during my teenage years. This is one area of my life I don't think she should have to deal with any more than she is. It's too sordid.

I grab some clothes I'd thrown to the side and put them

on. Then I cast one last glance at Anastasia and walk to the door.

When I step out of the room, Ehlga catches a glimpse of Anastasia on the bed with the sheet covering her, and her cheeks flush.

"I'm so sorry to disturb you two. I didn't know what to tell her. I didn't want to be rude. She seems quite fragile."

"That's okay. Did she say what she wants?"

"No, not so much. Just that she wanted to speak to you. I've just left her in the living room with a cup of tea."

By Odin. What the hell am I going to do with this woman I never really wanted to speak to? *Ever.*

Not only that. It's barely eight thirty. I got home after two in the morning because I was busy as fuck at the office. With my takeover, I've had meeting after meeting after meeting with all sorts of people. I didn't realize I was going to be so busy, but it is what it is.

"Alright, I'll go see her."

Ehlga nods, and I head to the living room.

I find Mira standing by the large Van Gogh painting hanging over the fireplace. Vittoria Butyrskaya used to fuss over that one a lot. It was one of her favorites. I left all her paintings up on the walls the same way I kept the classic books in Pavel's office.

Mira was admiring the painting, but turned to face me when I walked in.

She looks terrible and just as fragile as Ehlga described. And thinner than when I saw her at the wedding. As if she hasn't eaten since. Someone could easily snap her in half.

Despite that, the black fur coat she's wearing and her hair in that tight bun maintain her elegance.

"Good morning." Her accented voice has a slight quiver to it.

"Morning."

When I first learned about my father and his other family, I always imagined what I'd do if I met them. I always knew I'd find it hard to talk to Viktor and his mother. Zakh or Malik didn't feel like my competition, but Viktor and Mira did.

Now Mira is standing before me.

In my eyes, she's the woman who had the life my mother should have had. All her diamonds and pearls should have been Mom's. All the times Mira went to fancy restaurants or dressed up for a party or some high-end prissy function, it should have been my mother in her place.

"I apologize for coming here so early, or at all. I don't expect you to welcome me into your home." She pauses for a beat and takes a quick breath as if to calm herself. "I hope I didn't disturb you.

"It's fine. I was just in the shower." *If only it was just that.*

"I promise I won't take up too much of your time. Leif told me how busy you are. I wanted to talk to you before I fly out to Russia."

"What about, Mrs. Volkova?"

"Don't worry. I'm not here to ask you to reconsider anything. I'm so ashamed of how my husband treated you and your mother. Whatever you do is understandable." Her frail hands shake, so I decide to tone down my fury.

"Then why are you here?"

"Is it okay if we sit?"

"Of course." It's probably for the best because she looks like she might fall over and shatter if we stand any longer.

I motion to the leather sofas, and we sit opposite each other. Me in the armchair and her in the double seater.

"I wanted to ask you to confirm something Leif won't. His silence speaks louder than anything, but I just want to hear the words."

With that said, I know exactly what she's going to ask me. There's only one thing that no one has talked about.

It wasn't relevant at the time, but it is now. For *her*. If I'm right, and I think I am, it's to do with my father's fidelity.

A topic I'd rather not talk about.

"What is it?" I ask the question, but I can see she knows I've guessed.

Her throat works, and she swallows hard, then her trembling hands come together. "I know I have no right to ask you this, but I just wanted to know a few things. I, um...I assume you know why your mother waited twelve years to tell your father about you."

"Yes, I do know."

"Will you tell me?" Her voice shakes, and I actually feel sorry for her. She's clearly another woman who made the mistake of loving my father.

"Maybe you really should speak to Leif about this."

"Leif is a decent man who's known me for years. He knows I'm hurting, and he won't hurt me any more. But you don't know me, and I don't expect you to feel anything for me. Sometimes it's better to hear the truth from someone like that. So, please, tell me."

I guess I'm going to have to do it, then. "They were having an affair."

The moment I say the words, her pale eyes cloud like the

sky on a stormy day, then tears stream down her cheeks faster than an untamed river.

I was sixteen when Leif told me about my parents' affair. That was the gritty part of my past he wanted to leave for last.

He told me my father would see my mother every time he had business in Russia.

I never saw him, or them together, but I'd had suspicions long before I was twelve. I remember her acting like she did whenever she had a new man in her life.

THE LAST TIME they saw each other was serious.

Serious enough for my mother to tell me who I really am and who my father was. She wanted me to meet him.

That was mere days before she died. I remember us speaking about it over breakfast that day, then by nightfall, we were on the run.

Mira continues crying, so I reach for the box of tissues at the end of the coffee table. I hand her the whole box, and when she takes out a wad of tissues, she breaks down.

"I'm so sorry." She dries her tears and tries to compose herself. "I promised myself I wouldn't fall apart. Especially when I knew in my heart it had to be that. What else would make a woman come clean with such a truth? Then Evgeni killed her for it and chose to live with me. I'm so sorry."

"It's all his fault. Not yours." I feel strange comforting her, as if I'm betraying my mother, but I'm compelled to say something to console her.

"I still feel terrible. And like such a fool for thinking my husband was true to me." She wipes her face again and sets her shoulders back. "Thank you for being honest with me."

"That's okay." Deciding to change the subject, I think of the things I spoke to the family lawyer about that involve her. Everyone is still waiting to hear my plans, but as she's here, we can talk about what I'm doing with the assets that affect her. "I won't be doing anything much with some of your assets."

"Oh my. I haven't even thought about that. Do I still have a home to go to? I've been staying at a country house my family owns, just in case. I wasn't sure what you were going to do."

"You can keep your home. I won't be touching your personal assets or anything you held jointly with my father."

"Thank you. I'm very grateful."

Of course, she's fucking grateful. The house and the assets combined are worth several million. I'll bet she imagined me throwing her out on the street. That's what I thought I'd do, too.

I don't know if I'm acting like a chump by not doing it, but I decided I wouldn't because of Leif.

I search Mira's eyes and wonder if she knows about the vineyard or the original plans for Anastasia. Of her three children, Viktor seems closest to her, but there's that old adage of keeping women out of business.

In the Knights, women are expected to be submissive and subservient, treating their husbands like masters. The only place I'd want to treat my woman like that is in the bedroom, where she can worship my dick.

"Is it okay to ask about Anastasia?"

"She's fine." I try to say that as succinctly as possible so she doesn't prod.

But either Mira doesn't notice the hint, or she does and is taking the risk, because she looks like she's gearing up to ask me more questions.

"This is going to be hard for her."

"Because of Viktor?" I fill in, using the same concise tone.

"He's just one very important element of her life. I'm sure you must have done your research on her background."

"I have."

"She's been like a daughter to me, and I've been many things to her, so I know how she must feel."

"And how do you think she feels?" If Mira knows what's good for her, she'd better not tell me some fucking lovey-dovey shit about how much Anastasia loves Viktor. If she does, I won't hesitate to tell her that Anastasia's tight little pussy tells me otherwise.

"I think Anastasia feels like her world has been turned upside down." Her expression softens. "She's just a girl who's been through a lot. I've watched her go through real pain and suffering. And I've watched her overcome grief. She wants to be a therapist and work with children, pretty much like I do. Except she has real life experience."

"I will bear that in mind." I try to sound as polite as I can given the awe in which she speaks of Anastasia.

"Thank you. I felt you needed to understand her a little more in case she needs to lean on the people she's grown up with. Like me, or Viktor. We're like her family. Viktor was almost her husband. That's going to mean something to her, too. They have an attachment."

I bite the inside of my lip. There's nothing I can say against that because it's true.

"Well, you've given me much to think about." My voice is stiffer than a freshly cut board.

"Thank you for your time and everything else. I'll leave you to get back to your busy schedule."

"I'll see you out."

We stand, and I lead the way. As soon as we get out into the hallway, hurried footsteps grab our attention. I turn to see Anastasia rushing down the stairs.

"Mira!" she calls out, her voice overflowing with emotion.

Her steps quicken, and Mira meets her halfway. Anastasia practically falls into her waiting arms, and I feel like the asshole I am for depriving her of her support system.

At the same time, I can't help but look her over and drink in the little knitted dress hugging her perfect body. She's wrapped her hair in a bun, showing off her swan-like neck.

I almost had her.

Almost.

I can still feel the tight walls of her pussy wrapped around my dick like a glove.

She was so tight I assumed maybe she and Viktor might not have been as active as I imagined. Or maybe she's just naturally tight.

"It's so good to see you," Mira gushes, cupping Anastasia's face, showing the mother-daughter relationship they have.

"You too."

"Are you okay?"

"I am."

Our girl is more than okay, Mira. I would have given her the chance to come at least twice if we hadn't been interrupted.

"It would be great to meet up, if you're free." Anastasia glances at me for confirmation.

I stare back, expressionless. I've already given the go-ahead to see Mira, and my terms haven't changed. She can see her as long as Viktor isn't there. It's simple.

"That would be amazing." Mira clasps her hands together with delight. "I'm in Russia for a few weeks, but I'll call you when I get back."

She's talking heartily, but I catch the moment she looks at Anastasia's hair and notices it's as wet as mine. Wet from the shower I told her I was having. I read into the questioning look that flickers over her face, and I know what she's thinking—that we showered together. *Which we did.*

Of course, there's every chance we could have been showering separately, or Anastasia could have washed her hair during the time Mira and I were talking.

But I don't think she's thinking any of those things.

If I cared, I might laugh. Mira all but told me Viktor was the love of Anastasia's life, but if I'm right about her thoughts, she must be questioning that love, too.

"I can't wait to catch up," Anastasia bubbles, completely oblivious to the shift in Mira's focus.

"Me too, I'll see you soon. Be well, my dear." Mira hugs her and looks back at me.

I walk her to the door and let her out. Then I turn back to face my wife-to-be and make my way over to her.

Her expression turns anxious when I stop too close for

her comfort. A shudder brushes over her shoulders as I lean in and inhale her feminine scent mixed with the hint of honey from the shower, along with arousal. It's a deadly cocktail of sin waiting to be consumed.

I give her one of my ruthless smiles and lean even closer. "Baby girl, next time anyone asks how you are, make sure you tell them how well I take care of you. You would have come all over my dick if we didn't get disturbed."

As expected, her cheeks turn crimson. "Do you have to be like that all the time?"

I throw her off by slipping the band from her hair and making a point of watching her wet locks tumble down her shoulders. "I want to fuck you, so yes."

She recoils at my words. "You are so vile."

She tries to step away, but I grab her arm and pull her to my chest, so she's pressing up against me like we were in the shower. I move to her ear, and her breath catches. "Don't deny that you want to fuck me, too. We came close, so we're not done yet."

I'm glad she doesn't deny it.

"P.S." I want her to squirm. "Mira noticed your hair was wet, like mine. I told her I just got out of the shower."

Anastasia's mouth drops, and her heartbeat quickens against mine. "That doesn't mean she knows anything."

"Oh, I think she does." My don't-give-a-fuck smile makes her tremble with more shameful humiliation. "Don't worry, I'm sure she'll understand. She was young once."

"You're just being an asshole. She doesn't know anything."

"What if she did? You know it wouldn't matter, right? You're mine. Not Viktor's. You never, ever were."

The hurt in her eyes grips me more than it should, and I want to grab her and shake her. There's no question of her guilt, nor the strong feelings she has for her beloved Viktor. And I despise it.

When she was ready for me to take her, I wasn't mistaken about the need and desire I saw in her eyes screaming at me to devour her. She wanted me. Then she remembered him, and she stopped wanting me.

Or rather, the more accurate description is that she felt guilty for wanting me.

It's an invisible war of shit. But I know I want her badly enough to fight.

I'm a possessive motherfucker that way. When I came here, it was to take everything, including her. It's not enough just to take her body. A body is a shell. It's what's inside that counts. Those are the parts worth stealing.

We'll continue our games—*her punishment*—until we can't.

Until one of us cracks.

Until I break her and get my dear brother out of her system, or she breaks me by my wanting her so damn much.

"Be ready for me later." I subsume my wretchedness and leave her staring after me.

While she questions her heart, I question myself.

I'm jealous of what she feels for Viktor.

That was never part of the plan.

Neither was obsession.

CHAPTER EIGHTEEN

ANASTASIA

I feel like a slut.

I can't shake the feeling, no matter what I tell myself or how I paint things in my mind.

Sluts don't normally have the clash of emotions I'm experiencing.

Usually, they don't care. I've encountered enough of them to know. There were tons of sluts in high school and even more in college.

They didn't care as they went from one guy to the other. And they certainly wouldn't have a problem with being with a guy's older brother.

Not like me. The girl who's committed her soul to its own shitty apartment in purgatory.

Here I am again, sitting on the sofa in the sunroom, trying to study but failing miserably because I can't get my guilt-riddled mind to think of anything else besides Desmier Volkova.

I've been back at college for a few days now. When I get home, I either study in here or by the pool.

Studying has been the only thing to distract me from the guilt I feel over the nightly *punishments* which send me deeper down the river of shame.

I just can't do it today.

I've been in here now for the last three hours with my cognitive psychology textbook aging in my hands. I'm supposed to be reading about the early onset of neurodegenerative disorders, but I haven't gotten past the first page.

My nightmares are still tearing me apart, but so is the tug of war in my heart.

Desmier and I haven't gone as far as we did the day Mira came to the house, but everything else we do is just as potent.

Every night for the last six days has either seen me on my knees with his cock assaulting my mouth, or me on my back with him eating me out like he's been marooned on a deserted island starved for food.

I've experienced things with him I never even thought about or talked about with Lorelai—whom I get my sex education from. She doesn't sleep around, but she's more versed in the opposite sex than me, the virgin pretending not to be.

The pirate man has led me to the proverbial edge, and I don't know what will push me over. Him. Or me.

When it comes to him, I feel like my own worst enemy. Like he's my kryptonite and I have no choice but to bend to his will.

Ehlga comes in carrying a tray filled with sandwiches and some other pastries I like. A warm smile lifts her ruby-red lips, and her hair is done up like she's going out. Last week, she went to the opera. She'd extended the invite, but I wasn't in the mood.

"Hello." Her face lights up as she sets the tray on the table next to me. "I thought you'd want something light before dinner."

The food is enough for at least four people. "This is what you call light, Ehlga?" A light chuckle I don't expect falls from my lips. I savor the feeling, as few things make me laugh these days.

"Well, you didn't eat much yesterday, and I don't consider the bite of toast you had this morning as breakfast." She sits opposite me and crosses one ankle over the other.

"I see. I guess I wasn't hungry." With all my worries, it's a wonder I can get anything down my throat at all. When stressed, some people stop eating altogether, some eat too much. I'm somewhere in the middle of the scale but closer to those who don't eat.

"Just eat what you can. I'm going to a poetry reading, so I wanted to make sure you ate some of the things you like."

"I will. Thanks for making them." I'm grateful she's so caring, but I probably won't eat a lot because my appetite is nonexistent.

"You are very welcome."

We've grown closer, which has been nice. Talking to her sometimes eases the tension, and she's taken care of all the wedding arrangements, as if she understands how difficult it is for me to marry another man.

"How's college been going?" She rests her hands on her lap.

"It's been good."

What's even better is not being here, and I love seeing all my friends. The only downside is everyone—the good, the bad, and the stuck-up bitches—know what happened to me. Whoever wasn't at the wedding would have been fully informed when the gossip spread like an Australian bushfire.

"I'm glad. How are you doing otherwise?"

The mood of our conversation shifts with the question, and I'm stumped for an answer.

"I'm okay," I answer by default. Of course, it's a lie. But I lie so often now that even the air I breathe, the walls of the house, and the trees surrounding us believe me.

To keep up the façade, I give her one of my sweet smiles —the mask I slip on to make me look like I won't end up like my mother.

"What time is Desmier coming back?"

"I'm not sure, dear. His schedule is all over the place this week."

I just hope he's not back soon. His schedule is all over the place anyway, but he's busier this week because he's going on a business trip tomorrow. He'll be gone for over a week. The break from him will be great, but his return will mean I'm that much closer to becoming his wife. I'm still as terrified as the first day I found out.

"Try not to worry about Desmier too much." Ehlga taps the back of my hand.

I stare at her, wondering if she's going to elaborate. She never says anything about him, other than letting me know when he's here, wants me, or has some asshole order for me to follow.

"Sometimes he can come across as being... intense." She nods as if she really believes what she's saying.

I stifle a groan that I knew would sound rude. I want to tell her that *intense* is when your college professor gives you a B- on an assignment you thought you aced because he wants you to do way better next time.

Desmier Volkova is not intense, and I'm beginning to think I was right about Ehlga not using swear words. If she did, she'd be using something along the lines of *motherfucker* or *fucking asshole* to describe him.

"Ehlga, I appreciate your effort to make me feel comfortable here, I honestly do. But I'm sure you know Desmier's intentions for me. And you know what he did to me."

The light in her expression dims, and discomfort settles in the seal of her thin lips. "I do. I just want you to know there's more to him."

"Like what?"

"A different side. Something softer."

"Something softer?" If I knew I wouldn't get in trouble, I would totally taint her perception of him and tell her what he makes me do at night.

"Desmier is not always the version you've seen. It might help you to keep your mind open to that, as you'll be married soon."

Married. Married to a stranger who makes my head spin and my body speak to me in a language I don't want to understand.

"I'll keep that in mind."

"Good." Her radiance returns as she smiles. "I'll leave you with something to cheer you up."

My interest piques. "What?"

"This." She picks up one of the teacups from the tray. I assumed it was empty like the one next to it, but it's not. Dark tea leaves have settled at the bottom, looking like a shadowy butterfly. I remember using this cup at breakfast to drink her special Slovenian blend.

I guess she's about to tell me my fortune, so I try like I did the other day not to look like I think it's a crock of shit.

"Look what the stars hold for you." Her eyes beam like she's about to hand me a check for a million dollars.

"Is that good? It looks like a butterfly or some sort of insect."

"Very good. It's the butterfly. It means success and happiness."

"That's nice." I can't even try to keep the sarcasm out of my voice. I don't believe in the whole divination thing anyway, but now I definitely don't. The only success I'm going to have here is not going crazy in this house. And if I accomplish that, I guess I'll be happy.

"Don't say it like that. My skills have never failed me." The light ends of her gray waves bounce as she nods.

"Alright, Ehlga, if you say so."

"I do say so." She laughs. "I'll leave you to eat. I'm around for the next fifteen or so minutes. If you need me, just call."

"Okay, thanks."

She dips her head and saunters away.

I pick up a chicken mayo sandwich and eat it. It tastes amazing and is a good distraction. When I'm about to grab another, my phone rings. I'm expecting a call from Lorelai, but I thought she'd call later.

I grab my phone but freeze when I look at the screen and see it's not Lorelai calling me.

It's Viktor.

CHAPTER NINETEEN

ANASTASIA

Viktor's name continues to flash across my phone screen, like the blaring red and blue lights of a police car.

A gamut of emotions assails me, and my heart doubles over in a triple beat.

There's trepidation and fear, happiness and hope, and shame.

Shame for the scandalous way I've been with Desmier.

Shame for the secret parts of me that feel pleasure during those forbidden moments when I come undone in his arms like a slut.

Or a cheater.

I feel like I'm cheating on Viktor now even just thinking about Desmier.

I stare at the phone, wanting to answer, but the consequences of doing so stop me. I'm supposed to see Viktor sometime in the next two weeks. Talking to him now might jeopardize that.

The phone rings on and on and on, quivering in my hands.

Or is that me?

I don't know. What I do know is, if I know what's good for me, I mustn't answer the phone.

I need to let it ring out and tell Viktor I'm sorry when I get to see him.

That's what I need to do, but I don't want to because, God, this is Viktor.

The man I used to call my prince.

How can I ignore his call?

He knows he can't call me because I told him in the *one* text I was allowed to send. And he would have known anyway.

But I'm still the same girl who screamed with delight when Dad first allowed him to call me, and I'm still the same girl who swooned every time he sent me a message.

Lorelai said Viktor was trying to get me back.

What if he found a way?

Even if he didn't, wouldn't it just be good to hear his voice?

Or maybe it might fix me. Remembering how I loved him always made me stronger.

That thought does it. I answer the call. The ringing stops, and I press the phone to my ear.

"Anastasia. Baby, is that you?" Viktor's deep voice fills me with the same elation I used to feel every time I was with him. But then I remember the danger.

"Viktor, I can't talk. Talking to you is going to make it worse for me. Desmier is—"

"I don't give a fuck. I needed to know how you are." His tone, that authoritative yet protective tenor, envelopes me. It's a reminder of what felt safe and what we used to be. "I'm going crazy not knowing what's happening to you."

My breath hitches, and the backs of my eyes sting with those tears that still want to fall. "I'm okay. I wish things were different."

"I miss you."

"I miss you, too."

"Awww, isn't this touching." Desmier's voice carries across the room, crashing into me like a tsunami.

My body jolts then flushes with a maddening cacophony of fear and heat from his piercing stare.

He's leaning against the door frame, his black Armani suit making him look like the businessman he's supposed to be. But he still looks like the Grim Reaper to me.

Being caught again doing something I'm not supposed to do is just so typical of my fucking bad luck.

So no, Ehlga, I don't believe your predictions of success and happiness. The idea of wishing for either of those feel like bullshit to me.

"Anastasia, what's happening?" Viktor's voice speeds up in my ear, like when you put a song on fast forward for far too long. "Is Desmier there?"

"Yes, I have to go." I barely manage to get the words out.

"No, what's he doing?" Viktor's voice is loud enough for Desmier to hear.

Desmier walks up to me, and the moment he snatches

the phone out of my hand, I know he's going to do something bizarre.

"Desmier, Viktor was just checking to see if I was okay." I study his face. "He didn't mean any harm."

He walks me into the wall with one of his I-don't-give-a-fuck stares, and I crash into the hard surface.

Pressing the phone to his ear, Desmier clears his throat, and a mirthless smile floats across his lips. "Hello, little brother. Listen very carefully, and you'll know what I'm doing."

He puts the phone on speaker and sets it on the window frame next to us.

"What are you doing?" I try to stay calm, but my pulse jumps in my throat, throbbing so hard I can't breathe.

"Reminding him who you belong to."

The malevolent flicker in his eyes keeps me rooted to the spot. I don't get the chance to brace myself before he drops to his knees and swoops under my skirt like an eagle catching its prey. In the next split second, he shoves the skirt up my hips and buries his face into my pussy.

"Stop it, you bastard," I manage, but I'd sound more convincing if there weren't a moan laced in my voice.

"Desmier, what the hell are you doing?" Viktor's voice echoes around the room and through me. "Come back to the phone."

I attempt to push Desmier away, but when he spreads my legs wide and moves my panties aside with his tongue, I shriek. At his touch, raw pleasure hits me.

One flick of his tongue over my already swollen clit injects me with raw ecstasy that overpowers my every thought.

My mind recedes, and I forget who I am, where I am, and who I'm supposed to love.

He sucks on my clit harder, then rips my panties off and hoists my leg over his shoulder. Then he deepens his suckle, sending pleasure coursing through my body.

My emotions shatter like tiny shards of glass, and a loud, uncontrollable moan rips from deep within my chest. It rises straight from the place which craves him the most—*all of me*. Another one follows, and another, and another.

He continues devouring my pussy with his mouth, alternating between licking, sucking, and tasting me.

"Oh God..." My voice hits every wall in the room, and the vicious wave of my orgasm grabs my insides. It builds and rises like hot lava ready to erupt and burn everything in its way.

My brain snaps back into reality when the pirate man stops his wild suckle, giving me a moment of respite.

But just a moment. Rising to his feet, he holds the leg that was on his shoulder up with one hand. With the other, he cups my sex and shoves two thick fingers back into my passage.

And... Jesus. It's too much.

He finger-fucks me, and my back arches to take his thrust. The overload makes me grab his jacket.

He leans toward my ear and licks over the lobe, sending a shiver of delight through my brain. A nip at my neck spreads it over my body.

"Ahhhh...." I moan, but that shouldn't have felt so damn good.

"Good girl." Desmier's voice is spitefully loud. And loud

enough so anyone nearby can hear him. I'm sure they'll hear me, too. "Clearly, Viktor didn't fuck you properly. But I can."

The mention of Viktor's name and the allusion of fucking tug at the sexual haze covering my mind. But the pirate man knows exactly how to keep me where he wants me, because he knows what my body wants.

Needs.

He touches me like he's studied my body for millennia and knows how to pass every single test on *me*. So, when he rips open my top, making my breast pop out and sucks on my diamond-hard nipple, he knew I'd come.

I do, writhing against his hard body like a trapped animal. At the sound of my obvious unmistakable sex moans, he sucks harder, making an exaggerated sucking noise right next to the phone. Then he returns to my ear and breathes over my skin.

"*Krichi dlya menya*," he husks in Russian, telling me to scream.

One hard shove of his fingers against my clit, and I come again, obeying with a scream I don't care who hears.

"Anastasia." Viktor's voice barely registers in my mind.

Until it does... and I'm so ashamed.

I glance at the quiet phone, and it's like I can see him watching me with disappointment. And so much hurt.

Then I look at Desmier's smiling face and quickly fix my top, covering my breast. With the utmost disgust, I shake my head at him. What he just did was so mean and cruel, and so damn fucked up. Just like him.

He drops my leg and picks up the phone. "As you heard, dear brother, I take great care of my things." Although his slight accent deepens and it's sexy, he sounds like he could be talking about a car or the asset he once called me.

"You fucking asshole." Viktor's tone is overflowing with so much fury, I can almost feel his wrath burning my skin.

"Goodbye, Viktor. Do not call her again." Desmier hangs up the phone and sets it back on the window ledge. Then he hardens his stare.

He really is evil. "You asshole. Why did you do that?"

"Because I can."

Rage like I've never felt before possesses me, and I slap his cheek so hard my fingers leave a print.

I go to slap him again, not caring what he'll do to me, but he grabs my hand and shoves me harder into the wall.

He pushes his body into me, and I feel his hard cock pressing into my belly.

"Watch it, baby girl. You haven't seen me mad yet. You won't like me mad."

"Fuck you. I don't like you anyway."

He laughs. "If it makes you feel better, you keep telling yourself all the lies you want. But you came for me, Anastasia. Your naughty little pussy doesn't lie."

"It was a natural reaction because you touched me."

"You were already wet for me when I touched you. Meaning you wanted me."

"No," I choke out, feeling like I've just been called out on a secret I would have taken to my grave. "I don't want y—"

His mouth crushes to mine, cutting off my words like a short circuit in a wire.

He gives me the kiss I never got that night when this craziness all started. And it's every bit as raw and unapologetic as it is seductive.

The provocative pressure sends a shockwave through my system, numbing my brain. Hunger unlike I've ever known stirs to life in my soul, and I'm so stunned and helpless against him that when he yanks me flush against his hard chest, I kiss him back.

One large hand clamps the back of my neck while the other laces through my hair to deepen the kiss. My lips part against the assault of him, and he uses the chance to push his tongue into my mouth with a deep masculine groan that turns my knees to water. The delicious taste of him melts me as he gives me something I never knew I needed.

It's hard to imagine that a devil like him could kiss like this, rivaling every heart-fluttering kiss from the movies and raising the bar for all Prince Charmings— past, present, and future.

How strange that we've done so many other things but never kissed. Now that we are, it feels like I'm tasting the real him.

I press my hands against his chest, feeling granite muscle as I drink in his scent of sandalwood and power and sex. It erases everything I warned myself about when it came to resisting him.

Then he pulls away and releases me. Leaving me breathless, and like I wasn't alive until just now.

He glares at me, staring into my eyes like he can see everything I try to hide from the world. "You do like me. And I like you, too, or we wouldn't be here. This wouldn't be so hard."

I want to deny his stupid, stupid words, but I can't because they aren't stupid.

"Let me save you some time and heartache, Valkyrie. You don't love Viktor."

His venomous words spike my nerves like a thousand needles piercing into me at once, shaking the foundations of my world even more.

"How dare you?" My voice is so quiet I might as well be talking to myself.

"I do dare, baby girl. And I'll take your phone away if you speak to him again. Be ready for me later."

He walks away, leaving conflict gripping my core.

What the hell just happened?

And what did I just do?

Dread fills my soul when I think of how Viktor heard me come.

And I kissed Desmier. I actually kissed him.

Oh, Viktor, I'm so sorry.

And it's not true. I do love you.

I do love you.

I do love you.

The mantra repeats loudly in my mind.

But something in me *has* changed, and I realize I'm not the same girl.

I'm not the same Anastasia I was before Desmier Volkova.

The thought twists me inside out, but when I turn around, all the blood stills in my veins when I see Gytha standing on the second-floor balcony opposite the sunroom.

She's a good distance away with the entire pool between us but close enough for me to see the hatred ingrained in her expression.

She was watching *us*—Desmier and me.

I don't know how long she was watching, but I feel she saw everything. I also sense that she knows, too, about the shift in the air between Desmier and me.

That's one more thing she'll hate me for.

I'm trapped in her stare for eons before she walks away.

It's only when I can't see her anymore that I'm able to breathe again. But my mind and body feel so mangled, I'd swap this world for my nightmares any day.

At least I know what happens there. Out here, the monsters still reign, and they still want to destroy me.

They just might.

CHAPTER TWENTY

DESMIER

Zakh steeples his fingers on his desk as I sit in the leather chair in front of him, relieved that we're finally meeting.

Today is another crazy busy day. I also fly out to L.A. tonight with Leif for what should hopefully be a ten-day business trip, but seeing Zakh couldn't wait any longer.

He got back from Russia last night, and by the time I return from L.A., we'll be days away from the inauguration.

I can't remember the last time I was this keen to see anybody, and I never thought I would feel this way about one of my brothers.

Zakh's office isn't that different from mine, but his has less décor. There is only one painting on the wall behind him, depicting the battle of Heaven and Hell.

When he smiles and sits back, I imagine him right at

home in the infernal underworld. Probably sitting next to me.

"I assume you found the information okay?" A mischievous grin lights up his face, making him appear more lighthearted than when I last saw him.

"I did. My assistant says she had to jump through hoops, though."

"Assistant? Gytha doesn't look at you the way an assistant would." He makes a point of using her first name, as if he's looked into her. I'm sure he has and tried to do his research on me, too. It's no more than I did on him and the others. "Or is that perhaps *your* version of an assistant?"

I chuckle. "We're not like that anymore."

He quirks a brow. "Because you're getting married to Anastasia Sidorov?"

Just hearing her name stirs my cock.

Yesterday's wild encounter was definitely my personal favorite to date. I can just imagine my dear Viktor's face after he heard his beloved coming for me. Teaching his pompous ass a lesson was satisfying. At the same time, I lost myself in her pleasure. And that kiss.

Fuck. The thrill was like sailing into the eye of a storm.

She felt it, too. Even though I devastated her with my jab about not loving Viktor.

Do I believe that? *No.* But I said it to be a vindictive, coldhearted bastard.

Since she's supposed to be nothing more than a ploy, the best way to answer Zakh is with something as vague as I feel because the woman drives me crazy.

"Gytha and I are just business partners."

"Okay. Brother." He nods, but it's clear from the mischievous smirk on his face that he doesn't believe me. "I was just curious. We have years to catch up on, you and I."

"It would appear so."

"Speaking of which." He glances at the tattoo on my wrist of Odin's rune and smiles wider. "If I had that, I'd at the very least challenge the Pakhan for the Bratva."

I chuckle and sigh. Zakh seems like the kind of man who would start a war to conquer countries. I'm not that guy because I don't choose to be. I just want one thing.

"I'm getting what I want. And it's enough, so the Pakhan can relax. I won't be challenging him for anything."

A spark of reverence invades his dark eyes. "That deserves respect."

"I appreciate that."

"Where did you train?" He's asking about my Reaping and initiation into the Knights.

"Across the old Viking lands." That's Denmark, Norway, and Sweden, but the people who trained me still refer to them by their old names and still consider themselves Danes.

"All of them?"

"Yes, all."

His brows disappear into his hairline. "You're kidding me."

"The Reaping was the hardest, obviously. A hundred days of survival tasks and challenges with the clan's berserkers that could have killed me on any given day." For a sixteen-year-old boy, any of those were horrific and barbaric, but that's why it's done—to assess the survival of the fittest. "My journey ended at the old temple in Uppsala." In the eleventh century, the temple was dedicated to the

Norse gods: Thor, Freyr, and Odin. In the Knights' training, the final task shows you your destiny. Mine led me straight to the temple door. That's where I received the rune, but I had to earn it first. With blood.

You have to kill one of the men who held the rune before you. It's kill or be killed. He was my first kill. To this day, I still wonder how I did it. We both fell over the side of the mountain. I grabbed on to the edge, but he fell to his death with my knife stuck in his neck.

Zakh looks more than impressed. "We should talk more about that someday."

"We should."

"Indeed, and with that said, I'm sure you're eager to talk about the *vineyard*."

"I am. Thank you for the heads-up." I give him a curt nod.

"I felt it was something you should know. Have you told Anastasia about it?"

"Not yet."

He levels me a curious stare as if he can see through to the parts of me that are so taken with her. "Be careful with that one, brother. She's a real beauty but she thought the sun shone from Viktor's ass even before she understood what marriage was."

"I believe you." I've seen the evidence for myself. She might easily change her mind if she knew about Viktor's involvement with the vineyard. But part of me fears she might not. "In any case, I don't want anyone becoming aware that I know about this yet. I'm sure you can understand why."

"Oh, yes. That's very wise given that it means death

under the Knights' law if anyone were plotting things they shouldn't against their brother."

The way he speaks makes me think he wants to get rid of Viktor. I've already assumed he doesn't trust him, or he wouldn't have ratted Viktor out about the vineyard. I want to be clear on why, among other things as I sense there's more than meets the eye with Zakh.

"How the hell did you find out about the vineyard?"

He gives me a confident smile, and I realize I'm right.

"I have a special penchant for getting information. I might be on a par with your lady friend there, or slightly better. She left a trace here and there, but I cleaned it up."

I raise my brows. "You can hack?" Or maybe it's a little more than that if he can detect Gytha's traces. She's not messy in the least.

"It's my thing, but I don't announce it. Sometimes it's better when people don't know everything about you. That way, you can keep more things to yourself."

"Do the others know?"

"Malik. Not Viktor."

I could have guessed that. Zakh seems closer to Malik than to Viktor. It was just something I picked up on at the wedding.

"Leif knows, too," he adds.

"I guess that's why he wants me to get to know you guys."

"I suppose so. He wants us to get to know you, too."

"What's your take on that?" I've never cared one way or the other about being a part of them. I always thought they'd reject me, but I'm curious to hear his thoughts.

"I won't lie; the situation is strange. I'm close to Leif,

maybe closer than the others, so I feel betrayed that he didn't tell me about you. But I get it. I trust the decisions he makes are for the best. So, I'm on board."

I'm surprised by the lightness that fills me at being accepted. "That's good to hear."

"And you? What about you?"

"I'm on board, too." I am, though not with Viktor, but that goes without saying.

"Does that mean I earned some element of trust?" He keeps his gaze trained on me.

"You did." I'm not going to give my wholehearted trust to him because I never do that—except with Leif and Ehlga—but this is a start I think I need. Zakh gave me a lead to check out that I wouldn't have had. "I guess I don't have to ask why you told me. You want to be Obshchak. Don't you?"

"When our family got the opportunity to join the elite, I was always going to be the Obshchak when Father retired. I want it to stay that way."

Well, this is the first moment I've felt that I can now choose my subordinates.

"What about Malik? What should I do with him?"

"Whatever you choose."

"Can I trust him, too?"

"He's in a weird place, but he's on board. And yes, you can trust him."

Leif told me that Malik had been captured and tortured by one of our father's enemies years ago. He was held in captivity for close to a year. I assumed that's why Malik seems calculative and quiet. Shit like that can change a man in ways no one knows unless they've been through a similar experience. It happened to me once, but I was only gone for a few days.

"Malik and I work together in the accounts department. When Father became the Sovietnik, our role extended to taking care of the Raventhorn Bank." That is the bank that holds all the Knights' money. "Malik is the only one of us who trained with the Pakhan's security force, and he served in the Navy for two years."

"Impressive." I especially like the Navy part.

"Well, I feel like I should put in a good word for him since I'm trying to get a position that could be his."

"I'm assuming I can trust Viktor as far as I can throw him?"

"Man, if you can do that much, I give you credit." He chuckles.

"You don't trust him?" I decide to cut to the chase.

Zakh grins. "That's debatable. We're Volkovas. Power-hungry men. But let's just say a few things have happened to make me question my brother."

That sounds important. "Like what?"

He pulls in a breath. "You might not care to hear it because of what our father did to you and your mother."

I see. It's to do with him. Zakh's right. I don't give a shit about our father. But perhaps this is something I should hear.

"Tell me anyway."

"I don't believe his illness was brought on by natural causes."

I narrow my eyes. "But he had a heart condition."

"Yes, but it didn't make sense. A man doesn't suddenly go from being active one day to so sick he has to be hospitalized because his heart is bad, then collapsing straight into a coma."

That doesn't sound right. "What do you think happened to him?"

"There were traces of oleander on the desk in his office. I had the place swept for it when he first fell into the coma. I suspected it could be something like that. I'm sure you know how deadly and undetectable that poison can be."

"I'm aware of it." I bite down hard on my back teeth, willing myself not to care. I don't for the old man, but what Zakh is suggesting is that there's something else going on. "Does anyone else know this?"

"No. I didn't want to say anything yet until I have more proof of *who* put the poison there. And what their plans are. If they slow-poisoned our father, they could be up to anything."

"How come you're telling me?"

"Our father is going to die, and even if he makes it back, his position has already been dissolved with your arrival. But before you, the person who stood to gain everything was Viktor. Now he's a sitting duck waiting on you."

"You think Viktor poisoned our father?"

"Yes. As such, I don't want him to have what he so desperately desired. Or *anything*. But now you have it."

"Didn't you want the chance to take over the company and be at the Pakhan's right hand?"

"Of course, I did. We would have all wanted that, but I knew it would never be mine. You can't want something that was never yours to begin with. It's fruitless. What you do is secure what is yours, or what should have been. If I'm doing it, I'm sure Viktor and Uther are doing the same thing.

They'll be looking for ways to either supplement their loss or get it back. So, I guess I don't have to tell you to watch your back."

"No, I have eyes on them."

"I have eyes on them, too. I want to find out if Viktor really did poison our father. You do know that if he did, and he's plotting your death, too, it makes him *our* common enemy. It would be one more nail to hammer into his coffin." He intensifies his stare. "But if it's not him, that means it was someone else who might have another agenda which could be the same as Viktor's."

"Yes, it does mean that." And it's something I have to be aware of. The worst thing that could happen is to get blind-sided by someone I never saw coming.

"You have more eyes than me and our father's personal security team at your command, as well as your own. If we were working together, it would be more hands, less work."

He's right. And that's a very clever way of asking for my help. It's just that even if Viktor or whoever hadn't poisoned the old man, I planned to kill him the same way he had my mother killed. Knights' law or not.

Nevertheless, Zakh has raised points I would be foolish to ignore. I don't have to care about our father to work together with him and accomplish a common goal. Zakh has already proven his worth by telling me about the vineyard. I wouldn't have gotten that information on my own.

"I agree."

"Does that mean you'll do it?" He looks hopeful.

"Yes. And I think I just chose the new Obshchak."

He smiles wide and stretches his hand out to shake mine.

"Thank you, brother. Pleasure doing business with you."

"It certainly has been."

Viktor is going to be more enraged with me when he finds out I've chosen Zakh, but that's his problem.

I won't rule him out completely, though.

The best thing to do with an asshole like him is keep him right where I can see him. That way, I'll know if he's planning to kill me or trying to get his woman back.

Good luck on both, Viktor.

You'll need all the luck in the world if you plan to come for me.

CHAPTER TWENTY-ONE

DESMIER

I rest my hands on the windowpane, gazing at the beautiful, platinum-haired Valkyrie sitting by the poolside.

I'm standing by the floor-to-ceiling windows on the second floor, and she's completely unaware of my presence.

I'm home in the breath of a break to see Anastasia for two reasons.

The first is my dick misses her mouth. The second is to give her *my* engagement ring. Jayce is on his way with it now.

I've used the ring as the perfect excuse to come home and kill two birds with one clever idea. As I'm heading out to L.A. within the hour, I needed to get my fill.

Anastasia is reading what looks like a boring-as-fuck textbook. The sight of its thick pages turns my stomach, but the woman holding it makes the whole studious-bookworm look sexy. Especially while wearing those black-rimmed fuck-me-I'm-a-hot-librarian glasses.

A blue skater dress clings to her body, lifting her tits and showing off smooth thighs. The only thing I don't like is that bun on top of her head.

She wears her hair like that a lot. I don't know why when she has the kind of locks a man likes to run his fingers through, or grip when he needs to fuck properly.

Still, I couldn't care less about her hair when her body is made for all sorts of sin.

She's completely engaged in her book, but the waning sunlight highlights the disturbed look on her beautiful, angelic face.

Is that look about the crest? Or *me*?

Or is she thinking about Viktor?

It's understandable if she's thinking about the crest. That's the only thing I'll allow because I haven't stopped thinking about it either.

Gytha is still trying to find a connection between Uther and the Butyrskayas, and Leif said he didn't know of one. Of course, he found the idea of Anastasia recognizing the crest as odd as I did.

It's definitely a worry I'd like to get answers for. Just not enough to distract me right now from wanting Anastasia. Given our last few wild encounters, I'm leaning toward believing she's just as worked up as me. But I can't push aside the fact that I know she's conflicted over Viktor.

I'm supposed to understand because everything is still fresh for her, but like a teenage brat, I don't want to, whether I believe that she loves him or not.

Maybe it's because I'm leaning more towards *not*.

When a woman loves a man, she wouldn't be easily tempted by another. She'd fight tooth and nail for that love, and nothing would be able to sway her.

She wouldn't look at another man the way she looks at me, and there would be no desire.

I'd have to be a sick motherfucker seeking my own pleasure, forcing her into something she doesn't want.

But maybe I am.

I can't be sure of anything, and I'm too fucked up to stop what she started.

My annoyance makes me dig my fingers into the hard wood of the window frame.

"Hey, boss."

I turn at the sound of Jayce's voice. "Hey."

"I got it." He walks up to me, pulls out a blue velvet box from his pocket, and pops it open.

Inside sits a ring with a tiny princess-cut diamond nestled in the center of a platinum band.

I picked it from a brochure the other week and got Jayce to use Viktor's engagement ring as a size guide.

Seeing it in real life hits home that I'm about to give a woman my name and make her my wife.

My wife.

What will being married to my enemy's daughter be like? I can only imagine.

"Is it alright?" Jayce gives me a tentative stare. "The jeweler said you can contact him if something's wrong."

"It's fine." I take the box and close it.

"Getting cold feet?" He smirks, casting a glance through the window at Anastasia. "Or maybe from the look of you, it's something else."

I chuckle, then sigh. "There's no harm in enjoying my work."

His smile widens. "Definitely not. And she's a nice piece."

I slip the ring box in my pocket. "Tell my wife-to-be to meet me in my office."

Thinking of how my little Valkyrie will react when she gets my message makes me grin.

"Sure thing. After that, I'm hitting the streets with the team."

"Okay, report back tomorrow unless anything changes."

He dips his head and leaves.

I make my way to the office down what I call the haunted passage. As far as I know, no one died in this house, but I've always felt that the Butyrskayas' presence remained here because this was a real home to them.

Once I'm inside my office, I sit in my chair and wait.

Anastasia won't be in a hurry to get here, but she also won't want to take too long and suffer my wrath.

Ten minutes pass before her hesitant footsteps echo on the other side of the door. Although I left it ajar, she knocks.

"Come in," I call out, leaning back into the soft leather of the chair.

She walks in, her face a pretty mixture of fear and arousal when she sees me. I smile at that, loving the effect I have on her.

She's taken off her sexy librarian glasses, but there's never been a time since I've met this woman when her look didn't scream *fuck me*.

"Didn't know you wore glasses." I sit forward, resting my elbows on the desk.

A flicker of annoyance flashes in her eyes as she processes that I was watching her. "So, now you're a stalker?"

"I just happened to see you by the pool, reading."

"Of course, I forgot there's no privacy here."

Wow, I like the fire. Although she seems more hot-tempered today than any other.

Have I cracked her?

No, not yet... this woman doesn't fracture easily. If she did, she wouldn't talk to me like that.

It's not that she isn't scared. She's terrified, but she's a fighter. Broken people fight because they've tasted darkness no one else could possibly comprehend.

What's working her up the wrong way is me.

"Need I remind you that everything is mine?"

Her eyes blaze, and I can see she wants to tell me to go fuck myself, but by Odin is she holding back.

"What do you want, Desmier?"

"You know what I want." I give her a shit-eating grin that makes her cheeks flush and her ice-blue eyes darken with desire.

"This is ridiculous."

"Bad girls deserve to be punished, don't you think?"

"You never said how long this stupid punishment would last."

"No. I didn't." I give her a measured stare. "I figured we have so much fun, why stop now?"

"You're such an asshole."

"Yes, I am. Anyway, before we get down to business, we have another matter to tend to."

She swallows hard. "What is it?"

"Come here to me."

She thinks for a moment, then moves, her steps hesitant.

I swivel my chair to face her and retrieve the ring box from my pocket. Her eyes round when she looks at it, then her gaze drifts up to meet mine.

"What is that?"

I flick the box open, revealing the ring inside.

Surprise washes over her face, and I know she's impressed. The ring is beautiful. More importantly, it's better than the one Viktor gave her.

"Give me your hand."

Without arguing, she obeys. I slip the ring on her finger, and she gazes at it.

I look, too, and it feels like a mark of possession, branding her mine.

I don't know if I'm fucked up for being more satisfied about this than everything else I stand to gain from owning her. Like the oil company masquerading as a vineyard she doesn't know about.

Maybe I'm so taken with her because she's different from any other woman I've ever been with.

"I'm amazed that a brute like you has such good taste."

Brute?

I don't know anyone who uses words like that. It's like she's stuck in a classic novel like *Jane Eyre* or *Pride and Prejudice*. I only know about those books because Mom was obsessed.

"Then again,"—she pauses—"it suits you to put something so beautiful on someone you loathe, like a *Sidorov*."

Her words slice into me deeper than they should, flaring my temper.

"At least the ring is yours and not some dead woman's." I know Viktor's ring belonged to his grandmother. "I bought that ring for you with my hard-earned cash."

"Hard-earned cash? You own a multi-billion-dollar business."

"I do now, but every cent in my bank account is money I worked for." On the ships, no one was above the other, so I worked my ass off.

"In any event, it was an honor to wear Viktor's grandmother's ring," she retorts in a matter-of-fact tone that pisses me off.

"I'm sure it was. And I bet he was the perfect gentleman proposing with flowers and music and wine."

"Of course, he was. Not like you." She issues me a cruel smile that shouldn't look as sexy as it does or enrage me as much as her words do.

When I grind my teeth, I know I'm going to make her impression of me even worse. But I don't fucking care. "How about you put that mouth of yours to good use and suck my cock?"

Her mouth drops as if it's the first time she's heard me talk so crassly.

"You're such a dick."

"We've crossed that bridge, baby girl. Now do as I say. And take your clothes off, too."

A flush of crimson steals her color, and her eyes become pools of rage.

She takes off her clothes, and her perfect naked body drives me insane. The scathing fury on her face could incinerate me, but her hard nipples tell another story.

I look her up and down, committing her beauty to

memory. Her shapely breasts, the soft creamy curves of her hips, and her bare clean-shaven pussy.

All mine.

The thought moves me, and I catch her waist, pulling her closer.

"Bend over and show me your pussy first." I can barely speak past the arousal clogging my throat.

"What?" Her face pales.

"Just do it."

She stifles a groan and bends forward, showing me her sweet round ass and the slit of her pussy lips.

I bury my face into her ass cheeks, and she gasps, then grabs the edge of the desk as I lick the line from her pussy to the tight rosette of her ass.

I wonder if she's a virgin there. It would be something left for me to stake my claim to.

Tightening my grip on her waist, I push my tongue deep into her pussy and suck her clit. In response, she clenches her thighs, trying hard not to like what I'm doing to her but failing. *Badly.* Oh so badly.

Her needy moans of pleasure tell me everything I need to know, so I keep feasting and slide my hands up her body to fondle her gorgeous tits.

Moments pass with us like this, then she climaxes with pleasure-filled moans.

I hold her tighter, enjoying the flow of her juices flooding my mouth and the way she writhes against me, rubbing her pussy on my face. She's fucking kidding herself if she thinks this isn't *fun,* because it is.

I squeeze her breasts, massaging her nipples until she

comes down from her high, then turn her to face me so she can drop to her knees.

When she does, I steal a moment to loosen that godforsaken bun so I can grip her hair. As the silky strands float down her elegant shoulders, she stares up at me with hooded eyes, no longer able to maintain the mask of fury.

I undo my belt and take out my cock, fisting my straining length as she watches in fascination. "Suck me, baby girl."

At my command, Anastasia secures one hand around my dick, lowers her head, then takes me into her mouth.

She sucks my length, running her tongue over the head of my dick, and I pump into her hot, wet mouth, owning her face and her emotions.

Fisting her hair, I guide her to take me deeper, then fuck her mouth the way I want to own her cunt.

This game of ours has made lust consume me. Every time we do this, she does something to me I can't shake.

When I eventually blow my load, I truly hate that I'm not inside her, and she almost, almost makes me wish I were the kind of man who could do second best.

I pull my dick out of her mouth and tuck myself back into my pants, watching her swallow my cum and look ashamed.

Seeing her look that way ignites my temper and the jealousy simmering in my veins.

She stands to retrieve her clothes, pulls them on, and turns to flee as if she's disgusted and tormented by what we just did—what *she* just did with *me.*

Fury makes me catch her before she can even take the first step.

She gasps, and I move her into the wall, pinning her there so she can't escape.

"What are you doing now?" Her voice breaks as if she might cry.

"Giving you a rude awakening."

"I've had enough of your wisdom for a lifetime, thank you very much."

I press into her soft, lush body that's still hot with need. It's as infernal as mine. The chemistry between us is off the fucking charts, so I can't let her run off to pine over Viktor.

Smoothing my hand up her neck, I hold her face so she can't look away. "What's harder for you? Hearing the truth? Or resisting me?"

"I don't know what truth you're talking about."

I sneer, trying to tamp down my rage. "Let me remind you. You don't love Viktor."

"How the hell can you say that to me when you barely know me?"

"My eyes never lie." I'm talking as though I'm sure, but I'm not. I'm still being a vindictive dick, trying to get the girl. I'm right about some things, though. "If it's that hard for you to accept what's happening to you, maybe I'm right."

"Nothing is happening to me."

Fuck this. I cover her mouth with mine, stealing away her next breath.

I don't allow her the chance to think before I consume her lips with a cruel kiss. Within seconds, her body softens and she yields, opening her mouth for me.

I kiss her with the same greed and hunger that's driving me fucking insane. And she kisses me back.

This kiss is more potent and brazen than yesterday's,

awakening everything inside me, even the parts I keep locked away where not even I can find them.

I want to consume her as badly as I need air, but she needs another rude awakening.

Pulling away from her lips, I move to her ear. "This is what is happening to you, Anastasia. This. And you need to admit you want me."

"No..." Her voice is but a whisper, tainted with denial.

"Yes, you do. And I still want to fuck you."

"Then do it." She turns her face back to me, brushing her nose over mine. Her ice-blue eyes darken with desperation and a hint of madness that looks like the same thing that's possessed me, too. "Do it and get it out of your system."

I should. I really should. My dick is hard again and ready to go, and everything in my body is singing to me, telling me I should.

I *would*, but it's not going to work. Fucking her right now won't get anything out of my system because we both have another problem.

I run my thumb along the smooth skin of her neck, and she gazes at me with expectancy. "If it were as simple as that, I would have done it already. But we both know that. And we also know once won't be enough. Not for me. And not for you."

Her face turns to stone, and she looks like someone siphoned some of her life away, but she doesn't answer.

I step back, breaking the spell, and I'm glad she's made no attempt to deny what I've said.

"See you when I get back, baby girl."

Blinking rapidly, she stares at me for a few brief

moments as if she has something to say, then she turns and walks out, her back ramrod straight and her legs shaking.

The door swings shut, but her essence still lingers, haunting me once more.

I always knew Viktor and I would never get along because my father chose his life over mine. But my real problems with him were amplified because of Anastasia Sidorov.

Whether she loves him or not, he has a hold on something I can't steal—her heart.

But if I could… I'd steal that, too.

The same way I stole her.

CHAPTER TWENTY-TWO

ANASTASIA

I'm at Raventhorn University, sitting under the oak tree near the quad with Lorelai and our friends Willow and Eilish, whom we met at the start of our freshman year.

We've just finished our classes for the day and are hanging out like we usually do until it's time to leave.

With the radiant afternoon sun beaming down on us, this could be the perfect day.

Three weeks ago, I would have done anything for this oh-so-normal opportunity, with normal conversations like the latest campus gossip Lorelai is filling us in on. But I have so much going on in my life, my head could implode.

Everything has come at me in a vicious circle—Desmier, Dad, the crest, Viktor, and the wedding, which is now eleven days away.

In the sea of so much chaos, I've been thinking about

Desmier more than anything. And I can't get him out of my head.

He's been gone now for twelve days. His trip ran over, and he's expected to return in a few days' time.

Instead of the break I thought I was going to get from him, every time I look at the gorgeous engagement ring on my finger I feel bad for liking, the things he said to me before he left ravage my mind. They replay in my head like a movie stuck on repeat. Scene by scene, line by line.

Whether I like it or not, the rude awakening Desmier hit me with about wanting him and wanting more than just one time with him was the truth.

I couldn't refute it then, and I can't now. And that's the problem.

I thought I was in love with Viktor, but how could I claim to be in love with him if I can admit to wanting another man?

And so quickly?

If I were in love with Viktor, I shouldn't be tempted at all. And I should hate the way I don't despise everything Desmier makes me feel when I'm with him.

When we're together, something ignites in me and there is just me.

Me without the memories of decency and duty.

Me being me, acting on impulse, instinct, and arousal the same way any other unattached woman would.

I never thought I'd end up in this crazy triangle where I'm questioning my love for Viktor and the pirate man who stole me has sown havoc in my heart.

The trouble with that is, things are not simple when it comes to Desmier. Succumbing to anything I feel for him, even a little bit, is dangerous. Nothing has changed when it comes to what brought us together. My father is still my father, there are still important things I don't know, and I'm still a pawn in a game.

"Hey, are you okay?" Lorelai taps my knuckles.

"Yes, I'm fine." I straighten and paste a smile on my face, praying no one can see past the mask. My friends still think I'm crushed about losing Viktor and feel sorry for me. They've gone above and beyond to make me feel better, which I appreciate, but I don't want to always look like the needy one among our group, hogging all the attention. "Sorry, I just lost track."

"I think that's my fault. I was talking about my trip again," Willow says, looking guilty.

It's me who should feel guilty. I didn't even realize when the conversation changed. "No, please don't think that. I'm just a little tired. I love hearing about your trips."

"I'm glad. I don't want to bore you." She giggles.

"Never."

Willow is married to Caspian Ivanov, the Pakhan's son and campus god. No one would ever get tired of hearing about the trips he takes her on. She's also the heir to all things Raventhorn. *Literally.* Her great-great-great-times-a-hundred grandfather was Raventhorn himself. The way people talked about her when we started college was like the excitement in the wizarding world when Harry Potter went to Hogwarts.

"You sure you're okay? I know you must be on edge with Desmier coming back," Eilish states, tilting her head. Her electric-blue bob makes her look like a character from an anime.

"Yes, I definitely am."

"Try not to worry. It's not good for you."

"Sure, I know." I wish I could try, but I think it's impossible with so much going on.

"Do you think you might be able to go out with us tomorrow?" Lorelai cuts in. "They have an open-air cinema in the park."

"I'd like that."

"Yay. It'll be fun, and we can do dinner as well." Willow clasps her hands in glee, and her entire expression brightens.

"That would be amazing." I nod, agreeing

Willow starts listing out our favorite restaurants, which leads us back to her trip with Caspian. As they fall into conversation, I get lost in my thoughts again.

It's not long after that, that Caspian and Lucian, Eilish's fiancé, come to get them, leaving me with Lorelai, who gives me a curious look the moment they're out of earshot.

"Okay, now we can really talk." She shuffles to face me.

"What? What do you mean?"

She sighs in frustration. "We need to talk about that *thing* we haven't spoken about yet."

I know exactly what she means. She's referring to Desmier, although I've only called him an asshole when I'm with her. But since she's my best friend, it would be weird if she hadn't sensed something else was up with me even when I did that.

"Come on, Anastasia." Lorelai pushes her ponytail over her shoulders. "I know you don't entirely despise Desmier. If you can't talk to me, who else are you going to speak to?"

I could ask her the same thing about Zakh, but as her

friend, I'll always be understanding. Especially since her story is a forbidden one that could revive an old family feud.

"I'm in a really messy situation." My voice reflects my trepidation.

"I can see that. Tell me what's going on."

"I don't know where to start, or if I should even start when there are other things to worry about." Like not seeing Dad for close to a month and my nightmares still tearing me apart. I haven't spoken to Lorelai about the crest since she essentially told me to leave it alone, but it's still a big deal to me.

"None of those things are important now. Talk to me about Desmier."

My gaze darts to the water fountain near the science building, and I stare at the stream of water flowing from it while I think of what to say. It's hard to release my thoughts in words. It makes everything real. "I've just never met anyone like him before."

"That's not always a bad thing. It could be why you like him. Aside from the fact that the man is seriously hot."

"Lorelai." I shake my head at her.

"It's true. Come on, you noticed, right?" Her brows rise.

"Yes. I did notice." I don't know who wouldn't. "It's just that I'm supposed to love Viktor."

"Do you?"

"Yes, of course." I stare at her as if she just slapped me. I pray she's not about to echo Desmier's words. It would feel worse if she did.

"Okay."

I search her understanding expression and decide to risk asking her outright. "Don't you think I love him?"

"Yes. Yes, I do believe that."

My shoulders relax, until apprehension fills her eyes.

"But I don't think you were in love with him."

And there it is. The answer that would devastate me, if my soul hadn't already whispered to me and told me to open my eyes if my heart was conflicted.

"You really don't think so?"

"I don't. Please don't hate me for saying that."

"Of course not."

"Good. And disclaimer: I don't think it because Viktor isn't my favorite person. I do believe he loves you and you would have had a nice life. But loving someone and being in love with them are two different things. Because of chemistry. One has it, the other does not."

Once again, I know she's speaking from experience, but her words hit me hard.

"I don't know what to do. Everything is a disastrous mess."

She takes my hand into both of hers and smiles. "Take the mess away. Just pretend it doesn't exist and think of the man. What happens when you do that?"

"If I did that, I think I would lose myself."

Lorelai smiles and brings her hands to her heart. "Oh my God, I've never heard you talk like that before. Something's happened between you two, hasn't it?"

An angry blush crawls over my skin, instantly giving me away. "I shouldn't talk about that."

She sucks in a sharp breath. "So, something *has* happened?"

"Yes. And no."

Her jaw falls open. “Have you slept with him?” Her eyes hold me in place, begging me to elaborate.

“No. We... just did other stuff.” Things that set my body on fire just thinking about. On the nights when I haven’t had nightmares, I dream of him and all the things he’s done to me.

Our conversation is interrupted by the loud roar of a motorcycle engine ripping through the air. The sound commands the attention of everyone around us, and we give it because motorcycles aren’t allowed on this section of the campus.

There’s a massive sign saying so right at the entrance of the driveway.

Despite that, the biker dressed in full black continues up the path, not caring who he’s upsetting or which rule he’s breaking.

Lorelai smirks when he guns the engine louder and tears up the hill like he’s riding out of a *Mission Impossible* film.

“Someone’s asking for trouble.” She laughs.

“I think it’s more the case of begging for it.” There are a ton of badass guys who attend the school, but they know that the kind of trouble they’d get in with the dean or even the Pakhan isn’t worth it.

This guy clearly doesn’t care.

When he gets closer and I take note of his familiar muscular build, my nerves spike.

The bike stops at the edge of the hill, a little over twenty feet away from us.

My poor heart stops when the biker pulls off his helmet and I realize it’s Desmier.

“Oh my God.” Lorelai’s voice pierces through my shock.

But I'm still staring at Desmier, trying to figure out if what I'm seeing is real. Or rather *who.*

Desmier is here.

He's back.

A bubble of excitement rises in me at seeing him, but I push it away as quickly as it forms.

He's back, and he's here to do what?

I feel I should have guessed it was him the moment I heard the bike, but I didn't know he owned one. Even so, only someone who lives by their own rules and completely disregards everything else would ride a motorcycle through the restricted section of Raventhorn University like they own the place.

Since he's never picked me up before and I thought the guards were on their way to get me, I can't imagine he's here looking for me.

Desmier swings one powerful leg over the bike, stands, and gazes at me. With his hair messy, a fuller beard, and all that leather wrapped in his bad attitude, he looks sexier and forbidden.

A twinge of annoyance—and what feels like jealousy—hits me when I realize I'm not the only girl who notices. Every female with eyes in our vicinity has formed the same opinion, and they can see Desmier looks like the seriously hot and dangerous guy most mothers warn their daughters to stay away from. I'm sure mine would have been the first in line to issue the warning if she were still alive today.

"Hey, Valkyrie. Come on, let's go!" he shouts, and something inside me withers away.

He's talking to me. And he said *let's go*? As in home?

On that bike?

"Valkyrie?" Lorelai gives me a salacious smile, and her face becomes as animated as it does when she hears juicy gossip.

I glance at her, but shock is preventing me from speaking. From the alabaster look of my hands, I know the rest of my skin has turned ghostly pale.

"This is not happening," I mumble when I notice people now casting curious glances my way.

"Hey, baby girl, come on!"

I wish I could jump into a black hole and allow it to take me far away into another dimension. What the hell is this asshole playing at?

And how dare he do this?

I'm not riding on that thing with him.

"I think maybe you should go with him." Lorelai giggles, rubbing her hands together.

Go with him?

No, I don't think so. But I will give him a piece of my mind.

I grab my satchel and march down to him with my hands balled into fists.

Stopping a few paces away, I set my hands on my hips and glare at him.

"What the hell is the matter with you? This is a respectable place with important, decent people."

Of course, in true Desmier Volkova style, all he does is give me that mocking smirk which grates on my nerves and fans the flames of my fury.

"Decent?" He raises his thick dark brows. "I'd bet my left nut most of them are thinking of either getting high or fucking."

He might not be wrong, but I don't care. I hate any sort of attention being drawn to me, and I've had no end of it since he stormed into my life.

"Can't you just be normal?"

"Normal is boring as fuck. Now, get on the bike."

"No." I try to sound firm but fail because now I'm terrified. I've never ridden on the back of a motorcycle before, and it was never on my bucket list of things to do before I die. "I'm not going anywhere with you on that monstrous thing, riding around like some hoodlum. Christ knows what will—"

Like the first time we kissed, he steals my words away by sealing his mouth to mine. Just like then, I never saw him coming. He just slipped his arm around me and brought me to his lips in one swoop then kissed me.

Unlike then, we have an audience. One that blends into the ether as

his lips devour mine.

I melt into him, my body awakening. Then it's left feeling cold and lacking when he pulls away and gives me his sexy trademark grin.

"I missed you, too."

My awareness flips back into focus and I look around, my skin flushing as I think of how he just kissed me in front of everyone.

And did he just say he missed me?

The thought makes me lightheaded, but I'm still looking around at the people watching, including Lorelai, who has the biggest smile on her face. And that look that tells me she thinks Desmier and I have chemistry. *Which we do.*

Thank God I came clean moments ago, or she'd find out

tomorrow—or later—like the other girls will when people start talking about how Anastasia Sidorov was kissing the long-lost Volkova son who stole her away from his brother at their wedding.

Knowing these people, though, they'd probably add a lie here and there and say we were having sex on the lawn.

My stomach twists, and I decide I can't care. Not when the pirate man before me is looking at me like he's going to eat me.

"Get on the bike, Anastasia, and hold on to me real tight. You know how." Desmier's smile widens, turning seductive, and I think of those moments when I hold on to him as he eats me out.

"What if we crash?"

"We won't. Just hold on to me and enjoy the thrill."

He hands me his helmet, and I put it on, praying we don't die. Then he helps me get on the bike.

It already feels dangerous, but when he gets on and I wrap my arms around his thick waist, I feel safe against his body.

He puts on a pair of sunglasses, guns the engine, and I shriek when we take off like we're heading to the moon.

That thrill he mentioned is the same that keeps getting me in trouble with him.

It's happening again. This time, I'm taking off on the back of his motorcycle with my ass in the air. Thank God I wore jeans today and carried my satchel.

I screw my eyes shut, unaware of when we leave campus or when we reach the road. All I do is hold on, and I don't know which emotion is worse right now—the terror of this ride or the temptation of being so close to him.

We go faster, at light speed, and my body fills with the sound of the engine and him—his heart beating and the fiery, dangerous essence that makes him the rebel he is.

Soon, it feels like we're flying and the excitement of living on the edge ripples through me.

I chance opening my eyes and see the trees and houses flickering past in a blur.

We ride like that for close to an hour before we start to slow down as we approach the house. In a car, I'd still be traveling and probably stuck in rush hour traffic.

The gates open for us, and a slow ride up the driveway takes us right to the door.

I release Desmier, and he gets off the bike, pulling off his glasses with a grin.

"That wasn't so bad, was it?"

I roll my eyes at him and relax a little because it was fun. "No."

"Perfect. Next time, you'll feel like a pro."

"Next time?" He's picking me up again?

"Yeah, next time."

He lifts me off like I'm weightless, and when my feet touch the ground, I stumble like I just got off a rollercoaster ride. Laughing, he catches me, but then the playfulness in his expression is replaced with the seduction from earlier.

"Come." He takes my hand and leads me up the sweeping stone steps.

"Where are we going?"

"Bed. You and I have unfinished business." His husky voice, filled with molten desire, steals over me, sending thrills up and down my body.

I want to protest and tell him about the paper I have to

write, but my traitorous body wants us to finish business, whatever meaning that holds for today.

My hand in his feels so good, and the rest of my body yearns for his touch.

The guards standing by the doors open them for us, and we walk in.

But we don't make it to the stairs because Viktor walks out of the living room with Gytha next to him.

CHAPTER TWENTY-THREE

ANASTASIA

At the sight of Viktor, my throat goes dry and panic rattles my brain.

Although Gytha is standing next to him, I don't really see her.

All I see is him.

Him dressed in his usual attire which, minus the leather, isn't that different from Desmier's style. Like Desmier, Viktor is wearing dark clothes, but he looks like the same man I was counting down the days to marry.

That familiar air of authority and desire to protect me emanates from his presence, and he still looks at me with the same adoration.

"What the hell are you doing here?" Desmier's angry voice rips into my daze, and I shudder from deep within. The playfulness we shared moments ago is gone and the ruthless devil is back once again.

He drops my hand like a steel weight, and when he marches up to Viktor, I instantly realize this is my fault. My one and only text weeks ago resulted in this visit. This is around about the time Viktor said he would drop by. I just never got a set date or hour, and then I forgot altogether that he was coming.

I can't believe I actually forgot. When I first got here, holding on to the idea of seeing him was all that kept me going.

"I was invited," Viktor replies with a smug grin.

"Fucking invited by whom?"

I rush forward, resting my hand on Desmier's arm. "Me."

His gaze snaps to mine, and rage flares in his eyes like the untamed fires of hell.

"You?"

"You said, remember?"

"When the hell did I say—?"

"When I first got here, that's when. You allowed me one text."

He narrows his eyes, and I feel the hard muscles on his arm flexing beneath my fingers. "You didn't know I'd be back today. I specifically said I needed to be around if he was going to come here."

"That's my fault." Gytha speaks up, standing a little taller, setting her shoulders back like she's posing for the camera. "I informed your brother you'd be back, and I didn't think it would be a problem for him to come today since Anastasia had invited him."

She really is one messy bitch. One look at her tells me

she's loving this. She took what I started and fashioned it into something else that worked for her.

I haven't seen her since that day she was watching me with Desmier. It was clear she hated seeing us together when she's supposed to be the queen.

People like her look for any opening to screw with you. Especially when you allow them to.

Like I have to do now. No matter how conflicted I am about my feelings, I owe it to Viktor to speak with him. Even at the cost of Desmier's wrath.

"I need to see him, Desmier." I tug on Desmier's arm then drop my hands at my sides.

The same fury continues to blaze in his eyes, but if there's one thing I know about him, it's that he's a man of his word.

"We'll just be in the living room." I nod as if he asked me something and I'm giving a response.

All he gives back to me is a stony glare with no words and no other emotion besides rage.

This is the first time I've seen the brothers together since the wedding. I knew they didn't like each other by what Desmier did during that phone call, but I didn't realize how much he hated Viktor until now.

"Come, we have things to talk about, too." Gytha takes Desmier's arm and tugs on it, but he doesn't look away from me.

I already know he's going to be mad at me when Viktor leaves, so I just walk into the living room with Viktor following.

We sit opposite each other, and neither of us speaks

until Desmier walks away, Gytha in tow with her runway strut.

Viktor sighs and relaxes his shoulders as he softens his expression.

I can't believe how long it's been since we last saw each other. Nor all that's happened to me since.

But what's happened to him?

Seeing him has brought everything home and pushed me out of the fantasy I was in with Desmier. Now I'm back in reality, I remember how our dream wedding was ruined, and so was the life we thought we were going to live.

"I'm sorry about that." I speak first because I should. "I should have made sure he knew you didn't know when you'd be able to see me."

"That's not your fault, Anastasia. It's his. He's the psychotic asshole who made me wait this long to see you. I'm sorry I couldn't give you a specific day. Things have changed a lot for me since he took over the company, and the delay in his trip delayed me, too."

As his voice seeps into me, the familiarity of him returns, but I know I've still changed.

"It's fine. I understand."

"Are you okay, Anastasia?"

I feel like there's no right way to answer him, given that last phone conversation where he heard me orgasm and Desmier told him not to call me again.

"I'm fine." I decide on the simple answer as it feels safer, although it sounds wrong. "Are you okay?"

"Don't worry about me. I'm still pissed as fuck that I haven't been able to do anything about this situation."

"I know you would have done what you could."

"I did. Has he told you any of what's going on with the family?" He searches my eyes.

"No."

"What *has* he told you?"

Straightaway, I think about the shit about Dad and know I should hold my tongue. It's strange how I was able to confide in Lorelai, knowing she'd take my secrets to her grave. But these are secrets I don't think Viktor would keep. He's a Knight. A high-ranking one who lives by the oaths they take and would die for them, too. If my father's crimes are as terrible as Desmier says they are, it would be Viktor's duty to report them.

"He hasn't told me anything." I school my expression so he doesn't suspect the lie. "I just know what the marriage contract stipulates. Is there anything else I should know? You mentioned what's happening with the family." I guessed there was so much more outside of what my father did to Desmier but, as always with him, he's kept it from me.

"It's nothing you should worry about." He tries to school his expression, too, but his eyes give him away, and I can see he's keeping things from me. "That guy has issues."

I agree, but I have issues, too. And they didn't just come out of nowhere. Desmier doesn't like Viktor, that much is clear, but that deep-seated fury was there from hello. I saw it at the wedding, and I know it was directed at Viktor, not the others.

That is what he's talking about and won't tell me.

"Have you seen my father?" I decide to change the subject.

"Not so much. I heard he's making preparations to go to Russia."

"Russia? To live?"

"Most likely. He hasn't said much to anyone."

Because he can't. Knowing my father, he'll do his best to cover things so seamlessly no one would question his moves. But him going to Russia means it would be even more difficult to see him than it is now.

Viktor reaches out and takes my hand. "Don't worry about your father, Anastasia. He can take care of himself. His one mission in life was always to take care of you, so please focus on that."

"I will, and I am okay. I'm back at school and just focusing on my course."

As he studies my face, I know he's thinking about me being here with Desmier. I sense if Lorelai picked up on the shift in my emotions, he does, too.

He's the only other person I'm close to who would know me that way.

I feel that I have to say something, if only to apologize.

"I'm sorry about that phone call." My words come out in a stutter.

Now that he's right in front of me, I realize how right I was about him being hurt. He is.

"Has he done anything else to you?" His jaw clenches. "Like force himself on you?"

"No."

"Are you sure?"

"Yes. I didn't mean for what happened to happen. It just did."

"It doesn't matter."

"Doesn't it?"

"No, it doesn't." A shadow of worry washes over his face, and his eyes turn dark. "Listen to me, Anastasia. Desmier is a dangerous man. Try to remember that and don't get fascinated by him."

God. Don't I already know this? But it's too late, and I'm embarrassed that Viktor has to give me this warning, because he already had firsthand evidence that I'm fascinated with Desmier.

"Are you listening to me?" His voice takes on that hard edge of authority he uses with his guards.

"I'm listening."

"I'm telling you this for your own good because I love you."

All the time we've been together, he's never said that to me. Those three words of deep sentiment every girl longs to hear—*I love you.*

And I'm so stunned, I'm speechless. Speechless at hearing him confess his love, and by my reaction.

I've waited all my life to hear those words from him. Now that he's said them, when it should matter most, I don't know what to say. Or feel. My heart should be leaping, but it's still conflicted.

"Nothing has changed the way I feel about you." His gaze intensifies. "I know you feel the same way about me. We had dreams we wanted to fulfill, children we wanted, a life we wanted. Do you remember that?"

My heart squeezes just listening to him talk with such fervency, and I feel so much worse. "Of course, I remember."

"Then they're worth fighting for. So, I won't stop trying to get you back. If there's a way, I promise you I will find it."

"I would just love to see you try," Desmier answers from the door. His voice carries across the room hard and loud.

Neither of us saw him standing at the door, but now that my gaze darts between him and Viktor, I can see Viktor doesn't look fazed, and I feel like he would have said what he did in Desmier's face.

It's the perfect vision of the alpha when standing his ground.

But what happens when you meet your match?

I hope I don't find out. Because Desmier looks like he's ready to kill Viktor.

CHAPTER TWENTY-FOUR

DESMIER

I can't remember the last time someone pushed me to this level of rage.

I'm furious Viktor is here. And I heard what he said to Anastasia.

He told her he loved her and sold her a vision of the future any girl would give her soul for. Dreams, children. A life.

A nomad like me who came from an unstable home, watched his mother die, and prefers the company of the sea couldn't offer a girl like her anything of the sort.

I don't have dreams, and I can't see a future. When I try to, all I see is darkness and doom.

I know, in whatever is left of my heart, that's because his father—*our father*—took my mother away from me. She was my home.

Viktor stands and stares at me head on, squaring his

shoulders like he's ready for the fight I want to give him, but he doesn't know there's no way back when you fight me.

"Like to see me try? Really?" His nostrils flare. "Well, I already am trying."

"She's mine, and you're not getting her back." When I move forward, Anastasia shoots up to step in front of him.

"Who the fuck do you think you are? Do you seriously believe I'm scared of you? I'm Viktor Volkova!" He sounds like a lion staking his claim to the pack.

"I'm Desmier Volkova, and I don't give a fuck who you are. I will fuck you up from here to Valhalla."

"Think I'm actually scared of you? Or that fucking rune makes you a god?"

"How about we test how much of a god my rune makes me." The fucking asshole really doesn't know who he's talking to.

"Desmier, please." Anastasia's eyes plead with me to calm myself, but I'm not backing down. "Please don't make this worse."

"Stay out of this." I look away from her because she still wears that expression that tells me she loves him.

God, would I love to tell her about the vineyard and taint her perfect vision of him. I'm only fucking holding back because I still need to keep that secret, but also because it feels like grabbing for scraps in shit when you have nothing left and know your opponent has one over on you.

Regardless of what I think or what Viktor stood to gain from marrying Anastasia, he was telling the truth—he does love her.

I could tell. She could, too.

Anastasia steps closer. "Desmier—"

"You heard me."

"Why are you stopping her? She deserves to fight for what she wants." Viktor seethes with blazing eyes. "What kind of man steals a woman seconds before she's about to take her wedding vows?"

"This one." I'm not about to sugarcoat who or what I am just because he's trying to make me look bad. I know who I am, and I've never pretended to be anyone else. "This entitled motherfucker who wouldn't hesitate to kill you."

"You're seriously threatening me?" Viktor rushes me and makes the mistake of shoving me in my chest.

I'm like an unmovable wall of steel, so he doesn't even move a hair on my head. But that little mistake fucking does it. I land a fist in his face that would have taken him out if he weren't a Knight.

Anastasia screams when he stumbles back.

"Stop it! You guys are brothers," she wails.

Neither of us wants to hear her or cares for her words because we don't want to be brothers.

When he recoils and comes at me, I'm ready for him and glad no one is around to stop me. Gytha, who helped plan this shit, is on a call that came through when she was trying to speak to me. Ehlga is out, and the staff who can hear the commotion know to stay the fuck away.

I throw myself at him, and we crash into the wall, exchanging blow after blow, pretty much equally matched.

I grab him by the throat when he digs his thumbs into my shoulders, and Anastasia screams again.

"You're just a fucking asshole with mommy and daddy issues," Viktor grates out, and I see red. A wall of red fire covers my eyes, and I'm like a rampant bull in an arena.

"What the fuck did you say to me?" I start, choking him, but he's fucking resilient. He's not backing down either.

"You heard me." He coughs. "It's a pity Father did such a poor job of taking out the trash."

Trash.

In my flash of fury, I see the unforgettable image of my mother's face staring back at me, her dying eyes still pleading with me to run and save myself. She died because my father thought she was trash. A mere loose end he was tying up, together with the bastard child he didn't want.

His beloved son just echoed my thoughts.

I release him, but before he can blink, I grab my gun from my back pocket, hold it to his head, and cock the hammer.

At that moment, Anastasia's shrill scream pierces through me and the same dainty hands that made me bend my will earlier to allow this visit grab my arm.

"Desmier, no, please don't," Anastasia begs, but it's best I don't look at her. Not while I'm like this, in full-on berserker mode, ready to kill.

To my surprise, Viktor laughs. It's a haughty, holier-than-thou laugh that continues to mock me. A stream of blood runs out the corner of his mouth, making his bloody smile look as psychotic as he called me.

I don't look away from him. I'm one breath away from ending him, and nothing short of a miracle will stop me.

"Go on, do it. Show us what a savage piece of shit you are." Viktor raises his voice.

"Viktor, fucking stop it!" Anastasia yells. "Desmier, put the gun away."

"No, go on, kill me." Viktor's voice rises even higher.

"Dig that hole deeper for yourself, motherfucker, because she loved me first. I can see what's happening here, and she doesn't want you. Force her however you want to, but you'll still be trash."

His words fuel my rage, and I want to release my bullet right into his head, but he's clever. He's figured me out and knew exactly what to say to stall me.

He used her against me. If I kill him now, I'll fall into my own trap, and she'll hate me as much as I wanted her to when I first started this game.

Anastasia's grip tightens on my arm. It's the feel of her desperation sinking into me that makes me the loser, and I lower my gun.

Viktor's unwavering smile becomes triumphant, and he straightens, hardening his stare.

"Get the fuck out of my house." I don't know how I can speak. "And don't contact Anastasia ever again. Stay the fuck away from her."

"As you wish, brother." That's the first time he's called me that, and his words were dripping with poison. He looks at Anastasia, and I hate, hate, hate the sparkle that enters his eyes. "Baby, remember what I said. I mean it. I'm still fighting for you."

With that, he walks out, and she lets my arm go.

The sound of the front door closing moments later pierces the tension. I turn to face Anastasia, who looks pale and frail like she might pass out.

The two of us are filled with so much indignation it's hard to believe we're the same guy and girl who walked into this house not even half an hour ago.

Her gaze falls to my gun still hanging limp in my hand,

and her porcelain skin flushes. The freaked-out look on her face and the rapid rise and fall of her chest tell me that despite her anger, she's afraid of me. *Really* afraid of me.

I put the gun away, but I'm still seeing red.

"You would have killed him," she stutters, holding back tears.

"Yes."

She sucks in a sharp, shocked breath. "Are you serious?"

I'll never know. Chances are I might not have, but I can't be sure I would have come to my senses.

"I told you I'd never lie to you. What about you? What would have happened if I'd walked in on your conversation a second later? Would I have heard you confessing your undying love for him? Or maybe you would have been fucking him. Bet he really misses that."

She goes from scared to livid in the blink of an eye, and I can't blame her. Even I know I'm being an asshole.

"I'm not talking to you when you're like this." She whirls around and heads through the door.

I follow on her tail, still seeing red, and at the same time kicking myself because I know I fucked up. Me and my uncontrollable temper lost whatever magic we had before we encountered Viktor. But I still want an answer to my question, and I'll go crazy if I don't get one.

I catch up to her as she's about to take the stairs and grab her arm.

"Let go of me, you asshole."

"No, answer the fucking question." I release her arm when she wrenches free.

"Leave me alone Desmier." She runs to the dining room.

I'm right behind her, and this time, I slam the door shut so she can't double back and escape me.

I grab her again before she can reach the back doors and go out on the terrace.

Her eyes snap wide when I move her into the wall, and her body goes rigid.

"Answer the fucking question, Anastasia. What would you have said to him?" I grab her wrists and pin her against the wall.

"You're hurting me and acting like a fucking child. Stop it."

I get in her face, her beautiful, beautiful face, and hover before her, my teeth bared.

"Give me an answer, and I'll stop."

"Whatever I say will be the wrong thing." Her panicked voice rips into me, and something I never expected hits my heart because the only reason she'd say that is if I'm right—she would have returned his confession of love.

"Why didn't you tell him you love him, then?" I'm a fucking fool for allowing this woman to drive me mad with lust and wanting to make her mine. And I'm a bigger fool for still wanting her.

But I do.

"Because..." Her breath hitches on a shudder.

"What? Because I stopped you? Well, you're mine, not his."

"Yes, I forgot I'm just an asset to you. Part of my father's collection, like a thing." Her eyes turn glassy. She looks so vulnerable I want to hold her and shake her at the same time.

"No. You're my girl." I sound like the child she accused me of being.

When her lips part in shock, I take advantage and claim her mouth.

At first, I don't expect her to kiss me back. I thought she'd be hesitant like she always is. But she kisses me with the same greed and recklessness that I give her, and it feels like I was never alive until just then.

She has my cold, dead heart pumping and color filling my black soul.

Her hands press into my chest and grip my shirt, bringing me closer, as if she wants me just as badly as I want her.

I pull her top over her head and take off her bra, freeing her gorgeous, puckered tits. I suck on them evenly, making her nipples harder. Then I quickly rid her of that stupid bun so I can run my fingers through her platinum locks.

Keeping my lips pressed to hers, I take off my jacket when she pushes it down my shoulders and slip my finger through the belt loop of her jeans. I feel for her zipper, pull it down, and shove her jeans down her legs.

We pause for nanoseconds so she can step out of them and her shoes, then I yank off my shirt and undo my belt and pants. I shove them down and bring her back to me so I can move her panties aside.

I need to be inside her. Touching her wet passage and eating out her pussy aren't going to satisfy me today.

I kiss her harder, devouring her when she tilts her head back and she moans into my mouth.

I can't help it. I rip her panties right off her lush body so

I can have all the access I want to her. Then I take out my cock and lift her leg, hooking it around my waist.

I line my dick up with her slick opening and drive into her, making her gasp.

She's still so fucking tight, I can't get deeper inside her than the entrance.

Anastasia grabs my shoulders and stares at me with a sexy cacophony of pleasure and pain.

I'm watching her face as the muscles of her inner walls squeeze around the head of my dick.

Savage need takes over, and she cries out loudly when I thrust in harder and deeper, impale her on my dick, and tear through something.

I freeze when what I just did hits me like an angry bolt of lightning flashing through a stormy sky.

Her glacier eyes meet mine, weary and drained.

A tear tips over her eyelid and slides down the rosy pillow of her left cheek.

In all the time she's been my captive, I've never seen her cry. Not even when I terrified her with her father's crimes and she begged me to spare his life.

That first time I ventured inside her, I think I knew then why she was so tight and why her body was trying to keep me out. I just didn't want to believe.

She was a virgin.

And I just stole her innocence.

CHAPTER
TWENTY-FIVE

ANASTASIA

I am the broken-winged angel who flew too close to the sun.

I got scorched then fell from the heavens, and now I'm here, staring the devil in the eye, wanting him.

He knows.

Desmier knows the truth now. And that I lied.

He knew it the moment he tore through my maidenhead. And now his face looks like that of a ghost.

In all the time I've known him, I've never seen him look so stunned. Like he truly realizes I just gave him the one piece of me no one else will ever have.

It's gone. My innocence now belongs to him.

My whole life, my parents went above and beyond to preserve my virtue and purity. All those times Dad micromanaged my life with the teeth of a fine-toothed comb, and I just gave myself to his enemy.

Desmier's cruel cock is buried deep inside me, ripping me apart, but desire slides down my body like sweat.

He continues to stare at me, his gaze unwavering, both of us frozen in the moment like we've been preserved in amber.

Something leaks from where we're joined.

That's the only thing that moves him. He pulls out a little, and we both look at the blood lining his cock—the evidence of my virginity lost.

His eyes flick up to meet mine, and he brings his hand to my cheek, a quiver in his fingers, pushing me back into awareness and this new feeling in my body.

He cups my face. "Why did you lie to me?" His voice is husky and saturated with guilt.

Guilt I never thought I'd witness in the pirate man who exudes so much vengeance.

"I don't know." Tears slide down my cheeks. Not from shame, but from the raw impact of him.

Desmier moves closer, the movement making his cock slide back deeper into my passage, and he kisses my tears away. It's tenderness I don't expect from him, especially not after the horrible things Viktor said.

There is much I haven't been told, but I didn't need to be to get the gist of what he was talking about regarding Desmier and his mother. I just don't know how bad things were.

Soft kisses tease the apples of my cheeks, pulling me back to this moment where the wall I put up has crumpled before my feet.

Desmier brushes his lips over mine, and the lighter parts of his eyes open the doors to his soul. "I had you first."

His fingers glide over my neck, awakening every cell in my body.

"I wanted you." The sweet truth on my lips feels as deliciously forbidden as we are. It's like touching fire, knowing you'll get burned but doing it anyway because you need to feel human.

The truth fractures the tenderness in his expression, replacing it with a dark desire which fuels my own. "Then I'm not sorry, my Valkyrie."

"I know." *And neither am I.*

He releases my face and grabs my hips, making me tighten my leg around him. I grab his thick shoulders, running my fingers over his muscles and tattoos, taking the pain as he inches deeper into me.

Then, with one hard thrust, he plunges his cock so deep inside me I see stars. Pain pierces through me as he thrusts harder, faster, rougher, stretching my body to take him.

I moan, tilting my neck back, my emotions confused and as conflicted as I have been since I met this man. Pleasure feels like pain, and pain like pleasure.

Then it's all the same thing and it feels good. God, he feels good.

My pussy spasms around his punishing length, and he increases his pace.

Every thrust of his cock pumps pleasure into me from head to toe, and I'm utterly lost in the sensation. My head is reeling, my skin ablaze, my soul dizzy with a potent cocktail of desire.

My fingers dig into his shoulders, my nails breaking the skin, feeling blood seep through the tautness. But he doesn't notice, and I'm so lost in the mad rhythm of our bodies slapping together, I can't think past the explosions of pleasure detonating through me.

I moan again, louder this time, and that's when he truly starts to fuck me. I come instantly, my orgasm burning through me like fire racing over gasoline.

His hard body hammers into my passage, lifting me higher and higher with each relentless thrust.

I arch my back, pressing my breasts into his chest, and he catches my face again so he can kiss me. This kiss is savage and unlike any other we've shared.

His mouth devours my lips while his cock does the same to my pussy, and time lulls us into thinking it's standing still. Only for us. Only for this moment when we're feasting on each other without restraint.

Lorelai told me to think of the man and take the mess away. I realize now I was always doing that.

Desmier pulls away from my lips but keeps hold of my face, and his expression becomes that of the possessive man who followed me in here.

"Tell me you're mine," he demands, his voice dark and demanding.

"I'm yours."

He leans close to my ear. "Remember that when I make you scream."

His words of warning shift the mood, giving me the only heads-up. When he returns to my lips, kissing me rougher than before, it's like he's the merciless Desmier I've grown to know.

He picks me up, keeping his cock buried inside me as he lifts me off the ground, and I instinctively wrap my legs around his hips. Then it's like we both go crazy and whatever madness that has possessed us takes full control over our bodies.

We crash into a tall vase when he carries me over to the table, and it falls to the marble floor, smashing. The plates that were on the table join it, shattering on impact and joining the sexy sounds of my moans and his deep masculine groans.

He sets me on the table and fucks me into the wood. All I can do to take the impact is rest on my elbows and dig my fingers into the surface.

Desmier fucks me faster, showing no mercy as he drives me to orgasm while exerting his dominance.

He fucks me like he still wants to hate me, and like he wants to break every piece of my body and put it back together again, simply because he can. And I love it.

I love it the way an addict loves their favorite drug, and he's my favorite mistake.

He fucks me like there is only me and only him, and whatever vendetta exists between him and my father is exactly that.

The mad rhythm makes me climax again, and as I throw my head back, crying out from the wicked thrill, I remember that I told him I was his, and I feel like he owns me.

My body is spent and claimed, but he's not finished with me yet.

He pauses his wild thrusts, pulling out of me so he can lift me off the table and bend me over it.

I've orgasmed twice, but his cock is still perfectly erect like he was made for fucking.

. . .

His warm, soft lips meet the shell of my ear and lick over the lobe. "This is how I wanted to take you when you first looked at me at your wedding."

The wedding.

I remember how I felt, too, so I'll stop pretending I didn't feel that invisible thread of attraction drawing me to him.

I gasp when he plunges into me again, grabbing my hip with one hand and a fistful of my hair with the other.

When he starts moving his hips again, tunneling his cock into me, my senses explode, and my soul is ripped apart by the havoc he's wreaking inside my body.

"Oh my God!" My scream does nothing but join the chaos devouring me.

In this position I can feel all of him. The full extent of his cock and his desire.

His relentless pounding pushes me into a state of delirium. My head is spinning, my mind dancing on the edge of insanity, and I'm not even sure if I'm breathing.

A lifetime might have passed with him holding me in this state where all he does is own my body and give me pleasure.

Finally, his cock goes rock-hard inside me and the warmth of his cum floods me, conquering the rest of me as he growls like a beast who's captured his prey.

The force makes me climax once more, but I'm battered beneath him.

My hair is all over the place, and sweat has drenched my body.

With his slick body pressed against mine, we stay silent for several heartbeats.

The room smells like us. Like sex, passion, and uncertainty.

I'm sure he must smell and feel it, too. It hit me as soon as I caught my breath. But he continues to hold me, and I don't want him to stop.

When he does and pulls out of me, I feel like a piece of me is gone. His absence takes the pleasure away, leaving my body sore and sensitive.

Desmier turns me to face him, and his cum runs down my thighs mixed with my virgin blood. We both look at it as if we're analyzing the meaning of our essence combined.

For me, it's hitting home that I just gave myself to him.

I did it despite Viktor telling me he loved me, reminding me of the future we planned, and promising me he wouldn't stop fighting to get me back.

I did it, and it felt right. It felt like my choice. As if it was the first time in my life I'd been given true freedom.

But what happens now?

What is Desmier going to do?

The problem with pushing the mess aside is that it's still there when you turn back to it.

In silence, he grabs a couple of napkins, and I'm surprised when he crouches down to clean me off.

As I scan his perfect body, I can't believe I just had him. While he was inside me, he was mine, too.

A knock on the door ruptures the silence, and I jump.

Desmier's fingers are still on my thigh, pressing into my skin.

"If you're finished, we have things to do," comes Gytha's brazen voice.

Embarrassment rushes over me as I realize she heard us.

She listened to us. The displeasure is in her voice, and I can imagine how much she's seething.

It's one thing to see us fooling around, but knowing we just had sex is another. Now I'm left to wait and see if he's going to leave me to be with her.

He's staring at the door like an internal war is raging in his mind, and all I can think is *please don't leave me.*

Please don't think of me as Uther Sidorov's daughter, but just Anastasia.

I'm just Anastasia.

As if he can hear me, he turns his head to face me and stands, towering me like a colossal giant. I'm already tiny next to him, but now I feel like I'm shrinking away.

Desmier keeps his eyes pinned to mine, his throat working as he swallows.

I continue to stare at him with the same anticipation Gytha must feel waiting for his answer.

"I'm busy," he calls back to her, and my eyes snap wide. "I won't be available until tomorrow."

With that, he reaches for me and scoops me into his arms, lifting me off the ground again.

"What are we doing?" I manage, pressing my nose into his hair when he pulls me closer.

"We're not done yet."

CHAPTER TWENTY-SIX

DESMIER

I'm sitting naked on the balcony outside my room, stargazing while I smoke a Cuban cigar.

The starry sky is perfect for sailing on a long voyage like the sea captains embarked on in the past to unknown lands.

I used to be obsessed with the sea.

Now I'm obsessed with a woman, and I don't want to stop being obsessed, even if I know the crash will be mightier than the burn if I fall.

I take a long drag on my cigar and savor the memory of how Anastasia gave herself to me.

She became mine officially the moment my cock sliced through her maidenhead and her virgin blood coated my length.

The feeling that came with knowing I was the first man to have her was euphoric, but more than anything, knowing she chose me and not Viktor was something else I don't know how to describe.

Anastasia might have loved him first, but she gave her body to me and told me she wanted me.

I had her all night. Over and over again. We went from the bed to the hot tub, to the shower, and back to the bed again, where she practically passed out.

Unable to sleep, I left her there in a deep slumber. That was hours ago. It's nearly four a.m. now.

There was too much on my mind to allow sleep to take me. The number one thing being her.

As fascinated as I am with her, part of me feels as cursed as the ancient mariner did on his haunted ship.

Viktor said enough to pique Anastasia's interest, so I know she'll have more questions than she already asked.

There's too much to talk about that I'm still not ready to discuss. It feels harder now that I've been with her. In ten days' time, she will be my wife, and I'm sure my struggle will feel even worse.

Then there's the matter of the vineyard. It's bad enough to keep my secrets about the past from her, but withholding information that essentially constituted a plot to steal from her makes me no better than Viktor or her father.

Still, it's in my best interest to keep hold of that information a little longer. Just until I think she really needs to know. I don't want to worry about her confronting Viktor or her father about it.

Although I told Viktor to stay away from Anastasia, there are going to be situations I can't control where he could pop up. There will also be events in the upcoming weeks where they'll see each other.

None of what happened last night between Anastasia and me means she hates Viktor. And she's never said she doesn't love him. That's a threat I can't ignore for more reasons than the obvious.

So far, that vineyard is the only heads-up I have regarding Viktor and Uther's plans. All these long weeks of watching and investigating haven't turned up anything else. That doesn't mean they're not planning a vicious backlash to my attack.

I still have to be ready to counter whatever they throw at me and use the resources I have. Even if it's as small and as simple as silence.

It's bad enough I'll see Viktor again in two nights at the leadership meeting.

I'm not looking forward to that in the least. I don't know how he's not dead after saying the things he said to me, and I don't know how I'll be able to restrain my temper when I see him.

My skin is as tough as dragon scales, but that fucker pushed me to a place I didn't even know I could go.

Maybe it's because I've never met a motherfucker who thought it was okay to make fun of the way a guy's mother was killed.

The soft pad of footsteps draws my attention away from the sky, and I look at the platinum-haired beauty walking out onto the balcony as if she just strayed out of one of my dreams.

Anastasia has the cream bedsheet wrapped around her decadent body, and when the silver moon kisses her long, flowing hair—which I fucking love seeing down—she really does look like a Valkyrie. If she is, then I think Odin loaned me his finest.

Like the weary sailor I am, I'm lulled into her ethereal beauty and just like that, my thoughts slip away. It's understandable that her beauty is more than enough to make a man fight for her, and fight even harder to keep her.

Nerves take over when she looks at me, and it's not because I'm naked.

Uncertainty hangs heavily in the air, but so do all seven deadly sins.

Her beauty is her pride, and I'm greedy for her. We're both lusting after each other enough to indulge like mindless, gluttonous fools who would sloth around all day, fucking. But my wrath will keep that line between us. So will my envy, because nothing will change the fact that she loved my brother first.

"Missed me already?" I smirk, looking her up and down.

She presses her hand closer to her chest, where she's gathered the ends of the sheet. "I wasn't sure if you were here. Or if you left."

Left and met up with Gytha, I mentally fill in, reading into what she's not saying. I can see why she'd think that.

I made a big choice earlier when I chose her. I wasn't quite aware of the weight of that choice until I carried her up to bed and buried myself deep inside her again. I still don't think I'm fully aware. All I know is I want her again.

"I'm here." With one last drag on my cigar, I blow out a ring of smoke and put it out, then straighten so she can see my cock is hard for her once more. She swallows hard when she realizes it. "Come here to me."

She glides over, and when she stops before me, I take off that sheet, exposing her naked body.

"What if the guards see us?" she mumbles, looking around.

"I pay them enough not to see anything." I pull her into my lap, slipping my arm around her tiny waist.

"But—"

"Shhh, just kiss me. I need you again." I lean in to gently kiss her lips and suck on her tongue when hers tangles with mine.

It's best if we don't talk. Definitely not now. I don't want to think about anything else besides being inside her.

I cup the heavy weight of one delicious breast then the nipple of the other between my thumb and forefinger. She moans into my mouth, and I grip her wrist, bringing it to my dick.

I've trained her well, and she's a quick study, so she knows to stroke me the moment her fingers touch my straining length.

She rubs my dick up and down until it's unbearable, and I pull her closer so she can straddle me.

I hold her in place, and she gasps as I slide into her already wet pussy.

She's still tight, and I'm sure she's sore, but not once has she stopped me.

It's like she's as desperate as I am to stay in the fantasy.

I plunge deeper into her, buried to the hilt once more. Her walls squeeze me, and I have to fight to control myself.

Her lips part in sweet agony as a soft whimper escapes her, and I caress her smooth thighs, running my hands up to grip her hips.

Her moans become louder when I start to move inside her in a slow grind, working my way deeper. Inch by inch, my balls brushing over her ass.

I catch her face and lick over her cheek and lips, tasting her before I kiss her. Then she trembles, releasing a shaky breath into my mouth that pushes her ripe nipples into my chest.

I grab her breasts and massage them the way I know she likes, tweaking her nipples between my fingers. Instantly, she arches away from my lips, her pussy spasming around my cock as she comes.

Fuck, she must have really needed me to climax so quickly.

"Bad girl," I mutter, kissing the milky hollow of her throat. "If you wanted me so badly, you should have come outside before."

"I..."

"What? Tell me what you need."

"Youuu," she breathes, and I swear to Odin I would give everything to hear her speak that word to me forever.

"What do you want me to do for you, baby?" I nibble on her throat. Then I can't resist tasting her erect nipples as she grinds over my cock.

"Fuck me."

"Oh, I will." I'm going straight to hell for corrupting this good girl; it will be worth it. "I plan to do all sorts of filthy things to your body. How about you do something for me first?"

Her eyes become more rounded. "What?"

"Ride me."

She blinks several times, pressing her hands against my shoulders.

"Ride... you?" Her breathy voice is sexy as hell. So are the intense nerves wrinkling her pretty face as she looks at me like I just asked her to speak a language she's never spoken before.

God, I love this. She's entirely clueless. And mine. Mine to do with as I please and teach whatever the fuck I want. "I want you to fuck me, baby. Ride my cock."

She moves her hips over me, sliding up and down my length. It's fucking magic, but nerves are holding her back.

"I don't know if I'm doing it properly." She bites back a withered smile.

"You're doing it just fine. But how about we practice a little more and this time you ride me like you want me?"

That seems to do the trick. She moves her hips quicker, and when she starts bouncing up and down my length, there's no question about whether she's doing it right.

If anything, she's too good at it.

Her movements send me over the precipice of madness, but I don't want to finish just yet. I have other nasty things in mind to do to her. I wait until she comes before I grab her hips and pound into her even harder, then lift her off me.

"Let's switch up, Valkyrie," I husk.

I take her over to the wall and turn her to face it. She presses her hands flat against the rough, stony surface and glances back at me.

"Stick your ass out for me, baby girl."

She does, submitting to my domination of her will and her body.

I stare at her glistening pussy in the moonlight with her arousal leaking down the inside of one thigh.

Dipping my fingers into her slick, wet slit, I rub her clit, eliciting a needy moan from her. I like her like this, and I like fucking her from behind because I get to see her ass and dominate her body.

I drive my cock back into her, grab her hips, and pound into her sweet pussy, relishing her cries of ecstasy and the way she fits me. It's like she was made for me. Made to be with me. Made to redeem me.

She comes again, her walls pulsing. But I'm not finished with her yet.

I pull out again, and she glances back at me with panic flaring in her eyes when I massage the tight rosette of her asshole.

"This is mine, too, Valkyrie." I rub her juices into her asshole, and her face pales. "Say red if you want me to stop."

I smile because I know she's not saying anything other than yes to me. Her silence is enough.

I push my dick into her tight hole. It's even tighter than her pussy was. My fucking dick feels like I'm going to crush it.

She winces, grabbing at the wall for support.

"It hurts," she moans out louder.

"Say red, and I'll stop, but I promise it will feel good really soon."

The lure of my promise keeps her there, and I keep pushing until my dick is deep inside her ass, claiming another piece of her body.

The same groan of agony rips from her throat when I start pumping, but seconds later, I hear her pleasure. Her passage opens more for me, and I drive into her harder and faster until I lose control. My balls draw up and my release erupts, blowing my seed inside her like a hurricane.

My fucking body feels drained like someone sucked the life out of me, but my skin is buzzing with the experience of finally fucking every hole in her body.

Her knees buckle, and I catch her, pulling out of her at the same time.

When I turn her to face me, she flops against my chest and holds on to me.

She's exhausted, in mind and body, but the look she gives me as she gazes up at me makes me believe we really could have this.

It's a sweet lie I want to believe, if only for this moment.

"Come, you need to go back to bed. You need to sleep."

"You too?"

"Me too."

I pick her up, carry her back to bed, and lie next to her. She falls asleep straightaway, but I don't.

I watch the sun come up, and with it comes a message from Gytha, as if she was waiting for sunrise to send it to me.

I open it, hoping it's not one of her attempts to screw with me.

It's not.

The message says:

"Can't find anything linking Uther to the Butyrskayas.
I've officially looked everywhere. My last lead came up with nothing.
I'll keep looking, but I don't think there's anything to find."

DAMN IT.

Looks like I'll be making that visit to my future father-in-law sooner than later.

I look at his beautiful daughter lying next to me, and the fantasy fades from my eyes the way I knew it would come sunrise.

But my feelings for her don't change.

I'm still obsessed.

CHAPTER
TWENTY-SEVEN

DESMIER

"He's still in bed. Can't you come back later?" Uther's butler argues, trying to block my path.

"It's fucking eight o'clock. He should be up already." And it's Thursday, not even a weekend day. There's no reason for the asshole to be in bed sleeping at this hour.

Since I don't give a fuck, I push past the wiry little man and make my way up the steps to Uther's bedroom. The fool, however, follows, clearly afraid of me but more terrified of what his boss will do to him if he allows me to disturb him.

"Please, just wait," the man continues, but I ignore him.

I'm already cringing at the thought of seeing Uther again before the wedding, but I need to do this. I was really hoping Gytha would find something, but I know she would have exhausted all avenues before sending that message.

When I reach the landing and draw closer to Uther's

bedroom, the distinct sexual sounds of moaning erupt from his room. I realize then why the butler was hellbent on stopping me.

When I glance back at him, he looks ashamed, an obvious suggestion of guilt.

Disgusted, I march up to Uther's door and practically kick it open just in time to see his nasty old ass moving rocket fast as he pounds into a naked girl kneeling on the edge of his bed.

Another naked girl screams when she notices me, and Uther stops, pulling out of the girl he was fucking.

When she scurries away to grab the sheet to cover herself like the other girl has, I realize they can't be any older than Anastasia. If not younger.

At least Uther grabs a sheet and covers his dick, but he looks at me as if he still has some power.

"What the fuck are you doing here?" he roars, nostrils flared.

I look at the girls, and the two of them shudder. "Get the fuck out."

Within seconds, they grab their clothes and scurry out of the room.

"I'm sorry, sir," the butler attempts, but Uther waves him off.

"Just pay them and get the fuck back to work," Uther snaps, and I feel even more disgusted.

When the butler leaves, I close the door. Uther puts on his dressing robe and looks more like someone's dad instead of an old, dirty perv. He's still a disheveled mess, though.

His eyes are bloodshot and his curly hair wilder, grayer, and unruly. The same as his messy beard.

"Fucking around with young girls now, Uther?" I smile at my soon-to-be father-in-law.

"That's none of your business."

"Need I remind you that everything you do is my business?" A quick glance around the room shows me the mess. There are empty cigarette packets, food cartons, cans of beer stashed in the corner, and white powder splashed across the table as if someone was doing lines. The room is a wreck. Just like him. And it smells like animals have been living in here.

One short month has taken a massive toll on him.

"What the hell have you done to the place?"

"Don't worry. It will be cleaned before I leave."

"It better fucking be."

He still has two months before he needs to clear out of here. The look he gives me shows he would answer me with a bullet to my head if he weren't scared of what I could do to him. My visit is unexpected, and I've only been to this house once before. That was the night I stormed into his life and threatened everything he owned. He was in bed then, too. That's how I knew which was his room.

"How is my daughter?" His eyes are glued to mine and hold that same pleading look they did the last time we saw each other.

"She's fine."

"You haven't hurt her, have you? Or done anything else?" His jaw clenches, and I know exactly what he means by *anything else*.

My lip twitches with a malicious smile as I mull over all that I've done with his precious baby girl whom he doesn't realize is a full-grown goddess.

"I haven't hurt her."

When his cruel face tenses, taking note I've only answered part of his question, I give him a shit-eating grin.

"What else have you done to her?"

"Nothing she didn't want."

His flinty gaze hardens even more, and so does his face. "What do you want, Desmier?"

Time to cut to the chase. "I came here to find out if you knew the Butyrskayas."

His eyes narrow to slits. "No. I of course know *of* them, but I've never met them."

I stare back at him, not knowing if he's telling the truth. Men like him are trained to be professional liars, so I'd never know one way or the other. With people like him, you'd never be able to tell from the usual signs that they're screwing with you.

"Are you sure?"

"Of course, I'm sure. Why are you asking me about them?" The wrinkles in his forehead deepen when he frowns, making him look like a bulldog.

This is where I have to play this conversation by ear. I'm going to mention the crest, only because I'm sure Anastasia told me she'd told him about her nightmare about a million times. Of course, I won't give him the meaning behind the crest. But I'll see if he knows.

"The house I live in previously belonged to the Butyrskayas." There's a slight shift in his eyes I'm not sure is something I need to pay attention to. "Anastasia recognized something that belonged to them."

"What did she recognize?"

"A crest. She's told me she saw it in her nightmares. It

made me wonder if you might have known the Butyrskayas before her accident."

At the mention of the accident, his eyes turn glassy and his face a dark mask of grief. "She's had those nightmares for years. Whatever she's seeing must be something imagined because we didn't know the Butyrskayas."

That's exactly what failure to find any connection means, but I remember how Anastasia looked when she spoke about the crest.

She was certain it was what she'd seen in her nightmares.

All I have is her word. And my suspicion. But I'm not even sure I know what that is yet.

"Tell me more about her accident and where you lived before." I have brief details in my reports, but I want to hear him explain. Just in case I can pick anything up.

The press of his lips unveils his discomfort in the topic. "I'm sure you know we lived in Russia. We were only here when we were visiting family and friends during the holidays. However, before Anastasia's accident, we hadn't been back to Boston for close to two years. When I got a permanent role here, we returned. I thought it would be good to take the family camping before Anastasia started school. That's when the accident happened." He pauses, then draws in a slow, shallow breath like a man who's just been given terminal news. "Anastasia was playing hide-and-seek with one of the kids at the campsite. She went off the trail onto a road... and, um, was hit by a car."

I know what happened next, but hearing the story like that makes me think of what Anastasia must have gone through at that age.

"What's this really about, Desmier?" He lifts his chin higher, seeming to regain his composure. "What the hell do the Butyrskayas have to do with me?"

His question is correct. What is this really about?

I am suspicious of him whether I have evidence or not.

I'm standing in front of the shadiest man I've ever met in my life, and his daughter recognizes a crest she shouldn't know about. Of course, something is up. So, he must be lying.

If I didn't think something was up, or trust Anastasia's judgment, I wouldn't have asked Gytha to check it out.

The problem is, if there's any link between Uther and the Butyrskayas at all, I'm not going to find it this way, so there's nothing more I can do here.

"Nothing to worry about now," I decide to say so he knows I haven't dropped the topic. "See you at the wedding. Make sure everything is ready for me."

"It will be ready." His stiff glare tells me he wishes he could try to kill me again.

"Perfect, because every time I see you, I want to kill you and I have to remind myself why I won't give you death just yet."

One last scrutinizing stare, and I leave.

Maybe time will tell his truth.

Or it won't.

Either way, he will meet his end.

CHAPTER TWENTY-EIGHT

ANASTASIA

"Oh my God, wow." Lorelai gasps when she walks into the hall and sees my wedding dress.

She just arrived. As she does work experience at the theater off campus on Thursdays, this is the first chance we've had to see each other. Normally, she's at the theater until much later. But after the way I left campus yesterday with Desmier, I knew she'd find a way to maneuver her schedule and see me.

My head is still spinning from everything that happened and my body buzzing with sexual heat. I don't even know if I can talk the way she wants me to because I haven't been myself since I hopped on Desmier's motorcycle. It's like we rode into an alternate universe and my head is still stuck in the clouds.

Lorelai saunters up to me, gives me a quick hug, then we both stare at my dress.

"That is gorgeous, Anastasia." She brings her hands to her heart and smiles at me.

"Thank you. It really is gorgeous." Now I'm grateful I had Ehlga's help when we went to the bridal store. That day, I wouldn't have cared if I got married in a trash bag.

Wedding dress number two is not designed by Vera Wang, but it's more breathtaking than the previous dress I chose. It's a beautiful, beautiful Lord of the Rings style Elvish gown that looks like it could have been made by the elves themselves in the film. Or like an angel should wear it.

It's hanging on the body of a mannequin in the center of the hall, where it will stay until I'm ready to wear it.

I came home from school about twenty minutes ago and saw it—ready and waiting for me. The seamstress was here, too, and she explained the final plans for next week. Ehlga insisted on keeping the dress on the mannequin in here because it looks so good, and she didn't want the fabric to wrinkle. As this hall is mainly used to display the paintings lining the walls, she thought it would be the perfect place to store it.

"Your dress will be ready in a few days." I glance at Lorelai as she walks around the mannequin, lifting the light chiffon fabric. Hers will be a similar style but in burgundy.

"I can't wait." There's a bounce in her step as she walks back to me, and I swear she looks happier than when I was getting married to Viktor. "Can we please talk now? I swear to God, Anastasia, you could kill a girl with suspense."

My cheeks heat, and I bring my hand to my head, biting back that same smile that kept trying to come out all day whenever I thought of Desmier.

I'm like a silly high school girl with a crush on the most

popular guy. I shouldn't be because I still have to keep my head above water. It's just that last night was unreal.

"Well?" Lorelai prods, yanking my arm. "Tell me what happened. The clock's ticking, and I have even less time than I had one minute ago."

We laugh, but there's a dimness in her eyes. She has an hour with me because she'll be going to a family dinner with the Konstantins. They're at that stage where her family and theirs are trying to get close.

As I haven't been anywhere for a while, I don't know if she's still seeing Zakh, but I assume she is.

"Okay, let's go talk." I nod and she links her arm with mine excitedly.

We go to the terrace and sit on the bench. I'm glad no one is out here and the closest guard is way across the garden, completely out of earshot.

When she looks at me with expectancy, I bite the inside of my lip, and curiosity washes over her face.

"You slept with him, didn't you?" she asks in a quiet but excited whisper-shout.

"Yes." I bring my hands up to my cheeks, and she squeals a little too loudly.

"Lorelai." I don't know why I'm telling her off, but I feel I should.

"What? Leave me to be happy. And ignorant. It really is bliss."

I laugh and shake my head at her. "You are so crazy."

"Sometimes you have to be. It helps." She nods. "How are you feeling?"

"Strange. I know I'm not supposed to read into it, because it is what it is, and everything is still so bizarre, but part of me wants to slip away into ignorant bliss." I borrow her words.

"Why can't you?"

There are so many reasons, but I keep thinking about everything Viktor said. "There were other things that happened yesterday that troubled me."

The hope I witnessed seconds ago slides off her face. "What else happened?"

"Viktor."

"What?" Her eyes bulge.

Quickly, I fill her in on the horrible parts of yesterday and the parts that left me torn.

"My God. I can't believe they were fighting."

"It was awful, Lorelai. I've never seen anything like it." My father kept me away from anywhere and any situation a fight could arise, so that was my first. "Desmier looked like he was going to kill him, and the things Viktor said were just terrible."

"I guess that's to do with the family secrets we aren't privy to." She lifts her shoulders into a listless shrug.

"It must be. And I'm caught in the middle of it."

"What are you going to do?"

I look away from her and gaze at the roses in the garden as if they can help me.

The more appropriate question is, where will my heart lead me? The worrying thing is, I already know the answer. My heart and body led me straight to him yesterday, but I'm scared. And there is too much uncertainty.

"I don't know, Lorelai." My voice comes out in a gentle whisper. "I just don't know."

"Maybe you need to think about it a little more."

I turn back to her and shake my head. "There's nothing to think about. Desmier isn't the kind of man you fall for, or even rely on."

We had fun last night, and I don't regret it. I wanted him and still do, but only a fool would entertain the thought of being with a man who's already told you who he truly is and what he's like.

"What if he could be?"

"No. I don't think he could. Desmier is the rebel who could make you drop your panties with one look. He's darkness and wild adventure. The guy who can make your body experience things you never thought possible." Just talking about him makes my nerves scatter. "But he's the same guy who said he doesn't want kids—absolutely not with a Sidorov—and he's going back to sea the moment he wraps this up. As in me, the wedding, and whatever else he's doing with my father and Volkova Inc."

And worst of all, there's Gytha. She keeps popping up at the worst of times like a bad rash you can't get rid of, and I know they have something going on.

I haven't told Lorelai much about Gytha because I don't like talking about her.

"And Viktor?" She holds my gaze with her pensive stare.

"Viktor is stability guy. He's the cereal box husband. The guy I imagined having the house with the white picket fence and our kids playing in the yard with a big shaggy dog." One guy represents a stable future. The other doesn't. "But it's not like I have a real choice anyway. Next Saturday, I'll be Desmier's wife no matter what I want." It feels like that's when the real battle will begin and I'll be even more torn between the two brothers.

"The wedding doesn't matter. You can choose who you have feelings for." She drags in a measured breath and straightens. "I agree Viktor is stability guy, but how do you feel about him after being with Desmier?"

My shoulders sag like steel weights are attached to them. "Not the same." Yesterday, I made a choice. As I made it, I knew I was pushing aside the part of me who loved Viktor. And it didn't feel wrong. "He said he wouldn't give up on me and that he would fight for me. What kind of person am I if I don't take that into account?"

"The normal, sensible kind." She smirks. "You can't base your decisions on your sense of duty to Viktor."

"But it should mean something to me."

"Not if you don't feel it." Lorelai reaches out and takes my hand. "Remember what I said about one thing at a time."

I nod. "You're going to tell me the same thing again?"

"Kind of. I think it's different when it comes to what your heart wants." Her eyes become open with emotion. "I think you have to look at the things that are important to you and hold on to them. Even if you can't have what you want, or you have to hurt people along the way, you know where your heart lies."

Her words sink into me, opening my heart. But I know a sentiment like that can only come from someone who knows what they're truly talking about and has lived it. I look at her and think of all the times she's been there for me—which is every time I've ever needed her. Literally. Every. Single. Time. And I'm that friend who is always in need. Lorelai is always, always there no matter what time of day or night.

How many people can say that about their friends? I've been lucky to have her, but I don't feel like I've supported her in the same way. It's time to change that.

"Do you know where your heart lies?" My breath stills while I look at her, hoping she won't find some way to change the subject.

"Yes," she answers after a long moment, her expression turning self-conscious and knowing. "But it might be better to be torn between two men who want you than the situation where you know one wants you and the other just sees you as a thing he has no plans to love, or treat like a human being."

Thank God, she's trusting me. A weight lifts from my shoulders, and I step into the shoes of the friend I've always wanted to be to her.

"Is that what it's really like?"

"Yes."

We stare at each other for a few awkward moments of silence while I wait for her to elaborate.

"You know about Zakh and me, don't you?" She speaks finally in a hushed voice. As if she's scared the trees might hear her.

"I do. Why didn't you tell me?"

"I was scared. I'm still scared."

"Don't be."

The vein at her temple pulses. "I love my parents with all my heart, but no one knows what they're really like. They show everyone a different face, but behind closed doors, they're something else. I'm not sure who is worse—my mother or my father. Thank God for my brother, but he has his moments."

I've had my thoughts about her family, but I didn't want to cast judgment since I've had so many things happen in my family that were in the public's eyes. Her family aren't like that; they're more like the ones you know have dark secrets they keep locked away in the same desolate place Pandora hid her box.

My father is overprotective, but hers is strict, strict, strict and treats her like cattle. He loves money and power more than anything in this world. Her mother is the same. Lorelai's brother, Leo, is more like the way a parent should be, but he loves power, too.

Because the Konstantins are filthy rich and are an old Knights family, Lorelai's marriage into their family will benefit everyone. It will carry the same prestige that my family feels for me marrying into the Volkova family.

"Wouldn't your father like the idea of you marrying a Volkova?"

"No, because there's no route for him to progress financially. The Konstantins have everything he's ever wanted. Even if he did, Zakh doesn't want to get married. He knew he wouldn't need to because the spotlight was always on Viktor. Now it's even better for him."

"How long have you been seeing each other?"

She blushes and chews on her bottom lip. "Since I was legal, but we fooled around before."

My brows shoot up. "Oh my God." I can't believe I only knew when I saw them together.

"I know, and I'm sorry. I just thought keeping the secret was better. My family is just starting to really get on with the Konstantins. The wedding is next summer, and they want me to use that time in between to get to know Dmitri. I can't fuck it up."

"I understand. What are you going to do?"

"I'm in the same boat as you with that one, because I don't know. When we first got together, we were just fooling around, but things changed when my father arranged for me to marry someone else."

"What about Zakh? How does he feel?"

She laughs without humor. "That's an even bigger mystery. He's the irrational rebel. You never know what those types of guys are thinking because they don't tell you. I know the day will come when we have to break up, and that's what will break me."

"Oh, Lorelai." I cover her hands with mine.

She blinks back tears then tries to regain her usual easy smile. "It's okay. It is what it is. But enough about me. Let's focus on you. I think the best thing you can do is to try not to worry. You're in a weird situation you have no control over, but there will come a time when you'll have to choose what's right for you. Or you'll go crazy."

I think that's already happened. "I want you to do the same thing."

"I will. I'm glad we spoke about it. I promise not to keep secrets from you again."

I give her a warm smile. "I'll hold you to that."

"I mean it. I promise." She brushes over my shoulder and smiles. "Hey, maybe in sixty years, we'll be two super sassy older ladies, talking about all our adventures. And our men. I'll be receiving my tenth Emmy for best actress, and you can be the celebrity shrink, like Dr. Phil. But you still give me friends and family discount."

In typical Lorelai style, she switches the subject effortlessly and even manages to make me laugh like I don't have a care in the world. I wish that were true.

"You are so crazy."

"It's a nice thought, though, right?" She gives me a one-shouldered sassy shrug.

"Yeah."

"I got half an hour left. Tell me what the final plans are for the wedding. I'm so glad I get to be there and be part of the wedding."

"I really am, too."

My worries about my wedding day are now mostly about Dad. I don't know what to expect when I see him, or how I'll feel. Every day, the secrets between us drive me further away from him.

Lorelai and I talk about the wedding, and she leaves right on the mark.

I head back into the hall to put the protective covering back over my dress, but I find Gytha inside, admiring it.

The sight of her makes my insides quiver, like jagged pieces of glass are slicing into me.

I'm not afraid of her, but I hate contention or any kind of unnecessary confrontation.

Since I've been in this house, she's spoken to me one time only, and it was vile. The other times I've seen her, we haven't spoken. That includes yesterday, which didn't go well for her.

Her presence here in this room, near my wedding dress, can't be good.

"It's very pretty," she states, keeping her eyes on the dress. Instead of acknowledging me, she circles the mannequin, lifting the light fabric of the hem, then allowing it to float back in place.

"Is there something you wanted?" If she were expecting me to say thanks, she's not getting it. She's not here to be nice to me, and I know no matter how much I harden my skin, whatever jab she's conjuring to throw at me is going to hurt.

"I just came to see what all the fuss was about." She stops a few paces away and straightens with the elegance of a swan. "Sounded like you had fun yesterday."

My heart constricts at the same time as my lungs. She's talking about when she heard Desmier and I having sex in the dining room. "That's none of your business."

An arrogant smile spreads over her red lips and her haughty glare pierces into me. "Look at you, all defensive and loved up. Don't fool yourself when it comes to Desmier Volkova. Whatever you think you have with him won't last, so enjoy it while you can. When we go back to sea, he won't even remember you. But I guess that's why he has me."

Just like last time, she walks away leaving me feeling like shit. On this occasion, her bite and sting carry the same vindictive blow.

And the void in my heart grows wider.

CHAPTER TWENTY-NINE

ANASTASIA

The tension drains from my body the moment I pierce through the water.

The neon blue lights at the bottom of the pool come on, and I feel like I'm swimming in the sea. In my angst-filled state, I'd probably feel better in the sea, with the crashing waves rippling over me. But at this hour, I'd probably get myself in trouble.

It's nearly one in the morning.

I was awake yesterday at this time, too, but I was in the hot tub with Desmier, where we seemed to be two different people who'd lost themselves to lust.

Now I'm by myself, faced with the sting of uncertainty. And the sting of Gytha's words, because Desmier didn't come home.

Of course, I assumed he was with her, and I couldn't sleep. Then I made the mistake of going through my emails and found one that was sent yesterday morning from the lawyer in Russia who is dealing with the vineyard I inherited from my grandfather.

I'd forgotten all about it since I had so many other things on my mind, and I'd already started the process of transferring my share of ownership to my father. Seeing the email asking me to get in touch reminded me of the situation.

Everything like that will change because I'm not getting married to Viktor anymore. As my husband, Desmier will be the new co-owner, which feels like one more awkward thing I have to worry about that I don't want to.

The ache in my mind actually made me drift off to sleep, only to be woken by another full-blown nightmare.

That's why I came out here.

It might not be the best idea, but I know what works when I get like this.

Freeing my mind of my worries, like unhooking the links on a chain, I swim underwater and do a few laps up and down the length of the pool.

After my tenth, the shadow of a man on the water's surface looms ahead of me, so I swim up to check who it is.

My heart trips when I find myself staring at Desmier. He's standing by the poolside watching me. All he's wearing are his boxers, which he pulls down his legs, revealing his massive, erect cock.

My gaze lingers on it, and he flashes me a sexy smile.

As if on command, my nipples harden and arousal gathers between my thighs. Like my volatile body was designed to respond to him in every way.

He dives into the pool and swims as if he was born to live in the water. I'm fascinated to see he barely moves his arms. All the work to propel him forward is in his body. He swims the length of the pool underwater then moves toward me on his way back, surfacing like a shark in one of those *Jaws* movies.

My fascination morphs into raw arousal when he reaches me and clutches my waist. He lifts me into the air, and I gasp, but the air completely leaves my lungs when he pulls me to his lips and kisses me.

His kiss leaves me feeling air-light, and I swear I'd float away with the wind rustling through the trees if he weren't holding me.

"Don't tell me you're trying to relive your team-captain days at this hour," he whispers over my lips.

I barely register him talking about me swimming in high school, and I can't help but be impressed.

"You know about that?"

"I made it my duty to know the important things."

Wow. It's hard to remember all the things I'm worried about when he knows all the right things to say to me. I didn't know what we were going to be like when I next saw him. Especially after my run-in with Gytha.

Pushing her out of my mind, I slip my arms around his neck, and he holds me closer, ushering me over to the wall at the shallow end, where he sets me down.

I lean against the wall with most of my body still immersed in the water. But Desmier is so tall the water catches him around his chiseled waistline.

He looks like he stepped out of a Davidoff advert. The X-rated version where he's naked.

"You know you're going to have to tell me why you're

out here at this time, right?" He smirks. "And in this bikini that should be for my eyes only."

I hold back a smile and watch the water dripping off his hard body when he rests his hands on either side of me.

"I don't want to have to kill my guards for looking at my wife."

My wife.

Those words, and in his deep voice, stir my soul and warm the corners of my heart.

I search his eyes, loving how the mingle of moonlight and the poolside lights gives him an otherworldly look.

"I'm not your wife yet, so they can live," I answer as nonchalantly as I can, trying to hide the effect his words have on me.

"From the moment you entered this house, you were my wife, married or not. So, they better not look at what's mine if they want to live." He's smiling as if he's talking about something simple, but I know he's serious.

I chuckle, and he catches my face, looking at me now as if he's inspecting me.

"What? Why are you looking at me like that?"

"That's the first time I've ever heard you laugh."

Really? I would never have noticed if he hadn't pointed it out.

"Maybe it's because you seem less evil. You're also naked. Aren't you worried about the guards seeing you?"

He gives me a wolfish grin. "They know not to look when I'm out here. Now, back to you. What's going on with you, Valkyrie?"

What do I start with?

I'm not going to talk about Gytha and look like I need

Desmier every time I have a run-in with her. I also don't want to think about him being with her—which I hope he wasn't. So, I think of the safe things we can talk about and start with those.

"Where were you?" My voice is meek and mellow. Different from how I thought I'd sound if I ever asked this question.

"Working."

"So late?"

He leans in and kisses my forehead. "Yeah. I have a million and one things to do."

"Why do you have to work so much? And all the time?"

His expression becomes lighter as he looks deeper into my eyes. "Do I sense that you'd like me not to work so much?"

"Well, I thought it's odd if you're going back to sea soon. Aren't you?"

Something dims in his eyes, and he glances down for a second. "Yeah, I guess I am."

"When?" All these long weeks have passed, yet he's never said.

"I'm not sure yet. Things have to be running smoothly here before I leave."

I decide not to ask when he'll be back as I already look a little clingy for bringing up the topic. I definitely won't ask about Gytha going with him.

I guess things will be like when he was gone to L.A. Just longer. And worse. When he was in L.A., we hadn't gotten this close.

I don't even know why I'm worrying over that because I

don't know what this thing is between us. The only thing I know is what I shouldn't want it to be.

"I don't think that's what brought you out here, though, is it? Ehlga said she heard you screaming like you were having a nightmare. Another one."

"I didn't know she was awake." *Or that she could hear me. God, that's so embarrassing.*

"She's up sometimes at this hour, baking."

"Oh."

"You're still having the same nightmares?"

I nod. "They don't stop. I have the same one over and over again."

"With the crest?"

"Yes." I bite the inside of my lip.

His shoulders relax, and he looks like he's considering something, but I don't know what. We haven't spoken about my nightmares or the crest in weeks. I thought he'd brushed it off, even if he believed me.

"I spoke to your father about the crest, and I looked into it."

A rake of shivers climbs up my spine, and my jaw loosens. There's no way he would have spoken to my father or looked into anything if he didn't think it was important. Or suspect something.

"Did you find anything out?"

"No. And your father said he didn't know the Butyrskayas. He thinks you must have seen something similar to the crest here."

When I sigh and look away, he guides my face back to his.

"I still believe you." He nods.

"But it's just my word."

"It's enough."

"Thank you for believing me. What do you think it all means, Desmier? You wouldn't have asked him about the crest if there were no meaning. Please tell me." I can see there's more on his mind, but he's holding back. Like always.

"Maybe we shouldn't talk about this now. You're already distressed."

My nerve endings spike, pushing me to try and get him to tell me what he knows. "If you know something, *please* tell me. I've been like this for nearly ten years. Everyone has told me not to worry about my nightmares because they aren't real, but I know my mind is trying to tell me something. Something that will help me remember things I shouldn't have forgotten. Please."

Although he keeps his gaze on me, I can practically see his mind working.

Working and churning through his thoughts. Everything he's allowed me to know has been carefully thought out and microscopically calculated. Whether it's him or Ehlga telling me. Nothing has been divulged to me simply because it's fair for me to know.

I wouldn't even dare ask him what Viktor meant about his father taking out the trash when he spoke about Desmier's mother. He knew I heard, and he hasn't said anything. Granted, the opportunity hasn't come up, and I don't think it will unless I broach it. This is different because we've already spoken about it. And we're talking about it now.

He presses his lips together and releases a breath. Hope fills me when he looks like he's going to tell me.

"That particular crest is special," he breathes. "But your father doesn't seem to know that. In fact, I'm sure he doesn't. So, you are not to make him any wiser. I mean it. You have to keep that secret, Anastasia."

The lump in my throat grows bigger, and my body feels numb like it does after I've woken up from my nightmares. "I promise I won't say anything. What makes the crest special?"

"You don't have to worry about that part. What's odd is, you shouldn't have been at wherever it was you saw the crest. And not during the time period you're talking about."

"Oh God." I bring my hand up to my head and breathe deeper past my shallow breaths.

"This has to do with your father, and it can't be anything good."

"Do you believe he didn't know the Butyrskayas?"

"No, I don't. Even though I can't find anything that links him to them. Everything he said checks out. But my gut tells me different."

Oh, Dad. What did you do? What more did you do? "I think something really bad happened to me. If so, I don't know why my parents wouldn't tell me. They told me about the car accident, and that was horrific."

"Maybe whatever happened was something worse. Or something else."

Knowing my dad, it's both.

I think of the email from the lawyers about the vineyard, and my stomach knots. I don't know what arrangements are being made now that I'm marrying Desmier, but I don't want my father owning the vineyard anymore. That vineyard is the last untainted thing in our family, and its care lies with me.

"I inherited a vineyard from my grandfather. I was told it was his pride. He owned Sidorov Developments and other businesses, but that vineyard was his everything. I was going to give it to my father and Viktor to take care of because they had plans. I don't want to do that anymore. I'm sure you won't either. I got an email from the lawyers today asking me to get in touch, but I can't deal with it."

He brushes over my cheek with his thumb. "I'll deal with the lawyers. And we'll talk more about things like the vineyard after the wedding. Okay?"

"Okay."

"Good. Now, enough of this business talk." He kisses me, and it feels like he's trying to distract me.

It works, and I kiss him back.

After a few moments, he moves away and smiles, the seduction in his eyes luring me to get lost in him. "It's one a.m. Anastasia. Do you remember what we were doing yesterday at this time?"

I don't know if I'll ever forget. "Yes."

He lowers his face to my neck and places a line of kisses over my skin. At the same time, he undoes the strings holding my bikini top together and takes it off. My bikini bottoms come off next, leaving me as naked as he is.

My bare nipples brush over his chest, hardening on impact when he pulls me closer. Then he grabs my ass, lifting me so I can wrap my legs around him.

My body erupts with pleasure the moment his cock pushes into my passage. He slides against my walls, his cock filling the void that previously left me empty and wanting.

He groans into my ear, muttering words in Russian I can barely make out because he feels so damn good inside me.

Then, slowly, he moves in and out of me, stretching me again and going deeper with every thrust.

"Ah...oh..." I breathe out, holding on to his shoulders when he speeds up. "Desmier."

"That's right, baby girl. It's me. Always me."

Pinning me against the wall, he angles me so he can fuck me harder and faster.

His body pounds into mine, and I savor the sounds of us, our bodies smashing together against the water. Like everything about him, he overwhelms me with consuming fire.

Thrusting harder and rougher until it's painful, he takes me over the edge. My body shudders, unable to stop the ravenous dose of raw pleasure he's giving me.

"Valkyrie," he growls, his voice sexy and strained as he climaxes.

Desmier hammers into me one last time, and twinkling stars erupt before my eyes when I come. My skin sizzles like it might burst into flames and my mind scrambles.

I cling to him, feeling the rapid fiery beat of his heart pounding against mine. Then I find myself choosing again.

This time to be the fool who wants him, instead of the worrier.

It hurts less.

I don't think I can go back to what I was.

Even if this—whatever we are—destroys my heart.

CHAPTER THIRTY

DESMIER

Aleksander Ivanov stands and looks at me.

His dark gaze then wanders to all the men in the room who make up the Bratva leadership.

We're at the headquarters building in the city. There are thirty of us seated around the large rectangular table in the center of the boardroom.

I'm sitting on Aleksander's right with the senior Brigadiers. My brothers are opposite me in order of age with Leif next to them.

This is the leadership meeting everyone has been waiting for, to hear my official decision. Apart from Leif, the only other two people in here who know my choices are Zakh and Aleksander.

Tonight, I also become the official Sovietnik. The tension in the air is the same—if not worse—than when I retook my oath at Raventhorn Hall.

My choices will affect everyone here, and I know they won't be happy when they find out I've demoted Uther.

Aleksander already knows and is fuming, and the others are like sharks trying to catch the scent of blood as they analyze me.

From the moment I walked into the meeting, I knew I couldn't allow my thoughts to slip.

Not even to wander to the beautiful woman in my home who I can't stop thinking about. Or Viktor, who's wearing that smug-as-fuck expression which overshadows the bruises he still sports from our fight.

The taunting expression is supposed to mock me, showing he doesn't accept my power and he really thinks he's going to get my woman.

We'll see about that.

My decision tonight will be one more thing to put his ass in its place. I'll bet this motherfucker thought Leif would have encouraged me to choose him to be Obshchak.

Viktor being the Obshchak is logical if I am the Sovietnik, since roles are normally chosen by age.

I might have at least considered the idea under other circumstances.

Or not. I've never been able to stand him. Not even when Leif tried to paint him in the brightest colors of the rainbow.

Right now, I hope I find something to put his ass in the ground. *Forever.*

"Welcome, everyone, to this month's leadership meeting." The authoritative tenor of Aleksander's voice commands the men's undivided attention. "As we know, tonight is another special meeting for the Brotherhood. So, without further ado, I wish to introduce you to Desmier Volkova, Evgeni Volkova's eldest son."

When he points at me, I dip my head briefly with respect.

"As the leader of the Knights, and the Pakhan of the Komarovski..."—Aleksander keeps his gaze on me—"I hereby declare Desmier Björn Volkova the presiding Sovietnik of our Brotherhood. He will be my second-in-command, so in my absence will take over making the decisions for the organization as a whole. His first act of leadership will be to choose the Obshchak and other subordinates who make up our esteemed elite."

"Thank you, Pakhan," I say and turn to face my brothers. "After much consideration, I have selected my brother Zakh to be the new Obshchak. I have also chosen my brothers Malik and Viktor to jointly hold the position of head of our security."

Of course, Zakh doesn't look surprised, but Malik looks taken aback. Viktor, on the other hand, glares at me as if he wants to rip the skin clean off my body.

Since the head of security role previously belonged to Uther, the men around the table are visibly shocked and disgruntled.

"Very well. We all welcome the new members of the elite. We are now whole as an organization." Aleksander bows his head respectfully, but his face displays the displeasure Leif warned me about when he spoke to him. Leif thought it was respectful to tell him early enough because we knew he would try to fight it. Aleksander would have also needed to call Uther to release him from his duties.

The meeting continues for an hour, during which the new changes and other business matters are discussed, then Aleksander dismisses us.

Before the men start filing out of the room, Aleksander taps my arm.

"You stay," he mutters. "I'd like a word."

"Of course, Pakhan."

I catch Leif, Zakh, and Malik looking at me just before they walk through the door.

Once the room is cleared, Aleksander gives me that sterner look I've grown accustomed to with him.

"What did you want to speak to me about?" I straighten and assume my usual poker face.

"I'm sure you knew I'd have questions even after speaking with Leif."

"I did."

"Why have you removed Uther Sidorov from his position?"

Of course, I knew would get backlash from him, so I came prepared. Everything I tell him needs to sound like the truth so he stops being suspicious of me. At the very least, my explanation needs to be sufficient to hold him off from digging around. Things are set up so no one can find out what I know about Uther's crimes, but nothing is ever certain. I've always been one to keep my mind open to all eventualities.

"I felt the time had come for a change, and I wanted the role to be held by one of my brothers." I felt Malik was perfect for the role, but I only chose Viktor so I can keep an eye on him. Uther will still be working in the same division, so I can watch him, too.

"Be that as it may, I'm sure you're aware of Uther Sidorov's level of skill and years of experience. That makes him trustworthy."

No, Aleksander, those years of experience made him a tool others could use for their benefit. All Uther did was use his position to screw with you.

That's what I want to say, but I don't. Nor do I tell him that it was Uther's fault Aleksander lost twenty of his best men to his enemies when they walked into a trap Uther set in Uzbekistan last year. Uther was playing sides and set them up, using them as a decoy so an international terrorist could flee the country. Aleksander's son and nephew were present at that expedition and barely made it out alive.

I also won't tell him that early last year, Uther leaked information to the Feds and that's why Aleksander was being investigated. Worst of all, I definitely won't tell him that it was Uther who killed one of his personal bodyguards when he found out what he was up to.

That's just a few of the worst things I have on Uther. There's more I collected because I knew I needed to come at him with a weapon solid enough to make him bow to my control.

"I believe you chose my family to take care of the Bratva because you believe we can handle things in the way they should be."

"That's exactly why I chose the Volkovas, but Uther has always been a part of that setup. You must understand my concerns." His voice echoes his displeasure. "To be honest, if things were like they were before I elected your father, I would have overruled this decision in a heartbeat."

"Maybe you just need to trust me."

He laughs without humor. "I'm going to need a hell of a lot more time to get to know you first before I can trust you. Last year, our organization almost fell apart. Over a thousand years of a formidable legacy, and it almost disintegrated on my watch. The Volkovas were my plan to rebuild. The setup your father put together *is* the Komarovski Bratva. That's why there was no question when it came to my decision to choose your family."

"Then rest assured I've done the right thing and I've chosen the right people."

He looks at me for a long moment, then a flicker of that suspicion that irks me enters his eyes. "I hope so, Desmier Volkova. I also hope for your sake there are no other reasons for removing Uther that I don't know about and should. He's certainly being dealt with in a manner that suggests there might be."

"No, Pakhan." I give no emotion away, although there is so much inside me.

"Like I said, I hope so. I'm sure you're aware that if there *were* such matters, I wouldn't hesitate to dole out certain punishments you might want to keep within your hands."

Aleksander is no fool. I knew if anyone were ever to suspect my vendetta against Uther, it would be him—no matter how much I may look like I'm fulfilling a marriage contract. The risk in telling him the truth was this. The chance that he might figure out Uther had something to do with my mother's death.

Aleksander also knows Uther. He knows how much Uther values his position in the Bratva and that he wouldn't have just accepted the loss of such an important role without a fight or some appeal if I didn't have something over him. Aleksander just doesn't know where to start looking for what I have. Even if he knew, he would never find it. It's hidden so deep, I'd need the type of clearance to get into Fort Knox to access it—that's the benefit of having someone like Gytha working for you.

Regardless, I need him to trust me.

"It would be a shame to start off on the wrong foot with me, especially since you'll have a wife to take care of in a matter of days." Cruelty curdles deep in his dark blue gaze.

At the clear threat toward Anastasia, my blood spikes and my nerves twist. The crimson haze of rage is a breath away, but I quell it only because I need to.

I have my rune, and I could challenge him, but there is always strength in numbers. Especially when you have a solid following and the devil's laws are on your side.

Now that his eyes are on me, if he managed to find out what I have on his own, he could kill Anastasia for any of the crimes Uther has committed. And what I suspect him of —as in the mystery surrounding the Butyrskayas. Guilt for that would be worse than what I already carry because of who the Butyrskayas were. When Anastasia marries me, she'll no longer be anything to do with Uther, but there are exceptions. Exceptions the Pakhan can make if he wishes to.

"I assure you, there is nothing to worry about." I sound like things really are what they seem. But I'm already planning his death if he thinks he can use Anastasia against me.

She's mine.

Mine to protect. Even if I have to come up against all the Knights in the world and beyond, I'm not going to allow anything to happen to her.

"That's good to hear. See you in a few weeks. I hope you enjoy your wedding."

"Thank you, Pakhan." I bow curtly and leave.

His eyes bore into me right until I walk through the door. It's only once I turn into the corridor that the intensity subsides.

When I walk into the passage, I'm surprised to see Leif standing with Zakh and Malik. They look like they were waiting for me.

"There he is," Leif announces, looking like a proud father.

"The man of the hour." Zakh smiles.

"I wasn't expecting anything," Malik says, extending his hand to shake mine.

I shake his hand, feeling more assured in my decision. "Are you okay with the role?"

"I most certainly am. It's more along the lines of what I'm trained to do."

"I thought so. I felt it would be more useful to put those skills to use."

His smile widens. "Thank you."

I glance at Leif, who nods his approval, then I look around for Viktor, who I'm sure has already left.

"Viktor's gone," Zakh fills in.

"That's okay."

"We thought maybe we could talk for a while," Leif suggests. "Maybe you boys could get to know each other a little better before things become more hectic."

"I'd like that."

I know what he's trying to do. Leif wants us to bond. As

much as I just want to get back to Anastasia, I have to do this for him. And maybe for me, too.

Strength in numbers is probably what I need, especially with the Pakhan clearly suspicious of me and having Viktor as my enemy.

CHAPTER THIRTY-ONE

DESMIER

Today is my wedding day.

The day is finally here, and I feel different to how I thought I would.

Leif and I are in the dressing room at Hammond Castle, the wedding venue. This place is more suited to me.

Anastasia and I will be getting married in the ocean view private gardens.

The wedding will take place in half an hour, and everyone, including her, is here and ready.

Leif adjusts the purple sash on my shoulder, making sure it sits perfectly against my Knights tunic. The bearer of the Odin rune wears this sash when he's getting married.

Leif was entrusted with mine after the Reaping. He's giving me that proud father smile again, and I slip into one of my moments where I appreciate all he's done for me.

He's dressed in his tunic, too, but as he's officiating the

wedding, he's wearing a white cape with a metal laurel leaf securing it around his neck.

"Your mother would have certainly loved to be here today to see you get married." Leif's voice carries that sentiment again.

The same sentiment he uses when he speaks about my mother in times when he knows she would have been proud of me.

There's more affection in his tone today, for her and for me. It takes me back to when I used to wish he were my father.

"She definitely would. She loved weddings and talked about what she would do at mine."

"That sounds exactly like her." He laughs, and there's an unmistakable sparkle in his eyes. "She'd be so cross, though, that we chose a garden. Fryeda liked churches. She wanted to get married in church with lots of guests and her wearing an extravagant gown people would be talking about for years to come."

That makes me smile.

He always talks about my mom as if she's still alive, or like she's gone somewhere and will be back any minute.

I'm compelled again to ask him about his feelings for her, but just like always, I feel like I'm overstepping boundaries. Maybe this is one time, or one moment, where I feel like I should and it might be okay.

"I... used to think you were my father," I begin, and his gaze shifts to mine.

He finishes adjusting the sash and stares at me.

"In fact, if you are, that would be fine." I know he's not. The paternity test gave me all my answers, but deep down, the boy in me hoped that Leif could have forged the test to make it look however he wanted. Just because he could. "It would be more than fine, actually. Of course, it would mean we just pulled off one hell of a stunt on everyone. But I wouldn't care."

He pulls in a deep breath, keeping his gaze on me. His eyes look glassy with emotion, which deepens when he rests his hand on my shoulder.

"You are my son," he says in that pride-filled tone again, and my heart jumps with hope that my make-believe could be true. "I might not be your biological father, but the same blood runs through our veins. I couldn't ask for more, and I feel selfish even saying so."

"Why? It means a lot to me to hear you say that."

"I know, but I feel selfish because I've always thought you should have been my son."

I think he's just given me an opening, and I'm going to take it. "You had feelings for my mother, didn't you?" Finally being able to ask that question feels like weights being lifted from my soul.

"Yes. I did. I do."

"What happened, Leif? She must have known. Why would she have chosen my father or anyone else over you?"

"It's just how it happened. I was the best friend. The friend who never told his best friend how he felt about her. Your mother always loved your father, and for a time, I thought he loved her, too." Regret fills his eyes, and he leans against the cobbled walls. "Your parents first broke up when our parents arranged for your father to marry Mira. They didn't even know he was seeing your mother. It wasn't allowed because she was a servant's daughter. Had it been me, I wouldn't have cared who she was. I would have fought to be with her. But she didn't love me like that."

"Are you sure?"

"I am. Trust me, she didn't, and I thought it was better to be the best friend who was always there for her than not have her at all." A moment of sadness passes between us, then his face brightens. "Maybe she will love me like that in another lifetime. One where you are my son and we have a nice life together. Today, we'd be here together watching our son get married and starting his future with his wife."

I nod. It sounds like a dream.

"She did love you, Leif. I know she did. It was how she looked at you."

"Thank you for saying that." He blinks and takes a quick breath. "I think it's time now. Are you ready?"

"Yeah, I'm ready."

He rests his hand on my shoulder again and gives me a stern look. "Don't be afraid to love your wife, Desmier."

Love...

A dark soul like me wouldn't know what to do with such a hallowed thing.

I didn't come here looking for love, but I think it found me just after obsession did.

"You hear me, son?" Leif hardens his gaze.

"I hear you, *Father*."

At my words, he touches his forehead to mine and smiles. "Good. Let us go."

We make our way out to the courtyard and then the garden, where we find Ehlga and the harpist. Jayce and Zane are with Anastasia. Gytha is not here. I didn't think it was appropriate for her to be.

Ehlga gives me a hug when I approach her, then we take our places beneath the gazebo covered in white roses.

Minutes later, Anastasia and Uther appear under the archway with Lorelai, who holds our rings.

The harpist starts playing an old Nordic wedding song, and Anastasia and Uther begin their march.

I don't even want Uther to touch her, but I wanted him to give his daughter away to me today because he doesn't deserve her. This march is symbolic of his defeat. And he knows it.

I was supposed to relish this, but when I look at my beautiful bride, all I see is her. All I want is her.

She looks every bit the angel in that dress, with her hair down and flowing in the wind, just for me.

She's mine.

Not Uther Sidorov's daughter.

Not the woman I stole from my brother, but the woman I made mine.

She left a mark on my cold heart, and I don't feel so dead anymore.

I'm not sure if that's a good or bad thing.

Death might be a friend I shouldn't be eager to part ways with, but when they reach me and Uther hands Anastasia to me, I see life.

Me alive in her and with her.

And a future she makes me want to try for.

Because I'm in love with her.

CHAPTER
THIRTY-TWO

ANASTASIA

"I now pronounce you man and wife," Leif announces with a proud smile. And just like that, I become Anastasia Volkova. "You may now kiss the bride."

Desmier leans in and kisses me.

The kiss, as soon as it touches my lips, feels different in all the right ways. It holds the passion we've shared mixed with lust and a promise for later.

It's a real kiss. Something I know my father wasn't expecting.

Can he tell it's real?

I know Lorelai can.

I'm all sorts of nervous, but this kiss takes me out of reality.

I wondered how I would feel today getting married to Desmier. Not Viktor.

What I feel is that thrill. Like I'm flying close to the sun again, but I don't want to turn back. I haven't even thought about being bound to the Knights. Even though Desmier is in his tunic, I feel like I'm truly married to him, and this is the first time my heart hasn't been conflicted.

We pull apart, and our few guests clap. Dad doesn't. He keeps his hands at his sides and his face stern.

Ehlga is the first to hug me. Lorelai next.

"There are refreshments in the dining room," Leif announces, pointing to the reception room with the stone arched doorway. "Please help yourselves."

Desmier glances at my father when he approaches and leans down to my ear. "I will allow you some time with your father, then we're leaving."

"Thank you."

Lorelai gives me a quick glance before Desmier ushers her and Ehlga away. Zane follows them, but I notice that Jayce stays behind.

I expected Gytha to be here with them, and I'm glad she's not. With the wedding being so small, I'm sure I would have gone up in flames from her infernal stare.

I look back at my father, noting how haggard he seems. Although he's scrubbed up well, his bloodshot eyes and obvious weight loss give him away. His suit looks almost too big for him, and I felt smaller arms when we hugged as we met under the arch before the wedding march.

"Should we go and sit?" Dad motions to the stone garden bench next to the water fountain.

"Yes."

When he slips an arm around me, that feeling of safety he always provided covers me like an old familiar blanket you reach for when you need comfort. I curse myself for the feeling and becoming the daddy's little girl Desmier accused me of being weeks ago.

Although things are so different now, and we're different, it's a relief to see Dad and know he's okay. But all my angst and questions are still with me. I don't know how I'm going to speak to him knowing that if he gives me answers, the truth will hurt me more than the ignorant bliss of not knowing.

We sit facing each other, and he reaches out to touch my face as if he's memorizing me.

"Just making sure you're real."

"I'm real." I can't help but smile.

"You look so much like your mother."

My heart knots. He never talks about Mom. Never. Even when people said how much I looked like my mother, he never commented. Not even before she died.

"Thank you."

Tension slides into his expression and he straightens. "You looked taken with him. Desmier."

He noticed the kiss was real, and from the tone of his voice, everything else.

"Yes." I won't deny it. There's no reason when it's true, and no point.

He leans forward, cutting a glance in Jayce's direction. "What has he told you?"

"Just enough to scare the shit out of me when it comes to you. Crimes against the Knights, Dad? Crimes that could kill us both?" I keep my voice firm so he knows he can't just brush me off like he usually does.

"Anastasia, I have done terrible things. All of them unforgivable."

The knife already plunged deep in my heart twists. "And you did something to Desmier, too, didn't you?" I'm surprised when hope sparks in his eyes. My question shouldn't have given him anything of the sort.

"Hasn't he told you?"

"No."

"Then that is either a kindness I don't deserve or the same type of punishment as giving you, my daughter, away to him."

"What do you mean?"

"I didn't want him to tell you."

I understand the hope now, but that sickening feeling churns again, telling me what I don't know is so much worse than what I do. I'm sick of being kept in the dark.

"Tell me what it is. Tell me something *true,* Papa." That's what I used to call him when I was younger. I stopped when kids made fun of me at school.

I'm hoping the endearment will reach the father I thought I knew.

"I love you. That is true." He pulls in a deep breath.

"I love you, too. But I know you've lied to me many times before. Let it stop today."

"Everything I told you was because I love you."

"Lies destroy people."

"Sometimes, the truth does worse."

I stare at him for a long moment, realizing he's stalling. I know what that means. I'm used to it. "You're not going to tell me anything, are you?"

"Anastasia, some things are better off unknown."

I bite down hard on my back teeth to keep my rage in.

"Like my nightmares? I know Desmier went to see you about the crest."

"Your nightmares are just nightmares. It has nothing to do with anything."

"I don't believe you."

"I'm sorry you don't. But this isn't the time to be arguing when we haven't seen each other in so long." He swallows hard. "I'm going back to Russia in a few months. I have business I'm planning to set up there, and I'll be closer to the vineyard."

I haven't thought about the vineyard since Desmier and I spoke about the email last week. I'm sure my father isn't going to like that I've changed my mind about giving it to him.

"I'm keeping the vineyard as it was intended, between me and my husband."

His face pales, then the blood rushes back to his cheeks and his nostrils flare. "Why?"

"Dad, if we can't be honest with each other, then you don't deserve anything from me."

"This is him, isn't it? He's poisoned your mind against me."

"No, you did that. He just opened my eyes."

He grabs both my hands and brings them to his heart. "Do not put all your trust in him, Anastasia. Please don't do it."

"Who am I to trust? You?"

"My love for you is real. You and Desmier began in hatred and revenge. It won't end any other way. Let's talk about the vineyard properly another time, when we're allowed to see each other again and things are less heated between us. You might not think I deserve it, but that's all I have left. I don't even have you anymore."

My heart aches at his accusation, and I wish I could deny it. But this isn't on me. I'm merely caught in a game of thrones.

"We'll talk about it again, then."

Out of the corner of my eye, I spot Desmier walking out of the reception hall. He's changed into his normal clothes. The black biker jacket and black clothing. Dad notices him as well and goes rigid.

"Remember what I said. Don't trust him. To him, you are my daughter. That will never change, and he will always hate you for that."

I ignore the pang in my heart and stand.

When Desmier approaches and takes my hand, I give it. He doesn't say anything to Dad. They both just look at each other like mortal enemies.

We walk away, and I glance over my shoulder back at Dad, who's still looking at me with that warning in his eyes.

As soon as we turn the corner and I can't see Dad anymore, that vulnerability I first felt when all of this started hits me again. It's the opposite of how I hoped to feel today of all the days.

Then again, what did I expect?

And Dad is right. I'm his daughter, and it's enough to condemn me.

I suppose this beautiful venue is as special as today will get.

We reach the parking lot, walking in silence until we reach Desmier's Ferrari. It's the car he drives least. He has so many I can't keep up and is mainly on his motorcycle.

He opens the door for me, and I get in.

When he slides into the driver's seat, I expect him to gun the engine and drive away. Instead, he looks at me.

"What did he say to you? You look upset." He searches my eyes.

I shake my head and blink back tears. "He didn't tell me anything, and that's the problem." Telling me not to trust my husband didn't help either, when I feel like Desmier and I are just fooling around. "You don't tell me anything either, so I don't know why I bother. Let's just go home. I have a paper to write."

"No."

When he chuckles, I glare at him. "Why?"

He cups my face, and I try my best to remember the warning I was issued not two minutes ago, but it's so hard.

The corners of his lips curl into a sexy smile and he kisses my nose. "Because we'll be late for our flight if we don't leave now."

My pulse jumps. "Flight? What are you talking about?" I actually thought he'd drop me off home with Ehlga and go to work.

"We're flying to Miami, where we'll link up with my ship. Then I will sail you around the Caribbean."

My mouth drops, and all I can do is stare at him. Did I seriously hear him right?

"The Caribbean?" Like the cruise I was supposed to go on with Viktor. Except... "You're sailing?"

"*We're* sailing, and believe me, it's better than any cruise." He laughs, giving me a real laugh, and I see what he's like when he's not evil. When his laughter fades, he brushes my cheek and looks at the ring on my finger—the wedding band. "We just got married, Valkyrie. Forget what your father said, and what he didn't say. Let's forget all of this for two weeks."

"Two weeks? Desmier, I don't have any clothes."

"We won't need clothes."

He guns the engine, and we drive away.

But once again, I catch sight of my father, and he looks as broken as he did the last time I was taken away.

CHAPTER THIRTY-THREE

ANASTASIA

I feel like a new woman as I walk through the revolving glass doors of Mira's private practice. There's a lightness about me I'm sure people can see, and I feel more confident.

Desmier and I returned from our honeymoon last night. We had the most amazing time. He sailed me around the Caribbean, stopping at every island, where we frolicked in the sea and sun by day, then made love under the stars at night.

I didn't want to leave and return to the real world.

When we did, it was nice to get a message from Mira letting me know she was back from Russia.

Since I'm not back on campus until next week, I thought it would be great to catch up with her today.

As I walk into the elevator, I catch sight of my very tanned skin. A dead giveaway of the fun I had in the Caribbean with Desmier.

I hope I don't look like I had too much fun.

The last time I saw Mira, I was left worrying about what she thought of me. Now that Desmier and I are married, I'm still worried. Mira is someone I want to keep in my life, so I hope what's happened hasn't placed a wedge between us.

Once the elevator car comes to a stop, I walk up to her door and knock.

"Come in," she calls out, and it's good to hear her voice.

I push the door open, and when she smiles, I feel like we'll be okay and nothing has changed between us.

It's even more confirmed when she gets up from her chair and rushes around to hug me.

"Oh, my dear, look at you." She holds my shoulders and takes me in with a brighter smile than the one she wore when we last saw each other. "You're absolutely glowing."

"Thank you."

"Come, let's sit. I got those pastries you like." She points to the little table by the sofas with a white pastry box sitting in the center.

"Oh my God, thanks so much. I love those." They're the same type Ehlga makes.

We sit, and Mira opens the box, waving her hand over it as if she's displaying a case of jewels. We used to do this after every session I had with her, whether that was mentoring or talking. To me, it was therapy even though she couldn't be my official therapist.

I take a strawberry donut, and she does the same.

"How have you been?" I ask before we can get into any discussion about me. Mira is selfless that way. Things couldn't have been easy on her over the last couple of weeks, but she'll be more concerned about me.

"I'm better now. Going to Russia was reinvigorating. I saw my sisters and their kids and grandkids." She laughs heartily. "It was nice being away. And I'm stronger for it. Being away from Evgeni was hard, though."

It always feels weird when I ask her about him because I know his health is bad. Now Desmier is another reason to feel awkward, but I'm going to ask her anyway.

"What's happening with him?"

"He's still hanging on, and I still have faith. As long as his brain is active, I'm praying and hoping." She blows out a ragged breath. "And I will continue to stand by his side in sickness and in health."

"I'm sure he will appreciate you for that." I nod with respect. Although I still don't know the full story, I'm now sure Evgeni must have cheated on her. I've had to go by people's actions—particularly hers—and what Viktor said to Desmier.

"I hope so."

"He will." Everything I know might be tainted, but I feel I'm right about that.

"How have *you* been?" She holds my gaze with interest.

"I'm okay. I'm..." What do I tell her that won't sound awkward?

"Glowing," she fills in.

"Yeah, glowing. I had to try to do what I had to." Saying *move on* doesn't sound quite right, but I suppose that's what happened.

"And that's okay. I'm sad you're not my daughter-in-law, but that changes nothing between us. I just want you to be happy."

"I'm trying."

"That's the best thing you can do for yourself."

"I guess." I know no matter what she says, she would have wanted me to be happy with Viktor. There's a fundraiser tomorrow night at Volkova Inc. that I'm not looking forward to because he'll be there. God knows what will happen between him and Desmier. "Are you going to be at the fundraiser?"

"No." Her shoulders droop. "I'm still trying to lie low. I won't attend any of those events for a long time to come."

"I understand."

"Viktor will be there, though."

"How is he?" I'm wondering if she knows about the fight. It wouldn't be like Viktor to tell her, but these are different times.

"He's, um...well, he's still taking things hard. You know how much he adored you."

"I know." Maybe I shouldn't have asked the question.

"You can't think about him now. Viktor will be fine, Anastasia. It will take time, but there's nothing anyone can do now but move on."

"I know. I just worry about him."

"Don't. Promise me you won't."

I give her a little smile and nod. "I promise."

"Good. Now, tell me more about what's been going on with you. Did the nightmares stop? We never got a chance to talk about that."

I go with the subject change because it feels appropriate. In any event, this discussion is better for me because Mira helped me get rid of the nightmares the first time around.

"I still have them maybe four to five times a week, and sometimes several times during the night."

Her brows furrow. "Oh, Anastasia, why didn't you contact me?"

"I didn't want to disturb you."

"Don't be silly. Are you still getting the same dream sequence?"

"The same."

Worry fills her eyes. She knows about the crest because she knows the dream. But I will be keeping my promise to Desmier about the deeper meaning of the crest.

"Mira, did you ever, at any point, think something else besides the accident must have happened to me?"

She dips her head slightly, and the solemn look on her face is my answer. "I did. I just never knew what it could be. Recurring dreams are the mind's way of trying to reconnect and clarify an event. There's a block somewhere, and sometimes people have triggers that can help. You said you saw monsters, and if we were watching anything with monsters in it, you'd start crying. I often wondered if that was your childhood mind's way of creating something to cover something else."

"Like people?"

"Yes. Like people. You never dreamt about the car hitting you. Not once." She presses her lips together. "Of course, these are all just assumptions. *My* assumptions. Your father is a very secretive man, but your mother was secretive, too. When you first started having nightmares, I asked your father if something traumatic had happened to you apart from getting hit by the car. He told me no. But your mother always had that look about her, like she was covering something up. I'm sorry. I hate to say it like that."

"It's okay. I know what you mean. She was like that all the time."

Mira reaches for my hand and gives it a squeeze. "This thing has been bothering you for years. If we can't figure it out and no one will tell us, maybe it's best to let it go."

That's the hard truth I don't want to face but something I might have to do. "What if it's important, Mira? I don't know if I can just let it go."

"How about we set something up for next week?" she suggests, noticing my hesitation. "You could come to my house next Sunday, and we can spend the day together. Then we can start the process of doing what we did last time. It would be good if I can rid you of these nightmares forever and maybe dig a little deeper to see why you have them in the first place."

"I'd truly love that." But who knows what I might dig up?

It's even worse now that I know Dad lied to me.

SOFT JAZZ MUSIC envelopes me as Desmier and I walk into the foyer at Volkova Inc.

The fundraiser is being held in the grand hall, but quite a few people have spilled out here, drinking from elegant long-stemmed glasses and talking in groups.

Everyone is dressed in their finest, as usual for this year's event. Last year was the first time Dad allowed me to attend. This year, I'm here with my husband, who owns the company.

It's interesting how times change, but some things

remain the same. Last year, when I walked in with Viktor, there were women casting glances at him.

Women are looking at Desmier, too, and because he has that obvious dangerous sexy edge, they look like they can't help themselves.

He's dressed like he's going to the Emmys in his Boss suit and cropped cut hair. I'm in a strapless fitted gown, but I'm tired from the migraine that kept me up all night.

It's still bothering me now, but I'm putting my best face forward. This is our first event as husband and wife, and I know people are talking.

"We'll stay for an hour, then we're leaving," Desmier whispers in my ear.

"You? Stay at work for *only* an hour? I don't believe you."

He smirks, dipping his hand lower down my back so he can squeeze my ass. "You in this fuck-me dress had better believe me."

Despite people watching, he kisses my neck as if we're alone. Then I remember he's the rebel. The pirate man who doesn't care what people think.

He pulls me closer, and I'm about to say something when Zakh approaches us.

He's smiling, which I take as a good sign. I'd hoped Zakh and Malik would treat Desmier better than Viktor had. They were always more down to earth. I guessed Desmier would take to Zakh first before anyone else, and it appears I was right.

Seeing Zakh always makes me think of Lorelai, though. Now that I've spoken to her and she's aware I know their secret, I feel even more compassionate toward them.

"Hey, welcome back." Zakh beams, giving Desmier a one-armed hug, which I take as another very good sign.

"Thanks."

Zakh turns to me and smiles. "Anastasia. Welcome to the family."

"Thank you so much." I give him an actual hug because I've known him forever, but when we part, he dips his head respectfully the way I've seen the Knights address the wife of another Knight.

"Would you mind if I steal your husband for a few minutes? I swear I won't take him away for too long."

I notice the shift in Desmier's expression on hearing the request, and he becomes more serious.

"That's fine. I'll leave you guys to talk."

"Don't go too far." Desmier glances at me.

"I'll just be in the bathroom. I'll come right back."

"Okay."

While they head toward the stairs, I walk in the opposite direction to the bathroom I used when I came to visit Viktor here.

As those are full, I take the stairs up to the next level.

There's no one on this floor usually because it leads to the archive department, so it doesn't surprise me that it's empty.

When I get to the bathroom, though, the door is ajar, and the clear sound of a woman's moans and bodies slapping together filter out into the hallway.

I've heard enough of those types of sounds at frat parties to know what they are, so I turn around to leave, deciding to mind my own business.

But I stop in my tracks when the guy speaks, realizing I recognize his voice.

It's Viktor.

At least I think so.

"Take what I give you like my good little slut," the guy says, and I'm sure it's him. But talking like that? I've never heard him talk like that before.

Against my better judgment, I find myself moving back inside the bathroom.

Then I see him with his pants down, pounding into Megan, his secretary, who's naked and holding on to the sink as her hair flies everywhere.

I shouldn't be shocked. But I am to see him like this, and to see evidence of what Lorelai's told me. We're not together now, so this is none of my concern. It just shows me who he is.

"Fuck me harder than you did on your wedding day," Megan cries, her words shocking me further and freezing my mind.

Something shatters inside me as I process what she means.

Wedding day.

As there's only one wedding she could be talking about, there's no mistaking that it was ours.

"Greedy bitch, I'll destroy your pussy this time," Viktor growls, giving added confirmation they were together on our wedding day.

Disappointment and anger roil in my stomach, keeping me rooted to the spot. The incidents Lorelai told me about happened when Viktor and I weren't engaged, so while I was upset, I tried to deal with it. This is different, and I realize how foolish I've been.

I was the innocent, naïve fool whose father wrapped her in a ball of cotton to preserve her virginity for a man who couldn't even be true to her on their wedding day.

Viktor pulls her closer to him, and suddenly, he sees my reflection in the mirror, watching them fucking.

Immediately, he stops his furious pounding and stares back at me, horror tainting his face as he realizes I heard what they said. And I'm here witnessing what they're doing.

"Fuck, Anastasia. I'm..."

I don't wait for him to finish or pull out of Megan properly before I rush out the door. But in my clumsiness, I stumble and drop my purse, sending all my lipsticks, my phone, and keys rolling out.

Cursing myself, I bend down to pick them up and have the misfortune of hearing Viktor arguing with Megan.

"Are you kidding me? You're going to her? Didn't she just marry your brother?" Megan is practically shouting in that irritating squeaky voice I've always hated, so I'd be able to hear her even if I were on the other side of the globe. "We've been fucking nearly every day for the last five years, and you said we would never stop. What the hell is wrong with you?"

As more truth spews out of her mouth, I realize I'm an even bigger fool. Viktor was never true to me.

Never. And he was never going to be, no matter what contract bound us together.

A contract is exactly what I was. A person who was bred to be a wife and fulfill a business arrangement.

The tears that are never far away stream down my cheeks, and I curse myself again.

They aren't from seeing them together, but for the hurt I feel for believing so much in a man who was never going to love me.

I gather my things and run down the hall just before Viktor steps out of the bathroom, but I'm not fast enough. I just manage to get down the stairs to the floor I was previously on when he grabs my arm.

"Anastasia, wait."

"Let go of me, you cheating asshole." I try to wrench my arm free of his grasp, but he holds on tighter. And now we have the attention of people around us.

"She meant nothing. I wanted to be with you."

"That's bullshit. Let me go."

Instead of releasing me, he yanks me hard toward him and to my shock, crushes his lips to mine.

CHAPTER THIRTY-FOUR

ANASTASIA

Viktor kisses me like he never has before, and everything feels wrong about it.

Shock siphons the blood from my body, stealing my senses, and I'm like a rag doll in his arms, unable to break out of his hold.

"Hey!" Desmier's voice booms over us like a roar of thunder, and Viktor pulls away, leaving me feeling worse than I did moments ago.

Desmier saw us kissing. And so did Zakh and Malik and everyone else.

Viktor releases my arm when Desmier rushes forward. His hand is already balled into a fist, which connects with Viktor's face the instant he reaches us.

Viktor strikes back, catching Desmier in the same place, then they start throwing punches like they did weeks ago at the house.

It takes Zakh and Malik to pull them apart. Zakh takes Desmier and Malik Viktor. But they're still growling and cursing like hell beasts.

It's only when Desmier cuts me a glance and sees the tears streaming down my cheeks that he seems to realize something else happened before the kiss.

"Fucking stop it, Desmier!" Zakh yells.

While he struggles to hold Desmier back, Malik has Viktor in a lock that prevents him from moving around.

"Stay the fuck away from my wife," Desmier growls at Viktor with feral rage.

"I would if she didn't find me."

"Stop it," Megan cuts in, rushing up behind Viktor. Her hair is still a mess, but at least she's wearing clothes.

I glare at her, remembering all the times she was nice to my face and probably laughing behind my back.

"Anastasia caught us together," she explains, cutting me a sharp glance. "She was upset, and Viktor went after her."

The moment she says that, Desmier looks at me again and takes in my tears once more. Then his expression morphs into something I can't quite read, and I know he's not as angry at Viktor as he is with me.

"Clearly, she's still in love with me if she can be so upset," Viktor spits, making everything so much worse by using my fury to his advantage. "Look how distraught she is."

The change in Desmier is instant. It's like something drains from him, taking away the magic we shared not even an hour ago.

"No," I cut in. "I'm upset because I just found out they were together the whole time I was with him."

Despite my attempt to clarify, Desmier doesn't look like he cares for my explanation.

"I explained that," Viktor says to me, but I'm not even looking at him anymore. I keep my focus on Desmier.

This is bullshit, and it's best we get away from here.

"Desmier, can we please just go home?"

He doesn't answer, and he doesn't look at Viktor again.

Zakh releases him, and he takes my hand, leading me away.

By the time we reach the parking lot, Desmier is walking so fast, he's dragging me along in my heels. I almost regret being so eager to leave with him in this volatile state where I don't know what to expect from him.

He's undoubtedly enraged because he thinks I'm still in love with Viktor, and he's not looking past that part to understand what I explained.

When we get in the car, he takes off like we're in a high-speed chase. It's like he's stepped back into the shoes of the man he was weeks ago—when he was evil.

I catch him glancing at me while I dry my tears. When they subside and I'm calmer, I think of something to say to explain myself further, but no words come.

We get home in that dreadful silence and head up to our room. Desmier switches on the light, sending the darkness fleeing as if it, too, can sense his anger.

I'm about to walk into the bathroom because I just need some space from him, but he stops me, placing a heavy hand on the nape of my neck.

"Not until I'm finished with you." His fingers clamp down on my skin, cold, hard, and demanding, making my nerves jump.

"Why? What are you doing?"

"You'll soon see, my dear Valkyrie." I don't like the subdued hollow in his voice, or the way he didn't answer all my questions.

"Desmier... I told you why I was upset."

"I heard you. Loud and clear, baby girl." He steers me toward the bed and moves behind me to pull the zipper down the back of my dress. Chills curl down my spine and race over my body, making me numb.

"If you heard me, what are we doing?" My voice is as stiff as my body. "The kiss meant nothing to me. I didn't expect Viktor to do that. And what he said wasn't true. I'm not in love with him."

That's the first time I've said those words out loud, but no answer comes; Desmier just continues taking off my clothes. The dress, my bra, and my panties float to the floor, pooling at my feet as I'm left naked and vulnerable before him.

"Why don't you talk to me?" I try to step away, but he catches my arm.

"Get on the bed, ass up."

Despite the sexy glint in his eyes as they roam over my naked body and the lewdness of his command, I decide to stand my ground. "No. Let's talk."

"Oh, we will talk. Now, do as I say. Don't, and you know how I truly love punishing you."

"I didn't do anything."

"That's yet to be determined. This is a reminder."

"Of what?"

"Get on the bed. Don't let me repeat myself again, or you

will not like it." His eyes become hard and guarded. I can't even see past his fury.

This can't be the guy I was so fascinated by all these weeks. The one who told me I was his girl, sailed me around the Caribbean, and melted my last resolve.

Am I the fool again?

Defeated, I slip off my shoes and crawl onto the bed, then glance over my shoulder, watching him take off his jacket and shirt.

He walks up to me and rests his hand softly on the curve of my back. A shiver of heat coils down my spine, and I drag in a slow breath to keep my focus.

"Remember the other week when I said we'd talk about certain things after the wedding?" His voice takes on that Arctic edge. I shudder.

"Yes." I don't know what this has to do with what happened tonight, but it's so typical of him to be cryptic.

"We're going to talk about those things now, *wife*."

He plants a line of kisses down my back, trailing down to my pussy, where he pushes his tongue into me.

The maddening cocktail of arousal and tension jolts my body, and I wish we weren't in this weird space of uncertainty. I wish we could go back to mere hours ago when we devoured each other in this bed and barely wanted to leave.

I wish we hadn't left because this feels like something else.

"It's time you get another rude awakening about your beloved Viktor."

I snap my gaze back at him. "He's not my beloved. I told you what happened."

He replies by pushing two fingers into my passage,

pumping in and out of me slowly. I suppress a moan, but he teases it out of me.

"Always wet for me, though." His voice is a whisper that speaks to the secret parts of me that crave his touch. "Your beloved Viktor would never have been able to keep his dick in his pants, but there's something else you should know about him."

I don't like the sound of this. Desmier's fingers trail up to my back again and linger by my spine.

"What should I know?"

"It's about the vineyard."

I narrow my eyes when he returns to my face and brushes his nose along mine.

"What about the vineyard?"

He releases a slow, pensive breath, tickling my skin, then moves away.

I continue watching him, our gazes tangled and unwavering. He undoes his belt buckle, shoves his pants and boxers down his hips, then steps out of them.

I've seen him naked so many times, but my heart still skips a beat at how perfect he is. Perfect and closed off to listening to me.

Desmier climbs onto the bed, getting behind me, leaving the questions of the vineyard and the reminder hanging in the air. Then his cock is pushing into my passage and he's moving inside me. Slow at first, as if he's torturing me, then fast. And faster.

He grabs my hips and tightens his grip, so it's more painful. Then I see stars when he starts slamming into me.

Moments later, I come so hard my body feels like it might shatter, but he continues his relentless pounding, pulling me back toward him so he can fist my hair with one hand and pinch my nipple with the other.

"Des...mier. Ahhh." My voice crashes into the walls along with the wild sounds of us.

He's fucking me like he wants to unleash his rage and possess me all at the same time. Like he hates to feel anything for me. Like whatever we have between us is my fault and he wishes he'd never met me.

I'm not even aware when we crash down in a sweaty heap. All I know is that he's still pounding into me.

He flips me onto my back and slides on top of me, plunging his cock back into my now-sore passage. Catching my face, he keeps me there, locked in his furious passion when he starts pounding into me again.

Finally, he comes, unleashing his hot cum inside me, which is hotter than normal. When his pumps slow, he rests his forehead on mine, kissing my nose and cheeks.

My mind is a wreck, and I can't think past him and the new possession he's inflicted on my body

Lifting himself up on one elbow, he continues to stare at me and I wait for him to speak. That's when his guard drops and I see pain. That pain again that desolate souls carry. It's like looking into a black hole of doom.

"Your vineyard isn't merely a vineyard." He speaks after what feels like eons in a low, rusty voice, still thick with arousal.

"What?" I breathe. "What do you mean?"

"It's an oil company. Your father and Viktor tried to trick you into giving it to them."

My lungs squeeze and my heart nearly leaps out of my body. "What are you saying to me?"

"You own an oil company worth billions, Anastasia. They wanted to take the company from you. The ownership is currently being masked, but it's yours."

A stone drops in my stomach, and I feel like I'm going to have a heart attack. My heart won't stop racing while the thoughts in my head scramble like eggs being tossed around on a hot grill.

"No... Everything was all a lie?"

"Yes, they lied to you."

"*My God.*" And Dad telling me how much the vineyard meant to him was part of the bullshit, too. "When did you find out?"

"I've known for some time, but I wanted to keep it secret so I could watch them. When we got married, we became co-owners, and the only way to get things back on track is to kill me."

"Kill you?" My heart becomes a tight fist, clenching my chest.

"Kill me, and they get you back. Viktor marries you, and things go back to normal. But I have the last ace up my sleeve."

"What?"

"I've started the process of transferring my half of the company to you, so you own it completely. That way, no one would be able to take it from you." He gives me an uncanny smile and leans in closer. "I'm the fool, aren't I? The fool who wanted the girl more than the money."

I can't believe what I'm hearing.

"Desmier—"

"Shhhh, baby girl. It gets worse for me because I just figured it out. You do love Viktor."

I shake my head. “No.”

“Yes, you do. You always did, and you still do.”

“No. It’s not true.” Lorelai was right; I was never in love with Viktor. The truth sang to me the day I gave myself to Desmier.

“Yes, Anastasia. Here’s why. You’re not a crier. I’ve only seen you cry one time, and that was because you were in pain. You were in pain tonight. A different sort of pain for love lost. No matter what you and I have, you grieved the loss of the man you thought Viktor was. The man you wanted to be with. The man you love.”

His words seep into me, stalling my mind.

“I was upset because he was never true to me.”

“Exactly. And that’s the problem. You were upset. If you didn’t still love him, you wouldn’t be so hurt. You would feel nothing but relief that you escaped being with a cheater. But you’re so blinded by love for him, what’s right in front of you is not enough.” He pauses for a beat, and my mind stops, too, as I see the grievous error I made. And I regret it. “I can’t bleed Viktor from your heart or drain him from your soul. I can’t steal those parts of you because they still belong to him. That’s the reminder I needed. Along with the fact that you are Uther Sidorov’s daughter. My enemy forever. That’s what you are to me. No longer my Valkyrie.”

His crude words scrape deeper than the layers of my skin, cutting into my bones. I’m so fragile I dare not breathe in case I shatter into a million shards from which I’ll never be able to put myself back together again.

Desmier slips off the bed, and I lift myself up.

“Desmier—”

"Don't. Do not speak. You heard what I said, and I mean it."

I stare back at the man I just lost as he drags on his pants and grabs a T-shirt and his biker jacket from the wardrobe. Then he walks out the door without looking at me.

As the door slams, I realize I just lost the only man I've ever truly loved.

My husband.

CHAPTER THIRTY-FIVE

DESMIER

I rush down the stairs like a madman, shrugging into my jacket as I descend.

Fucking hell.

I need to kill something or at least shoot something. Anything to get Anastasia out of my head.

Fuck Viktor, and fuck everything.

Fuck my heart.

I knew better than this—to fall for a woman I shouldn't have.

I should fucking hate her just for being Uther's daughter. And yet, even as I think that word—*hate*—I can't do it. Even now, when the truth is laughing at me, telling me I couldn't break her love for Viktor and I was always second best.

My mind has been all over the fucking place since Anastasia Sidorov came into my life. I just made everything worse when I turned her into Anastasia Volkova and officially made her mine.

I was ready to kill Viktor when he kissed her earlier because I thought of her as my wife. Then a different type of fury struck me when I got the rest of the story and saw how crushed Anastasia looked.

I perfectly understood her reasons for being upset, but I didn't want her to be because she's with me. That's supposed to be better than Viktor.

But it's not.

How can it be when I stole her?

And there, that's the problem. I stole her because she was the daughter of my enemy. She was never supposed to mean anything to me.

We were always wrong, so no matter what I do, I can't make us right.

I was the one who blurred the lines between us. Now I need to heed the rude reminder of what she's supposed to be and pull my head out of my ass. I need to get back on track and cut this vision of the loving wife and a future from my head.

I came here and did what I needed to do. Once things are on track, I can head back out to sea in a few weeks, where I belong.

By then, my part ownership of the vineyard should be transferred to her and the threat removed. The lawyers said it would take about four to six weeks to do so, in keeping with the cooling period. I was hoping to wait until that had happened before I told her the truth, but she needed to know tonight. I just hope I haven't shot myself in the foot by revealing it. If I have, I'll need to be prepared for whatever comes of it.

I rush out to the garage, needing to feel the thrill of riding my motorcycle.

I don't know where I'm going yet, but I can't stay here.

When I get inside the garage and find Gytha there, I stifle a groan, but she can see I'm not in the mood for anything, business or otherwise.

A seductive smile spreads across her red, glossy lips, and she leans against the door of my sports car with the same air of seduction.

That's done on purpose to conjure my memories of riding around town with her, or times when I had her naked on the hood.

Fuck my life. I can't deal with her now.

"I saw you come in. You didn't look too happy. Thought you might come back out here." Her voice is as gentle as a cat's purr.

"I'm going out." I keep walking until I reach the bike, but she follows.

"Trouble in paradise?" She runs a finger down my arm. "I always had the cure for that. Why don't we go back inside and fuck whatever is wrong with you out of your system?"

If it were that easy, I wonder if I would do it.

Would I fuck another woman to forget Anastasia? Or to get her out of my head even temporarily?

Would it be her? Gytha, the first woman I thought I could love.

It would be so easy to do it. To take her, or someone else. A guy like me never has trouble getting pussy.

But I won't do it.

I can't.

Because of fucking love.

I'm not the guy to cheat on the wife he loves, even if she doesn't love me back.

"No, and do not ask me again." I glare at her, and her face hardens.

"I can't do this. I can't watch you like this."

"Like what?"

"Belonging to someone else." She swallows and blinks back tears. "There's a job in Denmark I'm going to take. It starts in a few weeks' time."

I stare back at her. This is the wrong time to speak to me, and not about this.

I've always thought of her as an integral part of my business, but I knew the day would come when she'd leave. I thought it would have happened sooner, after we stopped screwing around.

Now she's looking at me like she wants me to tell her to stay.

But I can't do that either.

"I was hoping we could work through this. Being with you was always reason enough to stay." She presses her lips together. "Do you think we could?"

Her eyes plead with me to say yes, but this is one question I don't have to think too hard about, or for too long.

"You should take the job, Gytha. We're not going to work anything out."

First, she stares as if she's stunned by my answer, then she turns away from me in silence and walks out.

Feeling like I'm going to implode, I jump on my bike and ride away at lightning speed.

I ride around for a few hours before I decide to head back to Volkova Inc. and finish up some of the work I put aside before I left on my honeymoon.

It was work that could wait then, and it can still wait now, but I need something to occupy my mind.

I take the back entrance and the elevator up to the floor that houses my office, hoping I won't get any more nasty surprises. I shouldn't because it's nearly one in the morning and the fundraiser ended at midnight.

When I step out of the elevator car, I see the light on in Zakh's office and hear voices. Him and someone else who sounds like Malik.

Zakh's office isn't far from mine, but since I always use the other entrance, I don't really see him unless we arrange to meet.

It occurs to me that he might have been here working late in the past and I wouldn't have known.

Earlier, he wanted to speak to me because he and Malik had tracked down the dealer who supplied the particular blend of poison he'd found in our father's office. He said he was looking into who purchased it—to see if it was Viktor—but hadn't found anything yet.

Maybe he's found something. Zakh has now shared his suspicions with Malik, so it would make sense for them to be here if something more was found.

I make my way over there. They look at me when I reach the door, and I can tell straightaway they were deep in conversation about something important.

"Hey, guys." I keep the annoyance I still feel out of my voice.

"What are you doing back here?" Zakh asks.

"Better to work."

"Trust me, it's not," Malik says.

"What's happening?"

"The short story is our dealer is dead." Zakh leans back and steeples his fingers.

I release a heavy sigh. "How?"

"Shot this evening just after I found the intel."

My brows knit together. "That's suspicious as fuck." I walk in and take a seat beside Malik. "Who else knew you got the intel about him?"

"Just me," Malik replies.

"Then you're being watched." That's the only thing that makes sense.

"That's exactly what we're thinking, so something else is definitely going on. And whoever is watching is tracking us from inside here, and our homes. I've been going through my computer looking for spyware, but I can't find anything."

I look from Zakh to Malik. They're worried, which they're right to be with

everything being so vague. "Did Viktor go home?"

"Yeah, with his secretary." Malik smirks. "He's been with her all day."

I shake my head with disgust, but that's an alibi that might excuse him on

some level.

"What are you thinking, Desmier?" Zakh asks.

"I'm not sure. It looks like someone else is involved."

"I managed to get a message to Eric Markov." Erik is the Obshchak in the Voirik Bratva. He was one of the people I went to see when I was in L.A. He creates and supports our antivirus software at his company Markov Tech. "I sent him the IP address I found. It was linked to the undisclosed recipient emails ordering the poison from the dealer. I won't take the risk and decrypt anything from here. Eric's looking into it now. We're just hanging around to see if he finds anything tonight."

"Good. How did you find the dealer's details in the first place?"

"That's my part," Malik replies. "Some things require street smarts. I looked at the toxicology report Zakh got from the lab and noticed the oleander was blended with a synthetic street drug. That was probably what made our father's heart condition look so real. I know there are only a few people you can get the drug from. Our guy was the best at what he did and an expert in poisons used by many assassins."

Zakh bites the inside of his lip. "I've asked Leo and Kill to go to the coroner's office to get more details on the dealer's time of death and whereabouts before he was shot. I trust them to keep things quiet."

Leo and Kill are enforcers in our Brotherhood. As Leo is Zakh's best friend and Lorelai's older brother, and Kill is their cousin, I respect Zakh's trust in them.

"So, it's a waiting game now."

Malik stands and pulls on his jacket. "We might be here for a while. I was about to get some food. Are you going to be here long enough to eat?"

I nod. "I'll stay. Looks like I'm needed here more." Home is definitely not where I want to be with shit going on behind my back.

"Alright. I'll be back in ten minutes. Call me if you hear anything while I'm out."

He leaves, and I look back at Zakh. He's so tense the vein on the side of his head is standing to attention. Earlier, he seemed hopeful that he was on track to find something.

Over the time I've gotten to know him, the main thing I've realized is how close he is to our father. What he wants is revenge.

I know what that feels like. But the same man he wishes to seek vengeance for is the one I would have killed myself.

"Desmier, this might not be Viktor." He leans onto the desk with gritted teeth. "Or there are others working with him."

"We'll have to wait and see."

"I'm not known for my patience."

"Neither am I."

"Yeah, I figured that out when you decked Viktor earlier."

"You know he fucking deserved it, and more." I make a fist and press my knuckles into the edge of my seat.

"Yes, which begs the question of why you're here and not with the wife you looked really taken with."

I shake my head. "I'm not taken with her." Instantly, I feel bad for the lie. The deadpan look he gives me tells me he knows it's a lie, too. "Or rather, I mustn't be."

"Why? I've never seen Anastasia look like that with anyone, and I've known her practically her whole life. She looked happy. So did you."

"I think she's just grown accustomed to me. That's all it is."

"She's your wife, Desmier. Look, she was bound to be

upset hearing that Viktor was a damn cheat because she was essentially raised to love him. But I get where you're coming from because I would be pissed, too. All I'm saying is, give her the benefit of the doubt."

I appreciate what he's saying, but my earlier decision needs to stand.

"I need to cool off, Zakh. That's the best thing for me now. I need a break to get my head together."

"And what will your head together look like? The guy you were when you first arrived?"

That gives me pause, but I know the answer. "Yes. That guy was fueled by fire and had his head screwed on." Each day was taken with precision. Then it changed the moment I tasted her. My own damn punishment backfired on me and led me here.

"You're a different person now."

"No. Believe me, I'm the same guy. It's just that time has passed."

"But you love her."

I look at him as if he just hit me with a truck. I'm amazed that a guy whom I've only known for roughly two months can see through me enough to know that. It's almost like when Viktor could tell I was fascinated with Anastasia, but this is different.

There is no ill will in Zakh toward me.

"That doesn't mean anything."

"In our world it does. In our world, you don't always get to be with the girl you love. I won't."

My interest piques. He's never been so open with me before.

"Why not?"

"Because she doesn't belong to me." Defeat invades his eyes.

"You don't strike me as a man who would let that stop you."

"I'm not. But on this occasion, I had to. Sometimes you have to choose your battles wisely."

I consider his words as I mull over everything that happened tonight, and how it made me feel. I can't allow anyone to have control over my emotions the way Anastasia does. I just can't. "Maybe that's what I'm doing."

"I don't think you are."

"Why not?" I'm really interested to hear what he has to say.

"I came across something I thought was odd at first, then I realized it wasn't."

"What did you come across, brother?"

"The change of ownership details for Sidorov Developments."

Shit. How the motherfucking hell did he find that? That was hidden pretty much in the same way everything else was hidden, and I got Gytha to mask the ownership like Uther did with the oil company. I clench my back teeth and slow my breathing. Finding that means he knows a chunk of my plan he shouldn't.

"Don't worry, your secret is safe with me."

"Is it, Zakh?"

"I think you know the answer to that."

My heart tells me I can trust him, but I'm not used to trusting anyone outside my circle.

"Then what about it?"

"It belongs to you. To my knowledge, we were supposed

to form a partnership of shares. The whole marriage contract was based on that. Uther was to get shares in Volkova Inc., and you'd get some of Sidorov Developments'. But all you left the man with is the clothes on his back. You took his daughter so he'd have no way of arranging another marriage, you took his position in the Bratva, and now you own the vineyard/oil field, too." He gives me a pensive stare. "Apart from what you knew about the vineyard, I suspected there was more going on between you and Uther when you demoted him. It didn't make sense given his years of expertise. But now I know there's more. You came for vengeance on him, too, didn't you? Not just our father. Am I right?"

I haven't known Zakh for that long, but from what I know about him, I've gathered that he wouldn't be asking me a question like that if he didn't already know the answer.

"Yes."

He looks me over. "Was it Uther who killed your mother?"

"It was."

"Why haven't you killed him yet?" He speaks respectfully, as if giving due regard to my mother.

"All in good time. I'm sure you understand death is too easy for some villains."

"I do. Does Anastasia know?"

"No." I drag in a breath and clench my jaw.

I've gone from feeling like I can't talk about the past with her because Uther is her father, to not wanting to hurt her even more than Uther has. The people she loves lied to her, including Viktor. She already knows I'm the devil, but maybe I don't want to be the man to break her heart even more.

"If all of that can happen to you and you can still love her, that has to be worth something."

He's right. He's fucking right. But the issues Anastasia and I have are deep-rooted and tangled with the problems I've always had with Viktor, with him being chosen over me. Except this feels like the time that matters most, because it's happening now. And it's not something anyone can help me with.

"I guess we'll have to see."

Zakh's phone starts buzzing on the desk, and I'm grateful for the diversion.

He answers it, and within seconds, I know it's an important call judging by the deep furrow in his brow. It's probably the call he was waiting on from Eric.

When he hangs up, he slams a fist on his desk. "That was Eric. He says the emails came from Uther's computer. He ordered the poison. He was trying to kill our father."

CHAPTER THIRTY-SIX

ANASTASIA

I stare at the rustic red brick wall before me, tapping the bricks with my fingertips to that song in my head.

Run and catch, the meadow's calling you home...

I tap one, two, three, four, five, six, seven, eight.

On the eighth count, I blink, then I'm running through the meadow. A bird flies high in the sky, and the sun is bright and warm on my skin, tempting me to chase it. I run toward the sun, but it disappears, and blackness swallows me whole.

It's so dark, I dare not breathe. I'm too scared that I'll disappear. But I walk on the unseen path before me, terror ravaging my soul.

Darkness fills my mind like a thick fog of smoke, suffocating me with the

ominous feeling of imminent doom.

Patches of light flicker in the darkness, and I see it—the crest with the wolf and the moon engraved into it.

I try to get closer, but shadow monsters rush out of the darkness, howling and gnashing their teeth like evil souls trapped in the pits of hell.

Faceless faces push out of the darkness, and a million screams wrap around me.

Blood pours from the sky. And a knife plunges into my throat, stabbing me again and again and again.

I JUMP out of my sleep and nearly out of my skin, screaming.

As usual, my hand is at my throat and I'm expecting blood to flow out and cover me. But there's nothing.

It takes me a moment to realize I'm out of the nightmare and still in bed. It's daytime, raining heavily outside.

When my breathing calms, I look at the unslept-in space beside me, and then I glance at the clock on the wall.

It's nearly midday, and it doesn't look like Desmier came home again last night, which means I haven't seen him now in three days.

It's Saturday, and tonight is Leif's retirement party. I'm sure Desmier will be attending. Originally, we were both supposed to go, but I don't know if I should.

Not seeing Desmier all this time, without even any instruction from him to Ehlga, has sent his message clearly that he wants nothing to do with me.

He's distancing himself.

I could go tonight, see him and talk it out, but I don't know if I could risk being hurt any more than I am.

I don't know which would be worse—getting there by myself and him not speaking to me or him sending me home like a child.

Or... he could even be there with someone else. *That* would crush me.

I can't believe this is me. Months ago, I sat in this same bed hoping I would get through the day without seeing him. Then I couldn't stop wanting him. Now I need him, and he's not mine anymore.

I get off the bed, take a quick shower, and put on a T-shirt and yoga pants. I look like shit, and I don't think my looks are going to get any better than they are today. They might get worse, but here's hoping they don't.

I make my way downstairs and hear Ehlga in the kitchen talking to one of the other maids.

I'm not in the mood to talk to anyone yet, so I grab my hooded jacket from the coat rack and head outside in the rain.

Knowing Ehlga, she'll try to feed me with pastries or some sort of casserole because she doesn't know what to do with me.

I presume she's spoken to Desmier because I can't imagine him not talking to her. Every time she sees me, she has that look of pity in her eyes. It's obvious she's aware Desmier and I aren't on the best terms. Or any terms.

For the last few days, she's tried to be there for me in whatever way she could, but today I just can't be around people.

And with that decided, I'm not even going to brave going to that party tonight. Desmier has to come home and see me at some point.

I just wish it will be soon.

Flurries of rain cover my face, making it difficult to see, so I walk around to the garage.

A silly idea comes over me, and I find myself heading inside through the side door. I don't usually come in here. Most times, I'm dropped off at the front door. It's only when I've been driving around with Desmier that I've ever been inside.

Inside are six of his eight vehicles. The black Porsche and the Ferrari are missing. I expected the motorcycle to be gone, but it's tucked away in the corner with the helmet and one of his leather jackets hooked over the handle.

I walk over to it and run my fingers over the helmet, remembering that day mere weeks ago when he first came to pick me up from campus. He did that a few times after, then it was the wedding.

Things were actually perfect, and I was happy. I was so happy as we sailed across the Caribbean Seas as if that was our life and all we had to think about.

No one would ever have known there were still so many secrets between us.

Or that my little mistake would remind him he's supposed to hate me.

I don't even want to think of Dad now. Or Viktor.

Both disgust me. God knows what else there is I don't know. I'm sure there's plenty, and I can just imagine what I don't know must be so much worse than the information I've been allowed to have so far.

I lift Desmier's jacket, bring it to my nose, and inhale his scent. That masculine scent of power, possession, and safety.

"I don't think Desmier would like you in here touching his things," comes a voice I really don't want to hear.

I turn around and see Gytha walking through the door.

She stops a few paces away with her hands on her hips and a pout marring her model-like features.

"I'm sure he wouldn't mind." I pray she leaves me alone and goes away. I don't have the strength for her today. I never had it before.

"I've known him much longer than you have, so I know he doesn't like his things being touched by anyone other than him."

She's such a fucking bitch. Why, *why* is she always around when I'm either at my lowest or I'm contemplating something important? Today I'm both.

"Gytha, I'm his wife. Just leave me the fuck alone."

My tone and choice of words piss her off and she moves closer, like she's going to hit me.

She stops in my personal space, and because she's much taller than me, I instantly feel more vulnerable.

"You think just because he gave you his name it means anything? It means shit, especially to the likes of you."

"What the hell do you mean by 'the likes of me'?"

"You need to remember why you're here. It's not to play house or act like the little family you think you are."

"Maybe so, but what about you? You follow him around like a desperate dog. Do you think he wants you?" I might have sounded more confident without the quiver and hurt in my voice, or that feeble undertone.

"Be glad I'm choosing not to mess up your face." She sneers. "My dear Anastasia, you are just something to fuck until he gets bored. And I have more chances of being with him than you. You are Uther Sidorov's daughter. There is no way he will ever love you after what your father did to him. You're just the little bitch he—"

"That is enough." Ehlga's loud voice cuts into Gytha's words, an attempt to stop her from doing any more damage. But it's too late. She's already sliced through my heart.

Ehlga marches in from the rain and walks right up to us, her face red with fury. I've never seen her look so mad.

"This doesn't concern you, Ehlga." Gytha looks at Ehlga as if she's shit she's trying to avoid stepping in. "Why don't you go and bake, or clean, or something a normal maid would do."

"Nothing against the maids, but I am not a maid. And you will not speak to me or Anastasia like that."

"What authority do you have to talk to me like this?" Gytha sets her hands on her hips and lifts her chin in defiance.

"Enough to throw you off the property, *my dear*. Desmier is like a son to me, so this is my home, and *you* are just a visitor. And to address your comment about having more of a chance with Desmier, you and I both know that's not true."

Although my body is flustered from the jabs Gytha threw my way, Ehlga has my attention.

"I don't know what you mean by that."

"Of course, you do, Gytha, but let me clarify what I mean. If you closed your legs and weren't the God-awful fucking cheating slut you are, you just *might* have had a chance with Desmier. So, don't get worked up when he's found somebody new, someone who's a million times better than you."

I never knew Ehlga had it in her to talk this way—and she *can* say fuck.

Gytha looks like she doesn't know where to put her face.

"I think it's best you leave for the day out of respect to

Mrs. Volkova," she adds, pushing her shoulders back. "I'll also advise you, woman to woman, it's poor taste to keep chasing a man who doesn't want you. Especially a married one. Even you can do better than that, dear."

Without another word, or a glance my way, Gytha walks out. I swear I catch a tremble in her step, but maybe I saw what I wanted to see.

With Gytha gone, and the roasting Ehlga just gave her, I should feel euphoric. Gytha deserved every word she got, and them coming from the least likely person to talk to her that way made it that much sweeter.

But the sharpness of her sting hit me deep because she was right.

Take out the bitchiness, and she could have been Desmier reminding me that I'm Uther Sidorov's daughter.

Before I can take my next breath, tears flow down my cheeks.

I cover my face, and when Ehlga moves closer, I break down and cry for everything.

Everything I lost. My memory, my mother, myself. The lie my life was, and the man who didn't need to steal my heart.

The last hurts the worst because Desmier is the only person I gave a piece of me willingly.

"It's okay, dear." Ehlga's voice has returned to its normal calm and warmth, but she feels far away from me. "Come, let's go sit for a while and talk."

I nod, and I manage to walk when she leads me out to the sunroom.

We sit next to each other on the wicker sofa, and I cry until the tears subside.

"Sometimes, we need a good cry." She strokes my hair.

"Thank you for defending me. I don't think I could have done it even if I didn't feel so wretched."

"That's okay. That was a long time coming. Gytha deserved it."

"Some of what she said was true, though."

"No, there was no truth to her words."

I dab away the last of my tears with the heel of my hand and nod. "Yes, Ehlga. I'm sure you know what happened between Desmier and me."

She sighs. "That doesn't mean Gytha was right."

"I understand how he feels about how I reacted that night, but there's nothing I can do about my father or Viktor." My voice comes out in a choked rasp.

"Has he told you anything more about the past?"

"Not much. He told me his mother was killed and that he lived here with her when he was younger, then Denmark, then Russia. That's essentially all I know about Desmier's past."

She searches my eyes. "Then I think maybe the right time has come for me to tell you."

My spirit lifts at this possibility. "Will you really?"

"Yes. There are things he wanted to keep secret from you, but since he's promised me he would tell you when the time was right, I think I should do it now. The time feels right *now* because *I* trust you. I trust what I see in you with regards to how you feel about him, and I think you should know. I don't think you would do anything to put him in danger."

"No, I would never." I say that like a vow. "Ehlga, please tell me what happened to him."

She drags in a breath. "He's had a hard life and experienced terrible things no one should have to go through."

"What are those terrible things?" What makes a man become as ruthless as him? He's still so young yet acts like an older man who's lived through a hundred wars.

"Things that left him with scars that run deeper than the surface."

At the mention of scars, I instantly think of Desmier's burn scar.

"He has a scar on his back. Was he caught in a fire?"

"In a manner of speaking, yes. It was worse when he first came into my care."

Confused, I narrow my eyes. "Your care?"

"I became his mother when he lost his. He was twelve."

Twelve?

My eyes widen.

"I didn't know that. I assumed he was much older when he lost his mother."

"No. He was twelve years old. Leif put Desmier in my care."

"Leif?" That's even stranger. "Why didn't he take Desmier in?" That's the obvious question for anyone to ask. Especially if they know of Leif's kind-hearted nature. A better question to ask would be about Desmier's father and Mira.

"Leif and his wife wanted to, but it wasn't possible."

"Why not?"

"At the time, it was important to keep Desmier a secret to make sure he was safe. So, Leif put him in my care because he trusted me. He and my family go way back."

"Safe from whom, Ehlga?"

"His father."

The answer squeezes my insides, and my shoulders go rigid. "Evgeni? I... I don't understand."

"Evgeni didn't know about Desmier's existence until he was twelve." Her skin pales, and she pauses for a moment before continuing. "When Desmier's mother told him, he ordered their deaths."

"What? Oh my God." My high-pitched voice bounces around the room, and my brain refuses to process this horrific news.

No way are we talking about the same man who was so nice to me and welcoming, calling me his daughter every time I saw him. "I can't believe what you're saying to me."

"It's true. Leif managed to save Desmier. That's why he's alive today. The order was given because Desmier's existence threatened everything Evgeni stood to gain from his marriage to Mira. That was based on Viktor being his heir."

"I'm so shocked." So much about Desmier makes sense now. And his hatred toward Viktor. "Did Mira know any of this, or anybody else?"

"No, they all found out when Desmier stopped your wedding to Viktor."

That would have been while I was being brought here. "Why was I left out?"

"Because of Desmier's vendetta toward your father."

Dread twists my insides, and I feel sick. Something hits me in my gut that feels like truth. The last time I felt it was when I found my mother in the bathtub and knew she was dead.

As Ehlga looks at me, I feel even more certain that I

know what that vendetta is. It's like it's staring me in the face, and I can't breathe.

My father is an enforcer who worked for Evgeni for years. They were so close I'm sure there was no question of a union by marriage to join our families. Evgeni ordered Desmier and his mother's death, so he would have sent men to do the job.

Men like my father. The senior guard.

"Ehlga, my... father... he killed Desmier's mother, didn't he?"

"Yes."

Shock jolts through me at the confirmation, and I feel like I'm going to fall over and keep falling through the earth.

My skin goes hot, then cold, then hot again, then ice takes over, sending a chill through me that's so callous I don't know how it doesn't freeze my heart.

"No... it can't be. Please, no." My head moves on its own, shaking as more tears come.

"Yes. Your father was the man Evgeni sent to kill Desmier and his mother. He killed Desmier's mother, then took Desmier and tortured him for weeks. In the end, he locked him in a barn and set it on fire."

By the time she's finished talking, I'm crying and shaking so much I see stars.

Ehlga gets up and approaches me, then she pulls me into her arms and holds me.

Gytha was right. Oh my God, she was right.

"Don't cry, Anastasia."

"I can't stop. My father is evil, Ehlga. He's evil." When I think of all he's done, I'm so ashamed. Yet part of me feels like I always knew something truly horrific had happened.

Just like my nightmares. I know Dad is lying about that, too. So, only God knows what the hell happened to me, or what I saw and can't remember.

All the pieces of the puzzle of how I ended up here have fallen into place, and the picture it's created is damnation.

"Desmier must hate me, too."

"No. He doesn't hate you. Listen to me." She cups my face. "I told you all of this because I can see you both love each other."

"You think he loves me?"

"I do, but I think you already know that for yourself."

When I think of all the things Desmier has done to show me he loves me, I know it's not a question I should even ask.

Look what he did with the oil company. He gave away his ownership to me so it would all belong to me. He told me he chose me over the money. The fact that he even told me about the oil company is everything. I've been kept in the dark for so long, but he pulled me out into the light.

"I do know," I mutter.

Ehlga smiles. "Then if you do love him, too, fight for what you have. Don't give it up. It will be something you'll both regret."

"How can I even face him?"

"You do it with an open heart and remember you are not your father. You are Anastasia. That's all you need to be. That's who he fell in love with." She nods and gives me a little smile. "You should go see him later. Okay?"

I think about it, pushing past the guilt ravaging my mind, and I nod.

CHAPTER THIRTY-SEVEN

ANASTASIA

I make my way up the wide, sweeping stone steps of The Langham Hotel and the gentle night breeze lifts the ends of my hair.

As Leif is so distinguished in the Knights, and generally throughout Boston, I'm not surprised his retirement party is being held at one of the city's finest hotels.

It's located right across from Boston Harbor, so the slight salty scent of the sea tickles my nose. A little distraction from my shaky thoughts.

I'm not a hundred percent certain about this idea of just turning up and seeing how things go with Desmier, but I'm doing it.

This is me trying. This is me fighting for the pirate man who holds my heart.

The doormen open the doors for me, and I walk in,

immersed in the music and people dressed in formal wear. It's almost a déjà vu moment from the fundraiser, but this time I'm by myself, and people notice straightaway.

The hotel's facilities have been booked out for the event, so everyone around me is here because of it. But there is no mixture of what I call *normal* people and those who belong to the Knights.

Those around me are either from the Knights or the Bratva. There are also those from the alliance. As such, there's a different vibe in the air. Something that commands authority and attention.

Immediately, I feel out of place, but I push those feelings aside.

I'm not here for these people. All I need to do is find the one man I came here for.

As I walk through the ballroom, I search the crowd, but I can't find Desmier anywhere.

I head across the room out into the other foyer, which has a balcony.

That's where I see him talking to Leif.

My heart warms just from seeing him. Instead of the few days that have passed, it feels like years since we last saw each other.

I hope I can fix this, but more than anything, I pray he can look at me as Anastasia again, not Uther Sidorov's daughter.

Whatever Desmier and Leif are talking about looks important as they seem deep in conversation. But Desmier must feel my eyes on him because he glances my way and our eyes lock.

We're about thirty feet away from each other, but the intensity of his stare is so potent he could be standing right in front of me.

Heat streaks through me, warming every particle in my body just from his stare.

But I can't tell what sort of mood he's in. He looks neither happy nor sad at seeing me. He's just looking.

I stare back, thinking of everything my father did to him. I almost feel like abandoning this plan and going back the way I came. But I know if I do, I'll regret it. Just like Ehlga said.

With a deep breath, I summon the strength from my heart and continue my path across the foyer to the stairs that will lead me to him.

It's only when I reach them that I look away from Desmier and take the stairs up.

When I arrive at the top and walk onto the floor, someone calls my name.

It's Viktor, and I'm determined not to make tonight go as badly as it did at the fundraiser.

When he rushes up to me, I stop, turning to face him, ready for whatever he's going to say to me. Good or bad.

"You're here." His voice takes on a softer tone than the other night, without that vindictive air.

"I am."

"I would have tried to call you, but I didn't want to make things worse."

"There was no need to call me." The coldness in my tone is new and invigorating. All my life, I practically worshiped this man. It's good to have the smoke cleared from my eyes.

"Yes, there was. Anastasia, I'm sorry. I'm sorry for everything. I still want to be with you. I'm still fighting to be with you."

"You don't need to do that either. Viktor, I don't love you. I'm not sure I ever did." I wish I could lash out about the vineyard, but remembering Desmier's words about the possible plan to kill him keeps it locked in my mind. "This has to end here. I'm in love with my husband."

Viktor's eyes narrow, becoming dark pools of venom. He doesn't answer, but when his gaze shifts from mine to over my shoulder and hatred amplifies his stare, I know there's only one person he could be looking at like that.

So, when I turn and see Desmier, I'm not all that surprised.

From where he's standing and depending on when he got here, he would have heard what I said to Viktor. He certainly would have heard the last words I said, which were the most important.

Without another word, Viktor turns and walks away. Although I know I just added another wedge into a messy situation, I made the right decision and my heart feels free.

I walk toward Desmier and stop a breath away, searching his eyes as he gazes back at me.

I hope he can see how I feel because this is the no-holds-barred version of me. It's everything. My heart is in my hands, and all that I feel is beaming from me like a beacon of light calling this sailor home.

His eyes roam over my long black evening gown, which isn't that different from the last one I wore. When he reaches out to lift a lock of my hair, I feel more at ease, and I realize the door is open for me now. I just have to take the chance and walk in.

"Valkyrie," he says, and parts of my heart heal just hearing him call me that. "Every man in this building has his eyes on you in this dress."

"I just need one guy looking at me."

"He is."

"Then I hope he can look into my soul and see how I truly feel about him."

The guard drops from his eyes, and he inches closer. I inhale him, committing his scent to memory.

"Be careful, Valkyrie. The angel shouldn't fall for the devil."

I have the perfect answer. He thinks I'm the angel, but I'm not. It's him. He's the avenging angel, while I'm the devil's daughter.

"Then maybe you shouldn't fall for me." I feel like I'm crawling over thin ice just by saying that, but I needed to. And I need to trust that this strong connection between us is solid enough to keep us together.

Desmier touches my face, bringing his nose to mine. As he looks at me, I wonder if he can tell that I now know about the past and what my father did. It's the only reason why I could have said what I did.

"It's too late. I've already fallen for you."

A brush of his lips over mine renews my strength. I touch his cheek, running my finger over the scruff on his chin.

"It's too late for me, too. I think if I lived my life a thousand times, in many different ways, something would always lead me back here to this point where I choose you."

He guides my face closer to him. "Then I will always find you in every lifetime."

When he presses his lips to mine, time fades into the ether, taking everyone and everything with it. All I feel is him, all I want is him, all I need is him.

We kiss as if we need each other for our next breath, then suddenly, he's moving me away.

"Come. I need you," he whispers over my lips, then he takes my hand and leads me down the hall away from everyone.

He opens the first door we find. Dim lights pop on, revealing the interior of a storage closet holding boxes and shelves. Before I can even take note that we're probably somewhere we shouldn't be, he pushes me up against the wall.

His lips return to mine, and I no longer care where we are.

Hungry kisses rule my lips, then my mind, then my body.

When he shoves my dress up to my hips, lifts my leg, and hooks it around his waist, I'm ready for him.

My pussy is aching to have his cock inside me, pounding my mind into oblivion.

Desmier stops kissing me for a moment to shove his pants down and take out his cock. Then he grabs me, moves my panties aside, and slams right into my passage.

I gasp, throwing my head back in pleasure, and he takes that chance to push me harder into the wall and fuck me like he wants to keep me forever.

He pins my wrist to the wall, binding me in pleasure, and I savor him.

I savor the feeling of him, and us joined together. The way we should be. Always.

When he looks at me, I know he sees me for who I am.

Not the devil's daughter.

CHAPTER THIRTY-EIGHT

DESMIER

She's like a dose of fire to my soul.

Scorching and consuming everything in its wake. Owning it. Owning me.

I pound into her body like I own her, but it's Anastasia who owns me.

She owned me the moment she chose me.

I heard what she said to Viktor, and my heart tells me she knows more things that I couldn't tell her about the past and her father.

It's the way she looked at me and how she thought she was the devil, not me.

That means Ehlga told her. I trust Ehlga wouldn't have done so if she didn't think it was right, so I'm okay with it.

When I look at Anastasia, I see nothing but the woman I love. My wife.

Her blue gaze, filled with pleasure, pain, and love, is

everything, and I need nothing more in this life than what she can give me.

I try to hold on and control myself so I can keep going, but I never stood a chance. I've wanted to take her again from the moment I walked away the other night.

I come, and she does, too, digging her nails into my shoulder.

She wraps her legs around me as we kiss once more, and when we calm down, I know I need more.

"We're not done yet." My voice is thick with my desire for her.

"No, I need more. I need you."

"Let's get out of here."

I don't even know what the fuck state we're in when we walk out, but we manage to cover the parts that shouldn't be showing and leave.

Thank God I drove my car tonight. We jump in and arrive home in record time, but I'm already tearing at her dress before we can get through the door.

We barely manage to make it upstairs, where we fall into our bed, and I devour her all over again.

That's what we're like all night. We don't sleep.

It's not until the early hours of the morning that we calm down and lie together naked on the bed with the moonlight shining on us through the window.

The Valkyrie is lying cocooned in my arms with her hands on my chest. Her soft body is pressed against the hard planes of mine, but our hearts beat together as if we're one being.

In the calm, I sense even more that she knows about my past. She hasn't stopped touching me in some way. It's like she's scared to stop. I know the feeling because I don't even want sleep to take me away from her.

Or the truth. Talking about the truth will pull us from this moment. I don't want it to.

In the real world, I've spent the last few days with Zakh, Malik, and our men looking for Uther, my childhood monster, who has mysteriously disappeared.

Disappeared as in no one has seen or heard of him for days and his house is empty, as if he's moved town and country.

That motherfucker managed to blindside me and slip away under my radar. And I don't have a fucking clue what he's up to.

Him being the wielder of the poison that leaves my father hanging on to life adds to the theory that something else is going on. Something weird, considering Uther has worked for my father for a lifetime.

It's going to be something that will undoubtedly wreck my plans at some point and seek to overthrow all that I've accomplished. We're looking for Uther, but there's no way Viktor isn't involved.

He's still the only person this points to, but at this stage Viktor looks clean. Too clean, in my eyes. Which is just as much a sign of guilt as a dirty motherfucker.

I have eyes on him, but I don't know if I'm looking in the wrong place and missing all the things I'm supposed to see.

Anastasia's warm fingers trace the outline of the flowers tattooed on my shoulder, and I switch my attention back to her.

"Why flowers?" Her voice is low and cautious. When she looks at me, I see pain in her eyes again. Along with guilt.

Guilt that prompts me to address the elephant in the room. Since I got that tattoo in memory of my mother, I decide to start with that.

"They're lisianthus. They were my mother's favorites." I keep my voice even, trying not to show too much emotion as I remember how Mom used to always have fresh flowers in the house. It was her thing to do every Friday. "I wanted to carry a piece of her close to my heart. If you look closely, you'll see I have another scar, just underneath."

I look at Anastasia. Tears fill her eyes, showing her pain for me. They stream down her cheeks and she looks away from me.

"Ehlga told you what happened to my mother and me, didn't she?" I lift her chin, guiding her gaze back to me, and wipe the tears from her cheeks.

"Yes, and I'm sorry. I'm so sorry."

"I know you are. I am, too, but I don't blame you. I've never blamed you in that way. So, you mustn't either."

"I feel terrible. I can't believe my father did all that to you and took away your mother."

"Your father was just the instrument. The biggest monster is *my* father."

"I know, but it was my father who killed her and did so much to you. He's killed the love I have for him. And I know there's more. So much more. I know in my heart that my nightmares mean something. There's something terrible locked away in my mind that's to do with my father."

"There's a lot going on with your father, Anastasia. Things that will soon become out of my control. I need you to prepare yourself for the worst."

"You allowed him to live."

I have to be real with her. No more beating around the bush. "I allowed him to live for the moment. I wanted him to lose everything first because that's how you truly punish a man like him."

More tears slide down her cheeks. "I wish I could fix it."

"Nothing can fix it, baby girl. All we can do is move forward. You and me."

"Do you think we can?"

"We're going to. Because I'm not letting you go. Ever."

She smiles through her tears and lifts herself up to kiss me.

My cock hardens again, and suddenly, I'm starved for her like I was the first time when I took her innocence. But just as our kisses become ravenous, my phone vibrates on the nightstand.

No one has ever called me at this hour. It's just after four in the morning.

A call at this hour is serious and needs to be answered whether I want to or not.

I pull away from Anastasia, who immediately looks worried when I grab the phone.

When I glance at the home screen and see it's Zakh calling, I answer straightaway and get off the bed.

"Hey," I say first.

"Sorry to call so late. We got the guy who killed the dealer, and it seems like he's the one who's been watching us."

"Who is he?"

"An asshole who works for the Triad. One of their trackers and assassins."

"Triad?"

"Yes, looks like they're involved somehow. He had pictures on his computer." He pauses for a beat. "Pictures of you and Anastasia. And old pictures of your mother."

My blood temperature rises then spikes. What the actual fuck? That doesn't make any sense. "Where is he now?"

"We're at the warehouse at the docks, in the back office. We've been trying to question him, but he's not talking. Desmier, I think Viktor's involved in some way, but this feels bigger."

"I'm on my way." I will get the fucker to talk. Why the fuck would this guy have pictures of my mother?

"See you when you get here."

We hang up, and I look at Anastasia.

"What's happening? Where are you going at this time?" She looks freaked out.

"It's alright. I have to go check something out." I feel like a liar. Especially when I take my gun out of the nightstand drawer and she sees it.

"Desmier..."

"It's okay. Please don't worry. I'll be back as soon as I can."

In the moonlight, her skin turns paler, and she feels cold when I touch her cheek and kiss her goodbye.

She watches me leave. Her worry stays with me even when I can't see her anymore. As I rush down the stairs, I wonder just how much blood I'm going to get on my hands.

I'll cover myself in it if it gets me the answers I need.

CHAPTER THIRTY-NINE

DESMIER

I walk into the warehouse and find the back office.

Leo and Kill are standing by the large metal door.

Leo is nearly as tall as the door and looks like the typical Bratva man with tattoos covering his arms and neck. Kill is tall, too, but is more built and has elbow-length black hair with shaved sides. He reminds me of a Viking warrior, especially with the runes for death, war, protection, and justice tattooed on his neck and arms.

"We're back here," Leo says, motioning through the door.

"Is our new friend still functional?" They were still trying to interrogate the guy while I was on my way.

"He is, and still not talking."

No surprise there.

They lead me inside, where I find Zakh and Malik standing together with their guns at their sides. Both acknowledge me when I walk in. I do the same then look at the bald-headed Chinese guy sitting in front of them. He's covered in blood and tattoos from head to toe. He has so many tattoos, I can't tell the blood and ink apart. I also can't tell how old he is.

The guys have him chained to a metal chair with shackles on his arms and feet, holding him in place. The chair looks like it was stolen from the set of *The Green Mile, b*ut I see why they needed it. The guy has so much muscle on him he could pulverize a man with just one look.

I can also tell why they had trouble getting him to talk. He seems to be the type to hold his silence. I haven't had many dealings with the Triads, but the encounters I've had haven't been good. I imagine, like most of us in the criminal underworld, they're keen to hold on to information.

"Who captured him?" I ask.

"Me," Leo replies. "I had to hit him with a tranquilizer powerful enough to knock out an elephant."

"Then I hog-tied him and brought him here for the roasting." Kill pushes his elbow-length hair over his shoulder, revealing the rune for death tattooed on his neck.

"What's his name?"

"Xiou Miu. That's all we have on him at the moment."

I move closer to Zakh, and he points to the table beside him that holds a set of pictures laid out across the top.

"There were more pictures, but these were the most relevant," he explains.

The pictures of Anastasia and me are the first I see. They show us in different places over the last few weeks. Some together, others by ourselves. Rage fills every cell of my body when I find the pictures of my mother next to those.

There are five of them, and part of my life drains from me when I realize she's wearing the same clothes she died in. A red jumper and a pair of black jeans, her hair in a ponytail.

The pictures are of her at a gas station in Russia. One I remember us going to when we were on the run. When I run my fingers over the image, Zakh moves closer.

Something sinister dawns on me, and I cut the guy a sharp glance before looking back at Zakh. "These pictures had to have been taken hours before my mother died."

Zakh's eyes go wide, and Malik inches closer.

"Are you sure, Desmier?" Malik asks.

"I will never forget. This guy is a tracker. He must have tracked us down."

I remember how we ran to the old farmhouse in the Moscow countryside. No one was supposed to be able to find us there, but Uther did. He came with men. It looks like this guy was one of them.

Fury makes me reach for my gun. I'm about to rain hell on this motherfucker's ass, but Zakh grabs my arm.

"Desmier, we need him alive."

I shove him off. "I'm going to make him talk one way or another. I don't—"

My voice cuts when I catch sight of another set of pictures on the other side of the table. They're of Pavel and Vittoria Butyrskaya.

"He has pictures of the Butyrskayas as well," I say more to myself than to Zakh.

"You knew them?" Zakh looks from me to the pictures.

"Yes."

I move around the table to get a better look at the photographs.

Pavel's dark eyes stare back at me. He looks exactly like I remember him. A long beard, light blond hair, and that air of authority. Vittoria looks as gentle as I remember, too, with her kind blue eyes.

"This asshole has a lot to answer for." I look at the man again and take in his expressionless face. He doesn't even look like he's in pain from whatever the guys must have done to him to cause him to bleed.

What is this man doing with pictures of these ghosts?

And what the hell is going on? I actually didn't feel like I was involved, until this.

I move over to our new friend and stare him down. I want to kill him, but I want answers more.

"My name is Desmier Volkova, but you already knew that." I'm only telling him my name because where I come from, it's polite to give a man the name of his killer so he knows who sent him to hell. "I won't hesitate to fuck you up if you don't tell me what I want to know."

Xiou gives me nothing. He doesn't even blink.

"That's all we've been getting from him." Zakh looks at me with sternness. "Silence and a few snide remarks here and there. I'm trying to find something that will make him talk."

"Good luck with that," Xiou mumbles, but he's looking at me. I keep my gaze trained on him, too.

"You don't know me, friend," Zakh spits. "I don't need luck. I just need time, and you are running out of yours."

Xiou switches his gaze from me to Zakh momentarily before he's looking at me again.

"He might not know you, but he knows me. He was following me after all." I tap the side of my head with my gun and smile like the psycho I am. "I'm going to give you a chance to tell us what we want to know. If you don't take that chance, you get to discover the real me."

Xiou doesn't look fazed by my threat. I didn't think he would, and I already know he's not going to talk for me. If he didn't for anyone else, I won't be the exception.

"Who are you working for?" That's the best place to start and, like I guessed, I'm met with his silence. "Why do you have those pictures? Did you follow all of us? Me? My wife? My mother? The Butyrskayas?"

My question garners no response from Xiou. He's little more than a stone statue with a heartbeat. Pretty soon, he won't even have that. It's time to up the game.

"Not gonna take that chance?" I try to clarify.

When he doesn't answer, I cock the hammer on my gun and shoot him right in the top of his left leg. That gets a response from him.

He howls with pain and shakes against the chair. Blood spurts from his thigh and flows onto the floor, joining the blood already there.

"Have you changed your mind?"

Still no answer, so he gets another bullet in the same leg, then I shoot him again in his other leg.

Now he's shaking, and sweat mixes with the blood that was already caked on his face.

"Anything yet?"

"Fuck you," he growls. "You won't get shit from me."

I fire a bullet in his arm, and he cries out like a wild animal trapped in a snare.

At this rate, I'll kill him and end up with nothing. But I think that's what he wants.

I've shot him in non-vital places, but he can still bleed out if he continues to lose this much blood.

That's okay. I have other methods of torture up my sleeve, and I can keep this fucker alive all month if he's willing to play like this.

While he's panting, I throw a punch in his face, cracking his nose. I keep going until his front teeth fall into his lap.

He's a bloody mess, as are my knuckles, but I'm not tired.

What I am is fucking annoyed. I've been at him now for at least an hour, and the suspense of not knowing what the fuck is going on could well kill me.

"Fucking talk!" I sound like a ravenous beast unleashed from the darkest place in hell.

"Fuck... you." Xiou coughs blood.

"Desmier," Zakh suddenly says, rushing up to us. He holds out his phone to Xiou, showing him a picture of a woman holding two small children at her sides and a baby in her arms. "Maybe this will make him talk."

Xiou's eyes go wide. He looks terrified. A sudden change to what he was before, as if he's just swapped personalities.

"No. Please." His voice takes on a higher pitch.

"I told you I just needed time." Zakh throws a punch in Xiou's face and kicks his shin. "Maybe you'll tell us what we need to know in return for the lives of your wife and children."

I don't know what the fuck Zakh did to find this information, but I thank Odin for it, because I was about to kill this guy just for being annoying.

"Talk. Now!" I shout. "Tell me what I need to know."

"Please don't harm my family. Please. They are not a part of this. Please."

"If you want them to live, you need to talk right the fuck now."

He nods quickly and off balance. "Uther Sidorov and I have been working together for over twenty years. I am his link to the Triad, but I don't work for him."

"Who are you working for, then?"

"The Mark."

"Who the fuck is that?" I've never even heard whispers of such a person or group, and I'm a man who makes it his duty to know his enemies. Those who are active, and those who could potentially become a threat.

"I've never seen their faces. All I do is take orders. I can find people no one else can. I track and kill if I need to."

"Did you track my mother and me?" I need to get it off my chest.

"Yes."

At his confirmation I want to kill him again, but I tamp down my rage. There's something serious going on here, and I need the whole story.

"Tell me everything about the Mark."

"They run a human and organ trafficking ring for which my people organize the sales. They sell everything from babies to young women, and when they can't sell them, they harvest their organs. The business is a multi-million dollar one that has been running for decades."

"Decades?"

"Yes, decades. At least twenty-five years."

"Does my brother Viktor have any involvement in this?"

"I don't know. I've never seen him or taken orders from him."

His answer seems to rule Viktor out. So does the time-frame and the presence of the pictures of my mother and the Butyrskayas. But I haven't completely ruled him out yet. My gut tells me there's some sort of link. I just have to find it.

"What about my father? Why was he poisoned?"

"Viktor promised Uther more money to pour into the oil business once he took over from your father. Since your father had no plan to retire, the poison was to make that happen quicker. Your arrival turned everything upside down."

His eyes flit back to the phone in Zakh's hand, then he looks back to me.

"Keep going. The pictures of the people you have all share something in common. What is it?"

"You are all threats to the Mark's plans. Everything we do is based on securing the funds we need to carry out the business."

"What sort of threat was my mother?"

He shakes his head. "I don't know. At that time, I was new. I didn't know much. I'm still not told the details of various plans, but I have ways of finding out."

"How about you tell me the rest of what you know?"

"Everything else was about securing the fortune from the oil field under the vineyard. It was important that Uther got it."

I glance at Zakh, who looks just as stunned as me.

"What about the Butyrskayas?" Zakh asks.

"Yes, even them."

"Where did they die?" I cut in.

"In this country, but that's as much as I know about them. I tracked them to New York, then they fell off my radar. Uther can tell you the rest."

I knew I was right about Uther's connection to the Butyrskayas. That motherfucker also knew there was nothing to pin on him. He knew I would have to get that intel from an asshole like this.

"What connection did the Butyrskayas have to the vineyard?"

"It's about his daughter. She's worth more to him than an oil company masking as a vineyard. That's why he's trying to get her back. The secrets from the past lie with her. Secrets she mustn't remember, or everything fails. The Mark doesn't want that to happen."

Instead of the rage and fury that were fueling me, a shiver of fear grips me. "What happened in the past?"

"She saw things she shouldn't have seen. I don't know what they are, only that those secrets must be kept buried deep in the earth."

Fuck. Fucking Uther.

I truly believe now that Anastasia's nightmares are memories, and I think I know what she saw. I think she saw what happened to the Butyrskayas. If Uther killed them, that would have been enough for the Knights to kill him and his family, wiping out any plans he had with this Mark person.

Xiou coughs more blood. "I was to watch you and find opportunities to take her back. They want to kill you, and when she is of no use to them, not even Uther will be able to protect her. She knows too much, whether she can remember it or not."

Damn it to hell. I can't let that happen. I can't. I can't lose her.

"What else do you know?" I grit my teeth as panic takes over my mind.

"Nothing, nothing more. I swear. That's everything."

"Then it looks like you're of no more use to me." I cock the hammer on my gun again, the sound drawing terror to his eyes.

"More will come to replace me. It won't end here. They'll just keep coming until they get your wife."

"Let. Them. Come."

I shoot him in the head.

CHAPTER FORTY

ANASTASIA

"Have more tea, dear. It will help." Ehlga taps the back of my hand.

She gives me a warm smile, but the worry in her eyes gives her away.

She looks just as worried about Desmier as I am and seems to be doing her best to not just calm me down, but herself, too.

Across the table between us are the cups of chamomile tea and coffee we've consumed. Only God knows how much we've drunk between us since before the sun rose.

We switched from tea to coffee about an hour ago.

I was already in the kitchen, sitting here at the breakfast table when she came downstairs. I couldn't sleep after Desmier left.

I assumed he must have contacted Ehlga at some point

because she knew he'd left the house on *business* before I told her.

"I think I'll pass, Ehlga."

Her shoulders slump. "Then I should make you something to eat. It's breakfast time now."

"No, I'm not hungry. I'm just worried." I've never seen Desmier leave the house with a gun.

I'd only seen the gun once before, when he pulled it on Viktor. I don't even know if it was the same gun, but it frightened me. It's silly because this is the world I live in. I grew up seeing my father with guns, and knowing what he did with them, as well as what could happen to him. Sometimes my father would get shot. He's sustained several injuries and been in the hospital more times than I can count.

It's the darkness of the mafia.

Desmier has been gone for hours. That can't be a good thing. I keep imagining someone calling us with news that the worst has happened.

"Try not to worry." Ehlga nods.

"You're worried, too."

She gives me a light chuckle, and her tension eases from her expression. "I always worry, and I'm used to him being away like this. You'd think I'd be less of a worrier by now."

"I don't think it's something you can get used to."

"You're right. I usually try to feel comfort in knowing that Desmier knows how to take care of himself."

I believe her. "Yes, I think of him that way, too."

"It's nice knowing you guys are okay."

"Yeah." I'd told her we made up, but I kind of think she knew that part already. Her room is on the other side of the house, but when we returned from the party last night, we were already tearing at each other's clothes, and not quietly. People would definitely have heard us. "Thanks again for encouraging me to go to the party and talk to him."

Her smile widens. "You don't have to thank me for that. Honestly. I just gave you a little push. You did the rest. Knowing him, I'm sure he already missed you."

"You think so?"

"I know so. I'm sure he knew you missed him, too."

"God, what am I going to be like when he goes back to sea?" I'm smiling and I sound like I'll be fine, but I don't think I will be.

"I think we'll be just like this, you and me. Then we'll hopefully get used to him being gone."

"Does he go away for so long because he has to?"

"I'm sure his work is integral to the company, but I think he genuinely loves living at sea. There's something about it that feels like home to him. I think it's because he's never really fit in anywhere, but he can make himself fit there. For most of his life, he's gone by one name or another, he couldn't be part of his family, and he wasn't really mine. At sea, he's just Desmier."

"I understand." I remember what he was like when we were in the Caribbean. It was magical to watch him, and I felt like I was in another world, living a different life.

"He's never had a wife before. That might change things."

"I hope it does." I can't imagine being away from him for months. Look at me now; I'm a mess. And I'm sure Gytha would try her best to get her hands on him.

The sound of the front door opening has us both turning

our heads.

I'm the first to get up and run through the door, rushing out to the hallway to find out if Desmier is home and if he's okay.

It's him, and he looks as okay as he did when he left.

I keep running right into his arms, only relaxing when he holds me.

"I was so worried." The words just fly out of my mouth, straight from my heart.

He holds me close, but I can tell something is wrong.

"I'm okay." He gives me a kiss.

We pull apart, but he still keeps his grip on me. Ehlga walks into the hallway and smiles.

"I'm glad you're okay, too," she says.

He looks at Ehlga with worried eyes, and I'm even more certain that something else is going on.

"Can you call Volkova Inc. and let them know I'll be away for the next few days? Just get my secretary to rearrange everything."

"Of course." Ehlga dips her head and leaves us, but there's a tremor in her step.

I turn back to Desmier and take in the tension clenching his jaw.

"Desmier, what's going on?"

"Come, we have to talk about some important things. And I have something to show you."

"Okay." I search his eyes, looking past the worry, and I see fear. Since I've known him, he's been a force to reckon with. I didn't even know he could be afraid.

"Come."

He takes my hand and leads me to the hallway near his office. The one with the ghosts and the crest.

I'm surprised when we reach the crest and stop in front of it.

"What are we doing here, Desmier?"

"You'll see. This is the purpose of the crest."

He touches the crest, pressing his hand to the wolf's nose, and I gasp when the whole face sinks in and the wall slides open, revealing a passageway.

"Oh my God."

"It's a doorway." He turns and holds my gaze. "So is the crest on the cliff."

"Secret passageways?"

I think back to what Lorelai said about Pavel Butyrskaya being a member of the secret squad, and this makes sense.

"Yes. This was a safe house. The crest was used both to identify the Butyrskayas' safe houses and link to secret passages."

A chill races over me. "So, I was at another safe house in the past?"

When he nods, I realize why he was so secretive about it before, and why he said the crest was special.

And... why I shouldn't have been there.

"What was I doing there?"

He touches my cheek. "I don't know, baby, but I think something did happen to you there. And I think you saw something else, too."

"What?"

"I think you saw what happened to the Butyrskayas."

My mouth drops. "Me?"

"Yes. I received some information that links your father to their disappearance, and I think your presence at the safe house suggests you saw something you shouldn't have."

I think about what he's saying and what he's showing me. This is all Dad again, and the evil he's done. "Why are you telling me this now?"

"Because I need to. I have to keep you safe. For the next few days, we're staying inside. There's a chance your father will try to take you, or we might be under attack."

"Attack? He would do that?"

"Yes. If that happens, you come straight here. If you're near the cliffs, you go through the crest opening there. Both will open just like this one and lead you away from danger. Do you hear me?"

"I'm hearing you. But what about you?"

"Don't worry about me. Just get yourself out."

"How can I do that? I can't just—"

"Yes, you must. Now come. There's more I need to show you."

Before I can say anything else, he's leading me into the passage. As soon as we step inside, lights come on and the wall closes behind us.

He leads me down the passage, which looks just like the rest of the other hallways in the house, only narrower.

"This part is a precaution in case you're followed or if anyone gets through the crest. There's a hidden wall below, with a passage that will lead you off the property. I'm going to show you the code to get in."

My mind is numb. I'm trying to pay attention and stop

myself from freaking out, but something familiar pierces through my being when we approach the brick wall ahead.

The feeling screams at me, ravaging my insides, and I don't know why the sight of the wall would produce such strong feelings inside me.

Until we get up close to it and I realize why.

At first glance, the wall looks similar to the other brick walls in the house, but I notice the difference straightaway in the line of uneven blocks. It's the slightest of differences you'd need to be told about.

The way someone told me. I just don't know or remember who. Only that I know because this is the wall I see in my nightmares.

My God... It is it.

It's it, and I think I know why I had that song stuck in my head in my dreams and why I was touching the wall.

My body becomes a dead weight and my steps slow.

"Desmier..." I tug on his arm to stop him.

"What is it?"

"I think I know the code."

"What do you mean?"

I'm about to find out.

I walk up to the brick wall. Desmier follows when I feel over the uneven blocks.

"It's here, isn't it?"

His face pales. "Yes. How did you know that?"

"The same way I know this." I tap the bricks with my fingertips and recall the song in my head. "Run and catch, the meadow's calling you home..."

I sing and tap the bricks the same way I have been in my

nightmares for years. It's only now that I realize the count matches the amount of words in the song.

On the eighth word the wall opens before me, and I look back at Desmier's shocked face.

"You've been here before."

CHAPTER FORTY-ONE

DESMIER

I walk into the sunroom with a glass of water and take note of how Anastasia looks sitting on the chair.

She's slumped against the side and looks like she's had the life drained out of her.

We've been in here for about an hour now with the doors open. We both need the fresh air. She still looks ghostly pale, and my head is still spinning.

We've been trying to figure things out and decipher where she was in her dream. She's told me her dream multiple times. Each time she's recounted it, I've tried to pick up on everything she's saying.

All I can think when I see her is that she's been here in this house before, and somehow, her past is entwined with the first people I considered family.

I can't wrap my head around it. Nothing makes sense to me, and I thought it was best not to tell her what I learned from Xiou because I don't want to freak her out any more than she is.

Right now, I have Leif on his way over, Zakh going through the Butyrskayas' records to see where Anastasia could have been in her nightmares, and everyone else either watching Viktor or looking for Uther.

While they're doing that, I'm here, pushing aside my inner turmoil in order to take care of Anastasia.

I can't begin to imagine what must be going through her head.

She looks at me when I approach. I hand her the water. Her hands shake when she takes the glass from me.

I sit in the chair opposite and watch her take a few sips, then put the glass down on the table.

"You okay?" I ask.

"I don't know. I just... don't know."

I understand the feeling. I don't know anything either. And I don't know if I should be making her stretch her brain to find out something we might not find.

The only things we've processed so far are what we already know—the crest and the secret door with the code.

As I watched her open the door, everything shifted for me and made me realize there's more to this than where my suspicions had taken me so far.

Her recognition of the crest was one thing that was suspicious as fuck, but watching her first identify the secret door then enter the correct code was something else entirely.

Something that's got to be linked to the dark secrets she's not supposed to remember.

Pavel Butyrskaya himself showed my mother and I the

passages and taught us the code. We only received it because of what we meant to him.

Only family knew that code. Not even the other members of staff. It was one thing we were never supposed to utter to anyone else.

So, how would Uther know it to teach to his daughter?

Anastasia looks at me and brings her hands together.

"I think maybe you should go upstairs and sleep for a while." I lean forward and take her hands.

She shakes her head. "No. I at least want to see if anyone finds something. And I wouldn't be able to sleep anyway."

"Anastasia, we've gone over everything. I don't think you can do anything else."

"I'm just hoping something might turn up, or it might come to me. Like the door. The moment I looked at it, I just knew someone had told me it was a secret door and how to open it." Her voice shakes nearly as much as her hands. "Desmier, I know how weird this looks, and I can't figure it out, but's that's no surprise since I'm so fucked up. I've been living in a house for two months and don't remember ever being here before, but I can open a secret door."

"You can't think of it that way. You had an accident, Anastasia, and we don't know what else happened to you."

"Or them. The Butyrskayas." She brings her hands to her cheeks, and her shoulders sag. "I think I knew them, Desmier. From what you said, I can't imagine my father teaching me the codes for their secret door. So, I need to remember. I have to. Especially if I saw what happened to them. And if we figure out where I was in my nightmares, I am going there."

"Easy, there. That might not be best."

"I need to go."

The door opens, and Leif walks in looking flustered. I realize this is the first time we've gathered like this. I wish it were under better circumstances.

I'm not sure what having Leif here will do, but he wanted to come over. At least Anastasia looks brighter for seeing him.

"Hi, guys."

"Hey."

Anastasia walks toward him, and he gives her a hug.

"Are you alright?" he asks her.

"No. I feel strange, and I don't know what to do."

"I don't think there's anything more you can do." He ushers her back to the seat and lowers himself next to me. "I've been reviewing the safe houses I know were owned by the Butyrskayas in this country. None really match up with what you've said so far. That could either be because you were at another safe house I don't know about, or one that's not in this country. But I've been thinking that maybe you could have been at another house they owned, or some other property. Your dreams seem to be fragments of events pieced together."

"I never thought of that," I say. That's a good assumption.

"How would we find out?" Anastasia asks.

"By looking at the same things we did before." Leif nods. "Because you mentioned running through a meadow, I've asked my assistant to look for properties the Butyrskayas owned that either included a meadow or were close to one. But if there's anything else you can think of, let me know."

"I will." Anastasia nods. "I really wish I could remember

more. All I have is running through the meadow and a bird flying over my head. Then it's darkness and monsters."

Leif nods, and then he seems to contemplate something that furrows his brows.

"What is it, Leif? You look like you've come up with something." I sit forward.

"The bird. I just had a thought." He turns to Anastasia. "What kind of bird was it?"

She blinks several times. "I'm not sure. It wasn't a big bird, and it was high in the sky. I'd say it had a dark color. Brownish maybe. God, I know that doesn't help. There are a ton of birds that fit that description."

Leif pulls out his phone and taps at the keys. When he's done, he shows Anastasia a picture of a Peregrine falcon flying overhead through the air.

"Did it look anything like that?"

Anastasia nods. "Yes. I think it definitely looked like that."

Leif sighs. "The Butyrskayas were friends with the Dyshekovs. They raised Peregrine falcons for hunting." He looks from me to Anastasia. "Lucca Dyshekov, the Pakhan of the Yurkov Bratva in L.A., still raises them now. I think I might have an idea, but I'll need to speak to him."

"Really?"

"It's a possibility." He switches his gaze to Anastasia. "If I'm right, it might be worth going to L.A. to see if anything jogs your memory."

I look at Anastasia, who is already nodding eagerly.

"Yes. I want to go. I'll do whatever I need to," she says.

"Then we'll leave tomorrow." I give her hand a gentle squeeze.

"Alright. I'll make contact with Lucca." Leif stands. "Can I talk to you for a second, Desmier?"

"Of course." I give Anastasia's hand a gentle squeeze before Leif and I make our way to the living room. "What's going on, Uncle?"

He bites the inside of his lip and glances over his shoulder like he's checking that we're completely alone.

When he looks back at me, I note the concern in his eyes. "I'm sure you're thinking it's beyond strange that she'd know the code to the secret passage."

"Of course, I am. I just don't know what to make of it."

"Consider this as a possibility: Zakh contacted me earlier with some information we should consider. It makes sense to me."

My scalp prickles with heat. I asked Zakh to look through the records again because I felt he might be able to find things that Gytha couldn't. "What did he find?"

"Some medical records of the Butyrskayas when they lived in Austria. They had another child, Desmier. A girl they called Mischa. Of course, she disappeared the same time they did, but she'd be nineteen now. The same age as Anastasia."

Shock crowds my lungs, then they squeeze as if tightened by a mooring rope. "What are you saying?"

"I think you know what I'm saying. Safety was a big deal for Pavel and Vittoria. Knowing them, the first thing they would have done is teach their kids that code, especially with a song."

"Uncle, you think that she's their daughter?" Just saying the words rattles my brain.

"I'm saying it's a possibility we need to consider. Especially since Zakh also found out that Anastasia's medical records were tampered with."

"In what way?"

"He found two sets of blood groups for her. One that would make her Uther's daughter, and one that doesn't. Guess which one was hidden."

"Fuck...."

"The details of her accident were tampered with, too. There's something sketchy about the location and the reports the police took from the driver who hit her. It looks like there were different reports, but we can't find the original. I didn't want to talk about it in there with her. This is the main reason I came over. You need to talk to her about it, Desmier."

"How the hell do I tell her that her parents might not have been her real parents?"

"She's your wife. You have to find a way to tell her. The deeper we dig, the more darkness we might find. If that happens, everything will get harder. Don't keep her in the dark. Not about this."

"Okay. I'll speak to her later."

"I'll check in later, too."

I nod, and he rests a hand on my shoulder. "Take care of yourselves and try to stay focused. It's all you can do."

"I will."

He leaves me, but I stay where I am with a million thoughts racing through my mind.

Anastasia...

She might not be who I thought she was.

But she's still mine.

CHAPTER
FORTY-TWO

ANASTASIA

The cool night air wraps around my body, soothing my mind like ice against fire.

It's the only thing that can balance me and calm the myriad of thoughts clashing in my head like the rough waves against jagged rock in a tempestuous storm.

And yet, my chest still hurts, my lungs still feel tight, and my heart is still fragile, like it might shatter if I think too much.

I've been here for hours, sitting on the balcony outside the bedroom. It was just after midnight when last I checked. Usually when I get like this, the pool would have seen me by now.

But the cacophony of emotions tearing me apart feels different to anything else I've ever experienced. I'm scared that if I move, I'll fade away and become nothing, not even a memory. Like *Mischa Butyrskaya.*

Is that really who I am?

If that's me, what happened? How did I get to be here, living the life of Anastasia Sidorov?

And what happened to the real Anastasia?

Mischa Butyrskaya.

I've tried on the name several times in my mind and on my tongue since Desmier gave me the shocking news that pushed me further into the dark abyss of confusion.

While I can't get used to it, the concept of me being someone else makes sense. It makes more sense than anything I've ever been told.

When I think back to how my mother acted around me for years after the accident, it was as if she didn't know me. But I thought it was because I didn't know her.

That was the giveaway—I didn't know anyone. I didn't remember anyone, and those who were supposed to know me didn't know me either.

So, what the fuck happened?

Dad, what did you do?

Dad?

He's not my father.

I'm already thinking like this is true because it's just the kind of fucked-up thing Uther Sidorov would do.

I just don't know what he did. Did he steal me from my family? Is that what he did?

Jesus.

I've been living this life for so long, slipping into another person's shoes, and I never guessed things were off because I wasn't the girl people thought me to be.

I reach for the little picture in a golden frame I picked up downstairs earlier. It's of the Butyrskayas. Pavel, Vittoria, and their baby boy.

I've seen this picture and other paintings of them maybe a thousand times since I've been here. To me they are just people. I don't recognize any of them, and I barely look like them. It's just Pavel who has really light blond hair like mine. Vittoria's is brown, and so is their son's. But Vittoria has the ice-blue eyes.

My ice-blue eyes.

I can't believe I could be here looking at pictures of my family without recognizing them as such, and I don't remember them.

The soft pad of footsteps has me lifting my head.

Desmier comes outside and walks toward me. In my angst-filled state, I'm surprised I can think of him as the most gorgeous man I've ever seen in my life. And he just rolled out of bed with his hair a sexy mess.

He's wearing nothing but his boxers, and the moonlight bathes his dangerously gorgeous, tattooed body in a sexy silver glow.

I always want him, always need him even when I don't know I do. But is he still mine after we received this news?

He lowers his body next to me and takes the picture out of my hands.

"I wish I'd never had to tell you." His deep baritone voice, rusty with sleep, cuts into the silence.

"I needed to know. The time of truth that I've been waiting for has come. I'm just not ready for it, and if this is real, I'm not sure how to deal with it."

"Together. We deal with it together. The way husband

and wife should." He holds my gaze, and I wonder if he means those words.

Does he even know what he's saying?

"Until...you realize what this all means, and the truth hits you, too. Then you won't be mine."

He straightens and stares me down. "What are you saying that for, Anastasia?"

I can't even bear to hear him call me that. By that name. I would even prefer one of the endearments he christened me with. Valkyrie. Or baby girl. Anything.

"It's true. You took Uther Sidorov's daughter. Your enemy. If I'm not her, then you have the wrong girl, and the appeal of it is gone. All you're left with is me. When you go back to sea, you'll most likely make that your new home, and I will never see you again." I hate the way my voice shakes then breaks. And the tear that slides down my cheek.

I go to wipe the tear away, but he reaches out and does it for me.

The gesture brings more tears, and my heart warms when he kisses them away, then kisses me softly at first, then hard and desperate.

So desperate he awakens my own need and desire for him.

He grabs my waist and lifts me onto him, then picks me up so I can wrap my legs around him.

Desmier carries me back to bed, still kissing me in that devouring way I've grown used to. It makes my body come alive with spell-binding pleasure as the sensation sizzles through every part of me.

Thrills rush through my nerves when he sets me down on the bed and pulls off my nightshirt, leaving me in just my panties, which he rolls down my legs with that wicked smile he first used to charm me out of my dignity.

Now that I think back, he hardly had to do anything to charm me.

I was always his. Right from the moment we first saw each other.

I'm aware he hasn't said anything, but I want this moment so badly that I don't care. And while it would break me, if all we had was this moment where I could be with him as my husband one last time, I'd take it.

He lays me out on the bed and trails fiery kisses over my body, pausing to suck my hard nipples and lick and suck my clit.

When he has me moaning, he returns to my lips, and I taste myself on his mouth.

Moving to my ear, he licks the lobes. His warm breath strokes my skin, taming the fire into submission.

"Want to know how I feel about you?" he finally speaks. "Let me show you, my Valkyrie. Let me fuck the confusion and the pain and the sadness out of your system. Then you'll know where my heart lies."

My breath catches, stalling my senses, wrapping me in the protection of his words. I watch him take off his boxers, part my legs, then grab my hips to ram his cock into me.

The force is so strong I arch off the bed and cry out. Not in pain, but in pleasure. So much pleasure I'm robbed of every breath in my lungs.

My heart beats wildly, vibrating throughout my body in its own symphony until I'm lost in him and this moment where he's making me feel him.

He starts pounding into my body, fucking me deeper

into the sensation. I feel him everywhere. Inside and outside of me, fracturing time and reality so nothing matters but us.

He takes me higher and higher with every secret part of me screaming for more. I give myself to him, and he gives himself to me. We're no longer stealing; we're giving and taking equally. It's mindless ecstasy I want to remember forever.

The blissful pleasure turns to liquid fire, and I come hard and scream his name, pulling him under, too.

The savage energy burns between us, forcing another orgasm from my body as his furious pumps slow. When our breathing calms, he lowers himself on top of me and searches my eyes like he's looking for me inside this shell of a body I borrowed.

The longer he looks, the more I worry it's because he can't find the woman he married. But he cups my face with the gentlest touch and presses his forehead to mine.

He brushes his lips over mine and meets my gaze again.

"I have loved you since the first time I saw you." His voice holds a reverence I never thought possible from him, and his words fill me with everything I've wanted. "Love will always lead me back to you because you are my home. And wherever I go, on land or sea, you will always be at my side and in my heart. I belong to you, Valkyrie."

Elation reinvigorates my soul, and the tears that come now aren't caused by pain but by love pouring from my heart.

"I love you, Desmier Volkova."

He smiles. "I know."

CHAPTER FORTY-THREE

ANASTASIA

Leif drives down the country road at a medium pace, keeping his gaze ahead but still looking around the woodland area.

Desmier and I are in the back seat of the car. He's holding my hand in his lap the way he has been since we left Boston yesterday afternoon.

We stayed at a beautiful hotel in L.A. last night I would have loved to enjoy. But the ominous feeling in my heart forbade me.

We're on Highway 74. The route that will lead us to the lake house. One of the holiday homes owned by the Butyrskayas, and the first on Leif's list to visit. We drove onto this road about half an hour ago, and I think we're close to our destination. We're meeting Lucca Dyshekov there. He owns the property now, and Leif says he still uses the grounds to train his falcons.

My stomach is in knots of anxiety and fear. Desmier's touch is the only thing anchoring me to this world, keeping me sane.

"We're nearly there." Leif looks back at us and returns his gaze to the road. "We're probably about five minutes away."

"I'm not sure what to do when I get there," I say.

"Just look around. Have a good look around the place and see if anything triggers a memory."

"Okay. I'll do that."

If nothing happens, I'll feel terrible for dragging them across the country for nothing. But if it does...

Well, I don't know. I have no idea what I'll remember. Or if I can. I fear that part of my brain is damaged beyond repair.

If that's the case, I'll have to move on. But something in my heart tells me to keep holding on. The nightmares were gone for years before they returned. As if they'd never left. That has to count for something.

Desmier runs his thumb over my wrist and smiles.

"Just stay calm." His voice is gentle. He leans forward and kisses me, then continues to stroke my wrist. "This is only an idea we're testing out. Don't put any pressure on yourself."

I nod, but it's too late. The pressure is on, and I can't remember how to be calm.

If these people are my family, I want to remember them, and I want to know what happened to them.

Within exactly five minutes, we approach the meadow. My lungs clench at the sight of the lush green grass speckled with buttercups and daisies.

As I stare and stare and stare, that feeling from the other day when I stood before the wall worms its way into me. That feeling of familiarity. Of knowing you've been somewhere before. Even if you can't remember.

That's what I feel, and it calls to me. It screams to me the way I think it used to when I was little.

"Stop the car, Leif." My voice echoes my desperation.

"What is it? Did you see something?"

"I feel something."

Leif stops the car, and Desmier releases my hand so I can get out.

The moment I step out of the car and the air fills my lungs, the familiarity deepens. I move, walking slowly at first, then faster and faster until I'm running through the meadow.

Desmier follows me.

We stop in the middle of the field, and it feels so good to feel like I fit somewhere.

Desmier stares at me with curious eyes.

"Anastasia..."

"This is the meadow, Desmier. This is the place." I whirl around, and then I see the house way down at the bottom of the hill with the lake beside it and the woods behind.

"Oh my God. The house... it feels familiar, too."

"Come on, let's go there and see what happens."

He takes my hand and leads me back to the car. Leif then drives the rest of the way along a winding road that takes us right on to the drive in front of the two-story home.

We all get out of the car. I look over the house, hoping to remember because it's beautiful and exactly the kind of place I could imagine myself relaxing and roaming around in.

The front door opens, and a man with shoulder-length hair walks out.

He looks to be in his mid-thirties and moves with that air of authority I've seen with most Bratva leaders. When he gets a little closer, I spot Russian tattoos on his hands, and I guess he must be Lucca, the Pakhan of the Yurkov. I've never seen a Pakhan so young before, but I know there are at least three in the alliance.

"Morning," he greets us.

"Lucca Dyshekov, you look more and more like your father every time I see you," Leif greets him with a warm smile.

They hug instead of shaking hands, and Lucca smiles.

"I take that as a massive compliment, Leif Volkova. Your presence is most welcome."

"Thank you." Leif turns to Desmier and me and points to us. "This is my nephew, Desmier, and his wife, Anastasia."

Lucca dips his head.

"Thank you for accommodating us," Desmier says with a curt nod, too.

"That's not a problem. It's good to meet you both."

"And you."

I attempt a smile when Lucca looks at me. I notice the way he takes me in. I'm sure Leif must have filled him in on what's happening, so when he walks toward me, I'm not surprised by the wealth of concern in his eyes.

"Please feel free to go wherever you need to, inside and outside the house." He gives me a polite smile.

"Thank you. Do you live here?"

"No. I have a custodian who does. I come here most weekends to train my birds. When the Butyrskayas lived in the U.S, they used this home for breaks. I remember them from when I was a boy. They were one of the families who always provided my father with business because they loved his birds."

"When was the last time you saw them?"

"About twenty years ago, just before they left the U.S."

"Oh." I was hoping he might have seen them later than that.

"But I was told they came here several times a year. Have a look around."

"Thank you."

Desmier taps my arm. "Do you want me to come with you?"

I nod. "Yes. I need you."

"Then I'm here."

He ushers me ahead, and we go inside the house first.

It's beautifully decorated with a look of an old world meeting the modern, but nothing is coming to me. We head upstairs and look around the rooms before we go back downstairs, doing the same thing.

Other than feeling like I should kick my shoes off, light up the fireplace, and relax in front of it with a steaming mug of something hot, I feel nothing more than that sensation of familiarity.

Desmier opens the back door, and we go outside, heading toward the lake.

When I look toward the wood, something catches my attention and I stop. It's two twisted-looking oak trees standing opposite each other. Thick vines wrap around the branches, which grow high and wide like they're reaching for the sky.

I turn, and so does Desmier.

"What is it?" he asks.

"There." I point. "There's something about those trees."

I'm walking toward them before he answers. He follows, falling in step with me.

The closer I get, the stranger I feel. No longer feeling that sense of familiarity, but something else.

As I get closer, something pierces through my mind along with the flash of... An image?

I close my eyes briefly and see a face. It's the terrified face of a woman. The

image is there for a breath and gone the next.

When I open my eyes and my brain processes the face, I realize it's Vittoria Butyrskaya.

My God...

"Something happened here." My voice comes out in a hurried rasp.

"What happened?"

"I don't know yet."

I keep following the path, walking through the thicket of trees. The path continues, ending at a little shed ahead.

The sight jolts my brain. I stop again as a burst of memories pushes into my mind, forcing me to remember, and it's like I've stepped through the veil covering my eyes. I can see and hear, as if someone injected me into the action scene of a film.

The thud of heavy boots echoes on the ground along with the ferocious voices of men. Then Vittoria and Pavel run through the woods with terror marring their faces in the moonlight.

A tall, lanky guy runs next to Pavel, and Vittoria is carrying a little girl.

Little girl?

No...

That's me.

It's me she's carrying. She is my real mother.

And the guy next to us is my brother, Elmier.

We rush through the dark, formidable woods. Branches breaking beneath our feet as the men chase us.

Pavel—*Father*—raises his gun and shoots behind us, but the men keep coming. There were so many of them.

I see us running past the shed and hurrying deeper into the woods, where the oaks turn to giant sequoias, looking like sentinels. But the men catch up with us, and more come.

They shoot Pavel in the head, and Vittoria's screams rip through me even now.

The men get closer, looking like monsters in the shadows. But in the moonlight, I meet the face of a man with a mean-looking knife scar running from his left eye to the edge of his jaw.

The man I would come to know as my father—Uther Sidorov.

He shoots Vittoria, and she falls to the ground holding me. Then, in rage, he pulls out a knife and stabs her in her neck again and again and again.

Blood splashes everywhere, like it's pouring from the sky. When Elmier tries to help, Uther shoots him in his heart.

"Bury the bodies here where no one will ever find them and take the girl to the car." Is all I hear. It's Dad talking, but it's like his lips aren't moving.

I remember screaming and crying when someone picked me up.

Men come with shovels, and they start digging the earth.

I scream harder when they make me watch them throw the bodies of my family into the earth. All three of them. My mother, my father, my brother.

As the dirt is being thrown on their bodies in the shallow grave, I manage to kick the man holding me and bite his hands. When he loosens his grip on me, I wiggle out of his grasp and run just like I've always been told to do in danger.

The man chases me, calling after me by name. But I don't stop. I run for the road, and just as I step onto it, a car hits me.

I scream and fall to the ground, falling back to the present.

Warm hands pull me deeper to the here and now, but I'm still crying.

"Anastasia." Desmier says my name, but he sounds so far away.

"Shovel. I need a shovel," I mutter through my tears.

Leif and Lucca have now come to join us.

"I need a shovel!" Desmier shouts.

Moments later, Lucca returns with a shovel and hands it to Desmier.

"Where, Anastasia? Where do we need to go?"

Summoning my last ounce of strength, I get up and

follow the path that will lead me to what I know will be one last nightmare.

But I'll be awake for this one.

My mind takes me right to the spot by the giant sequoias where I was nearly ten years ago.

It looks the same, except the clearing of earth has a thin layer of grass covering it.

"It's here. They're here."

Desmier stares back at me for a moment, hesitation in his eyes, before he starts digging.

Lucca and Leif join him with more shovels. The three of them dig and dig and dig until they unearth the first sighting of bones.

And I see what remains of my family.

Another scream pours out of my lungs, and I faint.

CHAPTER
FORTY-FOUR

DESMIER

I make my way upstairs to my bedroom with a heavy heart.

Anastasia's sobs filled me the moment I turned the corner and head up the stairs.

We've been back for the last two days, and her tears haven't ceased. I don't expect them to. What Anastasia has been through is beyond anything I could have imagined. Or expected.

I've been with her all day, but I had a quick errand to run that took about an hour. It was already nightfall when I left, and she was asleep. I'd hoped she would continue to sleep because she hasn't in days.

I keep asking myself what I actually expected from that trip but come up with a blank every time.

Truthfully, in my heart, if I'd known that trip to L.A. was

going to destroy my wife the way it has, I would never have gone.

I would have sailed her across the globe and hidden her away from the certain pain, devastation, and despair.

Regardless of the answers we received, and the mystery solved regarding the Butyrskayas, I never would have traded that for her demise and this living nightmare she now finds herself in.

As of last night, we now know with certainty that she is Mischa Butyrskaya. We had a DNA test done on the bones to confirm everything, and it checked out. The people in the grave were the Butyrskayas, and Anastasia is their long-lost daughter.

All that confirmation, yet we still don't have the full story as Uther remains at large.

If I had to guess, my assumption would be he took Anastasia because something happened to his daughter. There is no record of anything, but there has to be.

And that begs the question of what happened to the real Anastasia.

Uther inserted my girl into his daughter's life, and no one knew the difference. I imagine they must have looked identical. I've seen pictures, and even I can't tell the difference. Uther's wife had the same white-blonde hair and blue eyes Anastasia has.

That accident Anastasia had would have helped Uther's plan massively because she lost her memories. Not to mention that the Sidorovs were gone a lot for years before that shit went down.

Children's features also change so much during that time of their life. A seven-year-old can look very different at ten years old. When you can get your hands on someone with a slight resemblance, what you have there is a solid plan and a doppelganger to make sure you still have access to a billion-dollar oil company when the daughter you stole comes of age.

Just one time I wish I could have been wrong about Uther, but I've always been right.

I push the door open, and my gaze falls on Anastasia on the bed. She looks like a doll lying there in the center. Her tiny shoulders wrack with her sobs that are louder in here and deepen the ache in my heart for her.

She's frail. That's not surprising either. She hasn't eaten since we found the grave, and whenever she's tried to drink water or juice, it doesn't stay down.

She's a mess, and I don't know what to do with her to fix it.

I walk around to her side so she can see me, and at least she reaches for my hand.

I sit on the bed, pick her up, and lie back down with her resting against my chest.

I stroke her hair, loving the feel of the silky strands between my fingertips.

"It's going to be okay. You will be okay." I whisper the words in her ear.

She clings to my shirt and lifts her head to stare at me. "I just feel so awful, Desmier. I keep trying to remember my family, but I can't remember anything beyond that night. Nothing at all but horror and death."

"I'm sorry, baby." I stroke her cheeks. "I'd like for you to see a doctor. Just for the shock."

That's the only thing I could think of that might help.

"I don't know if that will help me."

"I'm sure it will. You've been through a lot, and that will weaken you for a while."

"Okay, I'll go." She sniffles and dries her tears. "Desmier, I'm supposed to see Mira on Sunday. I think I'd still like to. She was the only person who was able to help me after my accident. We arranged to meet because she wanted to help me work through my nightmares. I think seeing her would help me now. If only to spend time with her. She's basically the only mother figure I have left who understands me."

I sigh, trying to hold back my disapproval of that idea. Mira is a nice person who genuinely seems to have Anastasia's best interest at heart. They have a special bond I never wanted to interfere with. But she's Viktor's mother. That's not going to change any time soon.

When I last spoke to her, she mentioned allowing Anastasia to have her support. This is the time when I should be considerate of that, no matter who it is.

"Please, Desmier." Anastasia's voice is small and meek, like a child's.

"Of course, that will be okay."

"Thank you so much. I also want to tell her what happened. She told me the other day that she knew something was off, but my parents never acknowledged it. She said my mother, my... other mother, always looked like she was hiding something when she mentioned it. Now I know why."

"I'll speak to Mira, so when you see her, you guys can just talk." I want to keep those who know the truth down to a minimum for the moment.

"Thank you so much."

I'm only agreeing to tell Mira because she's going to be helping Anastasia, and I've also told Zakh, Malik, and Aleksander.

He had to know because the situation has escalated to a crime the Knights will have to deal with. My saving grace now is that Anastasia is not only my wife, but she's also a Butyrskaya.

The fact that days have passed and there's been no sign of Uther meant I needed more eyes and the resources that only the Knights can give me.

I'm hoping like fuck we find that bastard soon. He has far too much to answer for to enjoy freedom even for one day. Now I regret not killing him when I had the chance.

I could have done it at the wedding, but I didn't think blowing his brains out in front of his daughter would go down well.

"What's going to happen now? How do I move forward?" she mumbles, resting her head on my chest again.

"Together, baby. We move forward together."

"I'm so glad I have you."

"And I you."

"Desmier, can you tell me more about them? My family. I mean from what you remember."

"Yes, of course I can." I would have offered before, but I didn't want to make her feel worse. It's different if she asks me.

"Your... mom loved Sundays. She used to bake these amazing cakes. I'd eat a ton before dinner and always get in trouble, bust she didn't mind."

She tries to smile. "Tell me more."

I do. When her breathing slows, I know she's drifted off.

Just so I don't wake her, I decide to stay where I am and fall asleep, too.

It seems like I only closed my eyes for a moment before my phone rings and I wake up to bright sunlight beaming through the window.

Anastasia is still out cold on my chest. When I slide her off me and onto the pillow, she doesn't stir.

I grab my phone, answering straightaway when I see it's Leif calling.

I pray he tells me they found Uther.

"Hey," I greet him.

"Morning, are you up?"

"I am now. What's going on?"

He pauses for a moment and then sighs. "It's your father. He's just woken up and is asking for you."

CHAPTER
FORTY-FIVE

DESMIER

When I walk through the hospital doors, I don't know if I should walk fast or slow. Or just turn back and go home.

I don't even know how the fuck my father knows I'm here.

Or alive.

To him, I should be dead and no longer a concern of his. How did he suddenly wake up from a five-month coma we were told he wouldn't make it back from?

And ask for me? Me, of all the people.

What about fucking Viktor? His fucking beloved. Or my other brothers. Surely, he wants to see them, too. Maybe they're already here.

With every step I take, I ask myself what I'm actually doing.

What kind of fool am I to want to see the man who ordered my death and had my mother killed?

But that's just it—I *do* want to see him.

Months ago, when I was here, it was different. Talking to someone asleep is not the same as when they're awake and they can see all that you want them to.

I guess I have today to do that. I'm just not sure it will go the way I think.

I'm meeting Leif here; we're going to see my old man together. That's what Leif decided.

I take the elevator up to the floor my father's room is on, and when I step out, I see Leif ahead waiting by the room door.

He notices me, too, and meets me halfway.

Worry taints his face, but he still rests his hand on my shoulder for his usual greeting.

"You okay?" he asks.

"I don't know. How did he know about me?"

"The doctors explained that you can hear what's going on when you're in a coma. You just can't wake up. Someone must have told him about you. Or maybe it was you."

Maybe it *was* me. "I don't know what to expect or if I should be doing this."

"Me neither, but when I got the call, I realized this is something you might regret if you didn't do it. The doctors said he's very weak and it's nothing short of a miracle that he's awake. And alive. The others are on their way, but he's asking for you."

I grit my teeth. "Alright. Let's do this. Let's go see him. Maybe he really wanted to see for himself if I was alive. I can face him and let him see he didn't win."

"Spoken like a true Viking. Let's go."

We walk toward the room, and Leif opens the door.

Numbness fills me when my gaze falls on my old man in the bed staring back at me.

He's slightly propped up on his pillows and is still attached to a multitude of tubes, but he's awake, and we look at each other.

Leif takes the lead, walking ahead of me like I still need protection, like I'm still the helpless boy he rescued from the fire that should have killed me.

My father keeps his eyes on me the whole time, and there's a sad look in his eyes that doesn't quite fit the situation.

"Evgeni, you are awake," Leif states boldly.

"The life is draining from my body." He sounds weak and like his voice is hanging on to the edge of the wind. And he's still looking at me while talking to Leif.

I wonder if he's taking in our striking resemblance the way I did weeks ago. Seeing him awake now makes me do it again, and I almost think I'm looking at the older version of myself in about thirty years from now.

"Maybe you should rest." Leif sounds tense, like when he's doing something he really doesn't want to do.

"No." My father lifts his hand, and the heart monitor spikes. "I fear I haven't got much time left, and I need to speak to my son."

Leif looks at me, but I keep my eyes on the old man.

"Why do you want to speak to me, *Father?*" I can't keep the angst out of my voice.

"It's amazing. I could be looking at myself." Something that looks like pain fills his eyes.

"I'm sure that's not what you wanted to tell me."

"No. I heard you. It could have been a lifetime ago, or maybe it was last week. I don't know. You were here, talking to me, and I heard you. Since then, I fought to come back so I could look upon you and make sure you knew the truth before I left this world."

"You know the truth," Leif cuts in, showing his rage.

"Brother, look me in the eye and tell me you believe I tried to kill this boy and his mother."

His comment throws me off kilter, and I give him a narrowed stare.

"I do not care what your eyes tell me," Leif snaps, looking like he might rip my father to shreds. "Truth is truth. You sent your men to kill Fryeda and Desmier."

"I did not," he replies, and that numbness I felt previously returns tenfold. It increases when he returns his gaze to mine and intensifies his stare.

"You deny it?" I challenge.

"I don't have to deny anything, because I am not guilty."

What the hell is going on here? This is not the conversation I thought I'd have with him. "You expect me to believe that?"

Determination shines through his eyes. "I am on my death bed, and I have no reason to lie. It won't serve me in this life or the next to tell you anything other than the truth. The truth is I would never have hurt either of you. I was told you died in a fire. Uther Sidorov gave me evidence of both your deaths. He said it was an explosion. I flew back to Russia myself because I needed to see. All these long years, that's what I believed." He looks back at Leif now. "And you kept the truth from me."

"Fryeda told me your men were hunting her and her son. They actually said *you* sent them." Leif raises a fist. "She was getting ready to meet you when *your* men attacked her at home. She barely managed to get away and call me for help. There was no way I would have told you I rescued Desmier when I believed you wanted them dead."

"It was not me, brother. You knew how much I loved that woman. I would have loved my child the same way." My father's voice is more forceful, but it looks like the energy it took for him to speak has drained him immensely. I'm drained, too, for hearing him because it looks like he was set up. "I swear it on what remains of my life. I would never do that, but someone did."

Holy. Fucking. Hell.

This is Uther's doing. Fucking Uther again. And this must have been part of the Mark's plan, too—to set my father up.

But why? I'm missing something.

Something key. Something which, once again, fucking Uther will know.

He was the harbinger of death and had to make sure all of this happened.

My father looks at me again and reaches for my hand. My stubbornness keeps me rooted to the spot, confused by the years of hatred, but that compassion Ehlga taught me touches the human parts of me, and I move to him seeing nothing but truth engraved in his face.

His hands feel so cold when they touch mine, but there's a warmth in his eyes now, just for touching me.

"When your mother told me about you, I wanted to meet you." His voice sounds even weaker now. "We were going to meet that night at the park. I waited for hours, but she never came. I feel like I'm still waiting, but I finally got to meet you, Des...mier. I was finally going to do what I wanted and marry the woman I loved. That's what I was going to do."

"Would you have?" My voice is softer as I imagine what my life would have been like if that happened.

"Yes." He coughs, and his eyelids look heavy. "I would have. It was what I *should* have done when my parents forced me to marry a woman I didn't love and deserved better. Now I love your mother with my last breath, and you the same. Desmier Volkova. I'm glad you took my name."

His lips move slowly then stop. His hold on my hand loosens, but his eyes still hold me in place, keeping me frozen in time and the deep sentiment of his words. As if we could experience all the years we lost and the life we never had in this moment.

When his heartbeat on the monitors flatlines, I don't want to look away from him and accept he's dead.

But he's gone.

CHAPTER FORTY-SIX

ANASTASIA

I gaze at Desmier sitting on the beach in the distance, smoking.

He doesn't smoke often, and not like this.

This broken version of him where he looks like the lost boy again.

The last few days have been terrible for the both of us. First for me. Then for him.

He returned from the hospital a few hours ago and told me what happened with his father.

I didn't know what broke him more—finding out the truth and not being able to do anything about it, or watching his father die and knowing it's the end.

Both were too much. Like everything else.

To say I'm still a mess is putting it lightly, but I know I need to be there for him now. The way he has been for me.

The last few days have been like none other. I previously thought the day my mother killed herself was the worst day of my life. Finding the bones of the family I forgot in that grave went beyond that. I don't think I'd ever be able to explain to anyone how I felt then. And how I feel now.

The memory I relived is still slicing through my mind with razor-sharp edges, and still burning through my soul.

One of the worst things I've had to deal with is not remembering anything or anyone else beyond that point.

The only good thing is that my nightmares have become fragments that I hope will fade eventually.

I haven't spoken to Lorelai properly yet, but she knows I've had a tough time. I wanted to see Mira first before anyone else. Just to see her and comfort her. I don't expect her to help me after losing Evgeni today. I called her assistant earlier to find out if I could still visit tomorrow, and they said she still wanted to see me.

I cross the distance to Desmier. He turns when I get closer. The waning afternoon sun beams down on him, picking out the lighter parts of his eyes and his hair.

He blows out one last ring of smoke, puts out his cigarette, and stretches his hand for me to take. I do and sit in his lap when he places me there.

"I'm sorry I've been out here for so long." His voice is low and weak. "I didn't want to be around you like this." He gives me a brief kiss, and I touch his face.

"Desmier, you're allowed to grieve, and you're allowed to be sad."

"I like being stronger around you. You need me to be strong now."

"You need me, too. So, this is me being strong for you.

Talk to me." I can see he has every emotion under the sun bottled inside him, waiting to explode.

All because of my father. Damn, I keep calling him that. I keep forgetting who I am again.

He presses his lips together and releases a haggard sigh. "Baby, I don't know what to say. My life has been a lie. Pretty much like yours. Different but similar. Leif is beside himself, and I feel like I've shut down. Nothing was ever what I thought it was. My father loved me, Anastasia. You should have seen the way he looked at me."

That sounds more like the Evgeni I knew. "I'm so sorry, Desmier. I'm sorry things turned out like this."

"I know. At least I got to see him. Apart from Leif, no one else made it to the hospital on time."

That would have been hard on everyone. "I wish there were something I could do."

"This is helping. Us like this. Me being with you."

"Do you want to go somewhere? Just somewhere that's not here, or someplace we've never been before."

He gives me a little smile. "We could."

"Could we ride your bike?"

"Of course, we can. I knew I'd drag you over to the dark side eventually."

I smile, too, for the first time in days. "Maybe I need the thrill."

"I think I need it, too. Come on, let's go."

"ARE you sure I can't get you anything else before you leave?" Ehlga asks, clearing the table.

"No, I'm fine. I was thinking of having lunch with Mira if she's up to it."

"Okay, just make sure you have something."

"I will. Don't worry."

I'm about to head out to see Mira. I'm looking forward to spending time with her, even though I'm still not able to keep much food down. I think the shock to my system from the last few days has weakened me and I caught some kind of stomach bug.

Ehlga rests a hand on my arm when I stand. "Take it easy today."

"Sure, see you later."

She continues clearing the plates away while I head out the door.

As I'll be spending the day with Mira, Desmier went to Volkova Inc. an hour ago to catch up on some work. He'll then head over to Leif's and pick me up later.

When I step outside, my phone rings in my bag. I pull it out and check who's calling.

It's the doctor Desmier wants me to see, so I answer it as I continue walking toward the car.

"Hello, is that Mrs. Volkova?" comes a lady's voice.

"Yes. That's me."

"This is Nurse MacGregor. Do you have time to talk?"

"Sure." I was expecting a call to set up an appointment, but I didn't think I'd get one today because it's Sunday.

"Sorry to call you today. We were running an extra clinic and noticed some results in your blood work from the other day that we needed to talk to you about."

That sounds serious. A cold knot forms in my stomach. Trouble with my health is the last thing I need now. I had to give blood samples for the DNA testing. I never expected anything else to be found.

"Am I okay?"

"Yes, you're fine. But we didn't know if you were aware that you're pregnant."

My legs stop so suddenly I almost trip over my feet. Then my entire body goes so rigid I fear my spine will snap in two.

"I'm what?" I rasp out, my voice sounding hollow and frail.

"You're four weeks pregnant. It sounds like you didn't know."

"No." Four weeks? How can that be? Of course, I know how, but I've been on the pill every day. "I take contraception, though."

"You must have missed a day or maybe taken them later than usual."

Shit. I cast my mind back to four weeks ago and go through what was going on at that time. Then it hits me. Desmier and I had just started sleeping together and things were crazy. The days and nights blurred into one, and I can't deny that I didn't pay attention to the time when I was taking my pills. I don't at the best of times, and I didn't when it mattered.

"I... um..."

"Take some time to process. We would like you to come in over the next few days to see us."

"Okay."

"Will it be alright to give you a call on Tuesday to set up an appointment if we haven't heard from you?"

"Yes, that will be fine."

"Great, we'll speak to you soon."

"Thank you." I'm on autopilot and still like that when I hang up the phone.

I'm pregnant. Me.

No wonder I've been throwing up and I can barely keep water down. That was the only clue, and it suddenly emerged over the last few days.

I'm pregnant. There's a baby inside me.

I feel bad for being in shock, and I feel bad for not feeling happier. Then I start to freak. Desmier said he didn't want kids. But that was before. When... when he hated me. He doesn't hate me now, but how do I tell him?

Will he be happy or mad at me for being careless?

"Anastasia!" Jayce calls from the car parked paces away from me on the driveway. I don't even remember he was waiting for me, or seeing him. "Are you okay?"

"Yes. Sorry." I make my way toward him, and he opens the door for me to get inside the car.

"You look pale. Are you sure you should be going anywhere?"

"Yes. I'm fine." I'm not fine. I feel like I'm going to throw up again, and I'm sure that will be because of nerves.

"Okay. Just checking. The boss will have my head if I take his wife out when she's sick."

"Don't worry. You won't get in trouble." I give him a smile and get in the car.

He closes the door, and minutes later, we're driving off the property.

I get lost in my thoughts, feeling sicker than sick the closer I get to Mira's house.

Two hours later, we've arrived, and Jayce leaves.

Shaky legs carry me inside the house when the butler opens the door, and I'm led to the sunroom, where Mira sits looking like a shell.

She smiles for me, but her eyes are red, and she has that emaciated look again like when Evgeni first got sick. Only God must know what she's going through.

I hug her when she stands, feeling glad I came.

"I'm so sorry, Mira. I'm so very sorry."

She dabs away tears when we pull apart. "Thank you for coming to see me. I appreciate it in light of all you've gone through."

"I had to see you. Just to see how you are. I know you can't be okay, but I still had to come and check for myself."

She motions for me to sit. I do, and she sits next to me. "I have to be strong. I knew this was coming. Part of me prepared. Part of me didn't want to let him go."

"I don't think you could ever be prepared for death," I reason, giving her hand a gentle squeeze.

"No. You can't. It's been awful not having him here, but at least I could visit him at the hospital. Now I'll never see him again and I have to make arrangements for... the funeral."

"If I can help with anything, please let me know."

"That's really sweet of you. How are you doing?"

"Not so great." That's the truth, and with another bomb about being pregnant falling in my lap, I still feel tense.

"I'm still in shock, Anastasia. When Desmier told me what happened, it felt unreal, like he was talking about somebody else. But I feel like I should have known. Your father is truly despicable. Truly."

I nod, holding back tears. "I know. Do you feel differently about me?" I'm interested to know because things will be different now in ways I might not know yet.

For a start, the Butyrskayas were Knights. Things will be different just on the basis of that.

"In what ways, dear?"

"Because I'm not the real Anastasia." When I say it like that, it feels weird. I've decided to keep my name because I've gone by Anastasia for too many years to change it. In my heart, though, I know I'm Mischa Butyrskaya. "I'm not the girl you spoke so fondly of, who wanted your wedding veil."

Sadness enters her eyes. "I don't feel any differently about you. I will always love you no matter who you are. But my heart aches when I think of what must have happened to the real Anastasia. Your father hasn't been found yet, and knowing him, I doubt he'll be cooperative in telling anybody anything."

"No, I don't think he will be."

"Did you remember everything?"

"Just the incident itself and what Uther did." Saying his name like that feels better, but it still hurts. "At least I remembered how the accident happened. A man chased me through the woods, and I ran into the road."

"Did you see what he looked like?"

"No."

"My God. This is terrible. How are you feeling otherwise?"

How am I feeling?

Shaken, terrified, freaked out because I'm about to become a mother and I don't know the first thing about being one.

A wave of nausea hits me, and I place a hand to my stomach.

"Anastasia." Mira rests her hand on mine. "You look like you're going to fall off the chair."

I should tell her what's going on with me. Or, rather, inside me. If ever I needed to speak to anyone I trust urgently, it's now. Mira is probably the best person because she'll know what to do to calm me down.

"I... just got told on the way here that I'm pregnant."

Mira's eyes widen. "Oh, my goodness."

"It's sudden. And... I don't know what to make of it."

Her face hardens and she straightens, pulling her hand away from mine. "Well, that's such a shame. I was hoping you would have closed your legs to that filthy animal. But now you're carrying his offspring."

At first, I think I misheard her or imagined what she said, but her stony glare confirms I didn't.

"What, Mira?" I ask the question anyway because I've never heard her talk that way.

"I think you heard me perfectly. I never thought of you as a whore, but maybe I expected too much when it came to my husband's bastard son."

My mouth drops and something eerie races over my skin. "Why are you talking to me like this? I'm not a whore."

"I beg to differ. You were probably in that monster's bed days after you were supposed to marry my son."

My chest tightens, and I can't deny the accusation because I was. I just don't know why she's talking to me like this now.

"Mira..."

"It's okay, dear. My plans haven't changed, and you just walked right into my trap."

"What are you talking about? I don't understand. What's going on, Mira?"

Her face changes, morphing into someone I don't recognize. "I've always known you weren't the real Anastasia."

I stand, sucking in a sharp breath that stings my lungs. "How did you know?"

"Because the whole thing was my idea."

What the hell is she saying to me?

"What was your idea?"

"To kill your parents and take you."

Stars speckle my vision, and I back away. "No, it can't be. No. You did that to me?"

"Yes. As it stands now, it doesn't matter who you are. Mischa or Anastasia. Uther legally adopted you as a precautionary measure, so you are still his heir and I still get what I want."

"What do you want?"

"The oil company," comes a voice from behind me.

I whirl around and come face to face with Viktor, who catches my wrists.

He smiles, baring his teeth.

"Viktor..."

"Yes, baby. You won't get away from me this time."

"This time?"

"It was me who chased you through the woods."

More shock grips me, and I don't know how my head hasn't exploded yet.

"You?"

"It was me. Of course, I didn't mean for you to get hit by a car. But it was convenient that you forgot. Until now."

"You bastard." I look from him to Mira, and my stomach twists like someone rammed a wrench inside me and churned up my guts. "You're both evil."

"I suppose we are." His grip tightens around my wrists. "I told you I was going to get you back. And look at you here in my arms. You won't be keeping that baby, though."

"No, let me go!" I pull hard, trying to break free of his grasp, but he yanks me to him, and I crash into his chest.

"Never. I meant it when I said I loved you. You are mine now, Anastasia. You will never see my brother again."

"No."

He presses a finger to my throat, pushes into the pressure point there, and in seconds, blackness fills my vision.

My last thought is of Desmier.

And our baby.

CHAPTER FORTY-SEVEN

DESMIER

"I'll be with you in a few hours." I balance my phone between my ear and shoulder while I pick up the last contract document from the pile on my desk.

"Try not to stay at work too long," Leif says, his voice sounding raspy over the phone. It still holds that melancholic tone I feel. "Losing yourself in work isn't always best."

"I know. I still feel off." I swivel my chair around and gaze out the window toward the skyline. Rain is falling, so outside is a little darker than it should be for this time of day. It suits the sullen mood I can't seem to shake.

"I feel the same, my boy. I've been questioning my actions and decision to keep you a secret since we found out the truth. I can't express how guilty I feel about that."

"Uncle, you rescued me from certain death. Of course, you were in the right for keeping me a secret." I know if I were him, I would have done the same thing. And I pray I'll never be in that position. "I owe you my life, and I still think of you as my father. You did more for me than anyone could. Please remember that."

"Thank you, my boy. That means a lot. Everything is just going to be hard to process. And we have yet to get down to the crux of what's going on and find out who this Mark person is."

"Yes." I bite the inside of my lip, feeling the weight of my exhaustion.

It's probably a good thing I'm not around Anastasia today. I'm finding it difficult to find myself. At the same time, being with her would have soothed me and I would have gotten to take care of her.

Jayce checked in an hour ago, letting me know he'd dropped Anastasia off safely at Mira's house but that she looked sick. Ehlga said the same thing when she messaged earlier, so I'm going to call Anastasia in an hour and find out how she is.

"I'll let you go and finish up your work. I'll see you when you get here."

"Alright, I'll be there before the others." Zakh and Malik will be joining us later. Leif thought it would be good for us to meet at his house and have dinner.

"Good, be safe."

We hang up, and when I turn my chair back to the desk, I find Gytha standing by the door.

The door was already open, so I wouldn't have heard her come in.

"Hi." She gives me a cautious smile. I haven't seen her since my father died and I briefed my crew on the truth.

"Hey. What are you doing here on a Sunday?"

"Could ask you the same thing, but since I know you, I already know the answer."

When she walks closer and sits in the chair in front of me, I notice she seems to be different than she has been for the last few months. There's less tension in her expression and she looks more at ease.

Other than talking to her about business-related things, we haven't spoken properly since the night I told her to take the job in Denmark. I truly hope this isn't going to be one of those times when we end up arguing. I'm tired of the back and forth over a relationship that can't be resurrected.

"I had some stuff to do that I didn't want to run over into next week." She nods. "And I also knew you you'd be here. I wanted to talk to you and see how you were."

"I'm as good as I can be."

"I can imagine. All this time I've known you, the goal has always been to seek retribution. I'm sorry your father couldn't have lived to give you both the chance to make amends."

"I appreciate that."

She stares at me for a long moment, laces her fingers together, and rests her hands in her lap. "I'm sorry I cheated on you."

The apology is long overdue and respected, but it's too late. "It's okay."

"It's not. I will never stop being ashamed of myself. Not just for what I did, but because I knew you were serious about me. I got scared. Everyone I love, I lose. I thought it would be better not to be serious, so if I lost you, it wouldn't hurt. But I lost you completely, and the hurt is something that will stay with me forever."

I think about what she's saying and understand her more. Maybe the same thing happened to me, but in a different way. "Time will heal you."

"I hope so. With that said, I'm happy you found true love. You wouldn't have been able to love me the way you love Anastasia because I'm not her. And that's fine. You're going through a sad time, but I can see how good she is for you." She nods and gives me a small smile, looking more like herself. "I've accepted the job in Denmark, but I'm not leaving until all is resolved."

"I'm grateful, but will that be okay?"

"Yes. They'll hold it for me. It was part of my terms. So, I'm on board to do whatever you need me to do."

"Thank you."

"You are most welcome. See you in the morning."

I dip my head, and she leaves.

I take a moment to think about everything and then finish off the contract.

It takes me a little over an hour to get to Leif's three-story mansion in South Boston. There was a traffic diversion that took up extra time. I look ahead and don't see Zakh or Malik's cars, so it seems I'm still early enough to have some one-on-one time with my uncle. I'm looking forward to spending time with Leif and taking a break.

I park on the drive next to his truck and make my way up the steps.

When I reach the front door, I notice it's unlocked. That's strange for Leif even when he's expecting visitors. His butler, Jake, normally answers the door.

I push the door open and walk in, but the faint scent of

blood hits me when I walk a few paces in, and I stop in my tracks.

In my world, you pick up on things like that, and you know there has to be a lot of blood for you to smell it. My nerves spike in an instant, and worry cascades down my spine like a million spiders crawling down a drainpipe.

Carefully, I start walking again down the passage, noticing the house is unusually quiet. Especially for a Sunday afternoon. Leif loves football and basketball, so he'd normally be watching sports on ESPN.

Jake and some of the other staff would also be talking away or moving around the house. But there's nothing but silence. The sort of silence that tells you something is wrong.

I check the living room. It's empty, so I continue down the hall.

I turn toward the dining room, and my blood freezes when I find Jake on the floor, lying in a pool of blood with bullet holes in his body. Across from him are the maids, Helen and Jessie.

Fucking hell, what happened here?

I grab my gun and look around frantically, checking to see if whoever did this is still here. Keeping my gun close, I rush down the hallway, heading for Leif's office.

Seeing the door open when I get closer makes my heart pound like a sledgehammer against my ribs. I run through the door, and my soul shatters when I see Leif lying on the floor surrounded by blood and a knife plunged into his heart.

"No... no, please. No." I rush to his side. Although I can

see the knife and the blood, I foolishly hope, pray, and beg God and the universe not to take him from me.

Not him, not him, not him.

Please, not him.

My fucking hopes fade when I notice a few bullet wounds next to the knife, and when I touch him, he's cold. The life has already left his body.

Leif is gone. He's dead.

My uncle is dead.

I couldn't save him.

I couldn't save him the way he saved me.

We only spoke a little over an hour ago. How could this happen?

Damn it. If only I'd left work earlier, or not gone in at all, this wouldn't have happened.

I look at Leif, but my brain won't accept what I'm seeing. It can't because as much as I told him, and myself, that I'm no longer the helpless boy, I am. I'm that boy again, and my world has fractured.

"Leif..."

A creak sounds outside the door. Another follows, and another.

It's footsteps on the floorboards. Since it's not coming from the front entrance, I know it's not Zakh or Malik, so it must be someone else who's already here.

Readying my gun, I get up and charge through the door. Whoever the fuck is here, and isn't supposed to be, is going to die a very painful death.

I move out into the hallway, looking around frantically to see who it is, but find nothing.

When I turn around, something sharp enters my neck;

then there's a tingling pain that feels like I'm being stung by a bee.

I touch the spot and feel... a fucking dart?

I pull it out and look at the sharp needle at the end, quickly realizing when spots speckle my vision that it's a tranquilizer. Like the kind our enforcers use when they want to bring people in for interrogation. Before my mind can truly register what's happening, my arms go numb then limp at my side.

This can't be an ordinary tranq. I'd be out like a light by now if it were.

This is something else. Something worse.

Ice spreads from my neck to my shoulders then shoots up and down my body.

The gun falls from my hand, along with the dart, and I drop to my knees on the hardwood floor.

Seconds later, I'm completely on the ground and my vision blurs.

Those footsteps sound again, but they sound different this time. Like heels click-clacking against the floorboards.

At first, I'm not sure if I'm thinking that because my brain has turned to mush, but when Mira comes into my view wearing six-inch heels and a white fur coat, I know what I heard was right.

The smile on her face suggests I'm about to receive more answers I won't like.

But that smile... that sinister smile painted on her thin red lips as she watches what might be my last moments tells me everything I need to know.

It's like a punch to my gut and truth without words slapping me in the face like the hostile wave of a tsunami. One that devastates my mind when I think of Anastasia. She's supposed to be with Mira.

We both look at the dart, and that smile of hers grows wider, becoming the kind of triumphant a conqueror of nations would wear.

"It's a special blend I had the labs concoct for me." Her accented voice is dripping with power. It's no longer meek like it was months ago when we met and she appeared to be the grieving wife. "I got them to mix Deadly Night Shade along with a lower dose of etorphine and a phenothiazine, just so I could speak to you. I didn't want you to just hear me; I wanted you to listen."

"It was you, wasn't it?" I can barely speak. My mouth is hardly moving as the words spill out.

"Yes. It was me, dear boy. I am the Mark." She laughs.

"You're the Mark?" A pang of shock slams into my chest. I thought she was going to say she worked for the Mark. I never expected it to be her.

"Consider yourself lucky. Only a handful of people in my establishment, like Uther, know that. Everyone else assumes I'm a man. A powerful mafia boss with all sorts of wicked ideas up his sleeves. They never expect the psychiatrist, or the woman who does bake sales at her local church, or the organizer of the floral arrangement club at the country club. They certainly would never expect it to be Mira Volkova, wife of the recently departed Evgeni Volkova."

Fucking hell. I don't know how I missed this. During my entire time here, I never went soft, not once, but she blindsided me.

"Why would you need to become the Mark? Your family

is wealthy." I can't understand why she'd need to build an establishment based on shit like human and sex trafficking.

"That wealth was never for me. It was for my husband. The same husband who only married me to please his parents and fulfill his duty to the Knights." She grinds her teeth, and the vein in her neck tightens. "I sound like I hated him, but I didn't. Not the way you think. The poison I slipped him wasn't supposed to kill him either, but Viktor gave him too much. I just wanted Evgeni out of the picture so Viktor could take over. We needed the wealth from the Volkova empire after losing millions in a deal that went wrong."

"You fucking bitch." It was all on her—the bitch, and her son. At least my instincts were right about Viktor. He was involved, and she just covered his tracks so everything looked legit and switched the focus to Uther.

"The fucking bitch is what you have to become when you live in a world of villains and monsters who own you. I was promised to your father from birth. Just like Anastasia, my parents bread me to love him. But the difference between us was, I was madly in love with your father. Madly and deeply. That was never a lie." A tear runs down her cheek, and she quickly wipes it away. "It hurt me to no end that he never loved me, not even when I thought things were good between us. He never stopped loving your mother and grieved for her, and you, his bastard son, right up until he slipped into that coma. I found him looking at these mere hours before. I didn't even know he had them."

She reaches into her bag, pulls out a stack of pictures, and throws them down beside me so they scatter.

They're all of my mother and me. Pictures Mom must

have given my father. There are some of her holding me on a chair when I was too young to remember, and some of me as a baby. The others are a mixture of me when I was older and a bunch of my parents when they must have been teenagers.

My insides twist on seeing more evidence of how wrong and mistaken I was.

My father truly loved my mother and me. Both Leif and I were led down a misguided path of revenge on an innocent man. But Leif was still right to keep me a secret because this woman here is the real devil.

"I always knew about the cheating." She regains her former strength. "That day I came to see you, I was only there to determine what I was up against. When you took the fall for the meek little wife, obviously under Leif's instructions, I knew I had you right where I wanted you."

My lips move, but I can't say any more.

"I always knew Evgeni never stopped being with your mother even when she was with other people. She moved to Russia because she couldn't stand seeing him with me. But he took every chance he could to be with her. Then the day came when I overheard your mother telling him about you. That changed everything for him. He was going to leave me, so I sent the men to kill you and your mother. I thought my loyal dog, Uther, did everything right. Imagine my surprise when you turned up at my son's wedding and stole his bride."

I grunt, and she frowns.

"I didn't know what shocked me more—that or knowing Leif saved you. But poor Leif has finally met his end. Things are back on track now."

"Ana...stasia," I garble. My voice sounds like it's being chewed up by a shredder.

"Don't worry about Anastasia. Uther and I have a long-standing arrangement for his faux daughter. I scratched his back and helped him climb the Bratva ranks. Now it's time for him to pay his dues." She laughs again, and I have no voice left to ask any more questions about Anastasia. "You sent your wife right into my trap. All these long years, we watched her, making sure she didn't remember what happened to her and her family. The goal was to get her back, and now we have her far, far away from anyone who can take her from us. I'll get the oil company, and Viktor will get the girl he loves."

No. No. No.

She reaches into her bag once more and pulls out a black block with wires attached to it. My heart gallops when I realize it's a bomb.

"One last parting gift, Desmier Volkova. Sometimes you have to do things yourself to make sure they get done." She sets the bomb down right beside my face. On the front of it is a picture of my mother. Dead. Just like how I last saw her. She's lying on the floor with her neck broken and her eyes wide. "That picture is mine, but you can have it."

She gives me one last smile and then taps the top of the bomb, activating it to give her two minutes to get out.

The clock starts ticking, counting down in tandem with her steps as she walks away, never looking back.

The clock ticks, and as I watch my mother's face, my body continues to shut down.

Then I think of her—Anastasia.

My wife.

My Valkyrie.

My love.

She needs me.

I remember what Xiou said. That the Mark would get rid of her when they had no use for her. That's what Mira plans to do.

I can't let that happen.

I can't abandon my wife to such a fate. To death.

The thought makes me move my legs. God, there's still some life left in them.

Behind me is a window. If I can just get to it, I might be able to escape and land in the garden.

I can already feel the ice working down my body, and I have one minute left before the bomb goes off.

Summoning every strength left inside me, I move my body, wiggling at first, then I manage to get back up onto my knees without using my hands.

I push myself forward, slipping and sliding, my vision snapping in and out as the shit Mira gave me continues taking effect. But I fight, fight, fight, moving myself forward.

I reach the window, use my head, and ram it open. Then I push myself through just as the bomb goes off, exploding.

I'm falling. But I don't even know if I make it out alive.

CHAPTER FORTY-EIGHT

ANASTASIA

I roll my head to the side and groan. Someone strokes my cheek, and I open my eyes.

At first, my vision is hazy, but when everything comes into focus, I find myself staring at a gray concrete wall. The light around me reminds me of the kind you'd use for a storage room.

My cheek is stroked again, and I turn my head to find Dad hovering over me. He has a long beard, blood-shot eyes, and his face looks like someone did a number on him.

We're on the floor, and my head is nestled in his lap. It takes me a moment for my brain to connect and remember. Remember all he did and what he took from me. My family and my life.

The instant I remember, I scream and jump out of his hold.

"Get away from me!" The panic in my voice is mixed with rage and fear.

"Anastasia, please."

I back away into a wall, crashing hard against the surface. Then I notice the real problem we've found ourselves in.

We're in some sort of cell, and while I am free, there are chains attached to Dad's ankles, keeping him confined to the wall.

I look around the small unit that does indeed look like a storage room. Except I've never been in one that was equipped with chains to hold a person, or people, captive.

It's a standard box room with a metal door, but there are chains with manacles all along the wall Dad is on.

I recall how I got here and how Desmier has been looking for my dad, who isn't really my father. I've just found him, and he's in the same situation as me.

Mira and Viktor. I remember what they said and did.

I remember the truth Viktor revealed just before he knocked me out.

But what's happening now?

"Tell me what's going on." Although tears burn my eyes, I hold them back. I can't fall apart here. I mustn't. "Where are we?"

"At one of Mira's secret facilities. They're keeping us here for transportation."

"To where?" My voice rises by several octaves.

"Russia."

"No. They're not taking me."

"Anastasia, please calm yourself. It's not good for you to get worked up in your condition." He searches my eyes, and

I guess he knows I'm pregnant. "They told me about the baby."

"Did they also tell you they're going to try and take it from me?" Saying those words hurts my heart. I've only just found out about the life growing inside me and had it threatened in the same breath.

"Not if I can help it. I'm going to try and get you out." There's a different determination in his eyes I've never seen before, but I don't know how the hell he plans to do anything to help me when he's a prisoner, too.

"How are you going to do that?"

"I don't know yet, but I have to try. You are my daughter." A tear runs down his cheek, and he nods. "It's my duty to take care of you."

He sounds like the man I know, but he's too late to fix anything with me.

"I'm not your daughter. You killed my parents, and all of this is happening because of you."

He dries his tears and brings his hand to his head. "I'm so sorry."

"No, you don't get to say sorry. You killed them. All of them. You and Viktor were my monsters."

"I am truly sorry, Anastasia. I can't take back the past, but please know I love you."

He looks like he really believes that. Part of me believes it, too, but I no longer care how he feels. What I want is the truth. The rest of it. All the parts I don't know.

"If you love me, tell me what happened. Tell me how this happened. How did a woman like Mira become so evil? What the hell were you guys planning?"

"She was always evil. Always. But so was I. That's why

this is happening." He drags his knees up to his chest, looking like he's aged by a hundred years in just those few seconds. "I take it you know the majority of things."

"Yes. I know what happened to my family, and I know how my accident occurred. I know what you did to Desmier and his mother, and I know the vineyard is really a billion-dollar oil company. What I don't know is how you could be this evil. And what happened to the real Anastasia?"

More tears flow down his cheeks, and I swear I've never seen a person look more broken. "She... died."

Despite my turmoil, a wave of sadness hits me. In my heart I knew death had to be the answer because it always is. But I didn't want to jump to conclusions.

"How did she die?"

"She drowned." He drags in a deep breath and continues. "As a Sidorov, I was never going to have the chance to climb the ranks in the Bratva. Mira gave me a way to do so when I started doing her dirty work. The mission that defined me and set me up for life was killing Desmier's mother. That was how I first got close to the Volkovas and how the marriage contract first came about. When Mira wanted to secure her marriage and prosperity, I gave her that. Then, when we found out the vineyard had oil, it was everything to her, and her plans were a way for me to get some ownership of it. She pumped the money in to set up the company and kept it a secret. She knew if she could get her hands on the ownership, even through her son, it would be a done deal. He would own half, and so would I, providing it was given to me, then I'd give him forty percent more of the ownership. It didn't matter who was killed or hurt to achieve the goal because to Mira, it was worth it."

"So, when the real Anastasia died, that threw out all the plans." My voice is barely audible.

"Yes."

"Then you met me and my family?"

"Yes. Everyone was in Russia that year for the entire summer on a business trip. The Volkovas, the Sidorovs, and a few other families. We stayed at the same resort. While the men were working, the wives and children hung out. My Anastasia found a little girl who looked just like her. That was you, and it was how we first met the Butyrskayas. The two of you were always together. People thought you were twins, and you pretended to be sisters."

He pauses for a moment, giving me a chance to think through his words. It's devastating to hear these memories and not remember even a little part of it.

"It was so strange how you looked like her. The only differences were that my Anastasia had a little mole on her cheek, and her eyes were a slightly darker shade to yours. The differences were so minute no one ever guessed you weren't her." He swallows hard. "At the end of the summer, the day before we were scheduled to go home, Vittoria was looking after the two of you while you played hide-and-seek in the woods. She lost track of Anastasia, and we couldn't find her. We searched everywhere, knowing something terrible must have happened. The next morning, Mira found her washed up on the riverbank. Dead. She drowned."

"I'm... so sorry." My voice chokes. "Was... that my fault?"

"No. Of course not. But I blamed Vittoria for not watching her properly, and after all this time, I still blame her."

I remember how he killed her. It was with vengeance

and rage. Like he couldn't wait to get his hands on her and rip her apart.

"She was beside herself with grief for her carelessness, but your mother—my wife—lost her mind that day." He straightens and pulls in a measured breath. "I lost my sanity, too. I was already a ruthless bastard. But in my grief, I didn't think twice when Mira came up with the idea to take you. I wasn't even thinking straight when she told me to bury my daughter in Russia and keep it a secret. She didn't even have a proper funeral."

My heart aches as I listen to him telling me everything.

"I didn't want the oil company to go to charity either, or lose out on the partnership with the Volkovas, but most of all, I wanted my daughter back." He intensifies his stare. "When the Butyrskayas returned to the States, I tracked them down. Mira set up the entire operation and even got Evgeni to agree to me staying in the States. But I took the lead, and your accident just made things easier. Although you nearly died, Mira saw it as luck that you didn't remember anything, and she made sure you stayed that way."

A chill rushes over me. "What do you mean? What did she do to me?"

"Even though she wasn't ethically allowed to be your therapist, she gave you medication to stop you from remembering."

I cover my mouth, holding in the wave of shock that's ripping me apart. I can't believe what I'm hearing. Only God knows how hard I tried to remember, but I was never going to be able to because Mira was suppressing my memories with medication. I was such a fool to believe she was the person she portrayed to be. She was never the fucking motherly figure. All along, she was my enemy.

"You allowed her to do that to me."

"I had no choice. She did everything she could to control our lives and make sure you didn't remember what happened. But the nightmares were always a worry even when they went away."

"She told me it was my brain's way of trying to remember."

"It was, and we feared you'd see something to trigger those memories. Or you'd just remember everything by some miracle. The whole thing tormented your mother every day."

"Is that why she took her life?" She might not have been my real mother, but she was to me.

"It was one reason, but not the most significant. I'd even go as far as saying she wanted you to remember. Just so it would be over. She blamed herself for allowing Vittoria to take our Anastasia out that day without her. She was never able to accept that our daughter died or live with knowing I stole you from your family. She couldn't live with the fact that I killed them. Loving you and knowing the truth drove her insane. My wife and my daughter were the only two good things in my life, but I lost them both."

"You still acted like my father after she died."

"Because to me, I was. Men like me don't know how to love, but I loved all three of you. When Desmier rose from the ashes like some goddamn phoenix, I knew it was the end, but I didn't want him to tell you what I did, or for you to find out about my crimes because you loved me. You were the last thing I had left in this world to live for." He dips his head for a moment before his gaze climbs back up slowly to meet mine. "When Desmier came to talk to me about the crest, I knew I was in more trouble, and worse when he asked me if I knew the Butyrskayas. Before that, I never took any notice of the crest when you told me about it because I'd never seen it before. His questions made me realize Pavel Butyrskaya must have been a member of the Pakhan's secret squad. There were whispers about it when the Butyrskayas disappeared, but I never thought about it before. None of us did. Nobody even knew that Desmier's home used to belong to them. Not until he told me. Last week, when he captured one of my trackers, it was all over for me. Mira has kept me here since."

"What is she going to do to you?"

He gives me a wry smile. "Kill me. I'm like an animal waiting to be slaughtered. I've slipped up too many times and am a liability now. If the Knights know about Mira and Viktor's secret plots, they'll execute them. They're already out for me because they now know I killed the Butyrskayas. And right now, as we speak, Mira is trying to find a way to get rid of Desmier."

Desmier. My God, what are they going to do to him? He thinks I'm safe with Mira. I don't know how much time has passed since I was out, but maybe he knows by now that something has happened to me. Or not. I said I'd be away all day, and he was going to Leif's with Zakh and Malik.

When I asked him if I could see Mira, I knew he was hesitant. I wish I hadn't asked now. It was me who got myself wrapped in the trap.

"They want to kill him and invalidate any plans he has to transfer his half of the oil company to you. That way, you can marry Viktor, and it will be his. Then it will only be a matter of time before they kill you."

"Kill me?"

"Or keep you. But Viktor is a jealous man. He fell for you, and he loathes the fact that you want to be with Desmier. Before this day ends, you might not even have that baby in your stomach."

That does it. The tears I was holding back stream down my cheeks. "I can't let that happen."

"If they get Desmier, you'll be on your way to Russia at least by tomorrow. That's when you need to try and escape."

"Escape?"

He moves closer and lowers his voice. "I have a boat at the marina called *Silver*. I have ten thousand dollars on board and supplies that should last you for a few months if you need it."

"Dad, how am I going to escape them?"

"You have to try and find a way. I can't lose you again." As he speaks, I know he's looking at me like the daughter he lost. "I'm a soulless devil who doesn't deserve your forgiveness. Not even the devil will accept me in hell. But I love you like you were mine because you are. I stole you from your family, and it's my responsibility to try and save you. Even if it's to give you the last things I have left to help you get away from these people. I am truly sorry for what I have done to you...Mischa."

Hearing him call me by that name grips my heart, and I don't know what to say.

All my words are jumbled in my mind. I don't get the chance to unravel them because the handle on the door turns and Mira walks in holding a gun.

I marvel with disgust at how different she looks. She even seems taller. Not in height but personality and confidence.

"Your beloved husband is dead," she declares with a villainous smile.

Her words shut my body and soul down in an instant, then my heart turns over and weeps. Numbness cascades over my skin and I can't breathe. God...I can't breathe.

"No..."

Desmier. They killed him?

"I blew him up, my dear." She smirks and looks at Dad. "Finishing the job you couldn't do."

"Please don't hurt my daughter."

"You fool. You fell for our own game."

"Please, Mira. I'm sure we can come to some agreement."

"What, like her giving me the company and agreeing to keep quiet about everything? I don't think so. Besides, I'm afraid your journey has now come to an end."

"Mira, please," I choke when she raises the gun.

Dad looks at me, and our gazes lock. "I love you. I—"

Before he can get out another word, Mira shoots him in the head. Blood splatters everywhere, and I scream.

CHAPTER
FORTY-NINE

DESMIER

Everything is gray.

I'm not sure if I'm alive or dead, or in a dream.

My mind searches around the gray nothingness and the vast expanse of the void before me.

I feel nothing at first, then something warm caresses my cheek. My name is spoken, soft and sweet, and I wonder if it's her.

Anastasia. Did I make it? Did I find her? Did I save her?

My wife.

My eyes flutter open, but the grayness that looks like thick smoke prevents me from seeing anything. Then a light that's far too bright shines down on me, and I blink rapidly.

At first, the ceiling of my living room comes into focus, then a man's face hovers before me.

It's Leif's on-call doctor, Dr. O'Brien.

Leif...

Anastasia...

At the thought of their names, reality crashes into my mind and I bolt up.

"Easy, there," Dr. O'Brien says, laying a heavy hand on my chest and pushing me back down. I'm on the sofa, and a quick glance at the bandage wrapped around my body suggests I took a hit in the blast.

Gytha moves toward me, with worry in her eyes, and I realize it was her I heard. Not Anastasia.

"Desmier," she breathes. "How are you feeling?"

"Like shit."

"I had to remove some shrapnel from your back from the glass, and I've given you a low dosage of adrenaline," Dr. O'Brien explains. "Other than that, you should be okay."

"How long have I been down?"

"Nearly three hours."

Fuck. Who knows what could have happened during that time?

"Do you remember what happened?"

"Yes. Leif is..." I can't bring myself to say the words, but from the looks on their faces, I can tell they know. They know Leif is no longer with us. It hurts my soul to think those words, but I can't lose my mind now. "I have to find my wife. She was taken."

"What?" Gytha gasps. "Isn't she supposed to be with Mira?"

"It was a trap. Mira or one of her lackeys killed Leif, then she drugged me and blew up the house. She's taken Anastasia. I need to get her back."

Gytha's mouth drops open. "This is all so crazy."

"How did I get here?"

"Malik. He got to Leif's house and found you. Then he contacted us. He's in the sunroom, but there's something you need to see before you do anything."

"Gytha, I need to find Anastasia. I have to speak to Malik and see if he has any idea where Mira could have taken her."

"Trust me, you need to see this first before you talk to Malik. I'm not sure you can trust him." The worry in her eyes intensifies, gripping me and beckoning me to listen.

"I'll leave you two to talk." Dr. O'Brien backs away and leaves the room.

Gytha walks toward her laptop on the coffee table, switches it on, then looks back at me.

"We didn't know what happened, but when we found Leif and the others dead, it was clear there was an ambush. The surveillance got wracked in the bombing, but I managed to salvage this part of the recording."

"Show me."

She presses the button on the keypad, and the image of Zakh comes on the screen. He's kneeling beside Leif with his hand around the hilt of the knife that's plunged into Leif's heart. Leif is still moving, crying out in pain. Then the image cuts.

I'm so shocked my body moves on its own accord and I don't even realize I'm standing until I am.

Zakh...

Zakh killed Leif?

No, that can't be right.

"Play it again." I walk over to the laptop, crouch down so I can get a better look because I think my eyes must be screwing with me.

Gytha plays it again, and I see the same thing.

On the third and fourth go, I press the button, and it's only after I've seen the clip four times that the truth of betrayal sinks in.

Zakh. He was working with his mother and Viktor the entire time. He played me.

He fucking played me.

Even as I think of what logic is telling me and showing me, I can't believe the truth any more than I can that Leif is dead.

I look at the time on the recording and notice that Zakh must have gotten to the house just after I spoke to Leif.

And he killed him.

But it doesn't make sense. All this time, he helped me, and he was against Viktor.

Maybe that's all it was, and Mira welcomed him back into the fold with a price that enticed him enough. Everyone has their fucking price. He murdered our uncle.

And what about Malik?

"Give me a gun."

Gytha hands me her Glock.

"Now get Malik in here."

I'm still staring at the screen when she leaves.

A few minutes later, Malik walks through the door.

"Fuck, I'm so glad you're okay," he says, sounding genuine. But so did Zakh when he played the part of a brother who wanted to get to know me. "Desmier, Leif is—"

I don't give him the chance to finish. I stand and point the gun at him.

"Jesus, what the fuck?" He holds up his hands and looks at me as if I've lost my mind.

He has the haggard look of a grieving man, but I don't trust it.

"I'm going to ask you some questions, and if I don't like your answers, you're dead."

"What the hell is the matter with you? Our uncle is dead, and you nearly died."

"Your mother is behind everything."

"What?" He raises his voice and gives me an incredulous glare. "My mother?"

"She is the Mark. She drugged me and blew up the fucking house. But she had help." I press the button and replay the video for him.

He looks as astonished as me, and the blood drains from his face, leaving him sickly pale.

Despite me pointing the gun at him, he moves to the laptop, shakes his head, and does the same thing I did by replaying the clip again and again.

"This can't be. Zakh wouldn't do this."

"But he did. So, start talking, Malik. Are you in with them? Are you fucking playing me as well?"

"No, Jesus Christ, Desmier. I rescued you. Why the fuck would I rescue you if I'm with them?"

"Zakh looked like he was helping me, too."

"Think. You're not fucking thinking straight. If I wanted you dead, you'd be dead already. There'd be a bullet in your fucking head. What the hell have I got to gain from bringing you back here?" He slams a fist into the side of his leg and bares his teeth.

As I stare back at him, logic kicks in. He's right.

Mira wanted me dead. She immobilized me to make sure

I died, and she thinks I'm dead now. Why would he keep me alive if he was doing her bidding?

I lower the gun and shake off the shock. Time is ticking by, and I'm wasting it acting crazy.

"She has Anastasia. I have to get her back, Malik. Do you have any ideas about where she could have taken her?"

He thinks for a moment. "There are a couple of places we could check."

"Alright, let's go."

Grief and pain are pushed into the ether as we move.

I thought I had nothing left to lose, but Anastasia is everything. I have to get her back.

CHAPTER FIFTY

ANASTASIA

My heart has been smashed into so many pieces it's impossible to count them all. It's no different to all the grains of sand in this world.

My mind and body are disconnected, and my soul weeps for losing the love of my life. All that is left of me is an empty shell with nothing but a void inside.

The only thing I can feel is the spark of life created with love in my belly, calling to me to stay alive. But I've already failed as a mother because there's nothing I can do.

In my terror and grief, I'm here sitting on the floor of the bedroom I was taken to after Mira killed Dad, feeling sorry for myself.

I don't know what this place is. It seems like Mira conducts something medical here. Apart from the armed guards, on my way up I saw offices and labs with clinical staff. I also saw other storage rooms and bedrooms like this.

We're on the third floor, so quite high up with no possible way of escape. If I were to even try, I'm sure this shitty tunic Mira forced me to wear would get me the wrong kind of attention. I look like I escaped from a hospital, and I'm sure the rest of me looks that way as well.

Dad's blood was all over me from head to toe. I've been cleaned off, but as far as I'm concerned, I could still be covered in it. My skin remembers the feeling, and that copper scent still assaults my nose. The image of so much red and the man who assumed the role as my father dead will never leave me.

I don't know what the plan is for me once we leave this place, but if Viktor doesn't keep me, I can't imagine I'll have much more time left on this earth.

He and Mira will wait until everything is official then kill me in the same barbaric fashion they murdered Dad. Then most likely return to Boston to continue their normal lives.

I'll join the dead and become another secret. At least in some ways, I'll be with my husband.

Desmier... when I woke this morning in his arms, I didn't know it would be the last time. I didn't know I'd be in the breath of day and night staring at the waning sun through this window, and he'd be gone.

Dead.

I physically can't cry anymore. All the tears inside me have dried up like a thousand-year-old well, and the void has swallowed everything else.

The wooden door opens, and Viktor walks inside with a smug smile on his face.

I can't believe I ever had any kind of feelings for this man, or that I spent weeks in confusion trying to stay true to him when I knew in my soul that I wasn't in love with him.

He moves closer and stops a breath away, glaring down at me.

"Get up."

"Fuck you." I don't care what I say anymore. I have no fight left in me. I've lost everything, and I'm just waiting for him to take my baby.

Viktor smiles, uncanny and unfazed. In one swift movement, he reaches down, grabs my arm, and yanks me up from the floor.

I shriek from the pain that races up my arm, but he doesn't care. He shoves me into the wall, and that smile of his widens.

"You stupid bitch. You think you can talk to me like that?" He grabs my face and leans closer. "This was how it was always supposed to be. You and me. You get to determine how long it will be *you and me* if you play nice, because my feelings for you are the only thing keeping you alive."

"Feelings? Don't make me vomit. You never had any kind of feelings for me. You were always a fucking cheating bastard."

"All men cheat, Anastasia."

"No, they don't. My husband would have never cheated on me." The hollow inside me grows when I think of Desmier, and my soul continues to weep.

"You're not that special. Eventually, he would have."

"No. He wouldn't have. He wouldn't have needed to because he truly loved me, and I was enough for him." I've lost everything but my belief in the true love I shared with

Desmier. And Viktor doesn't like my answer one bit. "He wasn't you."

"No. He wasn't. He was a parasite, just like the thing you carry in your belly." His poisonous words have the desired effect.

They hurt my heart. But they also ignite the last shred of fire left in me to fight. I ball my hand into a fist and punch him straight in the side of his face, making him shout.

Viktor never saw my attack coming because of the angle he's holding me.

The shock on his face is classic, and worth the pain I feel when he slaps me back. With a savage growl, Viktor lifts me by my throat and carries me just like that across the room. He throws me onto the bed and slaps my face again and again and again until I see stars and taste blood.

I scream and cry as the pain shreds me to pieces, and I'm sure death is close. It has to be with such pain burning through my body.

"Fucking bitch." He delivers one last slap to my face. "Fucking whore. The doctors are on their way to remove it and fix you so you will never have children. That way, we won't have to worry about your whoring ways and having any other accidents."

"You evil asshole."

"It doesn't matter what you say. You are mine now." Another slap brings black dots before my eyes, and I scream again.

"I will never be yours." I can hardly talk, but my words are my only attack. "I will never love you. Never!"

"Then you will just be something to fuck until I'm ready to throw you away. Why don't I start now?"

He holds me down and pushes the tunic up my hips. When he tears off my panties, I kick my legs, trying to get him off me.

Nothing works. There's nothing I can do but lie here and allow him to destroy me.

"Stop it." My terror-filled voice fills the room. I'm sure people can hear me if they're nearby, but Viktor has no plans to stop anything.

He undoes his belt and shoves his pants down his hips, freeing his cock.

Grabbing my hips, he readies himself to shove into me, but just then the door flies open and Mira rushes in.

"What the fuck?" Viktor pulls his pants back on and sneers at her.

"We have a problem," Mira says.

I manage the strength to lift my head and look at her. She's gone pale, and her eyes are wide with fright.

"What the hell is happening?"

"We have to leave now. Malik is here with Desmier, and they have the Knights' enforcers with them, along with the Pakhan. It's over. We have to leave."

All I truly hear is Desmier's name. He's alive.

"How the fuck did Desmier survive?"

"I don't know. It doesn't matter. Let's go, Viktor. Take her. We still have the oil company if we have her."

He yanks me off the bed and pulls me along, blood streaming down my face and my body shattered.

The three of us rush through the door. The cold seeps into my bare skin when we step into the hall. We rush down it and get in the elevator.

The moment we go down, gunfire rips through the air. It sounds like a war zone.

Viktor takes out his gun, getting it ready to shoot the moment we step out of the elevator.

The passage is clear, but when we turn the corner, a host of men are coming our way. I spot Jayce and Zane, and they see me, too, in Viktor's grasp and Mira running beside me.

Viktor starts shooting, and when they return fire, Mira gets hit straight in the back of her head and several times in her back. She goes down like a rag doll, and Viktor doesn't even spare her a glance.

In his greed to get me away, he decides to retreat and hoist me over his shoulder. Now I'm used almost like a shield. The bullets stop because I'm too close to Viktor and we still have a good distance between us and the men.

We make it outside, and it's war out here, too, but he manages to reach a car. One of his guards is already running toward us to help him.

The guard shoots back at the men rushing our way while Viktor shoves me in the back seat of the car before he gets in the driver's seat and drives away.

I look around frantically, not knowing what the hell to do but thinking this is an opening. A possible chance to escape, just like the one Dad told me to find. All I have to do is summon courage and look for my chance.

We tear down the road off the building site, and then we're on a country road with the woods on either side.

The sound of a motorcycle rips through the air. A sound I will never forget.

The lazy day I remember at Raventhorn fills my head

with the image of me sitting next to Lorelai by the tree, watching the motorcyclist rebel drive onto the campus.

He's here again.

I look behind me and see Desmier on his motorcycle tearing down the road. He's fought death to come and save me. I also spot Malik's car not far behind.

Desmier shoots the wheels of the car. The tires blow, making Viktor lose control of the vehicle.

We run off the road, fly through the air for a few seconds, then land with a heavy thud on the ground. The car still has a lot of speed on it, though, so it keeps going straight into the woods. Viktor tries to swerve through the trees while I hold on, screaming as I know we're going to crash. I just manage to get my seat belt on when we do.

We smash right into a large, formidable oak tree. Despite the seat belt holding me in place, I still go flying into the back of Viktor's seat. My body feels like it's broken in several places.

Viktor is hurt, really hurt. But he's still moving. His airbags have blown out against him, but I can see blood on his head through the rearview window.

This is it, though. The opening I was waiting for. And come hell or high water, I'm fucking taking it. I can hear Desmier's bike not far away, so all I need to do is get to him.

While Viktor groans, I try to open my door. It takes me a few tries to push it open, but when I do, I don't hesitate to get out.

My legs are weak, but I will myself forward with my mind on my baby and my love.

I move as fast as I can, following the sound of the bike.

Desmier can't be too far now. I don't think he came the way we did, or he would have been just behind us.

"Stop!" Viktor calls out. Damn it, he managed to get out of the car, too.

I try to run but trip over a vine and go tumbling forward down the path.

Desmier's bike approaches, so I decide to do the only thing I can.

"I'm here, Desmier!" I scream. "Over here!"

Viktor may be badly hurt, but he can still move fast. Faster than me.

My ankle feels twisted, so I start backing away.

"If I can't have you, he can't either!" Viktor yells, pointing his gun at me.

He stops and cocks the hammer. I look at the gun in his hands, and fright unlike any I've known seizes me. My brain can't focus to get me to either keep crawling away or try to get up and run, no matter what's going on with my ankle and the pain in my head from the beating he gave me.

Viktor laughs, and just then, Desmier's bike launches out from the thicket of trees.

He shoots Viktor, but I know I hear two shots fired at the same time.

Viktor goes down, his gun still in his hands and blood coloring his white shirt. Desmier doesn't give him a chance to recover before he whirls his bike around and shoots him again in his head.

Viktor flops down to the ground, but Desmier doesn't stop there. He parks his bike by the tree, jumps off, and stalks up to Viktor to shoot him again in the same place.

It's only when his hand falls limp at his side and he

drops to his knees beside Viktor that I know something is wrong with him.

That moves me. My energy returns, and I get up, rushing forward on my ankle that feels like fire is burning me, but I don't care.

When I reach him, he falls onto his back, and I can see he was shot with the bullet that was meant for me.

"My Valkyrie," he mumbles.

I gather his head in my lap and look over the blood seeping through his shirt. It's right near his heart.

God, no, this can't be happening.

"Desmier, we have to get out of here. We have to get you to the hospital."

He grabs my hand and squeezes it. "No, I don't think I'm going to make it."

My heart doubles over on hearing that, but still, I refuse to give up. "Desmier, please, don't you dare leave me."

In typical Desmier style, he smiles and reaches up to touch my face with his free hand.

"I'll find you in the next life. I'll be waiting for... you. Always you. Always, always you. I have loved you since first I saw you."

"I love you, too. That's why you can't go anywhere."

"I'm sorry, baby girl. I think I'm going to Valhalla now, to the halls of my father and uncle and all those who have gone before me."

"No." Despite my belief that I didn't have any tears left, they pour out of me. "I need you. Desmier, I need you. I'm pregnant."

His brows rise, but it looks like it hurts him to do that. "Baby?"

"We're having a baby. We need you. Don't leave us. I need you."

His gaze intensifies, locking with mine. "Then we're not done yet."

The determination in his eyes almost makes me believe he's going to get up and walk, or fly to get help.

But his eyes flutter closed, and there's a deathly look about his face, as if he's already crossed over to the other side.

When I feel for his pulse, there's none.

CHAPTER
FIFTY-ONE

ANASTASIA

I keep my eyes on the door ahead of me. The one next to the snack machine the hospital's other visitors have been using.

The nurse came through it earlier to let us know the surgeons had started surgery on Desmier. That was over two hours ago. It's night now, but time has been messed up since I started this day.

Malik is the reason we even made it here and hopefully have a chance.

I lost Desmier in the woods. Actually lost him. There was no sign of life in him by the time Malik reached us. He had to start CPR straightaway and was able to bring Desmier back. Then there was no time to wait for an ambulance. Malik got Desmier into his car, and we drove to the hospital. I sat in the back holding Desmier while he basically bled out.

Now we're here in the hospital's waiting room. Lorelai

and Ehlga are on either side of me. Malik is sitting opposite us next to Jayce, and Zane and Gytha are standing by the corner near the window.

Everyone looks crushed, but the most broken person who feels the same pain I do is Ehlga.

She hasn't stopped crying since she arrived. First, it was sobs, then the sobs turned to the sort of quiet crying you do when you have no energy left in you.

I'm feeling a different sort of numbness now, and aside from the pain in my heart, my ankle and head are throbbing. I have twisted it.

When I arrived with my face and body battered and told the doctors I was pregnant, they checked me over to make sure the baby was fine.

The baby is okay, but I have a broken rib. I was given medication that was okay to take with the baby, and my ankle was bandaged, but that agonizing feeling is still there.

It's no worse than this waiting game. The waiting and wondering if this really is the end.

Another hour passes by. My head is on Ehlga's shoulder while Lorelai holds my hand.

I almost fall asleep, but when a hand with perfectly manicured fingers holds a small cup of water in front of me, my focus snaps back and I lift my head.

It's Gytha. She has three Styrofoam cups in her hand. One for each of us, and what feels like a peace offering to me.

"Thank you." I take it.

"He'd want to make sure someone is taking care of you."

I nod, and she gives me a polite smile before handing Ehlga and Lorelai their cups.

I watch her walk back to the wall and resume staring out the window. I look back at Ehlga, who seems appreciative of Gytha's turnaround. In a time like this, we need each other's strength.

I drink the water and savor the cold feeling soothing my throat.

Not two minutes after, the surgeon walks through the door.

I'm the first on my feet and hobble toward him.

"Easy, there," he says, putting out his hands to steady me when I stumble.

Lorelai and Ehlga rush to my side, trying to hold me up, but all I'm concerned with is hearing that Desmier will be okay.

"Please, tell me he's okay. Please." My voice is shaking as desperation ripples through every word.

The surgeon's eyes cloud, and sympathy takes over his face. "The surgery went well, but he's in a coma. The bullet hit just a few inches away from his heart, so his injury was quite extensive. He's lucky to be alive, but the next forty-eight hours are crucial."

"Forty-eight hours?" Malik asks.

"Yes. We'll be monitoring him during that time and running various tests, so it's best you go home and return in the morning."

"What happens after forty-eight hours?" I ask in a low voice.

"We'll know if he'll come back. Or not."

The last bit of energy I was using to hold on slips from me, and my knees turn to water, giving out.

Lorelai and Ehlga hold me up, but I have no strength left

and I can't breathe.

"I'm sorry." I hear the surgeon say, but his voice is so far away he could be on the other side of the world.

The tears come again, and I'm lost. It's Malik who picks me up and carries me out. After that, I don't know anything. I hear people talking, but I can't distinguish between who's speaking or even what they're saying.

Grief has hold of me now.

THE NEXT TWO days are awful, but Desmier is still with us.

I've been sitting next to his bedside watching him fight for his life and hoping he'll come back to me.

I pay attention to every sound on his monitors and watch for signs of anything and everything when the nurses and doctors check his vitals.

I continue praying as the next day passes with the same results.

His words keep ringing through my mind.

We're not done yet, we're not done yet, we're not done yet.

I just hope he knows I'm with him. Wherever he is, that's where I am, too.

Heart, body, mind, and soul. He always had me, long before I knew I'd given myself to him.

Two weeks slip by, and Desmier is still the same. I feel like I'm dancing on the edge of insanity.

The doctors have kindly arranged for me to sleep next to him when I can, so I stay all night.

Everyone is hoping he'll pull through and wake up soon,

so everything has been put on hold, including Leif and Evgeni's funerals.

On Friday night, I fall asleep next to Desmier instead of the cot the nurses set up for me, and I slip into a dream.

It starts with me running through the meadow. I run, and I'm happy. A bird flies over my head, but instead of the fractured dream—or memory—I see my family ahead of me. My real family. The Butyrskayas.

The bird flies to my brother and lands on his outstretched hand.

I run toward my father, and he picks me up, hoisting me in the air. My mother is laughing, and I feel so much love from all of them.

The memory fades, and warm fingers cover mine.

I almost think I'm still in the dream, but when I open my eyes and find Desmier looking at me, my heart soars into the heavens.

"Valkyrie..." he mutters in a faint voice.

"You're awake."

"I told you. We're not done yet."

I smile. That's the best thing I've ever heard. "No, we're not. We never will be."

CHAPTER
FIFTY-TWO

DESMIER

I lower myself into my chair. I'm in my office at home. A place I never thought I'd see again.

I've been home from the hospital now for a week, and it's been two weeks since I woke up from my deep slumber.

I don't know how I made it back, and my body is still weak, but I'm alive. Alive and grateful for a second chance.

I remember thinking my end had arrived when the bullet hit me, but it was worth it. I'd watched Viktor going after Anastasia with his gun to shoot her. To kill her.

At that moment, it didn't matter what happened to me. I had to save her by whatever means I could.

When his bullet hit me, I tasted death and got closer to the other side than I ever have. But now I'm back in the world of the living with a wife who loves me, a baby on the way, two funerals to attend, and a brother on the run for murdering our uncle.

Somehow, I need to get back on my feet and pick up the pieces that have been left behind after losing Leif. A month has passed since he was killed, and my mind still won't accept it. I keep expecting him to call me or come by and visit.

He left me a video message.

Ehlga gave it to me when I got home on Monday. She said he did it on my wedding day as a 'just in case' message. He knew once Anastasia and I got married, we'd have a clock ticking over our heads and it was only a matter of time before things started happening. Leif, as always, couldn't have been more right.

I've been trying to watch the video since Ehlga gave it to me, but every time I try, I can't bring myself to look at Leif alive, knowing he'll be forever trapped that way in a recording. Another memory for me.

It's even harder to watch knowing that Zakh, whom I actually ended up trusting, took Leif from me and no one has seen hide or hair of him. And with the skill set Zakh has, no one *will* find him. A man like that will know how to stay hidden.

But I will find him. I vow to avenge Leif in every way possible. It doesn't matter how well Zakh hides himself, I'll spend the rest of my life looking for him if that's what I have to do.

As for now, I'm making another attempt to watch the video.

Ehlga walks in with a jug of ice water. She gives me a warm smile when she sees me sitting in front of the computer.

"Are you going to watch it now?"

"I'm going to try. Is Anastasia awake yet?" Anastasia has been getting tired and falling asleep a lot more recently. It's a pregnancy symptom.

When I think of my wife pregnant, a feeling comes over me that I can't describe. If I were to try, I'd say it was eternal bliss and worth fighting death for. They both were worth the fight—my woman and my baby.

"Yes, she's out on the terrace. I told her you were probably up here watching the video."

"Thanks."

"Desmier, do you want me to watch it with you?" Another kind smile lifts her lips. "I can do that, if it will help."

I take her hand and bring it to my heart. "I'm okay. But thank you. Thank you for always being there for me."

Leaning forward, she plants a kiss on my forehead.

"Always. Let me know if you need me." She nods and leaves.

When the door closes, I pull in a deep breath and turn the video on.

Leif's face comes on the screen.

He's in his office sitting on the edge of his desk. He looks just like how I remember him.

"Hello, son. If you're watching this, it means I'm no longer with you in body." He pauses for a few beats and sighs. "I wish I could say I hope that doesn't happen, but in the world we live in, death is just around the corner. As you know by now, everything I own belongs to you. But what I wanted to leave you in this message is wisdom. So, my last lesson is this: don't grieve for me. Instead, live for me."

I take note of the change in his face as he speaks. As if this is the most important thing he will ever tell me.

"I devoted my life to making sure you lived to see happiness. I had the privilege of seeing you happy when you took your wedding vows. Our forefathers believed that fate would bring you your true love. I believed that happened for you, and a new leaf has turned over in your life with your marriage. So, love your wife and look forward to everything you'll do together. Those are the priceless moments that are worth fighting for. I had most of mine with you. Thank you for thinking of me as a father to you. That really did mean a lot to me, son, and I will always be with you."

He dips his head, then the screen goes blank.

Just like that, he's gone, but his words stay with me, giving me a newfound strength.

I sit there for a moment processing his wisdom, and I think of everything that's happened, from as far back as I can remember.

I've never truly lived until now. There was always something stopping me.

But Leif is right, and I've been given more than a second chance.

With that in mind, I stand and block out the weakness I still feel gripping my body. The strength in my heart is enough to keep me going.

I leave the office and find Anastasia on the terrace standing by the balcony. She's resting her hands on the stone surface, looking ahead at the garden.

Fate truly did bring us together. To think this was her family's home that I lived in as a boy before she was born, then she lost and found herself here with me. It must truly be fate.

When I get closer, she turns and looks at me. A smile lights up her face, and the twinkle in her eyes brightens.

I close the space between us and kneel to kiss her stomach through the fabric of her dress.

"I'm not going to get tired of this." I kiss her stomach again. "I hope you know that."

"I didn't know until just now." She giggles.

"Well, now you do. You'll have plenty practice for the next baby, and the one after that, too, and the one after that."

"Desmier, how many kids will we have?"

"As many as we can manage. It's not like we'll ever get tired of trying to make them." I stand and kiss her properly. "I love you, Anastasia Volkova."

"I love you, too, Desmier Volkova."

"Good, we should go to bed now."

"I agree."

EPILOGUE

ANASTASIA

"It's going to be so strange coming back after the summer and not seeing you," Lorelai says, sitting straighter.

"I know. I was thinking that the other day."

We're under the tree on Raventhorn's campus. I'm waiting for Desmier to pick me up, and she's waiting for Dmitri. This is the first of many dates her father has arranged with him, and I know she's not happy about it.

Although she's smiling, I also know she's still putting on a brave face because of Zakh. By now, everyone knows what he did and that he's basically being hunted.

Lorelai and I haven't spoken about it much, but I know she's hurting deeply.

"You know you'll still see me, right?" I smile. "I just won't be at college for a year." Today, I did my deferment for next year. I'm due in January, but I have no plans to walk around campus in my pregnant state. We have another month of classes before the summer. By the time I get back, I'll be just over five months pregnant. I plan to resume my course the year after next on a part-time basis.

"Of course, I'm going to see you. That's not up for discussion. I'm already planning your baby shower. It's just going to be strange not having you here, but for all the right reasons."

She looks so proud of me, and I feel lucky to have her. But once again, I'm left feeling like she does more for me than I do for her.

"Thanks for being you, Lorelai."

She laughs. "Thanks for being you, too. I don't think I could have ever had a better friend, or one who knows me so well."

I tap her hand and give her a reassuring squeeze. "I'm happy to hear that because I know you're not doing so well now."

"I'm trying my best."

"You're doing well. How are you feeling, though? Truthfully."

"Like my world is ripping apart every day and I spend my night trying to patch it back up. I just can't believe what Zakh did, and I feel selfish for feeling like shit because I know I'm never going to see him again. There was never any hope for us."

I still can't wrap my head around the truth and accept the things that were done by those who betrayed us. Zakh, though... Like everyone else, I never saw his actions coming. The damage he did will be reopened next week at the funeral.

"You will get through this," I assure her.

"I believe that. You inspire me to find my strength. You've been through hell, Anastasia. And you got what you wanted in the end. Your happiness gives me hope."

"Thank you, but I don't think I would have gotten very far without your help."

I know I'm right when it comes to that. Over the last few weeks, she's supported me with so much while Desmier was recovering. She's done everything and even dealt with the lawyers for me when it came to the oil company. Apparently, because Uther adopted me, the company is still mine. Lorelai convinced me to keep it and do good with it, so I've made arrangements for the charity my grandfather chose to get a massive percentage of the profits each year.

I pull her in for a hug, then, moments later, Desmier's car comes up the drive, but Jayce is driving. If Desmier were a hundred percent and I weren't pregnant, it would be him storming in on his motorcycle again, defying all the rules.

The car rolls to a stop near us, and Desmier gets out, holding the door open for me.

"Go be with your guy. I'll see you tomorrow." Lorelai smiles.

"See you tomorrow."

I give her another quick hug before I rush down the path to skip into Desmier's arms.

Without even thinking, we kiss right there for the world to see, and I get lost in him all over again.

Every day is a happily ever after for us because I have him and he has me.

~

DESMIER

One week later

I've had far too many sad days in my life.

This one is right up there with the rest.

I buried Leif and my father a few hours ago.

We held a double ceremony and buried them next to each other in the family plot. The turnout was astounding, and the deep appreciation for their lives by all who were there was just as impressive.

Since we got home, I've been in my office sorting things out, just to get my mind off the day.

While Ehlga and Anastasia are baking in the kitchen, it seemed like the thing to do to suppress my grief.

A knock sounds on my door, and I wonder who it is. It's been a while since anyone has knocked on that door. Gytha still knocks, but I'm not expecting to see her until next week when she leaves for Denmark. She's been helping us look for Zakh, but as the days have gone by with no results, I didn't want her to miss out anymore.

"Come in!" I call out.

The door opens, and Malik walks in. Although it's odd for him to be here, it's good seeing him.

"You okay?" I ask when I notice the troubled look on his face.

"Not so much. This was at my house waiting for me when I got back." He pulls out a note and shows me. "It's addressed to the both of us, so I opened it."

He hands it to me, and I notice our names on the envelope. I open it, pull out the note from inside, and read it. It says:

I didn't kill Leif. I've been set up.

I can't clear my name right now, but you're not going to find me until I can prove my innocence,

Zakh

I look at Malik and take in the stern expression on his face. Part of me would love to believe this, but I know what I saw on the surveillance recording. And I know now that I have to be careful.

"He was at your house?" I ask.

"Yes. And no one saw him, but that's the kind of shit Zakh can do. We're dealing with someone who can walk around in plain sight and be invisible if they want to."

"Fuck."

"What are you thinking, Desmier?"

"We saw what he did for ourselves." I squeeze my hand into a fist.

"We did. He held the knife in Leif's heart. How can that be a setup?"

"Exactly."

"What now?" He holds my gaze, clenching his jaw.

"Either I find him, or he proves his innocence, whichever comes first."

Whatever happens, there will be retribution for the dead.

Whoever is responsible will pay with their life for those who lost theirs.

Thanks so much for reading.

If you liked Desmier and Anastasia's story, you will love Zakh and Lorelai's story in Villain's Obsession, coming to you in a few weeks xxx

If you want to read more of my sexy Mafia Men, try any of these:

Hugs and Love xx

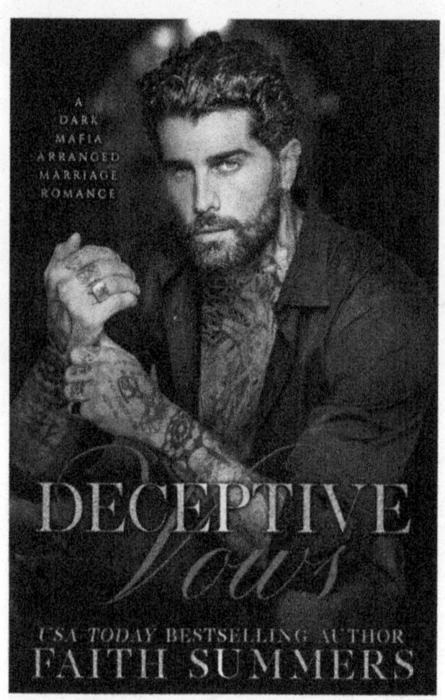
A
DARK
MAFIA
ARRANGED
MARRIAGE
ROMANCE
DECEPTIVE
Vows
USA TODAY BESTSELLING AUTHOR
FAITH SUMMERS

# ACKNOWLEDGMENTS

For my readers.

Always for you.

Thank you for reading my stories.

I hope you continue to enjoy my wild adventures xx

ABOUT THE AUTHOR

Faith Summers is the Dark Contemporary Romance pen name of USA Today Bestselling Author, Khardine Gray.

Warning !! Expect wild romance stories of the scorching hot variety and deliciously dark romance with the kind of alpha male bad boys best reserved for your fantasies.

Be sure to join her reader group - The Dark Odyssey

https://www.facebook.com/groups/462522887995800/